DEFIANT DESIRE

"'Tis you I want, Ashton," Bethany said quietly.

He fixed her with a challenging stare.

"You'll not find me gentle."

She lifted her chin defiantly.

"You'll not find me fearful. By all rights, I should show you the mistake you've made."

Ashton placed her on the bed and lowered himself beside her, taking her lips with a raging thirst. Her hands crept tentatively, searching around his neck, and she offered her lips again. Her body shuddered to life beneath his questing hands.

"Perhaps," she whispered, "you'll find we've not committed such a terrible mistake."

By Susan Wiggs

Winds of Glory
Vows Made in Wine
Briar Rose
Circle in the Water
Lord of the Night
The Mist and the Magic
The Raven and the Rose
The Lily and the Leopard
Embrace the Day

Available from HarperPaperbacks

Winds of Glory

⊰ SUSAN WIGGS ⊱

HarperPaperbacks
A Division of HarperCollinsPublishers

HarperPaperbacks *A Division of* HarperCollins*Publishers*
10 East 53rd Street, New York, N.Y. 10022

Copyright © 1988, 1995 by Susan Wiggs
All rights reserved. No part of this book may be used or reproduced in any manner whatsoever without written permission of the publisher, except in the case of brief quotations embodied in critical articles and reviews. For information address Avon Books, 105 Madison Avenue, New York, N.Y., 10016.

A paperback edition of this book was published in 1988 by Avon Books. This edition has been revised by the author.

Cover illustration by Bob Sabin

First HarperPaperbacks printing: July 1995

Printed in the United States of America

HarperPaperbacks, HarperMonogram, and colophon are trademarks of HarperCollins*Publishers*

❖ 10 9 8 7 6 5 4 3 2 1

For Jim and Charlotte Wiggs, with love

ACKNOWLEDGMENTS

My thanks to:
The Preservation Society of Newport County,
Alberta Lloyd-Evans,
and
Joyce Bell, Alice Borchardt,
and Barbara Dawson Smith

Winds of Glory

Prologue

**Fort George, Rhode Island
9 December 1774**

The musket ball entered Private Ashton Markham's body at an angle, ripping through the flesh of his left side and fortunately missing his vitals before lodging itself into the dry wooden planks of the ordnance house behind him.

As he was slammed against the side of the building and sank down into a snowdrift, he found himself thinking—inasmuch as he was able to think—that the heat of the lead ball was the first warmth he had felt in weeks. There was something oddly comforting in that, and in the soft winter silence that followed the single report. He heard his own breathing—ragged, labored—and saw a wisp of steam rising as his blood crept down into a cushion of new snow. He smelled the blood and the clean scent of the snow and the acrid burn of the powder that blackened the hole in his red woolen frock coat.

A strange whir began in his head as he looked away from his wounds and gazed out across the gentle, rounded snowscape of Goat Island, where as a lad he had gone to the turtle races; they had decked the winners in ribbons and eaten the losers.

Moonlight, white and shimmering, silvered the area surrounding the fort and carved deep shadows in the drifts. It was a scene of quiet beauty, one that, had he been free to do so, would have sent him galloping across the island on Corsair, his favorite mount. But Ashton had not been free to ride since the British army had claimed him with a shilling and a pledge four years earlier. And now, any movement at all was out of the question. He had never felt so light, so groundless.

He blinked his eyes. The moon-dusted scene before him shimmered and quaked and lost form. In its place came other fragmented images, crowding into his mind. He saw his father and their cottage on the estate called Seastone, the huge stable of blooded horses in their care, the summer races and autumn hunts. God, had life ever been so simple?

He grimaced at the pulsating pain in his side. Life had been uncomplicated, even sweet, back then. Each day had slipped effortlessly into the next. He trained horses, he raced, he won. Closing his eyes, he remembered the feel of a swift mount's sinew beneath him and the bite of the sea air on his face.

He had not thought about that other life in a long time. Not since the summons had come, calling him to serve in King George's army. He felt the corners of his mouth lift in a self-deprecating smile. He had made a poor soldier, having no taste for endless drills, marching through marshy wilderness executing pointless maneuvers. . . . But most of all he had never been able to put his heart into subjugating the gathering storm of rebellion in the Colonies.

He tried to summon rage at the patriot who had shot him, some unseen sniper lurking in the woods, trying to raid the ordnance house. But it was hard to feel anger when he felt as light and insubstantial as the snowflakes that winked and sparkled in the moonlight, dancing before his eyes until he had to close them against the brightness.

Above the vague whirring in his head he heard a shout. Then another. And then footfalls thudding, cushioned by the snow. Dragging his leaden eyelids open, he saw torches bobbing across the compound. In seconds a circle of faces surrounded him.

"Markham? Markham!" That was Sergeant Mansfield, his cockney accent thickened by drink. "Hold that torch higher, private. Christ, he's been hit!"

Ashton felt himself being lifted onto a litter, heard exclamations of concern and angry oaths directed at the patriot sniper. He was borne away to the infirmary, only vaguely aware that a detachment of soldiers had been sent out to comb the woods.

A lantern hung overhead, and the surgeon, roused from his sleep, peeled Ashton's frock coat away. He hissed, drawing in his breath.

"'Tis bad," he muttered, grabbing a pile of linen. "Though not mortal." He lifted Ashton's head, offering a bottle of rum. "Hell of a way to get yourself discharged, Private Markham."

Discharged . . . Ashton felt himself begin to smile, and a warm feeling spread through him.

The patriot in the woods—God bless his rebel hide— had set him free.

1

Newport, Rhode Island
May 1775

"Get your head inside the coach, miss," Carrie Markham said. "You'll lose that bonnet I spent hours trimming."

Bethany Winslow ignored her maid and leaned farther out the window for her first glimpse of home in four years. Like the great rocks brooding upon the cliffs of Aquidneck Island, Seastone had not changed since she had left for the Primrose Academy in New York at the age of fourteen.

The wide avenue leading up to the house was lined by budding larches. Box hedge, filling the air with a dry, pungent aroma, edged the massive stone house and wound through gardens graced by a springtime array of flowers. The huge gambrel-roofed building sat in quiet splendor amid a crowding abundance, a fullness of leaf, bud, and blossom.

"We're home, Carrie," Bethany said over her shoulder, hat ribbons and honey-gold hair flying in the wind. "Home."

"Hmph." Carrie tossed her bright red ringlets and settled back on the bench across from her mistress. "I much prefer New York. The gentlemen are so much more sophisticated there, and I didn't have Ashton and my father questioning my every move."

Bethany refrained from suggesting that perhaps Carrie did need someone to watch over her. In New York the pretty young woman had managed to get herself into several romantic scrapes. But Bethany was too pleased at the moment to argue with Carrie. They were home, and nothing could dampen her delight.

By the time the coach rolled up on the pebbled front drive, she could barely contain herself. Ignoring another admonition from Carrie, she burst from the coach and hit the drive running. Her feet flew beneath her full yellow skirts as she mounted the wide stone staircase and opened the door to the foyer.

Familiar odors, the smells of home, wafted to her: the clean scent of verbena polished woodwork, the aroma of fresh bread from the bake house, the faint tinge of the pomade her mother used on her absurdly lofty hairstyles. . . .

Mrs. Hastings, the housekeeper, turned from her fussing at a plant stand near the library door. "Miss Bethany!" She straightened her mobcap and came forward to enfold Bethany in her plump arms. "You're home at last! And look at you! Who would have thought our gawky colt could have become such a beauty? Turn around, child, and let me look at you."

Smiling, Bethany sketched a graceful turn. "'Tis grand to see you again, Mrs. Hastings. Where is everyone?"

The housekeeper's grin sagged and she flushed, wiping her hands on her apron. "The library, miss. But—"

Bethany ran to the door, not of a mind to scold Mrs. Hastings for her life-long habit of nosiness. A loud metallic crash sounded from within. Bethany paused, her hand closed over the polished brass knob.

Her father's voice rose in anger. ". . . never countenance this sort of dissension under my own roof!" Sinclair Winslow blustered. "By God, Harry, you're an Englishman, do you hear? I won't have you speaking treason against your king. I am shocked that you deem the rabble-rousers at Lexington Green worthy of anything more than a stint in the pillory."

Harry's muttered reply was followed by the sound of a blow; flesh cracking against flesh. Bethany's heart lurched, and she squeezed her eyes shut.

"This time you've gone too far, boy. Just look at your mother, barely able to raise her head for the shame of it. 'Twas bad enough, your taking up with the popish trash last month, parading her at our Junto reception like she was our equal. And now this—this talk of grievances against our king, waving Otis's scurvy pamphlet in my face—"

Bethany pushed the door open and stepped into the library, her hand at her bosom, covering her pounding heart. Her eyes focused briefly on an iron fire back bearing the arms of King George III. The piece lay facedown in the grate. The people in the room fell silent as her troubled eyes swept the scene.

Lillian, her mother, sat in a Townsend armchair, wringing a dainty handkerchief and pressing it carefully to her powdered cheeks. Behind her stood William, Bethany's elder brother, patting his mother's shoulder with one hand while swirling a cup of Jamaica water in the other. Harry and Sinclair were paired off in front of the great stone mantel, the father flushed and glowering, the son grim and defiant. The livid imprint of Sinclair's hand blossomed on Harry's cheek.

Like an untimely shadow, dismay eclipsed Bethany's delight at coming home.

William, less handsome and more ambivalent than Bethany remembered, seemed to come to himself first. He rounded his mother's chair and approached Bethany, arms outstretched. Unsmiling, she went to him, smelling the rum on his breath. Then she kissed her parents, each in turn. They greeted her stiffly, still not recovered from the row.

Finally she turned to her twin brother. From birth their spirits had been linked in an almost mystical way. They knew each other as thoroughly as a person knows his image in a looking glass.

Harry was in pain; she could feel it almost as if it belonged to her. She stared into the depths of his eyes— hazel flecked with tawny gold, like her own—and read a deep inner turmoil that caused her insides to twist in sympathy.

"What is it, Harry?" she asked softly, taking his hands.

"I'm sorry to spoil your homecoming like this, Bethany. I've been sent down from Rhode Island College."

"Among other things," Sinclair grumbled.

Harry directed a look of unconcealed loathing at the iron fire screen. "Aye," he said with soft defiance, "among other things." He led her to the library door. "Let's go out into the garden, where we can talk."

"Just a minute, you young whelp! We've not settled anything—"

"Yes, we have, sir." Harry's eyes narrowed. "I think the conclusion of this discussion is clear. You'll not tolerate my views or the woman I love, and I'll not allow myself to be bullied by you. I shall leave. As soon as I've spoken with Bethany."

Dumbfounded, she stumbled along behind him. He didn't speak as he hurried down the narrow path to the summerhouse, passing a bench of straw beehives and, farther on, their mother's dovecotes. Bethany was holding her side by the time they reached the summerhouse. The small, decorative building sat upon a rise, overlooking the shores of Aquidneck Island to the east and the spires of Newport to the south.

She sat upon a bench, facing the restless waters of Narragansett Bay through an unglazed window. She glanced over at her brother and caught his frank perusal of her yellow lutestring gown with its dainty ruchings and lace.

"You've changed," he said, a shadow of his familiar gamin smile flickering across his face. "You used to be a skinny little hoyden with bare feet and burrs in her hair."

"I? A hoyden?"

"Don't tell me you've forgotten all our old escape routes from the schoolroom, the scores of places we used to hide from governesses and tutors. You were more at home riding the grassy fields of Aquidneck than in some stuffy parlor listening to the pianoforte or following the stilted steps of the dancing master."

She sensed that he wanted to cling to the past for a moment, to remember the good times. Although her heart was breaking, she grinned at the recollection of the prissy Sylvester Fine.

"Miss Abigail tamed me," she allowed, "although in her own way she made me wilder than ever."

Harry raised an eyebrow. "So the rumors about Miss Abigail Primrose are true. The needy gentlewoman recently over from England is not so proper after all."

"She had us reading Locke and Trenchard and excused us from lessons in needlework and deportment. Polite accomplishments were never my forte, anyway. But you mustn't say anything, Harry. Miss Abigail depends on her reputation. She'd be ruined if people knew she introduced her students to Gordon and Cato."

"Glorious dissenters, all. I'm glad you took your schooling there. You've too fine a mind to waste on petit point and parlor games, mincing empty words with society matrons."

Bethany took his hand. It was so like her own—slender, long-fingered, the oval nails well shaped. "I think you'd best tell me what brought about the row."

His smile tucked itself away like the sun behind a cloud. He raked a hand through his hair. "It all started last year when I brought Felicia home to meet Father and Mother."

"You wrote me about Felicia. She sounds lovely."

His expression softened and he looked a bit like the little boy he had once been, sweetness mingling nicely with mischievousness. "She's more than lovely, Bethany. She's kind and bright and . . . she's everything to me. At first Mother and Father were civil enough, thinking me too young to know my own mind, but they soon realized I'm serious about Felicia. I mean to marry her."

Marry. What a strange and wonderful notion. Bethany knew full well that she, too, would be expected to marry soon, but she had always regarded it as a remote, abstract idea in some distant future. Hearing of Harry's plans raised a cool shiver on her skin.

He glowered down at the waves rising up to explode against the rocks far below. "I wanted to give Felicia everything she's lacked all her life, but it seems I'm to be cut off. Father's promised I won't have so much as a shilling once we're wed."

Bethany tasted the sharp salt air on her lips. Ah, she had missed being home, but so much had changed. "I can't imagine Father being so cruel. What is his objection?"

"She's Catholic, the daughter of a miller in Providence, and a few years older than I."

Bethany spent a pleasant moment considering the novel idea that her brother was in love. Then she turned her thoughts to the less pleasant situation with her parents. "What's this about your being sent down?"

"I burned a ship."

"You what?"

"There was a British ship, the *Antonia*, in the harbor.

She was stationed there solely to harass American traders. One night my mates and I got to drinking a bit too much at the Old Sabin Inn and decided to rid the harbor of the *Antonia*. We rowed out and set her afire. The crew escaped unharmed, but the vessel was burned to the waterline."

"Dear God, Harry. How could you—"

He waved a hand to silence her. "Do you remember Sykes, my valet? Seems he found my boots and some clothing soaked with seawater and presented the evidence to the dean. I could have been tried for treason, but the college officials didn't want to create a scandal. So I was sent down. Needless to say, Sykes isn't with me anymore."

"Oh, Harry—"

"Don't start in on me, Bethany. 'Twas a foolish thing I did. But I'm sick to death of British harassment. We're American, by God!"

"You talk of your countrymen—of yourself—as if they were the enemy."

"They could well be, if England continues this betrayal of her own colonies."

Harry had always been impetuous and quick to anger. "My brother, the rebel," she said softly, and took his hand in hers.

"Does it shock you?"

"Not really. But it saddens me. I must agree with one thing Father said. You're an Englishman. No matter what you or Sam Adams or James Otis or any of the malcontents in Boston say, you are an Englishman."

"England's done me no favors. Like you, I've grown up. I have a mind of my own. Father can't accept that, nor will he consent to my marrying Felicia, so I must go."

"Harry—"

"There's no other solution, Bethany."

"But what will you do?"

"Marry Felicia. We'll live in Bristol, where I've been offered a position with a man named Hodgekiss, who owns a shipping concern. I'll be keeping his books and such. Don't look at me so, Bethany. I shall be fine. And you must visit us once we're settled."

Together they stood and held each other briefly. She swallowed to loosen the tightness in her throat. "I'll come; you know I will," she said, blinking tears from her eyes.

He lifted a strand of hair from her cheek, where the breeze had blown it. Tucking the deep golden lock behind her ear, he smiled. He had a sweet, wistful smile. In childhood, she had always been the bold one, the one to comfort him when trouble arose. Could he manage on his own? Perhaps so, for in the resolute depths of his gold-flecked eyes she saw the courage of his convictions.

Her tears spilled while she watched him go, his tall, slender form framed by Persian lilacs bending over the path. She heard him call to a servant to get his things together.

This was hardly the homecoming she had envisioned while on the boat from New York. Instead of a happy reunion, she had found her mother in tears, Harry and her father hurling angry words, William unsteady with drink.

Enveloped by a feeling of loss, she did what she had always done when a shadow dropped over her life. Lifting her skirts, she ran through the winding garden paths to the stables, half a mile distant.

Ashton Markham's currycomb scraped over the gleaming coat of a tall Thoroughbred. The stallion's midnight color was as rare as his fleetness on the racing green. As head stockman, Ashton could have left the task to one of the grooms, but he couldn't seem to do enough for this beast. Corsair was the finest animal ever bred in the stables, the triumphant culmination of all the years Ashton and his father had been breeding horses for Sinclair Winslow. Every trait was carefully selected, from the clean, sharp lines of the large head and proudly arching neck to the elusive and highly valued quality known as heart. His fiery temperament perfectly matched Ashton's ambitions for him.

No one rode a stallion by choice, but this horse was different. He would be more than mere breeding stock. He would be a champion.

The currycomb moved restlessly under Ashton's hand, and suddenly his pleasure in the task was eclipsed by an overwhelming sense of futility. He was master of this horse in every way but the one that truly counted.

Corsair did not belong to him.

All that Ashton did at Seastone was for Sinclair Winslow. Admittedly, the man paid him well, but it grated on Ashton's pride to work for someone else. He wanted neither other men nor laws to tell him what to do.

Ashton was a man to whom the fates had been capricious. With the eye of an artist, he could detect beauty and promise in a horse, sometimes seeing those qualities while others were blind to them. Yet he was poor, and such horses were dear.

Thanks to his father, he had a gentleman's education and a scholar's mind. But aside from Roger Markham, he rarely conversed at length with anyone more erudite than a stable groom. And, hidden beneath the layers of a somewhat dispassionate and practical nature, Ashton had a heart that protested his lonely existence and a mind that cried out for companionship.

He was shackled to the Winslows by responsibility to his ailing father, not resentful of the burden but feeling its weight nonetheless. Roger was seriously ill; Ashton had no choice but to carry on the work for him despite an inability to understand his father's loyalty to Sinclair Winslow.

Thrusting aside the feeling of restlessness, Ashton turned his attention to the stallion. "You'll win every major race of the season, my friend," he said, setting a pail of mash before the horse. "'Twas a lucky turn I was discharged in time to train you for—"

The wide double doors of the stables burst open, bright sunlight streaming into the corridor between the stalls. Just as Ashton straightened, a yellow-and-lace-clad form hurled itself into his arms, sobs muffling against his chest.

Unthinking, he brought his hand up to stroke the waves of thick, honey-colored hair. A subtle fragrance of jasmine wafted from the soft, shuddering form. A few seconds passed before he became aware of just who it was he held in his arms.

"Bethany. You're home! What's wrong?"

But she wasn't ready to speak. While she cried as though her heart were breaking, snippets of memory stirred to life. He recalled her as a tall, skinny girl with features too large and vivid to be considered pretty. She had been a precocious, sometimes bothersome child who was never quite proper enough to suit her demanding mother. Then, as now, she had run to him when she was troubled.

Years ago a broken toy or a stubborn pony reduced her to tears. Feeling the yielding softness of a woman's body now, he suspected the trouble was something more serious. Placing his fingers beneath her chin, he tilted her head upward and, stunned, found himself gazing at an unexpectedly beautiful face.

High cheekbones, full lips, an adorable small nose, and huge amber eyes skirted by dark, curling lashes combined in an unlikely but irresistible harmony. Bethany had truly blossomed.

Hiding his amazement, he found a handkerchief in her sleeve and gently dried the tears from her cheeks.

"It's Harry," she said brokenly. Even her voice had changed: soft-pitched, low, and musical. "He and Father had a terrible row and he's leaving."

Ashton frowned. "I'd heard the servants' gossip, but I didn't realize the trouble had gone so far."

"Ashton, I don't want him to go. He plans to marry and labor as a clerk in Bristol. He's giving up everything, all for the sake of a woman and—and some foolish notion about fighting the British."

He grinned. "Most young ladies would find such a notion romantic."

"I simply don't understand. Is it possible for a person to love someone so much he'd turn his back on his family to be with her?"

"I can't answer that. But it sounds like Harry already has." Ashton paused. He knew Harry. The youth was fiery and passionate, never one to let common sense interfere with his convictions. "I know you'll miss him, pet, but let him go," he said. "His mind is made up."

She nodded. "I suppose I'm only being selfish." She caught her lower lip in her teeth as if to stave off more tears. Then she managed a weak smile. Once again Ashton was struck by her beauty. Ah, God, she was a rare one. What was she now, eighteen? The transformation four years of absence had wrought was staggering.

Somewhat cynically he told himself he shouldn't be surprised. Bethany was a Winslow, after all, a member of one of the oldest families in Newport, as carefully bred as one of Sinclair's prize fillies. And, like one of the Thoroughbreds or smooth-stepping pacers in the nearby stalls, she was being groomed, trained, and exercised for a very specific purpose.

To marry, and marry exceedingly well.

Some of that breeding showed as she dashed away the last of her tears and smoothed back her shining hair with an unconsciously graceful gesture.

"You must think me as impetuous as ever," she said with a self-deprecating smile. "Hurling myself at you as if I'd not been gone all of four years."

"I'd be offended if you behaved any other way, pet. I'd like to think our friendship hasn't changed." He eyed the fascinating new curves and swells of her body. "But you've changed a great deal."

"Harry said so, too." She frowned. "Miss Abigail did not approve of vanity, and so I did not dare to give such things much thought." Brows knit quizzically, she tapped a delicate finger on her chin and glanced down at herself. "I've grown larger, perhaps," she ventured.

"In the most intriguing places," he supplied with a grin, pulling her closer. The jasmine scent, dangerously enticing, nearly made his head swim.

A delightful blush stained her cheeks. "And wiser, in Miss Abigail's opinion."

"You were always wise, pet," he assured her, dropping a friendly kiss on her nose. "Most objectionably so."

"I am more accomplished." Her chin tilted proudly, and her topaz gaze caught and snared Ashton against his will. "I've learned French and geometry and can argue philosophy with the scholars," she finished primly.

He experienced an odd wave of depression. Admirable qualities, indeed, but how would they serve a young woman destined to become a rich man's parlor ornament?

Shrugging off the thought, he gave her a final reassuring squeeze before letting her go. "Welcome home, Bethany," he said.

Bethany stepped back and felt an inner stirring at the rich timbre of his voice, imbued by a distinct Kentish accent. The changes in him were subtle. He was as handsome as ever, though perhaps the lines of his face were a bit rougher, the look in his eyes harder. Yet his smile, flashing easily in his tanned face, was the one she remembered.

Ashton Markham had always fascinated her. He had been a serious youth, hard-working, although he had always managed to spare a moment for a little girl who, she now admitted, must have been a singularly annoying child.

He had bypassed all the gawky stages of adolescence, growing with maddening ease into this tall man with magnificent deep chestnut hair pulled carelessly into a queue at his nape. He had steady eyes, the blue of a wind-tossed sea, and rugged, sun-bronzed features alight with humor and a touching tenderness.

She wondered why she had never noticed the endearing cleft in his chin or the contained strength of his large, squarish hands. Catching herself staring at him, she flushed.

"Thank you. 'Tis good to be home. I think."

"Is Carrie with you?"

"Of course. Oh, Ashton, do forgive me. I was so wrapped up in my own problems that I completely forgot you haven't seen your sister yet."

"She'll keep," he said. "Unless she's had an epiphany, Carrie still thinks the world begins and ends with her. At the moment she's probably disturbing Father's afternoon rest, wheedling halfpence out of him to buy a new ribbon or bauble in town."

She blinked at the venom in his voice. "Ashton?" she whispered.

"Forgive me, love. I'd best find more charity in my heart for my sister. It's just that—" He grinned, shook his head, and turned to put up the curry combs.

His manner intrigued her. "Just what?"

He ignored her, and she stepped forward, putting her hand on his shoulder. She felt the dampness of sweat through his shirt, and for some reason her breath caught in her throat. "Just what?" she asked again.

Very slowly, he turned. She started to take her hand away, but he caught it and pressed it to the middle of his chest. It was fascinating, feeling the heat and contours of him through the thin homespun shirt. "Just that I'm trying to get used to the idea that Miss Bethany Winslow has become a woman of heart-stopping beauty," he said softly.

She took her hand away as if he had singed her. "You are a horrid tease!"

He stared at her hand, the one that still tingled from touching him. "I'm not the one teasing here, pet." His grin widened. "Who would've thought Miss Primrose would turn my gawky little filly into a consummate lady?" he mused aloud.

"Gawky! Ashton Markham, I was never gawky."

He ambled over to a tack box and seated himself on it, stretching his long legs out before him and crossing his booted feet at the ankles. His gaze moved over her in amused appraisal. "Sure you were, love. Legs and feet always too long and too fast for the rest of you." His eyes warmed in frank admiration of her bosom and narrow waist. "Don't take offense, love. The rest of you caught up quite nicely."

Once again she felt herself blush. It was odd and not entirely agreeable to feel uncomfortable around a person who had been her friend for years. But there was no denying the subtle tension that thrummed between them now. Studying the deep ocean blue of his smiling eyes, she realized she and Ashton were no longer childhood playmates. She felt suddenly wistful, wishing there were some way to recapture the easy camaraderie they'd once shared.

"Corsair is looking fine and fit, she commented mildly, grasping at a neutral topic.

Ashton gazed at the horse with almost fatherly fondness. "I'd lay a wager his qualities equal those of his great grandsire, Byerly Turk." He fitted two fingers into the corners of his mouth and whistled, a high sharp note followed by a longer, lower tone. Corsair's ears pricked forward, and an impatient whinny shivered from him.

Bethany felt a surge of admiration for the horse—and for the man who had trained him. "I'm impressed," she said.

"That whistle's never failed me yet. The lad comes to it every time, without hesitation."

"Have you raced him yet this season?"

Ashton shook his head and looked chagrined. "Corsair

may be fine and fit, but I haven't been. I've only recently recovered from an injury."

"What a goose I am," she said. "I haven't even asked about you." She took his hand in hers, feeling a delicious inner ripple at the texture of his large, blunt fingers. "How were you injured, Ashton?"

"I was shot."

"Shot! Dear Lord, by whom?"

"By a patriot, in an ordnance raid on Fort George."

"The bloody rebels again. Who are these scoundrels?"

He grinned. "Oh, farmers and tradesmen. Preachers, men of letters. Your neighbors, pet."

"How can you smile about it?" she demanded. "You could have been killed."

"I was dying a slow death in the army anyway," he said.

A sudden fear seized her. "Ashton, you're not . . . like Harry, are you? You don't mean to fight the British?"

He shook his head. "I don't mean to fight anyone."

Relieved, she absently stroked his hand. Ashton had always been one to nurse a bird with a broken wing or set Harry's collected butterflies free before they died. The memory made her want to stroke Ashton's tanned cheek and murmur something foolish to him.

"I'd best get back to my parents," she said, resisting the temptation.

He nodded. "And I to my chores."

She went to the door, then turned back. "Will you ride with me sometime? Like we used to do?"

His eyes swept over her one last time. "Nothing is as it used to be. But yes, pet, I'll take you riding."

"Good Lord, but you've become stodgy for a young man of twenty-five, Ashton," Carrie Markham said in irritation. 'Tis not as if I haven't earned a bit of fun after waiting on Bethany all day."

He glowered at his sister and picked up the supper utensils from the table, taking care not to wake his ailing father, who was napping in a chair, his breeders' journals strewn over his lap.

"Hector Northbridge is twice your age, Carrie, and crippled by gout. What interest could you possibly have in him?"

She laughed and stretched in her slow, catlike way. "Don't be naive. Why should Hector's age bother me when he gives me everything I want?" She brushed back her sleeve to reveal a bracelet of gold and garnets. "Pretty, isn't it?" She dangled her hand before him.

He turned away in irritation and began washing up. He addressed his sister over his shoulder. "If you've no regard for your own reputation, at least think of Father. He didn't raise you to be a rich man's plaything."

Carrie sniffed and regarded her sleeping father with distaste. "What has he ever given me that I should behave for his sake?" She gestured around the small cottage. "A drafty hovel with a puncheon floor, the life of a servant."

"You've a good room in the big house and an easy job as Bethany's maid."

"No thanks to him," she retorted, jerking her head at Roger.

"He's done his best for us, Carrie."

She narrowed her eyes. "For you, perhaps, Ashton. He spent practically every shilling he earned sending you to Rhode Island College. You had a gentleman's education while I was made to wait on that worthless Winslow girl." She glanced again at Roger, her face pinched tight with resentment. "Fat lot of good your fancy education's done you. You're still mucking out Sinclair Winslow's stables."

Ashton clamped his jaw shut to stifle a retort. What she said was true, but he refused to give in to resentment. Until Roger's health improved, he was forced to remain at Seastone in another man's employ.

"Where are you going?" he demanded as Carrie moved toward the door.

She tossed her head, spilling bright red curls down her back. She was a pretty woman, but her looks had a hard edge of bitterness and greed which lessened the appeal of her lovely face and figure.

"I'm going to town. Any objections?"

"Chapin Piper has been hoping to welcome you back from New York."

"That settles it, then. I want to be well away from here when Chapin arrives. For God's sake, Ashton, the man's a printer's son—a pauper."

"I'd sooner see you stepping out with an honest pauper than being dandled on the knee of an elderly libertine."

She sniffed. "Well, I'd appreciate it if you'd discourage Chapin from trying to see me in the future."

"I'm sure you won't need me for that. You'll chase the man off by yourself."

By the end of her first week home, Bethany felt distinctly depressed. It was as if Harry Winslow had never existed. When she mentioned her brother to her parents, she was immediately cut off, the subject turned. And so she missed him privately, feeling as if some vital part of herself was lacking.

Although Harry wouldn't have been able to help Bethany escape her mother's dreary social gatherings, at least his presence would have made them bearable; he would never stand for all the boring talk and overblown posturing. Today there would be no Harry to create a charming distraction while his sister loosed a mouse beneath the voluminous skirts of Viola Pierce, no impish lad chucking bombshell acorns into the parlor fire. . . . This afternoon Bethany had to brave the society mavens alone.

"There now, don't be puckering your brow like that,"

Carrie Markham said as Bethany scowled into her looking glass. The maid fetched a gold-worked muslin tea gown from the armoire. "No young man is going to notice you if you don't go down there with a smile on your face."

"I don't feel like smiling. It galls me that Mother parades me before every faintly eligible man in Newport."

"'Tis only that Mistress Lillian cares about you enough to want you to marry well."

"I'm afraid my mother and I have very different ideas about what it is to marry well. Her only requirements are a fortune and decent social standing."

"What else is there?" Carrie spread her hands. "I'd just settle for the money, never mind bloodlines."

Bethany turned while Carrie tied a tiffany sash about her slender waist. She recalled a conversation she'd had with Miss Abigail Primrose last year. Miss Abigail's views on marriage were charmingly unconventional. The lady believed that the union should be founded on a deep, abiding love, regardless of fortune or breeding.

"Not I, Carrie." Bethany stared out the window at a patch of foxglove in bloom, pink freckles on white blossoms. "I'd like to find some reason other than money and position to spend the rest of my life with a man."

"Nonsense." Carrie twisted Bethany's shimmering waves and pinned them into side-coils. "You only say that because you've never done without."

Bethany shook her head; they'd had the argument before. Carrie was convinced that money was the key to all happiness. Perhaps it was, for Carrie. And perhaps she would achieve her goal one day. She was pretty and bright and talkative; she handled men as skillfully as her brother handled racehorses.

"Will you be needing me this afternoon?" Carrie tugged at a fold in the full gown.

Bethany shook her head. She gave Carrie her freedom whenever possible. The maid led a reckless life, consorting

with whatever gentleman was willing to entertain her in
style. In New York, only Miss Abigail's boundless tolerance
had kept Carrie from being dismissed from Bethany's service for her escapades.

"You're free to go seek your fortune," she said with a
wave of her hand. "I only wish I had as clear an idea of
what I want."

Fixing a stiff smile on her face, Bethany descended to
the foyer. As she stepped down the wide hardwood staircase, she marveled at the perfection of her mother's prepa-
rations. The woodwork gleamed from meticulous polish-
ing; fresh flowers in pastel hues bloomed from costly vases
of crystal and colored Sèvres porcelain. Every detail, from
the freshly beaten Turkey carpets to the winking facets of
the chandelier above the entranceway had been arranged to
impressive advantage.

Beneath the vaulted plasterwork ceiling of the foyer,
Lillian Winslow greeted her guests. Her formal smile never
wavered, and her voice was rich with culture as she spoke
empty words.

Although Bethany admired her mother's skill in orches-
trating a social affair with such apparent ease, she couldn't
help but feel a bit sorry for Lillian. Mother's life was con-
sumed by doing things properly. Her every thought and
action—including disowning her son—upheld the unwrit-
ten laws of propriety. She made her daily appearance at
precisely eleven—meticulously gowned and pomaded—and
she stayed that way until precisely ten at night, retiring
with her coiffure wrapped and caged, hands creamed and
gloved.

Lillian offered her fingers to Hugo Pierce, holding her
head slightly to one side, just so. Bethany wondered if her
mother had ever done a spontaneous thing in her life.

"Miss Bethany!" She felt her hand gripped and raised to
a pair of lips.

"Hello, Mr. Cranwick," she murmured, extracting her

fingers from his after pausing just long enough not to seem rude.

"My dear, I can't bear such formality. Please call me Keith."

"Of course. How agreeable to see you again, Keith." She struggled to keep a note of cynicism from her reply. It was amazing the effect a woman's few extra curves had on a man. Years ago, Keith Cranwick had been one of her chief tormentors, taking snide pleasure in informing her governess that she had sneaked out of church or that she'd glued Master Fine's shoes to the floor during dancing lessons. But Keith seemed to have forgotten those childish pranks. He fairly simpered as he admired her gown and the topaz teardrop at her throat. She excused herself and went into the drawing room, which was jammed to the walls with Newport's perfumed and pomaded elite.

Guests moved about the room in a dazzle of silks and satin. The occasional flash of a scarlet coat and a burnished gorget betrayed the presence of British officers. Bethany wasn't entirely certain she welcomed the newcomers.

At the punch bowl she spied Godfrey Malbone, wealthy and fantastically ugly. She recalled a ditty from her childhood. "All the money in the place won't buy old Malbone a pretty face." It seemed cruel, now, and she made an extra effort to smile and greet him.

She lost count of the number of times she murmured polite, inane phrases to people she had absolutely no desire to know. Feeling like a puppet on someone else's string, she smiled woodenly at the Pierces and the Cranwicks, the Slocums and the Eastons.

Keith Cranwick maneuvered himself again to her side, every inch the dandy in his finery—ruffled shirt and cambric stock, embroidered ratteen coat, green velvet knee breeches. His heavily powdered hair gave off an oppressive perfume which robbed Bethany of her appetite for the thick chowder, delicate pastries, and thinly sliced meats.

Afterward some of the ladies demonstrated their skill—or lack of it—at the pianoforte. Under her mother's look of smug approval, Bethany was paired off with several more partners. The polite gentlemen seemed to meld and fuse in her mind, their sameness of manner and dress rendering them indistinguishable from one another.

Thus the afternoon dragged on, the men finally going off to discuss the politics of the day, the women gossiping and chatting about fashion. Finding herself alone for a moment, Bethany compressed her voluminous skirts and slipped through the French doors to a raised veranda.

Exhaling loudly with relief, she strolled through the lilac arbor and sat down on a stone bench. She was immediately startled by a crashing in the box hedge below the veranda. A leaping ball of brown and white fur careened from the bushes.

"Gladstone!" she cried as the dog leaped to cover her surprised face with kisses and her skirts with sandy paw prints.

"Naughty wretch, you've dug out of the kennels again," she scolded, laughing.

Gladstone regarded her with soulful brown eyes, the tip of his stubby tail quivering with shame and remorse. The spaniel had been Harry's Christmas gift to her seven years ago and was her special pet.

Hearing the music resume in the house, she reluctantly rose from the bench. "Come along, you," she said, patting her thigh. "I'd best put you up before you bother the guests. Somehow I don't think Mother's friends would appreciate being mauled by your sandy paws."

The dog followed her down three wide stone steps and along the garden path to the kennels. Promising an outing later, she put him inside, latched the gate, and started back toward the house.

A waft of fresh spring air and the sweet trill of a finch in the lilacs made her hesitate. Her mind rebelled at the thought of spending more stifling hours in her mother's drawing room.

She yearned to escape the luxury and stability her usual suitors offered. Seized by a sudden irresistible impulse, she obeyed her heart, not feeling even a twinge of regret as she slipped away from the house.

It was nearly time to light a lamp to chase away the dim shadows of the stables. The grooms had finished their chores for the day; Ashton stayed on to see that the horses were settled for the evening. It was a time to settle his mind, too, a respite from the endless chores of raising Sinclair's horses and worry about his father and Carrie. Hearing a light step behind him, Ashton looked up.

Suddenly he could think of no more unsettling a sight in the world than Bethany Winslow.

He almost didn't recognize her in her full, rustling tea gown with its plunging neckline, her hair beautifully coiled with a string of pearls. He still hadn't gotten used to the idea that she was no longer the sunny, gangling child who had dogged his footsteps years ago. At the moment her stunning face was a study in impatience and supplication.

"You promised to take me riding," she said. Without hesitation she pulled up the hem of her skirts and kicked off her high-heeled shoes. "I'm sure these boots will suit me." She extracted a dusty pair from a chest. Pulling them on, she threw Ashton a questioning look.

"Well? Are we going riding or not?"

He grinned indulgently, shaking his head. "There now, have you ever known me to refuse you?"

She returned his smile. "Never, Ashton. You never would."

In minutes they were trotting down the sandy lane to a broad field shimmering in the soft light of early evening. At first she felt clumsy riding astride, her full gown bunched up in front of her. But soon the years of her absence rolled away and she dug her heels into the honey mare's flanks.

With a joyful laugh, she felt the horse's muscles contract and extend beneath her in a wild gallop.

For the first time since arriving home, she felt a measure of the boundless happiness of childhood. She was doing what she loved most in the company of the only man at Seastone who didn't try to kiss her hand or tell her how charming she looked, all the while wondering what sort of portion her father would settle on her.

Ashton's grin as he passed her lit an ember of warmth in her heart. Unlike the gentlemen back at the house, who plucked handkerchiefs from their sleeves and pressed them to their rouged and powdered faces, Ashton's good looks were natural. His rugged features were adorned by high coloring and masculinity alone; his mane of wavy chestnut hair would never stand for a covering of pomatum. The dandies back in the drawing room were like stiff mannequins compared to the strength and vibrancy that seemed to emanate from him.

He raised his arm and gestured toward the edge of the meadow. She followed him down a path overgrown with gooseberry bushes.

"Where are you going?" she called.

"Just follow me." He guided his horse between a great tumble of rocks. Periodically he glanced back to see if she was negotiating the way. She sat Calliope with confidence, knowing the mare to be surefooted and responsive to a rider's commands. When they reached the bottom of the climb, she brushed a stray curl from her eyes and looked about.

"Oh, Ashton . . ."

He leaped from his mount in a lithe motion and helped her down. "Like it?" His touch lingered like sunlight on the sand.

"It's grand, Ashton. I thought I knew every inch of this island, but I've never been here before." She ran down a ribbon of fine sable sand and whirled around, embracing the scene with outspread arms. Still more of her curls

escaped their pins, but she didn't notice. She was capti-
vated by the wild beauty all around her, the singing sea
mists, the spray torn from the water by gusting windheads.
The cove was flanked by cliffs on either side, fringed at the
edges by wild roses in the first flush of delicate pink and
deep scarlet blossoms. Waves rumbled up and caressed the
sand with a hiss. The sky was painted amber and pink by a
sweep of clouds spreading over the horizon.

He took her hand and led her along the beach. "'Tis a fine
place to come when the world starts nipping at your heels."

She glanced up at him. "Do I look as though the world is
nipping at my heels?"

He stopped walking to face her. "Very much so, Miss
Winslow." He rubbed his thumb gently over her brow. "I
don't like to see you unhappy."

"I'm not unhappy," she countered, "but I miss Harry
and I don't seem to fit in with my parents' friends at all."

He sent her a dubious look. "Love, I've been thinking
exactly the opposite."

"What do you mean?"

He touched the necklace that rested upon her soft
bosom. "You're as perfectly suited to your mother's elegant
drawing room as this teardrop suits the color of your eyes."

She gasped, feeling the soft sting of his touch as he
turned the gemstone over in his fingers, then let it fall back
in place. "Ashton, the things you say—"

"You asked." One corner of his mouth lifted in a half
smile. "You, my dear, are the epitome of the well-bred
young lady: lovely and graceful, your speech cultured, your
manners impeccable."

He laughed at her goggle-eyed expression. "Come now,
Miss Winslow, I'm not one to listen to servants' talk, but
I've heard you already have half the swains of Aquidneck
panting after you."

"I liked you better when you didn't notice such things,"
she said glumly.

Still laughing, he swept the cocked hat from his head, pointed his toe, and dipped in an exaggerated bow. "I beg you, my dear Miss Winslow, for the favor of one dance." His simpering lisp was a convincing parody of a parlor dandy's speech.

Caught by his mood, she pretended to flutter a fan. "Certainly, Mr. Markham." She tittered, batting her eyes as she gave him her hand.

Humming off-key, he led her through the steps of a minuet, playing the part of the besotted young gentleman to perfection. She laughed and went along with the farce, grateful to feel the tension of the afternoon slip away.

But a new sort of tension arose between them as they moved through the imaginary ballroom. At first she thought it was only the relief of having escaped her mother's dreary party, but soon she became aware of something else, a sensation she had never felt before.

Although Ashton's decorum would put even the most well-bred dandy to shame, she was stirred by his closeness, the warmth of his large, callused hand clasped around hers, the scent of the sea breeze in his hair.

She thought it odd to be aware of him in this new, unsettling way. In all the years she'd known him, she had never been so fascinated by the play of muscles in his shoulders, the compelling appeal of his smile, the deep, scintillating blue of his eyes.

But she was aware of those things now. And she was startled. When the mock dance ended, she immediately felt a vague loneliness for his touch.

"Better?" he inquired, flashing her a dazzling smile.

She lifted her eyes to meet his gaze. Although he'd been a man fully grown when she'd left, he seemed larger now; taller and broader, more imposing. She swallowed, then returned the smile.

"Much better, thank you. But then, you're far more agreeable company than the gentlemen I left back in the drawing room. They're only concerned about their fortunes—and mine, alas—and what color frock coat they'll commission from their tailors this season."

Ashton laughed. "Lucky fellows. We workaday chaps haven't the time to clutter our minds with matters of fashion."

"I'm glad. I wouldn't be able to stand it if you were like that."

Not for the first time, Ashton caught himself admiring her. Lord, but she was something to see. Tall and well proportioned, with a proud bearing and those incredible eyes blinking at him. She had a mouth as delectably ripe as a dew-moistened berry.

Honey. That was the one word to describe her. All gold and warm and sweet, from the honey of her hair to the amber of her eyes to the high, pure color of her skin.

He tore his eyes away, pushing aside the tantalizing notion. It was unthinkable even to consider such a thing. Bethany Winslow, with all her ingenuous charm and natural beauty, was Sinclair Winslow's prize filly, probably just weeks away from being paired off with a Thoroughbred. Ashton cautioned himself to remember that.

Nodding at a semicircle of rocks to the right, he said, "Good fishing over there."

"I didn't know you liked to fish." She frowned. "There is too much I don't know about you."

He raised an eyebrow. "You've known me all your life."

"We both grew up here at Seastone. And, Lord knows, I dogged your footsteps like a lost puppy. But so much time has passed." She ducked her head shyly. "In some ways we're strangers now."

"Love, you make my heart smile," he said. "Did you know that?"

"No," she whispered, a blush painting her cheeks.

Ah, he liked being with Bethany. Despite the years that had passed, she was still fresh and young and guileless. He sat down in the warm sand and patted the place beside him.

"Very well, love, I shall fill in all the blank spaces. But I assure you, no stars collided on the occasion of my birth. What would you like to hear?"

She sank to the sand beside him, glowing with pleasure. She traced a lazy flowerlike pattern in the sand with her finger.

"Tell me about your mother."

A dim, sweet memory stirred. In his mind's eye he saw himself as a frightened five-year-old boy, although he didn't quite understand that his mother was bleeding to death after giving birth to Carrie. He remembered standing at the bedside, leaning close to hear his mother's whisper. What was it she'd said to him?

"Ashton?" Bethany's voice intruded gently. "If you'd rather not speak of it—"

"I don't mind. I was just thinking of my mother's last words. She told me all the usual things, I suppose—to honor my father, be a good boy. . . . I believe the last thing she said was, 'you were born a bond servant's son, but never forget who you are.'"

"A bond servant's son?"

He shrugged. "She must have been confused, so close to death. My father wasn't a bond servant; he always worked for his wage." With a twinge of guilt he recalled Carrie's resentment of the way Roger spent those wages. "I often wish he hadn't insisted on a proper education for me, but I suppose he believed it's what my mother would have wanted."

"Harry once wrote me that you were to graduate from Rhode Island College with honors."

"I felt the least I could do was be a decent student. But in the end it didn't matter; His Majesty's army summoned me before my schooling was done."

"Couldn't you have postponed your service? 'Tis what Father did for William—"

"Couldn't afford it."

"But that's not fair, Ashton. You were reading law—"

"In truth, the subject never appealed to me. If I'd pursued a career, I'd be sitting in some stale office right now, scratching a quill over someone's ledger books." He gave her a sideways look. "You must think it quite shocking, my not wanting to make a fortune as quickly as I can."

"Why would that shock me?"

"Isn't that how it's done in your world?"

"My world? What are you saying? You talk as though we come from different planets."

"So we might, in a way."

"I don't like the sound of that, Ashton."

"'Tis the way of things. You, my dear, have been born and bred for a very specific purpose. At summer's end you'll doubtless have caught yourself one of Newport's most eligible men and be well on your way to society matronhood. You see, it's simple—"

Ashton stopped abruptly to duck before the handful of sand that Bethany hurled at him hit its mark.

"Stuff and nonsense," she retorted, threatening him with more sand. "Listen to yourself, talking as though my fate were sealed by some divine stamp."

He tried not to anger her further by chuckling as he brushed sand from his sleeve. "Perhaps it's true."

"I don't accept that." Furious, Bethany leaped up and began pacing down the beach. She didn't notice Ashton following close behind.

"Maybe I don't want to catch a husband or be a hostess at tea or commission a wardrobe from London," she railed, throwing her hands up. "Maybe I want—" She swung around and stopped to find herself staring point-blank at Ashton. The evening sun had burnished his chestnut hair to an even richer hue. A soft breeze lifted a strand, blowing it against the tanned planes of his face.

"What, Bethany?" he asked, his voice soft and compelling. "What is it you want?"

She caught her breath. Lord, she could drown in his

blue eyes. A sudden, insistent urge possessed her; she longed to touch the tiny cleft in his chin, to run her finger, ever so lightly, over the upward curve of his lips.

"Ashton." Her voice was a whisper on the evening breeze. Then with complete honesty she told him, "I think . . . that I want you to kiss me."

For a dreadful moment she thought he was going to mock her. But, mercifully, he didn't laugh. He bent briefly and plucked a white flower from the grassy fringes of the beach. With a slow movement he brought it to her lips, running it over them as he spoke.

"Have you ever been kissed before, Miss Winslow?"

She swallowed, feeling her knees grow weak as he continued to caress her with the flower. The petals left fever in their wake, shading her complexion a deep, warm pink. He must think her so absurd, so childish. She lowered her eyes and slowly shook her head.

He tucked the rose behind her ear and placed his fingers beneath her chin, tilting her face upward.

"Then we'd best get on with your education, love," he murmured.

Bethany stiffened, bracing herself. The blush staining her cheeks rose to even greater heights until she felt as though her whole face were in flames. She had an abrupt urge to flee, but Ashton, smiling down at her, his hands now firmly gripping her shoulders, kept her in a thrall of fascination.

That odd, unfamiliar smile still played over his features as he lowered his face to hers. He brushed her trembling lips with his mouth, lightly, as if aware of her hesitation. Her mind emptied of all thought. She marveled at the softness of his lips and wondered that so light a touch could create such an intense wave of emotion within her. Her eyelids fluttered shut as the pressure of his mouth deepened. Within her, something powerful and secret awakened, leaving her unsteady. Her hands crept to his chest. Incredibly, his heart leaped as wildly as her own.

She wanted the moment to go on forever, to simply give herself up to the unfamiliar, surging sensations which swept over her like the waves rolling up to cover the sand. His nearness, the scent of his skin and hair, the movement of muscle and flesh beneath his cambric shirt, struck her with pleasure.

She thought she knew this man she'd grown up with. But the tastes and smells and textures so uniquely his were completely new to her. Bethany, who had always listened with wry amusement as her schoolmates waxed endlessly about stolen kisses, suddenly learned with keen awareness that there was, indeed, something magical about a kiss.

It was all Ashton could do to drag his mouth from hers. But he did, using his entire will. At one time he had believed nothing could be so harmless as kissing a girl. Now he could think of nothing so powerful as the longing he felt for this woman.

He pulled away and gazed into her flushed face. She looked so sweet, so vulnerable. Her lips were swollen and moistened by his kiss. The taste of the cherry flip she'd drunk at her parents' party lingered on his mouth.

Forbidden fruit, Ashton warned himself.

She searched his eyes as if trying to read his thoughts. "Ashton?"

"We'd best be getting back."

Bethany felt the warm stirrings inside her grow cold at the sharpness in his voice. She was a fool to think Ashton had been moved to kiss her by anything more than his own generous nature; he himself had often admitted he could refuse her nothing. The kiss, though it had set a torch to her blood, had been to him merely the fulfillment of a request.

"I'm sorry," she said in a small voice. "I had no business asking that of you."

He gave her a hard look, concealing his relief. Obviously she required nothing more from him than to satisfy a young girl's curiosity. Well, he'd done it, and far more thoroughly than he'd intended.

2

"Must you go this minute?" Ashton demanded, his voice tight and low with anger.

Carrie preened before a small looking glass above the fireplace. Her bright ringlets bobbed and shimmered in the candlelight.

"Mr. Northbridge has invited me to a game of piquet, and I intend to win at least half a crown from him." She pulled a knitted shawl around her shoulders.

"Father seems . . . worse tonight," Ashton said.

She knotted the shawl beneath her breasts. "Then send for Goody Haas. She'll cook up a draft of Venice treacle for him."

Ashton shook his head. "Her remedies do no good."

"Well, I have nothing better to offer. Good night, Ashton. I'm taking the Indian pony. You mustn't wait up. I do so hate it when you check on me. . . ." She swept through the doorway and ran lightly down to the stables.

Ashton went as far as the threshold, snapping out her name. Then he slammed the door against the sound of her laughter.

"Let her go, son," said a raspy voice behind him.

Ashton wheeled and crossed the room to the bedside. "Father, I didn't realize you were awake." He wondered if Roger had overheard the discussion about his condition.

"Can I get you anything?"

Roger shook his head. "Bring that stool over, son, so we can talk."

Filled with an overwhelming sense of helpless frustration, Ashton sat beside his father. Roger was but a pale shadow of the vital man he had been—unbearably thin, his once handsome face now haunted by ominous hollows beneath his eyes. The stool scraped the puncheon floor as Ashton drew nearer to the bed.

"A game of piquet . . ." Roger's voice was thick with phlegm. "Who is this Northbridge fellow anyway?"

Ashton looked away, focusing on the smoking, spluttering betty lamp above the fireplace. "A friend."

Roger nodded. Perhaps he knew of his daughter's trysts; perhaps not. Either way, he was as incapable as Ashton of preventing her outings.

"She must be very much in demand, our Carrie," Roger said. "Ah well, the girl seems happy enough. Should have had a mother to raise her properly."

"You've been both mother and father to her. To us both."

Roger's dry lips stretched into a smile. Yet at the same time he looked utterly stricken.

"Father, what is it?" Ashton tensed, ready to rush to do his bidding.

Roger raised a feeble hand. "Stay where you are. Ah, there is much I'll miss about you, son, much that I have loved—your seriousness, your devotion, even the stubborn streak of pride I see in you when you stride about Newport as if you own the town."

Ashton could only stare. Never had his father spoken to him like this, from the heart, with a desperate urgency that meant he knew he was dying.

Roger's sigh escaped as a wheeze. "There is so much to be said, lad, so much more I should have taught you. Perhaps, too, it is time to confess I wasn't the wage earner you always thought me."

Ashton frowned. "Sir, I don't understand. We've lacked for nothing."

"Aye, and there's a reason for that." An invisible weight seemed to press on his chest, and each breath he took required more of his fast-ebbing strength than the last. "Time for some serious talk, son," he whispered. "There now, we needn't mince about the point. I've lived longer than I deserve. Long enough to see you grow into a responsible man—" A fit of coughing erupted from him. Ashton leaned forward and held his shoulders. Roger waved him back to his stool.

"What I regret most about dying," he said matter-of-factly, "is that I leave you with so little."

"'Tis not true." Ashton's chest squeezed. "You've given me life. An enviable education. Being your son is a privilege, sir."

Roger's hand rose again to silence him. He exhaled, and the breath rustled like dry leaves in his feeble chest. "I've often wondered if I did right, bringing you and your mother here all those years ago."

"You had to leave. The situation was intolerable for Catholics in England."

"Aye," Roger agreed. "Thank God Newport is a free-thinking place. Sinclair Winslow—an Anglican—took me on to manage his stables. He valued my ability with horses over the way I chose to worship."

"'Tis as it should be." Ashton noticed a wistful look on his father's face and knew that Roger was thinking of the old days, back in Kent. Roger Markham had not learned about horses by slogging through the stableyards there. He had owned a country estate and had once ridden to the hounds on blooded hunters. But everything came crashing down around him with the arrival of Lord Sturgrove, fanatical in his hatred of Catholics. Roger could have retained his estate by renouncing his faith, but he had chosen the more rocky path of devotion instead.

"You did the right thing. A brave thing, sir," Ashton said.

"Not so very brave," Roger objected, "tending another man's stock. Your mother could never bring herself to do tasks she considered beneath her; she was always so much the lady."

Ashton looked at his hands as a few wispy impressions of his mother passed through his mind. She had died giving birth to Carrie, and Ashton had been only five at the time. He remembered her as a quiet presence, sitting at a window, seemingly unable to comprehend her active son leaping through the gardens with shouts of joy.

"Father," he asked, "why did you never take another wife?"

"Ah," Roger said with a wheezing laugh. "After one has ridden a Thoroughbred, one doesn't settle for a farm plug. But you." The old eyes narrowed. "You're the one of marrying age now, son."

Ashton looked away. "I've naught to offer a bride." He forced a careless grin to conceal his bitterness.

"Fetch the box with my rosary beads, son."

Ashton handed the beads to his father, wishing he could feel the comfort Roger seemed to find in the olivewood strand.

"There's something else in the box," Roger said. "Your mother's wedding ring."

Ashton extracted the slim gold band; plain, and shiny despite its age. His mother hadn't lived long enough to bruise the gold or wear it away.

"I'd wager," Roger said, "any number of girls would be proud to wear that. You've your mother's striking looks, my own horse sense, and a boundless self-assurance the Good Lord gave you. You call that naught?"

"I've never known one's looks or attitude to put food on the table or clothe a body."

Roger lifted one corner of his mouth. "Yes, exactly so." The half smile disappeared, and a furrow deepened his brow. "What's to become of you Americans? Civil war is an ugly matter."

"'Tis no longer agitation, but armed rebellion. There's a proper army now—Continentals, they call them. General Washington is putting Boston under siege."

For a moment, the dullness left Roger's eyes, replaced by keen probing. "You'll leave, won't you, Ashton?"

"I'm here for as long as you need me."

"We both know that won't be long."

"Father—"

"Never mind, just listen. Will you fight, Ashton?"

He remembered the punishing marches, the indifference of the officers, the air of indolence and cruelty that had hung over his regiment. "I've proven my aversion to soldiering. Besides, I'm no Loyalist."

"A patriot, then?"

"I'll leave the fighting to the rebels."

"Then where will you go, son?"

Ashton paused, regarding the betty lamp, which was down to its last drops of tallow. Where, indeed? Where did he fit in? He was educated; in addition to his schooling, Roger had taught him the manners of a polished—albeit penniless—gentleman.

He listened to the rush of waves outside, and another sound came chasing on its heels: the imagined rhythm of hoofbeats and the roar of a crowd. He had heard those particular noises often, crossing the finish line on the finest and best-trained horseflesh in Narragansett.

"I'll race horses," he said, so quickly he knew the idea had been at the back of his mind for some time. "I've gotten a decent reputation hereabouts. I know what it takes to win. There are those who will pay for that."

The cornhusk mattress rustled beneath Roger. "At least stay the season here; wouldn't do to leave Mr. Winslow wanting a stockman. You could train Barnaby Ames to take your place. And don't tell me you could walk away from Corsair."

Ashton hesitated. "I don't share your loyalty to Winslow, but it would be a shame to rob the stallion of a winning season. I'll stay for a while."

The troubled look in the pale old eyes was replaced by a contentment so sweet that Ashton almost had to look away. Roger's dry lips cracked as he smiled.

"I can ask no more, son."

Ashton could see his father's strength ebbing. Over the past few days no fewer than three doctors had been to see him. The physicians and Goody Haas as well had not been able to offer any hope. The lung ailment was eating up Roger's strength with alarming speed and finality.

Ashton battled a terrible emptiness. Too full of raw emotion to speak, he gripped his father's hand, wishing that, by some magic, some of his strength could flow into Roger.

"Carrie . . ." Roger raised his head a little.

"She's not here, Father."

Roger lowered his head back onto the pillow. "Take care of her, son. Don't let her own foolishness get the better of her."

Ashton nodded.

"And do not judge her too harshly."

"I won't."

Roger slept. Hours passed. Ashton moved about the room, tidying up and refilling the betty lamp. Roger awoke. A strange smile crossed his face. A single tear seeped from the corner of one eye, but oddly, there was no trace of sadness about him. A sigh slipped from between his parched lips.

Then, in a voice barely audible above the spluttering of

the lamp and the distant swishing of the sea, Roger said, "God grant you contentment, son."

The wick of the betty lamp guttered in its holder and the wavering flame died. Later that night, the light went out of Roger Markham's eyes.

In the garden a whippoorwill greeted the morning with three syllables, bright as liquid sunshine. But inside the shuttered cottage by the stables, all was dim and melancholy.

Unmindful of the roughness of the puncheon floor, Bethany sank to her knees by Roger Markham's body. As tears flowed down her cheeks, she choked out a prayer for the man she had known all her life. He had been so much a part of Seastone that, absurdly, she thought he would endure like the stones and the trees and the changeless rhythm of the waves.

After a time she rose and placed a kiss on the stark, cool cheek. Summoning all her courage, she faced Ashton. What did one say to a man who had just lost his father? No, not just a father. Roger had been so much more to Ashton. Friend, mentor, confidant, teacher . . . Roger's love for his son had been so evident that, guiltily, she remembered a time when she had actually been jealous of them.

"I'm sorry," she whispered brokenly, "so very sorry. . . . It won't seem the same without him." In the soft light of early morning she looked at Ashton's tense, haggard face and realized no words could comfort him. She crossed the room swiftly and placed her arms around his neck, crying quietly as she reached up and stroked his hair and soothed his cheeks with her hands. And as she did so, she was struck by the knowledge that she was, indeed, no longer a child, but a woman offering a comforting embrace.

Ashton stepped back and looked away. "I'll be all right," he said hoarsely.

His stiff restraint frightened Bethany. She sensed that he was riddled by a terrible grief he refused to show.

"You ache for him, Ashton," she whispered. "I can see it in your face. You must allow yourself to grieve; no good can come of holding back what you feel."

He shook his head. "Ah, don't look at me so. You make me wish I remembered how to weep, but—" He scowled and clenched his hands into a fists.

"But what, Ashton?"

His mouth thinned into a rueful, joyless smile. "Even now, you make me think of your softness, the way you feel when I hold you."

She caught her breath, and heat rushed to her face. "I wasn't trying to be . . . that is, I only wanted to comfort you."

"I know." He blew out his breath loudly. "It's my fault for not being prepared for how you've changed." His hands relaxed and then sought hers, holding them loosely. "I'll take your tears, love, because I have none of my own to give."

"It doesn't work that way." A fresh wave of sadness washed over her and more tears coursed hotly down her face.

"Ah, Christ," he said, holding out his arms to her. "Come here."

She pressed her face to his chest, soaking his shirtfront. "My weeping is selfish. You're the one in need of comfort."

He gave her a final squeeze and, as he had so many times in the past, mopped her tears away. "You are a comfort to me," he said gently. "I never realized my father meant that much to you."

"But he did." She looked wistfully at the crude fireplace at the far wall of the cottage. "How many times did I sit here, my head in his lap, listening to him talk? He had such a fine way of telling stories, I never minded when it rained and we couldn't ride. Your father was full of humor and affection. How many times did I run to him for comfort when my pony suffered a lame leg or the colic? He was always there, willing to listen, even when my own father thought my problems too trifling to bother with."

He dabbed carefully at her cheek with a handkerchief. "You had all a girl could ask for. Yet the things you treasure can't be bought with money."

"Exactly," she said, drawing in a shuddering breath. "Is it always so? Will we always want the things we lack and have no appreciation for the things we have?"

His fine mouth curved into a sad smile. "You ask hard questions, Miss Bethany Winslow."

Carrie Markham sailed into the cottage. Her pretty dimity gown was creased and sandy from riding, and her hair had a decidedly rumpled look. She was smiling broadly, humming to herself as she swept off her shawl.

"Ah, what a glorious time I had," she said. "And profitable, too—" She broke off, noticing Bethany for the first time.

"What brings you here so early, miss?" she inquired. "Oh my, you've been crying. Are you still troubled about your brother, or—"

"Carrie." Ashton's voice cut her off so sharply that she looked at him in surprise, catching her breath.

"Really, Ashton, 'tis not seemly for you to scold me in front of Miss Winslow." Carrie sent Bethany a conspiratorial look. "She, at least, has been generous enough to let me go about my business as I please."

Bethany looked away to hide the distaste she felt for her maid's escapades.

"He's dead, Carrie," Ashton said.

Carrie rushed to Roger's bed. She stopped a few feet short of him, staring, her back stiff, her arms hugging herself. Bethany expected a storm of grief. But Carrie merely stood and stared at the man who had been her father. A long, tense silence stretched over several moments.

Finally Carrie turned, her face expressionless, though pale. "God's will be done." Then she left the cottage, striding purposefully toward the main house.

Bethany caught her lower lip with her teeth, watching Ashton with pain-filled eyes. She noted the white furrows of fury around his mouth and the way he stiffened, his fists clenching and unclenching. Tiny ice shards of rage glinted in his eyes.

"Ashton," she said, fearing his anger, forcing herself to face him. "She didn't mean to sound callous. This is a great shock to her. Later she'll grieve for him."

"No," he said. She saw his anger ebbing away, replaced by a poignant, world-weary look that caused her throat to ache in sympathy. "Not Carrie. Perhaps it was a blessing she didn't love him. She won't feel the hurt."

Once again Bethany rushed to him and wound her arms around his waist. How could he be so strong, so implacably calm, when he had just lost his father? Without thinking, she leaned up and kissed his cheek and then his eyes, lightly, tenderly, as if to coax the healing tears from them.

The tears didn't come. Instead a groan ripped from his throat and he caught her in an urgent embrace. Taking her face between his hands, he crushed his mouth down on hers.

Unlike the time he had kissed her on the beach, there was no gentleness in him. He held her in a grip of desperation, as if clinging to her to ward off a dreadful emptiness inside him. His mouth ground down on hers, forcing her lips apart as his tongue sought the soft, untried recesses of her mouth.

She felt a shocking sensation; even grief didn't overshadow a heated longing that caused her to tremble. Not even his first kiss, its memory weeks old, could have prepared her for this reckless, sensual assault. She felt his need even more strongly than her own. He wanted her closeness, her compassion, and if he chose to take it in this way, then she would give it freely.

Relaxing against him, she invited the demanding caresses of his tongue and mouth, and moved her hands slowly over his back, trying to soothe the tightness in his muscles.

He released her abruptly. She watched the rapid rise and fall of his chest.

"I'm sorry," he said.

"Don't be. Don't apologize. 'Twas I who invited your embrace."

"I think you should go, Bethany."

"You shouldn't be alone right now."

"Nor should I be with you. Something about you causes me to forget myself."

"Ashton."

"Go, Bethany. I'll be fine."

She sent him a dubious glance, but he looked so hard and implacable that she dared not argue further. Stepping to the door, she turned. "I'll be back," she promised.

Sinclair Winslow frowned when his daughter rushed into the dining room that evening. Bethany understood her father's expression. He disliked any disruption of his well-ordered life; punctuality was a virtue he prized.

"We've held supper an hour for you," he said as William seated her. "What kept you?"

She didn't apologize. After the melancholy burial at the Common Burying Ground in Farewell Street, she and Ashton had talked idly for hours. She had cried again while he grieved in pained silence.

She said, "I was with Ashton."

"Really, Bethany, 'twas not necessary for you to linger over the man," Lillian said, echoing her husband's disapproval. "We've already sent him a basket of food."

Sinclair nodded. "I would have commissioned funeral rings, but the infernal Continental Congress included them in last year's boycott. I settled a generous bonus on Markham instead."

"And do you think that lessened his pain? Do you think a few coins can comfort him? Ashton needed *me,* Mother. Not food, nor money, but me."

"Bethany," William said in his slow, moderate tones. "We all feel for the man." He motioned for a footman to refill his wineglass.

"Then why don't you do something about it?"

"There now, Ashton will get over his father's death," Sinclair assured her. "He's a strong man. Lord knows, there'll be enough to keep him occupied now that the racing season is underway."

Her anger dissipated to silence. Nothing she could say would cause her parents to feel a thing for Ashton. With a sick jolt of understanding she realized they didn't consider him worthy of their compassion. To them he was an employee, not allowed to have feelings but merely to be worked like a beast for their gain.

William noticed she hadn't touched her meal of roasted squab hen and spiced squash. "Are you ill, Bethany? You've not eaten a thing."

"I haven't much appetite."

Lillian Winslow faced her daughter in agitation. "You mustn't be so morose, dear. You have been difficult ever since you returned from New York. Your fretfulness at the Malbones' ball last week was rather obvious."

Bethany was used to such criticism; her mother never failed to find fault with her. "I tried to be polite. I never once refused a dance."

"And you never once laughed or flirted or exchanged pleasantries with the guests," Lillian chided her. "Really, my dear, you must learn to enjoy the company of your peers. You don't want gentlemen to find you dull."

"I don't want gentlemen to find me at all!"

"She'll have no worries about that," William said. "She

could be daft as a dormouse and she'd still catch men's eyes." He grinned. "'Tis my misfortune that the most comely lady in Newport happens to be my sister."

"William, please." There was something objectionable about sitting around the elegant table receiving lavish compliments when Ashton was alone, sharing his supper with dim shadows and memories.

"Even Keith Cranwick, that cold fish, was remarking on the extraordinary color of those eyes," William continued.

"Appearances are important," Lillian said. "But Bethany, you must make more of an effort to be sociable."

"I don't like your friends, Mother," she said. Although usually respectful of her parents, she'd had a trying day and at the moment could not abide her mother's complaints about her behavior. "I don't like listening to Bach being mangled on the pianoforte by some lead-fingered ninny or being dragged around the dance floor by preening fops or pretending to be interested in endless discussions of who is wearing what at which ball this year." She stood up and flung her napkin onto the linen tablecloth. "I'd like nothing better than to be excused from all your dreary parties!"

Even as she fled to the haven of her room, Bethany realized it was hopeless. In time she would shed this black mood and once again be the dutiful daughter. Polite greetings and light, meaningless conversation would spring to her lips and she would play the role expected of her. What was it Miss Abigail had once said? The more distasteful we find a task, the stronger we become in performing it.

A warm breeze redolent of summer stirred the fine grass of the Common Burying Ground. Bethany stood beside Ashton, gazing at the mound of earth that, for a fortnight now, had covered the body of Roger Markham. Over Carrie's strident objections Ashton had spent most of Sinclair's bonus to commission a fine shale headstone from John Stevens's stonecutter's shop. Today the small monument had been placed where it would remain for all eternity.

The forceful, primitive melancholy of the carving arrested the eye and stirred the soul. Roger's name was inscribed beside that of his wife, with a verse from his favorite psalm chiseled beneath.

"'Our soul waiteth for the Lord; He is our help and our shield,'" Bethany read softly. "He would have liked that." She bent and patted the earth beside the marker, where she'd planted cuttings of yellow primroses.

Ashton nodded. His pain had dulled, although an empty, hollowed-out feeling persisted. He looked over at Bethany. Her eyes were moist, brimming with sincerity. She had come to him nearly every day, braving even his blackest moods to draw him into conversation. Sometimes she merely sat and let him feel her closeness.

He thought of her leaning on the desk in the stable office, her chin cupped in her hands, watching him record an entry in a breeding book as if he were penning an epic poem. The image was immeasurably endearing.

"What my father would have liked," he remarked, surprised at the fondness he heard in his voice, "was having a daughter like you."

"Oh, I wouldn't want to be your sister." She returned his smile, though hers was charmingly bashful.

"And why not?"

Her cheeks reddened. "Brothers do not treat their sisters as—as you've treated me in the past."

He felt his face harden as the memory of kissing her came back to haunt him. "'Tis best forgotten, Bethany," he said in a tight voice.

She turned an even darker shade of pink. "I shall never forget." Long, curling lashes veiled her eyes. "I kept the rose you gave me that day on the beach. It's pressed in tissue in a volume of Anne Bradstreet's poems."

He gave her a flinty-eyed look, concealing a surge of desire. At first he had been sure she would forget her attraction to him. Now he realized he was wrong. She was as tenacious as she had been as a child, only her desires were more complicated and dangerous now. The soft, winsome way she was looking at him left no doubt as to what she was thinking.

"I'll walk you back home," he said abruptly, leading the way down the grassy hill. They strolled together through the wharf area of Newport. Sailors in tattered working garb or in bright shore togs of flapping trousers, crimson sashes, and eelskin boots traded yarns and swigs of grog. Hucksters haggled over a few pence worth of calamanco. Gulls, attracted by the smell of fish and spilled rum, screeched, adding to the frenzied sounds of the waterfront.

They left the bustling activity of the wharves behind and wandered homeward, hand in hand. When they reached the quiet, elegant estate, Bethany slowed her pace, reluctant to leave Ashton's company despite his mood. She turned her attention to the gardens, which had blossomed into a summer fairy grove of color and scent. Tall Canterbury bells surrounded a plot of laburnums rich in streaming gold. Beneath a small grove of quince, the summerhouse offered a quiet haven.

She moved up the path, motioning for Ashton to follow, and paused at a low bush of lad's love, plucking a sprig and inhaling its pungent aroma.

"Goody Haas once told me this is a love charm," she said lightly. "Guaranteed to make me irresistible if I tuck a sprig in each shoe."

He grinned and shook his head. "You needn't worry about using love charms. Doubtless any number of men already find you irresistible."

She nearly asked him if he was one of them, but she didn't dare. Ashton was too kind to tell her he wasn't attracted to her and too proper to tell her he was.

Seating herself on a bench in the summerhouse, she laid the bit of lad's love aside. Far below, the sea pounded against the rocks. "'Tis peaceful here," she declared.

"Aye," Ashton said. "Though I prefer buildings that have a more practical use."

"I think it's perfectly lovely."

His mouth compressed into a bitter line.

"Why do you look at me so?"

He took a deep breath. "You just reminded me of the gulf between us." She opened her mouth to retort, but he held up his hand and continued. "You are charming, love, and impossibly naive. And I don't mean that as a criticism. You deserve a life of softness and indulgence. You have every right to expect things like an ivy-draped summerhouse."

"And what is wrong with enjoying beauty?" she demanded.

"Not a blessed thing. You should forgive my nasty mood." He drew his knee up to his chest and regarded her without expression. "I'll be leaving Newport soon."

Her jaw dropped. "You're leaving?"

"Aye, pet. Now that Father's gone, there's little to keep me here."

"Seastone is your home," she said. "You can't leave. You can't."

But he only shook his head. "This is *your* home, love. 'Tis only my place of employment."

She gave him a look of stricken disbelief. Tears of disappointment burned in her eyes.

Ashton turned his head away. "I'll not let you make me feel guilty," he said. Then, as if forcing himself, he looked at her. "Years ago I used to take you in my arms and tease you into laughter. But lately when I do that, neither of us end up laughing."

"Where will you go?" she asked, her voice low and shaking.

"I haven't decided yet. I'll be following the racing circuit after the season here."

"What about Carrie?"

"My sister lives her life exactly as she likes and will undoubtedly be glad to see me go. I'll send her money when I can."

Impulsively she took his hand. "I don't want you to leave," she said.

Ashton imagined he could feel the pain of her aching heart.

Heat leaped through his loins at the warm pressure of her hand on his. He filled his gaze with her beauty. Her hair was a long, loose cascade framing her face. Its color was extraordinary, like honey shot through with sunlight. A warm, ineffable scent of jasmine emanated from her. Her skin looked as smooth as cream, her lips full, begging him to taste their ripeness.

His hard-won resolve shattered when he saw her yearning. A groan of frustrated desire was wrenched from him as he pulled her swiftly to him and kissed her.

Bethany sighed sweetly in his strong embrace. Each time he held her, the bond between them strengthened; the silken cords of desire grew taut. As she fluttered her eyelashes against his tanned cheek, he heard her inhale as if drinking in his essence. Her hands began a compelling search over the muscles of his back.

His desire fueled by her mounting passion, he wrapped her closer. Under the increased pressure of his mouth, her lips softened and parted. He slid his tongue past the tentative barrier of her teeth and heard a muted sound of longing in the back of her throat. She tasted of summer's sweetness, and her warm, yielding body molded itself to his with innocent yearning.

The embrace lasted for an endless moment until he recaptured his resolve and reluctantly lifted his mouth from hers.

Bethany fell, trembling, against his broad chest, her heart

leaping wildly. "Ashton, don't leave me," she breathed in an unsteady whisper. "I feel as if I've only just found you."

"I've gone too far already. If you knew just what it is you do to me, you'd run in fear of your virtue. Let me go now, or I may not be able to bring myself to leave when the time comes."

"Then stay. Stay, so we can be together."

"That's just it," he said more harshly, his Kentish accent becoming more pronounced. "Even if I were to remain at Seastone, we could never be together."

"Of course we could, Ashton—"

His eyes grew stormy and his grip bit into the soft flesh of her upper arms. "Is this what you want?" He gave her a little shake. "A few stolen moments, groping in the garden like a pair of naughty children?"

She shook her head. With leaden sadness she stepped from the circle of his arms, conceding his point.

His sharp eyes scanned the garden for a moment, and a crooked, humorless grin crossed his face.

"What is it?" she asked.

"I was just thinking how dramatically my departure would be expedited if someone had seen us just now. Your father would arrange a regular rogue's march for me."

She tried to smile. Ashton wasn't afraid of anything, least of all her father's blustering.

Ashton stepped back, lengthening the distance between them. "I'd best see to my chores. Good day," he said abruptly, and retreated down the path toward the stables.

Bethany leaped from the figured brocade settee in the drawing room when her company announced that it was time to leave. She suffered the attention of her callers with cool politeness, not caring that people had begun to whisper behind her back that she was haughty and unapproachable.

She offered her hand to Keith Cranwick, her most frequent and least welcome caller. As he bent to press his lips to her hand, she looked away from the gleam in his eye. Behind him, Mabel Pierce aimed a dagger-sharp look at Bethany. Mabel considered Keith her private property and Bethany a trespasser.

Bethany's pasted-on smile wavered; someday she might tell Mabel just how groundless that jealousy was. For her, Keith had all the appeal of a toothache.

Extracting her hand from his, she gave it in turn to his companion. Unusually handsome, with dark hair and eyes, Captain Dorian Tanner was nothing like Keith. His features reminded her of a statue at twilight, full of secrets and shadows. Yet his uniform—a red frock coat faced with the dark blue of Hanover House—lent him a solid, trustworthy look. Dorian didn't actually kiss her hand, but bent over it with utmost decorum.

"Do come again," she said, remembering her manners. "Perhaps another time I'll be more attentive while we're playing cards. I lost dreadfully today, didn't I?"

"There's no pleasure in besting you, Miss Bethany," Dorian said.

She held her smile in place as she stood at the door, waving as their coach rolled away and wondering when she'd spent a more boring afternoon.

That evening she went to the stables, clad in a sleek dove-gray split skirt and matching jacket.

Barnaby Ames appeared, lifting his hat in greeting. "Always a pleasure to see you, miss. Shall I saddle Calliope?"

She opened her mouth to speak, but was interrupted by a rude snort from a nearby stall. Glancing over, she saw Corsair rearing his head and stamping his feet on the sawdust laden floor. A smile spread across her face. The stallion's restless mood perfectly matched her own.

"Saddle Corsair," she told Barnaby. "I think a more demanding mount would please me this evening."

He shuffled his feet. "Surely you can't mean to ride that infernal beast, miss. No one rides a stallion except a madman. The devil'd sooner toss you into a hedgerow as let you get the better of him."

"Corsair just needs a firm hand. Have you ever known me to fear a bit of horseflesh?" The stallion snorted again and tossed his head.

The groom argued, but Bethany wouldn't be moved. Soon she was seated high on the black stallion's back in the stableyard, concentrating doggedly on controlling him. He snapped his head back and sidled to and fro, behaving with unconscionable skittishness. When she tried to turn him toward the gate, the horse lifted his front hooves and raked the air, whinnying.

Suddenly the reins were snatched from Bethany's hands, and she found herself looking down into a pair of stormy blue eyes.

"What the hell do you think you're doing?" Ashton demanded, bringing the stallion in check.

She tossed her head, as defiant as the horse moving in protest beneath her. "What does it look like I'm doing, serving tea? I'm taking Corsair for a ride."

Ashton shook his head. "Sorry, pet, but I can't let you go."

"Who are you to forbid me to ride one of my father's own horses?" She felt inexplicably petulant.

He froze and went rigid. "I'm in charge of the stables, and I won't allow you to ride Corsair." Like a deserter from a battlefield, Barnaby Ames retreated to the stables.

"I shall do as I please," she replied.

"I see. The master's daughter expects complete obedience from a stable hand." Ashton's voice was bitter.

Bethany's hand flew to her mouth and she wished with all her heart she could snatch the words back. "I didn't mean to sound that way. I—it's been a rather trying day and—"

"Oh, yes. I'm aware of how exhausting cards and backgammon can be."

She looked away, refusing to let him see what his sarcasm did to her. "I intend to ride this horse."

"Then I wouldn't dream of stopping you, Miss Bethany." As he spoke, he ducked into the tackroom and emerged carrying a worn and dusty pillion. Before she knew what was happening, he had brought her to the ground and was securing the cushion behind the saddle.

"What are you doing?"

"Taking you for a ride."

She drew herself up in indignation. "I've not ridden pillion since I was two years old."

He leaned down until they were nose to nose, the angry blue of his eyes clashing with the obstinate hazel of hers. "You'll ride pillion with me," he said quietly, "or you won't ride Corsair at all."

She tried hard to cling to her anger. She tried, and failed. For beneath his imperative words, uttered from such close proximity she could feel the heady essence of his breath, she recognized concern. Lovely warm feelings swept in and softened the edges of her temper. Holding his eyes with hers, she gave him her sweetest smile.

"Shall we go, Ashton?"

Moments later they were atop Corsair. The horse wheeled and pawed the air, and Bethany had to fling her arms around Ashton's waist to keep from falling off.

As they cantered down the lane and veered out across fields of waving poppies, bright China red against the gray-green grass, she could feel Ashton's anger as acutely as she felt the awesome strength of the stallion's stride beneath her. She knew the ride would leave her sore for a week.

He drove the horse to a full gallop, and she could sense she was being tested. Beneath her, the pillion provided scant comfort. She gritted her teeth against each jolt to keep from crying out in pain as Corsair plunged across the fields.

Much later, miles later it seemed, Ashton relented and slowed the horse. Bethany moved gingerly in the saddle, squeezing her eyes shut against the pain in her thighs and backside. He glanced at her over his shoulder.

"Enjoy your ride, Miss Bethany?" he inquired mildly.

"Damn you," was all she could say.

His amusement began as a vague trembling, felt by her arms around his middle. Then he gave full vent to his mirth, laughing richly and mercilessly.

Bethany began to smile in spite of herself. Wondering where her anger had gone, she said, "'Tis not the first time I've humiliated myself on a horse."

"You always were a poor pupil," he chided, still chuckling. "Too impatient, never willing to consider caution. You still have a lot to learn." He patted her hand, then gave a light tug on the reins. They started homeward, taking the town route along Thames Street.

Although twilight gathered in purple splendor over the bay, Newport was astir. The wheels of commerce had brought the seaport to great eminence in the Colonies. Merchants achieved prosperity by ignoring the navigation laws and pursuing a policy of free trade, a policy the British officials had neglected for years.

There was plenty of money here, Ashton reflected. Glancing to his right, he saw tall ships, their billowing sails semifurled, wending in and out of piers looking for a likely spot to unload. Gimblets and rattinet were bartered right off the ships. The muted ochre and red houses of the shippers of Thames Street stood vigil over the busy scene.

"Ashton?" Bethany's soft query drew him from his reflection. "What are you thinking?"

"I was thinking about making a living."

"You make a perfectly good living at Seastone."

His expression tightened. Bethany, who had never wanted for anything in her life, should hardly be expected to understand exactly how little he had. "I want more than a position as someone else's stockman."

"That was enough for your father," she insisted.

"Not for me. I made him a promise of sorts, just before he died. This is America, for God's sake, not England, where a man's station is determined the moment he's born."

She folded her hands demurely about his waist as if in silent contemplation. He wanted to explain how he felt, why he was driven to build upon what his father had left him. But before he could speak, he heard a male voice calling her name. Swiveling in the saddle, he saw a British officer striding up Thames Street. A decidedly unpleasant feeling snaked through Ashton as he slowed Corsair.

"Hello, Captain Tanner," Bethany said.

The Redcoat executed a precise bow. "Miss Bethany. Delightful to see you again."

"Captain Tanner, this is Ashton Markham," Bethany said. "We were just starting back to Seastone."

"I see." Tanner's glance dismissed Ashton but focused with admiration on Bethany. "Good evening, then, miss."

With a nod as brief and curt as Tanner's glance had been, Ashton urged Corsair forward. "A friend of yours?" he inquired over his shoulder.

"He's called once or twice. He has a faultless hand at piquet."

"I suppose," Ashton said with unaccountable acidity, "Captain Tanner finds time to hone his skill in between harassing the citizens of Newport."

Her laughter sailed like bright music on the sea breeze. "Honestly, Ashton, you sound as radical as Harry."

Maybe I am, he thought, and then put the notion away as they left the town behind them.

As Corsair galloped past flower-studded meadows,

Ashton's thoughts turned to more pleasant subjects. He found himself contemplating the arms circling his girth so trustingly. Feeling the front of Bethany's body pressing at his back, he fought a sensation of arousal.

He began to regret his promise to Sinclair Winslow to stay through the season, racing his horses and training Barnaby Ames as his replacement. The sooner he removed himself from Bethany's company, the sooner he'd escape the wild, forbidden hunger she roused in him.

Bethany's hand drifted down his side to rest upon his thigh. At first he thought it was an accidental touch, but when she pressed him there, her caress seemed to burn through his buckskin breeches to his skin.

He cleared his throat. "Bethany, please . . ." She could not know what she was doing to him. Her very nearness was unsettling enough, but this little exploration was more than he could bear. "Didn't anyone ever warn you about teasing a man in that way?"

With a mortified exclamation, she took her hand away. Ashton couldn't suppress a grin, knowing she must be blushing to the tips of her ears.

They rode the rest of the way in silence. At the head of the avenue leading up to the house, a brown and white streak of fur hurled itself toward them. The spaniel circled Corsair, barking sharply and bowing his chest down, the wagging stub of a tail high in the air.

"Gladstone, shoo," Bethany said, laughing. "He's too fond of this horse."

"Much to the chagrin of Corsair." He helped her down in the stableyard.

Bethany scooped up the dog. "Gladstone forgives him, don't you, sweet?" She sighed. "I wish it could be so with people. Few humans can show adoration so freely, asking nothing in return."

Ashton regarded her keenly for a moment, then shrugged and walked the horse around the yard to cool him.

Bethany followed in quiet contemplation. Sometimes he baffled her. He could be warm and teasing one moment, sinfully sensual the next, cold and indifferent after that. As she watched him performing the familiar routine of putting up the horse, she admitted he fascinated her. And frightened her a little.

Miss Primrose had always told her to face her fears squarely. To get to know them like old friends, for who could ever be afraid of an old friend?

Very well, Bethany thought, no more mincing about the point. She squared her shoulders and went to stand behind Ashton as he slung the saddle over the side of a stall. When he turned, she was standing so close she could feel the warmth of his body.

Not daring to hesitate, she wound her arms around his neck and pressed herself against him. Immediately the lovely, melting sensations she had lately come to associate with Ashton washed over her.

He created a breathless yearning in her that she didn't quite understand. Full of questions, begging for answers, she tilted her head back and stared up at him. Passion and reason warred in his stormy eyes.

"God's blood, Bethany," he said, "what are you about?"

"What do you think?" She continued to gaze bravely at him, a mute message of longing in her eyes.

He exhaled loudly. Muttering a curse, he wrapped his arms tightly around her. His kiss was swift and impassioned, all-engulfing. He made no attempt at gentleness as his lips bruised hers.

Bethany burned from head to toe and she felt her legs grow weak and wobbly. His strong arms supported her. Lifting his mouth, he touched his lips to her eyes, her cheeks, the leaping pulse at her throat. She slid down to a soft bed of hay, pulling him with her. The nickering of horses and the distant pounding of the surf mingled with her own inner rhythm, and suddenly she no longer felt weak.

Fire raced through her veins as she pressed closer to him, covering his astonished face with kisses. She sampled the warm flesh of his neck, delighting in the taste of him. His loose white shirt gaped open, revealing a glistening chest with a patch of reddish hair and the tense, flat muscles of his midsection. She placed her hand there, wanting to know him, every part of him.

He relinquished her and sat up abruptly. "Enough, love."

"What is it?" she asked hesitantly, not yet recovered from the searing heat of their embrace. She reached out to place her hand on his shoulder.

He pulled away and wiped his sleeve across his face as if to rid himself of the taste of her. "We cannot do this."

"Why not?"

"By God, but you try a man. It isn't right. Can't you see that?"

"You're always saying that." She thrust her chin up in mutiny. "And yet, you always seem to forget."

He grazed her cheek with his knuckles. "You'll learn, as you get older, that a young lady doesn't dally with her papa's stableman. And she certainly doesn't enjoy it."

Bethany scooped up a handful of hay and tore savagely at the strands. "Since when can you tell me what I do and do not feel, Ashton Markham?"

He dropped his hand. "We're worlds apart, love."

"Only because you make it so."

"You don't even know what you want," he said, calm and resigned.

"I want *you*. I want us to be together, like"—she couldn't believe she was going to say it—"like lovers."

He eyed her keenly. "If it's a lover you want, Miss Winslow," he snapped, "you'll have to look elsewhere for a more docile studhorse than I." He turned away and left the stables.

Bethany leaped up and ran after him. Her passion had

been awakened, and the feeling raged like a tempest at sea. Windheads of desire buffeted her senses. "What about what just happened?" she demanded.

"You'll get over it," he said over his shoulder.

She kicked up puffs of dust in the stableyard as she walked beside him. "You're cruel."

He stopped in his tracks and grasped her shoulders roughly. She winced, and he softened and traced a gentle finger along the line of her jaw. "It would be far more cruel for me to indulge your urges, love. It may not seem so today, but it's true."

She searched his face, noting every detail: the tiny lines beside his eyes, the endearing dimple in his chin, the firmness of his jawline, the fascinating curve of his lower lip.

As she stared, something curious happened to Ashton. She thought she could see a slight gale of disturbance in the depths of his eyes. For the briefest of moments, he seemed to be mentally reaching out to her in a way so elemental that she shivered.

But he reined himself in so quickly that she was sure she had imagined the look of longing. The flicker had lasted only an instant, a heartbeat. Yet it was enough to tell her that Ashton was far from indifferent to her.

3

Bethany stood at the fence of the training compound watching Ashton break a new horse to saddle. Not break, she corrected herself; with Ashton, the process was a gentling, an instilling of mutual trust.

The fence she leaned on was an unmortared stone wall, laid as much to get the stones out of the way of the sandy track as to confine the stock. Heedless of the rough surface, she leaned on her elbows and cupped her chin in her hands.

The day was glorious, the air softly warm, the gentle breeze scented by sea and horse, bee balm and southernwood. Golden sunlight dappled the track; in her imagination one particularly bright shaft seemed to have singled out Ashton for illumination. His thick chestnut hair was alive with flames of light. The bleached muslin of his loose shirt glared to eye-smarting whiteness in the shadowless day. And those eyes, though so often stormy, were today as clear as the summer sky.

She boosted herself up to the top of the fence, swinging her bare legs to the inside. The rose-gray mare Ashton had just bridled caught sight of the movement and jerked her head.

Ashton flashed Bethany a grin. "Sorry, love, but it seems my lady friend here wishes a bit of privacy." The mare snorted.

Bethany was not offended, for she knew he took his work seriously. He was as concerned for the welfare of the horse as he was with succeeding in his training. She climbed down from the fence and retreated to the discreet shade of a hackberry tree, where she was able to see the training compound without threatening the mare.

Ashton gave his full concentration to the task at hand. His every movement bespoke quiet strength and self-assurance, as if the whole world existed as a forum for his skills. Watching him, Bethany shivered, feeling oddly chilled yet gloriously warm as well.

The rose-gray mare, aptly named Zoe for the sparks in her eyes, tossed her head in resentment of the training bit. Her flesh quivered beneath the saddle. Ashton approached the horse, sidling gracefully toward her, murmuring soothing words that sounded like a lover's endearments.

When he reached for Zoe's bridle, the beast jerked away with a grunt, nostrils flaring. Ashton planted himself in front of her as if daring her to accept his challenge. He continued his soft, inane patter.

The mare shied back, hesitant, yet at the same time intrigued by Ashton. Inevitably her nose pushed toward him a little. Moments later she was nuzzling his hand, hungry for whatever enticement he held there.

Chuckling, he fed her a bit of maple sugar and insinuated himself closer, reaching up to stroke the mare's neck and muzzle, his stream of low talk never ceasing. He whistled, too; he always whistled to the horses. Perhaps one day Zoe would be as responsive to the sound as Corsair was.

Before long he had hung the reins evenly over the neck. Then he angled himself against the mare's side, still stroking, banishing her fears with insistent gentleness.

Zoe hesitated still, stiffening and flattening her ears.

Again he put her at ease, whistled and fed her from his hand, then returned to her side.

In a movement so lithe and quick Bethany would have missed it had she blinked, Ashton was on the mare's back.

This sent Zoe into a panicked frenzy; she bucked and snorted, all four hooves leaving the ground at once. Determinedly Ashton clung with his strong thighs. The mare sidled and ran headlong, changed direction without warning, charged to and fro, until Bethany feared that even Ashton would be thrown.

But he rode out the storm, actually seeming to enjoy the ordeal. His will matched the proud obstinance of the horse; he used his strength gently yet compellingly.

He conquered the mare.

Bethany wasn't certain exactly when the change occurred. One moment the mare was resisting him with her every fiber and sinew; the next, she was being controlled by him, responding to his unyielding guidance at the reins and the pressure of his legs upon her sides.

He was not a domineering master; he did not press his advantage. Although in control, he allowed Zoe to gallop, to experience his guiding weight without learning to resent it.

Bethany's breath caught as she watched the soaring gallop, the beauty of the newly reined mare a perfect complement for Ashton's masterful riding.

Then he slowed the horse, drawing on the reins. He guided the mare to the center of the sandy track, where he brought her gradually to a halt.

The horse hung her head, looking replete rather than defeated. He spoke softly to her as he gave her sides a reassuring squeeze with his thighs and then leaned forward, draping his arms over her neck, still whispering.

Bethany had nearly stopped breathing. Her insides quivered and warmed as she stared. She had a sense of having witnessed something much more complex and dramatic than the mere gentling of a beast. The challenge, hesitation, soaring consummation, and wistful afterglow had less to do with horse training than it had with the sudden clash and fusion of two proud spirits.

Ashton dismounted and raised his face to the sun, revealing a profile so fine and purposeful that Bethany was seized by a sharp wanting.

Swathed in gold light, he looked like a mythical prince. Yet his rough, squarish hands and the ruggedness of his features gave him an earthy quality that was more compelling than the cold perfection of a storybook hero.

Ashton was a fantasy she could reach out and touch.

She leaned against the hackberry tree, feeling the rapid rise and fall of her bosom against her whalebone stays.

I love him. Her hand flew to her mouth as if she'd startled herself with the revelation. The notion had been fermenting in her mind for weeks.

"Oh, my God," she said aloud. "I do love him."

"Love who?" came a voice from behind her.

She swiveled around to see Carrie Markham standing there, mobcap askew as usual, holding a packet of calling cards. Invitations, no doubt, to a half dozen functions Bethany had absolutely no desire to attend.

"Love who, miss?" Carrie asked again, handing her the cards. Carrie grinned broadly. "About time you made up your mind, miss. The season's half over." The maid plucked a red-brown berry from the tree and rolled it thoughtfully between her fingers. "Let's see, could it be the handsome Keith Cranwick's finally found your favor? No. You've barely given him the time of day." Carrie tossed the berry over her shoulder. "I've got it! 'Tis the British officer, what's his name? Ah yes, Captain Tanner. And a good choice he is, miss. Probably has a fortune back in England."

Bethany barely heard her maid's prattle. Her mind refused to budge from the wonderful, absurd, terrifying notion that she had fallen in love with Ashton Markham. Her gaze moved back to the fenced compound, settling caressingly on the object of her startled adoration as he exited the yard with the mare in tow.

"What's the matter, miss? You look a bit dazed." Carrie followed Bethany's rapt gaze. "Sweet God in heaven," she almost shouted. "'Tis Ashton!" She grasped Bethany by the shoulders. "Are you saying you're in love with my brother?"

"I . . ." Bethany looked down at her hands, which nervously clutched the invitations. The feeling was so new, she wanted to keep it close to her heart like a precious secret.

But Carrie wouldn't stand for reticence. "You do love him, don't you?"

Bethany nodded. "I only wonder that the realization was so long in coming."

Carrie's mouth formed a surprised O. Then a range of emotions flitted across her face: derision, amusement, irony . . . and finally, satisfaction.

"Perfect," she said briskly. "Absolutely perfect."

Bethany blinked. "It is?"

"Of course, miss. Oh, I'll allow you're letting yourself in for trouble. Your parents won't like this a bit. Ashton's penniless, but your portion'll take care of that nicely. Quite nicely indeed . . . for all of us." She rubbed her hands on her apron. "Now, what to do next."

Bethany started walking toward the stables.

"Where are you off to, miss?"

"To see Ashton, of course."

Carrie planted herself in front of Bethany, barring her retreat. "Come now, you can't do that. You'll only blurt it out that you love him."

"That's exactly what I intend to do."

"Wait, miss. What'll Ashton do if you march down to the stables and announce that you've fallen in love with him?"

"Why, he—he'll . . ." What, indeed? She could just imagine the smooth smile, the barely discernible twinge of annoyance in those blue eyes. She had seen that look many times when he wanted to put her off without hurting her feelings.

"He'll tell you to forget him, to go get yourself a proper husband, the type of man your parents would want for you."

Bethany slumped against the stone fence. "You're right. That is precisely what your brother would say." She closed her eyes. "I have never known true fear until this moment. Do you realize how terrifying it is to know you love someone who might not love you back?" She raised troubled eyes to Carrie. "What shall I do?"

Carrie flashed her a triumphant smile. "For once you've asked my advice on something I can help with. I may not mend your smallclothes well or style your hair fashionably, but I can tell you how to handle a man. Even one as bothersome as my brother." She took Bethany's hands as she led her to the house.

"You can't run headlong into his arms," she said, adopting the attitude of a general plotting battle strategy. "There's no appeal for him in that. Men are thickheads. They often don't see the truth even when it stares them in the face. You must prove to Ashton that he wants you, force him to play the part of the pursuer. After all, who gets more enjoyment from the hunt—the hunter or the hapless fox?"

Bethany smiled ruefully. Hearing wisdom from the lips of Carrie Markham was a new and unexpected event. "What are you suggesting?"

"You must show Ashton he wants you by letting him know exactly what it feels like *not* to have you."

"You're not making any sense—"

"Hush up and listen. Trust me, I know. Remember when we used to steal persimmons from the Pierces' orchard?"

"How could I forget? I almost lost a foot to one of the dogs."

"But we always went back for more, didn't we? We could have had our pick of Seastone's orchards, so why did we risk our necks stealing the Pierces' persimmons?"

Bethany recalled the quivering anticipation of the child-hood plot, the artful thieving, the illicit deliciousness of warm, sweet juice running down her chin as she and Carrie giggled over their success.

"'Stolen waters are sweet,'" she quoted with a wicked grin, "'and the bread eaten in secret is pleasant.'"

Carrie clapped her hands. "Exactly as the Proverb goes, miss. 'Twas not so much the fruit as the act of getting it. Now put yourself in mind of Ashton. Don't offer yourself to him on a gilt salver. Make him *want* you."

"How, Carrie?"

The maid led the way into Bethany's room and closed the door. "Well, he can't very well steal you like a persimmon unless he believes you belong to another."

"But I don't—"

"Maybe not, miss, but there's no harm in letting Ashton think you've given your attention to another man."

A knock sounded at the door. "A visitor to see Miss Bethany," Mrs. Hastings announced. "A Captain Dorian Tanner."

When Carrie turned to face Bethany, her face was lit by a smile. "'Tis a sign from above, miss. This opportunity has just been laid before your feet. Captain Tanner is besotted with you. He's the perfect one to dangle before Ashton's nose." Carrie rushed forward to fuss at the folds of her mistress's gown.

But Bethany put her off. "I'll wear a riding habit. I'd like to take Captain Tanner for a ride."

Carrie looked suitably impressed. "You learn quickly."

Bethany kept a jaunty smile on her face as she led Captain Tanner down to the stables. Dorian's attention and light conversation made her feel pretty and feminine—and oddly powerful.

"I look forward to our ride, Miss Bethany." He held the

gate to the stableyard open for her. "It's been a long time since I've sat a decent horse."

She watched him as he closed the gate behind her, admiring the handsome fit of his scarlet uniform and his impeccably styled black hair, rolled at the sides and clubbed neatly at the back. The officer had a face so perfect that she had the sensation of looking at a statue. His straight brow, chiseled nose and chin, and sculpted mouth might have been rendered by an artist rather than by nature.

Dorian Tanner was an interesting man; his speech was strangely precise, as if he were concentrating more on how he spoke and less on what he said.

"Are you fond of riding, Captain?" she asked.

"Most assuredly, Miss Bethany."

A wicked thought occurred to her. "And do you favor a spirited mount?"

He drew open the stable door. "Is that a challenge?"

"We'll see, Captain." She called for Barnaby Ames and had him saddle Calliope and Corsair. When the groom led the horses out to the sandy yard, Tanner's pleasant smile vanished. He gazed in rapture at Corsair.

"He's completely black," Bethany assured him as she mounted from the block. "Some of the stable hands swear he's got a soul to match."

"We'll see about that, old fellow," Dorian said, taking the reins from Barnaby.

She heard the muted tread of a boot on the sandy yard. She turned in the saddle and was caught in the glare of Ashton Markham's disquieting look.

Oh, God, what was she doing? This wasn't her, playing the coquette and batting her eyes, playing upon the attentions of one swain to trap the other. It was madness. Madness!

And yet, as she studied Ashton's face, she saw a turbulence deep in his eyes, and it was not simple anger. When he reached for her mare's bridle and his hand closed around the leather, she realized what it was.

Possessiveness. He might not love her yet, but he considered her his to protect.

A glorious warmth spiraled up inside her. She wanted to reach for his hand, to tuck hers into it and tell him what was in her heart.

He would run like a hunted fox.

She knew this as surely as if Carrie had hissed it in her ear. It was far too soon to push him to admit his feelings. She forced herself to smile and tossed her head.

"Hello, Ashton. Captain Tanner and I were just going for a ride. I thought I might take him to that lovely private cove you showed me."

She saw him stiffen. His free hand clenched around the breeding log he was holding, while his other one dropped the reins. Oh, Carrie, she thought, what have you talked me into now?

"Haven't you learned your lesson about the stallion?" he asked in a low voice. "The beast's not used to anyone but me."

"Then obviously," Tanner drawled in a bored, upper crust voice, "the poor fellow's never had a proper master."

Bethany held her breath. Tantalize, Carrie had said, not infuriate. But it was out of her hands now. Dorian Tanner knew nothing of her game, yet he obviously knew plenty about masculine rivalry.

To Ashton's credit, he didn't rise to the barb, but stepped back. "Have at him, Captain. But he'll give you his worst, make no mistake."

Dorian swung up onto the horse. Corsair began his ornery antics, but Dorian brought the reins up harshly.

Bethany saw Ashton wince at the jerk of the bit in Corsair's sensitive mouth.

Dorian tipped his peaked hat, looking every inch the well-bred gentleman. With a lordly hand on the reins, he turned the horse and pressed in his heels. Corsair charged from the yard down the lane, leaving dust and the Redcoat's hat in his wake. Then Dorian wheeled the mount and started back, this time bringing both legs to one side, lowering himself until his boots brushed the ground. The impetus lent his feet wings; his legs came up and swung to the other side. The motion was repeated twice and then Dorian landed back in the saddle.

Bethany watched, dumbfounded and impressed. "Ashton! Did you see what he did?"

"Carnival tricks," Ashton muttered. "Could your captain have learned *that* while riding to the hounds?"

"My," said Bethany, feeling bold and saucy, "you do seem to hate it that another man can handle your horse."

On a splendid August day Ashton stared morosely into his tankard of ale at the White Horse Tavern in Marlborough Street. Earlier he had won a quarter-mile race at Cheltham's Green, earning a small silver plate and a decent-sized purse and, as always, the praise of Newport's elite. Yet he felt no flush of victory, no sharp satisfaction at having bested a dozen of the ablest riders in Narragansett.

Something was seriously amiss in his life.

It was not just the fact that his father was dead and Carrie was behaving more outrageously every day. Nor was it his own eagerness to get away; at month's end he would be leaving to take possession of the bit of Aquidneck beachfront he had been granted on his discharge from the army.

Still, something was wrong.

He scowled at his ale, reluctant to admit the source of his discontent. Yet, try as he might, he could not dispel the images that wove into his consciousness like some insidious illness of the mind.

He continued to stare into his cup, watching the bubbles rise laconically to the surface to cling and then disperse. He barely noticed a thin, tartly grinning wench who sidled up and, surmising his mood, retreated to a more friendly corner of the taproom.

In his mind's eye, he saw Miss Bethany Winslow, hurling herself into his arms for comfort like a hurt child, laughing as they held a mock ball on the beach, inviting his kisses with a budding sensuality that promised to blossom into passionate abandon. . . . But he hadn't seen that endearing side of Bethany in a long time.

He shifted restively on his stool, growing angrier by the minute. He should have taken her sweet offering weeks ago, and to hell with propriety. Instead he had nobly denied himself her charms. And for what?

So she could throw herself at the dashing Captain Dorian Tanner. The two were inseparable, tiring the horses Ashton cared for so diligently, spending long, lazy hours indulging in the very delights Ashton had forbidden himself.

So much for the idea that women preferred well-behaved gentlemen.

Ashton took a long draw on his ale, despising himself for caring that Bethany's fast-awakening desires were being sampled by another.

'Tis what you knew would happen, he told himself darkly. So why does it rankle?

The appearance of a newcomer in the tavern spared him from having to answer that question.

Captain Dorian Tanner—swaggering, scarlet-clad, infinitely confident—cast a disdainful gaze at the patrons. The White Horse was known as a patriot haunt, where seditious pamphlets were discussed and toasts were raised not to King George but to the other of that name, General Washington, who, that summer, had been directing the rebel siege of Boston.

At first Ashton ignored the intrusion; then Tanner's voice carried to his ears.

"Ah, 'tis Finley Piper." Tanner fixed a black-eyed glare on a middle-aged man in rumpled and ink-stained shirt-sleeves. "How goes it, Mr. Piper? I heard your printing press was working late last night."

Piper looked across the table at his son, a gangling youth called Chapin, but said nothing.

Ashton had known Finley and Chapin Piper all his life. The father was an ordinary man with a shrewd mind and a good education. Chapin was a few years younger than Ashton. Lantern-jawed, his throat all knots and cords, he said little but always seemed to have something—usually Carrie Markham—on his mind.

The Pipers adopted an attitude of quiet insolence as they regarded the Redcoat.

Tanner strolled over to the table and let his sword touch the edge. "What's the matter, sir? Have you something to hide?"

"Nothing at all, sir." Finley looked suddenly very unlike the simple tradesman he was. He straightened his shoulders, tipped his chin, and flexed his large, ink-stained hands. "There's no law says a man can't labor after hours."

"But I am intrigued, sir. You worked until dawn, yet I wasn't able to find a single copy of your product."

"My publications have become exceedingly popular of late, sir."

Tanner pressed his knuckles to the rough surface of the table and leaned forward in a menacing attitude. "Mr. Piper," he said, enunciating very clearly and quietly, "your seditious writings are but rumor today." He moved so close that his nose nearly touched Finley's. The printer didn't flinch as the officer added, "But I shall prove your treason; if not tomorrow, then the next day, or the next . . . and God help you when I do."

Ashton's stool scraped savagely on the floor as he got to his feet. "You wouldn't want folks to accuse His Majesty's officers of harassment, would you, Captain?" he asked mildly. "A spotless reputation is so vital in these unsettled times."

Tanner looked momentarily unnerved. Then he laughed. "Of course. Good of you to point it out, Markham, although I'm surprised a common laborer would concern himself with matters of state." With an exaggerated gesture he drew a watch from his waistcoat and made a great show of checking the time. "I must be going anyway. Miss Winslow is expecting me."

A fierce grin curved Tanner's mouth. "Poor sod. Your eyes catch fire at the very mention of her name."

Ashton's hands clenched. Only the slight pressure of Finley Piper's hand on his arm stopped him from driving his fist into Tanner's perfect face. He set his jaw hard against his temper and forced himself to remain still as the officer swaggered out into Marlborough Street.

"'Tis best you let him go, my friend," Finley murmured, pushing a fresh tankard of ale into Ashton's hand. "It wouldn't do to come to blows over a trifle when the future will offer us ample opportunity to fight for a much more meaningful cause."

"Not 'us,' Finley." Ashton felt a sudden distaste for battle-hungry agitators like Piper. "Leave me out of your fraternity. Such issues belong to those who are willing to kill for them. I don't happen to be that sort of man."

"But you will be," Finley vowed. "I already see the rage in you. 'Tis only a matter of time before the commitment nudges you in our direction."

Ashton shook his head, but when Chapin raised another toast to General Washington, he was surprised to see his mug lifted high in salute.

Bethany devoured Harry's letter, the first she had received since he had gone off to Bristol. Her brother's missive was optimistic; he and Felicia were abysmally poor but deliriously happy, expecting a child in the spring. Harry invited Bethany to visit and ended with postscript: "I entrust the enclosed letter to you, to be delivered with every discretion to Ashton Markham."

She picked up the folded and sealed enclosure and turned it over in her hands. Why was Harry writing to Ashton? And why did he want this letter delivered with discretion? Shrugging, she walked down to the stables. At the very least, the letter was an excuse to see Ashton.

Since she and Carrie had embarked upon their campaign to get him to notice her, she had seen far too little of Ashton. At times she questioned Carrie's tactics, although every so often she caught an unmistakable glimmer in Ashton's eyes that told her the ruse was not lost on him.

Sometimes she felt small and mean-spirited for pursuing the elaborate charade, but Carrie assured her the rewards would make it all worthwhile. Perhaps. But Bethany had already decided she would put an end to the scheme soon. Very soon.

Bolstered by the thought, she found Ashton in the small office in a corner of the stables. She paused behind his chair, feeling a rush of sensation at the sight of him. His head was bowed in concentration over a calf-bound breeder's journal. Roger Markham's handwriting covered the top part of the page; halfway down, the script changed to Ashton's.

He wore his father's spectacles, which gave him a look of pensive intelligence. His shoulders were taut; she experienced a sudden urge to touch him there, to knead the tension away with her hands.

For weeks she had been in the company of Dorian Tanner and was the envy of every young woman in Newport. Yet Dorian's classic handsomeness and smooth manners held little appeal for her. Each time she looked at that flawless face she found herself longing to gaze upon another, upon Ashton Markham's rough features. Each time she pasted on a false smile for Dorian and put her hand in his, she wanted to feel the earthy bluntness of Ashton's hands and to enjoy his unaffected personality. His flaws added up to a whole that was infinitely more human and approachable than Dorian's bloodless, studied perfection.

She took Harry's letter from her pocket. "Ashton."

He looked up sharply. Behind the spectacles his eyes narrowed. "Another outing, love?" He made the endearment a mockery. "Will your captain take time out from harassing townspeople to abuse Corsair again?"

She winced. "He doesn't mistreat the horse, Ashton. You know I'd never let him."

"Then how do you explain the oyster shell I found in the beast's hoof yesterday?"

"I didn't know about that, Ashton. Truly." Defensively, she added, "I apologize; perhaps we were too preoccupied to notice."

He came to his feet, tearing the spectacles from his face and flinging them on the table. "So the good captain preoccupies you, does he, Miss Bethany?" He stepped very close to her, so close she could smell the scent of saddle soap and horse that clung to him, so close she could feel the warmth of his breath on her face and see small, cold shards of anger in his eyes.

"I . . . we didn't . . ." Her throat felt hot with awkward embarrassment.

He chuckled, flicking his hand insolently over her cheek. "Doesn't take much to fluster you, does it?"

"A lady is always flustered by rudeness." Ah, she was getting good at this. Too good, perhaps.

His hand moved from her cheek to her hair, his fingers weaving into her curls. "Rude, am I?"

"Let go of me, Ashton," she said. "I did not come here to—"

He stifled the angry protest by covering her mouth with his.

She pushed her fists against his chest. For weeks she had longed for his embrace, but not in this way, this wickedly insinuating way. She wanted gentleness rather than anger, desire rather than demand. But, she reflected with sudden insight, her behavior had hardly invited gentleness and desire.

She felt dizzy and somehow violated when at last he relented and released her from his ruthless embrace. Tears stung her eyes as she gazed up at him. "Why did you do that?"

"You used to enjoy it, love."

"I used to enjoy your friendship, Ashton. Your approval. Without that your kisses mean nothing."

Flinging Harry's letter onto the desk, she fled.

A soft morning breeze, imbued with the scent of spicy honeysuckle and marybud gone to seed, dried the tears from her face. And with the tears went her feeling of hurt. Because suddenly, with startling certainty, she realized what had happened in the stable office.

Ashton had just given vent to jealousy.

Her mood was high the next day when she entered the library, summoned there by her father. Sinclair sat behind his massive block-front Goddard desk, smoking a clay pipe and looking over a small stack of correspondence.

He regarded his daughter with a satisfied smile. "Lovely," he said, eyeing her tawny gold outfit. "Not many women look so well in a riding habit. You've precisely the height and slimness for the style."

"Thank you, Father, though I doubt it matters much to Calliope." She wished he would notice more about her than her looks. "I thought to ride before breakfast."

"What I have to say won't take long. Your mother and I are sailing to Little Rest with William, and we won't be back until tomorrow. Your brother has decided to enlist in the king's horse corps, and I've a bit of business to do."

"William will be a British soldier?"

"Aye, if he manages to stay sober enough to sit a horse. His damned commission cost me a small fortune."

Bethany felt the color fall from her face. Harry had sided with the rebels and William with the British. They had grown up brothers; they could well die enemies.

Smiling across the desk at her, Sinclair said, "I want you to think about something while we're away." He tamped his pipe on the cork ball of an ash-salver and set it aside. "Captain Dorian Tanner has offered for you."

She stepped back, dumbfounded. "No."

His brows drew together. "Why so surprised, my dear? I daresay you've given him plenty of encouragement."

"But that was because . . . because . . ." She let her voice trail off. Her father would neither approve of nor understand her reasons for entertaining Dorian. "He's been pleasant company," she conceded hastily, "but I've no intention of marrying him."

"You will, my dear girl. In two months. Tanner has gone off on a tour of duty. He's promised to keep an eye on William, as a matter of fact. I've assured the captain that he'll find you most agreeable when he returns."

She curled her gloved hands into fists at her sides. "You should not have presumed to know my mind."

"In the end your sympathies matter not at all," he informed her coldly. "I need you safely married, and I need grandsons. Both your brothers are lost to me, William to his drinking and carousing, and Harry to his lowborn bride and infernal sedition."

"I do not feel obligated to provide you with an heir. If you're that interested in breeding, find a brood mare."

"Bethany, the country is being torn apart, even though we may not feel it here at Seastone. The rebels in Boston and Virginia have drawn the sword against our kind. I need to know you'll be safe if the conflict ever reaches Newport. Dorian Tanner is a good man, a committed soldier. I've been able to find out little about his family, but I'm sure he'll clear that up when he returns. You should be pleased to have attracted his notice."

"I will not have him." She trembled as her hand found the doorknob.

Sinclair gave her a genial smile. "Go have that ride, my dear, and sort it all out. You'll see I've chosen wisely for you."

She ran from the library to the haven she'd sought since childhood—the stables and Ashton Markham's soothing arms.

4

The deck of the sea-battered ferry lurched beneath Ashton as more passengers boarded from the small quay at Bristol Ferry. The August day had grown dark, the air heavy with impending rain. Ashton gripped the rail of the shallop and looked out across Narragansett Bay, puzzling over the letter Bethany had delivered the day before.

Harry Winslow was in some sort of trouble; that much he had surmised from the cryptic message. Something about documents to be delivered in secret and a British sympathizer who must not, at any cost, observe the exchange.

Ashton muttered a curse, calling Harry every kind of fool for involving himself in a matter that could only mean danger.

"Why me?" Ashton said softly through gritted teeth. Harry knew how he felt about the war, knew he determinedly favored neither side. Yet here he was, furious at the responsibility he felt toward the impetuous young man.

It had always been that way with Ashton and the privileged Winslow offspring. All three of them had spent their lives sparing nothing for prudence and responsibility. What should have been intelligent judgment in William had been smothered by his fondness for women and drink. Ashton had spent more than one sleepless night dissuading him from dueling over a lady or getting him out of a gambling scrape.

Harry was little better, although his ideals were somewhat more admirable than his brother's. Not that Harry was wicked, but forethought never preceded his actions. As a child he had been wont to climb trees he could not descend, to make promises he could not keep. The task of rescuing the lad had always fallen to Ashton.

And then there was Bethany. She was smarter than William, braver than Harry, and more spirited than both. In all fairness, as a child she had presented no special problems for Ashton. But the woman she had become did create a dilemma.

Lately she'd haunted his sleep and deviled his days. Large sparkling eyes and shimmering golden hair surrounding a powerfully pretty face seemed to live in his mind all the night through.

Thank God, he reflected, the girl seemed to have no notion of her effect on him. If she knew what her little flirtation with Dorian Tanner did to him, she would be insufferably proud of herself.

A gull wheeled overhead, hanging suspended in the moist air before winging southward. He watched the bird and tried to tear his thoughts from Bethany. But, unbidden, an idea took hold of his mind.

I miss her.

He scowled and nearly stumbled against a wooden grate as the ferry lurched again. He did miss her, damn the girl. He missed the easy rides and conversation and the way she used to need him, the way she ran to him to share a small triumph or disappointment.

A shout interrupted his thoughts. The ferrymaster had been about to cast off for Bristol when a slim, gold-clad figure leaped up the entry-plank. Ashton barely had time to react before he found his arms around Bethany and his shirtfront already damp with her tears.

"Ashton, I needed you this morning and you weren't there. I only found you because Barnaby said you'd asked about the ferry schedule to Bristol." Her gaze darted at the passengers on the boat, but she did not heed the scandalized glares they sent her.

There was an edge of hysteria in her voice. "I—I nearly winded Calliope getting here. But the ferrymaster's son promised to walk her for me." Her gloved hands twisted into the fabric of her riding habit.

Emotions too numerous and fleeting to cling to eddied through him: annoyance, elation, confusion, bemusement. He squeezed her hand and set her away from him, offering a handkerchief from his pocket. As he watched her mop her tears, the weeks seemed to roll away and he forgot his bitterness.

"There, love," he said, "what's troubling you?"

His tone of voice caused a new flood of tears to unleash, this one more torrential than the first. While he wondered how the girl could look so lovely even while weeping buckets, Bethany tried to choke out an explanation.

"I've gotten myself in such terrible trouble. My father said Dorian and I must—must—"

He laid his fingers on her lips. "Hush now. Calm down a little, and you can tell me about it later."

She quieted and leaned against him. He stroked her hair self-consciously, aware that at least half a dozen passengers had sidled closer, as if curious about the lovely young woman who was pouring her heart out against his chest. He experienced a sudden pang of fierce protectiveness. Taking Bethany's arms, he led her toward the canvas-sheltered bow of the ferry, away from the prying eyes and the mist of rain that had begun to fall. The ferry cut away from the quay with a shudder.

She gasped and stumbled, clutching her midsection. Her face went pale, and the color that returned was far from healthy; a curious shade of gray-green appeared on her trembling lips.

He gave her hand a squeeze. "What?" he asked, lifting an eyebrow. "An islander who has no sea legs?"

Her smile was thin and rueful. "I don't understand it. The voyage from New York was most pleasant." She swallowed hard.

He helped her to a lashed-down bench beneath the fulling jib on its taut forestays. Crouching beside her, he said, "At this rate we'll make port at Bristol in less than an hour. I gather this is an impromptu voyage?"

She nodded. "No one will worry. My parents and William have gone to Little Rest on the mainland." Her tear-drenched eyes grew shadowy with trouble as she added, "William has joined the king's horse corps and has gone on a tour of duty with Dorian Tanner."

Ashton's jaw tightened. So that was the cause of her distress. Bethany's suitor had left her.

"William has my sympathy," he said tautly. But you don't, pet, he thought. You don't.

Bethany gazed out at Hog Island, low and gray on the misty horizon. "In a way I'm glad I came. I've been trying all summer to get away to see Harry. What about you, Ashton? Are you going to see Harry, too?"

He nodded and looked northward. The ferry was closing in on the port.

"Why?" she asked. Then she placed her hand on his arm. "It was the letter I brought you yesterday, wasn't it? I meant to stay and see what it was about, but you . . . we . . ." The flush of pink in her cheeks contrasted with the pallor around her lips.

He patted her hand, amazed at the speed with which his resentment fled. For the first time in his life he apologized to a woman for kissing her. Bethany's dewy-eyed countenance made it easy. "I was out of sorts," he admitted dryly. "There was no reason to be rough with you. Sorry, love."

"Why were you out of sorts?"

He fastened his stare on the blue and ochre façades lining the port of Bristol. "Weren't you just asking about your brother?"

He thought she would press him to give voice to something he would not admit even to himself, but she relented, gripping the bench as the ferry rode a particularly rough swell.

"Tell me," she said. "Anything to take my mind off the sickness. Is Harry in trouble?"

"He may need someone to temper his rebel fervor a little."

"Yes," she agreed. "Yes, please. I simply don't understand why Harry is so sympathetic to the rebels. He was raised a proper Englishman."

"I see. Proper Englishmen keep their mouths shut when Lord North's hands rifle their pockets."

She glanced at him sharply. "Don't tell me you agree with that rabid dog, Sam Adams."

He grinned. "Never fear, love. I prefer my own authority to that of the patriots or the British."

"I am a Loyalist," she proclaimed. It was to be a prim announcement, but another swell caused her eyes to widen with acute discomfort.

"Perhaps you'll do your brother more good than I," Ashton said.

As they walked away from the rain-drenched wharves of Bristol, Bethany sent Ashton a grateful look; his mere presence had helped her weather her seasickness on the short voyage. The brisk walk to Hope Street revived her feeling of well-being, and now she was eager to see her brother.

She hid her surprise when a tall, thin African man opened the door of Number Ten Hope Street in a quiet section of the town.

"I'm Bethany Winslow," she said, dipping her head.

"And this is Ashton Markham." The man searched their faces, his eyes narrowed distrustfully.

"Who is it, Justice?" called a male voice from somewhere behind the narrow stairs of the modest town house.

Bethany burst past the solid wall of Justice's chest, calling her brother's name. In moments she was enfolded in Harry's arms. While Harry and Ashton exchanged a handshake, she studied her twin.

He looked different now, in ways that gave her pause. His clothes were somewhat shabby, though clean; the elbows of his frock coat had been mended by a meticulous hand. He was thinner, too, yet Bethany recognized his usual restless energy. His face lacked color; she reminded herself that Harry no longer took invigorating rides.

But beneath the look of worry and want, Harry's hazel eyes held a new, unfamiliar light. Despite his impoverished circumstances, he had the unmistakable look of a deeply happy man.

Before long, she learned precisely why. Felicia Winslow served a modest tea on chipped and mismatched china in the tiny parlor. Her manner was briskly friendly, unaffected by the traces of overprivilege and overbreeding Bethany saw in the ladies of Newport.

Like Harry, Felicia didn't seem to mind the lack of worldly possessions. She was attractive in an earthy way, with soft brown hair and fine, clear eyes of a startling green. Her smile was genuine, wide and big-toothed. The frank devotion with which she regarded Harry made Bethany warm to her at once. Felicia, Bethany decided, would act as an anchor to Harry's restlessness.

"This tea is most unusual," she remarked after they had caught up on the two months that had passed since Harry's departure.

Felicia gave a friendly chuckle. "Dreadful, isn't it? 'Tis a decoction of raspberry and lemon grass. A poor substitute for the China brew, but we make shift with it."

"I wasn't aware tea was so dear." Bethany set her cup aside.

Ashton laughed and shook his head. She glared at him, and he placed his hand on her arm. "I'm not laughing at you, pet. You've no reason to concern yourself with the politics of tea. Harry and Felicia make their own brew to protest the tax on imported tea."

Until today, the fact that outlaws in Boston and Norfolk had taken to dumping East India tea overboard had only been a bit of news for people in Newport's salons to shake their heads over. Now, in this drab town house where her brother lived, she realized that those outlaws had support.

"I find it perfectly ridiculous that English tea isn't served in an English household," she told Harry mutinously.

He smiled. "An American household, my dear."

"How can you say that?"

"I've lost my taste for English tea," he stated. "I've lost my taste for all things English when it comes to that. The tighter Parliament grips us, the more determinedly we shall struggle to be free."

"I am free," she insisted. "Free to do what I please." She blinked, realizing her foolishness. If her father had his way, she would surrender that freedom to Captain Tanner in two months.

Harry patted her hand. "Let's not quibble over loyalties. If England has your support, then perhaps there's hope for the empire yet."

She thought it an odd thing to say, but she forgot the disagreement as the conversation turned to other subjects and the afternoon slipped away. She forgot her initial worry about Harry; now she knew her brother was content with his gentle, adoring bride. He was even able to joke about his work at Hodgekiss's, proudly displaying his ink-stained sleeve as proof of his toil.

She felt faintly wistful about the intimacy Harry and Felicia shared—the fond glances passing between them, the occasional pat of affection.

"You're everything Harry said you would be," she told her sister-in-law. She had a sister. It was wonderful.

"So are you," Felicia replied. "Harry speaks of you often. But he forgot to mention how beautiful you are."

"Harry would consider it vain to mention his sister's beauty," Ashton said, "since she's his twin."

"That must be the reason." Felicia laughed. "Truly, only now that I've met you do I feel I know Harry. I've just made the acquaintance of his other half."

"You're his other half now," Bethany replied humbly, not at all disturbed by the change. "I've never seen Harry so happy."

They turned at the sound of a footstep in the doorway. Justice stood there and flicked his dark, somber eyes at the passageway to the rear of the house. Harry and Ashton excused themselves and left the parlor.

"Where are they going?" Bethany asked Felicia.

"I believe Harry has some business to discuss with Ashton."

"Rebel business," Bethany snapped.

Felicia sighed. "Can we not leave off this subject? I'd rather hear about what Harry was like as a child." Her eyes twinkled. "I'd love to talk about the baby we'll be having come spring."

As soon as she recovered from her shock, Bethany was suddenly glad she'd come to Bristol.

"Bethany's appearance surprised me," Harry murmured to Ashton as they made their way to the walled yard behind the house. Evening was approaching softly on the heels of the rainy afternoon.

"Your sister knows little about why I came." Ashton sat on the stoop beside Justice, whose gaze never stopped moving about the yard, scanning the shadows.

"'Tis just as well," Harry said. "I'm afraid I've gotten in a little thick."

Justice spoke for the first time. "A little," he echoed in a basso voice. "It's a wonder you're not swinging from the gallows, young man." The melodious notes of the West Indies rang in his speech.

"What happened?" Ashton asked.

"We've found a source of gunpowder for the patriots. This is a crucial time for us. We must keep the movement alive as militias are formed throughout the Colonies. Thanks to your training, Ashton, I excel at riding express. I've been entrusted with some sensitive material. We've got a chance to get our hands on some of the finest explosives known to man. It comes straight from the laboratory of Antoine Lavoisier."

Ashton frowned. "A Frenchman? Why would France supply a band of American rebels?"

"This has nothing to do with governments," Harry insisted.

"Aye," Justice said with a grin. "What can governments do if a private company happens to sell warlike supplies to the Americans?"

"They call themselves Hortalez et Cie," Harry explained. "We'll have their powder by winter if our negotiations succeed." He plucked a scarlet poppy from a small bed near the steps. "Things went smoothly for a time. I've slipped the British lines around Boston more times than I care to count." He drew in his breath and flung the poppy away.

"But . . . ?"

"But he was caught," Justice said mournfully.

Harry nodded. "By the cleverest infernal spy as ever swore allegiance to King George. The documents are safe, thank God, because Justice slipped away with them, but my face was seen. So far, no one's come banging on the door to arrest me. Perhaps my name is still unknown."

"How does this spy operate?" Ashton wished he were anywhere but in this drab little yard, about to be pressed into service for a cause he wished to avoid.

"That's precisely the thing," Harry said. "We simply

don't know. I was so certain all was well. We made an exchange a week ago Sunday in Brunswick Church, all according to plan. I'm sure not a soul noticed. People were all agog because Miss Abigail Primrose was up from New York. She was Bethany's teacher, remember? Anyway, the entire operation went off without a snag."

"Until that night," Justice supplied.

Harry nodded again. "I shall miss the courier work. Now I'll have to enlist to fight."

Ashton scowled. "That's nonsense, lad. You're no soldier."

"Neither are any of the farmers and tradesmen and parsons who took on the Redcoats at Lexington and Concord. Neither were the Boston merchants who fought on the hill where Mr. Breed and Mr. Bunker used to graze their cattle."

"What about your wife?" Ashton asked in annoyance. "And the babe that's coming in the spring?"

"Felicia feels as strongly as I," Harry countered. "We want our child to grow up free, not beneath the yoke of English oppression."

Ashton bristled at the familiar show of Winslow bravado. Perhaps because of his upbringing—so privileged, so insulated—Harry believed himself invincible, and always counted on someone to be there to pick up the pieces when he made a mistake. But he was no longer a youth embarking on a sophomoric prank; he no longer had his father's influence to buy him out of trouble.

Harry leaned forward, an avid look on his face. "You'd best go back in, Ashton. Justice and I will prepare the packet for you to transport, but 'tis best you know nothing of its origin."

"I've not said I'll do it."

"You've not said you won't. There's very little danger—"

"I'm not afraid of danger. I simply don't want to get involved."

"You won't be. All you have to do is deliver it to Finley Piper at the White Horse."

Ashton stood with the slightest of nods. It was far from the first time he had given in to the whim of a Winslow, and with an acute sense of self-disgust, he knew it would not be the last.

Bethany sat alone in the parlor, nibbling on a piece of toast and moving her hand pensively over a worn quilt on the settee. She looked up when Ashton entered. Even in the dimness, she could see a war being waged in his eyes.

"Where's Harry?" she asked.

"He'll be in shortly. Felicia?"

"She went to market. Today is the only day her favorite herbalist comes to town."

They sat together on the wooden settle, watching the shadows on the whitewashed wall across from them. Bethany picked up the teapot and filled a cup with luke-warm brew. "Tea?" she asked.

Ashton took it from her. Some of the agitation seemed to slip from his eyes as he raised the cup to his lips.

"Thank you," he said, then laughed. "Such a homely little scene. Anyone might take us for man and wife."

She nearly choked on the bit of toast she was chewing. All at once she remembered why she had followed him to the Bristol Ferry. Surely he would think of a way to make her father change his mind about forcing her to marry Dorian Tanner.

"Ashton," she began, "there is something I must tell you. You're the only one who can help. Dorian—"

"Dorian again." A tic of irritation leaped at his temple. "Why don't you ask him for help?"

"I cannot. You see, he is the cause of my trouble."

The front door crashed open and six British soldiers burst in, bayonets held ready. The officer, a sergeant, nodded briefly to Bethany.

"Sorry, Mrs. Winslow," he said curtly. "Duty, you see."

He fastened his gaze on Ashton. "Henry Winslow," he intoned formally, "in the name of King George, I arrest you."

Bethany was on her feet immediately. "But he's not—"

Ashton's hand bit into her wrist. "What crime am I accused of?"

Bethany nearly choked when she realized Ashton had assumed Harry's identity.

"'Tis not my place to explain," the sergeant replied, "but we rarely arrest men we don't intend to hang."

Bethany clutched Ashton's arm as he went calmly to the door with the officer. "You can't do this," she cried. "You mustn't let them take you."

Already he had stepped outside with the Redcoats, who flanked him front and back and on either side. As the soldiers prepared to march, he turned back and looked at Bethany, who sagged against the door frame.

"A last word with my wife, sergeant?" he requested. The officer nodded, cautioning him to be brief.

Ashton took Bethany in his arms. She bit back sobs of confusion and frustration. "Please," she whispered. "Please, tell them this is all a mistake."

"Of course it is."

"Let's tell them you're not Harry."

"So they can arrest your brother?"

She gave a gasp of alarm. Ashton spoke quickly. "Have Felicia get word to him. He's not to show his face in Bristol until this blows over."

"But you might be killed!"

He shrugged. "I won't offer your brother to the hangman."

"Ashton—"

He silenced her with a hand on her lips. "Come love, let me go. Give me a kiss like the good wife you are."

There was nothing reassuring about Ashton's kiss. It was desperate, hopeless, unbearably hard with passion and fear. And then he moved away, to be marched off to another man's trial.

5

The swirling sea mists of evening lent an aura of nightmarish unreality to the scene in front of Harry's house. The setting sun, filtered by shifting clouds, limned the impassive faces of the soldiers and the determined firmness of Ashton's profile.

This isn't happening, Bethany told herself, battling the panic that spiraled up her spine.

Yet the sergeant's barked order and the subsequent rhythmic tramping of soldiers' boots snatched away the dreamlike quality of the scene, lending it fearsome reality.

"Where are you taking him?" Her voice was shrill with alarm.

"The jail in Court Street, ma'am. He'll be brought before Colonel Darby Chason in the morning."

As the contingent disappeared down the street, Bethany bit hard into the back of her hand to stifle a protest.

Felicia found her in this stricken stance when she returned from market with a basket over her arm. "Bethany?"

Bethany gathered together the frayed shreds of her composure. "Where's Harry?"

"He'll be back shortly. What—"

"Ashton has been arrested."

"What's he done?" Harry asked. He and Justice had entered from the back. Harry clutched a hemp-bound package under his arm.

Anger stabbed at Bethany as she regarded the bloom of exhilaration in her brother's cheeks. This was all just a game to him, another adventure.

"Ashton has just saved you from the hangman, Harry. 'Twas you they came to arrest, and he let them think he was you."

Annoyance rather than consternation veiled Harry's face. His gaze dropped to the packet he held. "What now?" he asked Justice.

"Your friend did a brave thing, man," Justice replied. "He must know the importance of the cause."

"Ashton's only 'cause' is saving your foolish neck," Bethany told Harry. "You'll have to leave Bristol without delay. 'Tis only a matter of time before Colonel Chason finds out he has the wrong man."

Harry glanced down at his packet, cradling it like a fragile treasure. "Damn," he said. "How are we going to get these to Newport now?"

"I'll try," Justice offered.

Harry shook his head. "And risk ending up on the auction block?" He raked a hand through his hair, pulling strands from his queue. "Maybe Ashton—"

"I'm sure he has no interest in your documents now," Bethany said bitterly. "You're wasting time, Harry. I shall see to Ashton. 'Tis the British army holding him; he's an English citizen."

"The Redcoats are not to be trusted," Harry warned.

"Have you a better solution?" she snapped.

His shoulders sagged. "Still getting me out of scrapes, aren't you?"

She had softened to that boyish look many times in the

past, but not now. "I can only wait until court sits in the morning. By then you must be well away from Bristol."

Harry handed his packet to Justice. "Do what you can. And look after Felicia while I'm gone." Justice nodded and receded back down the narrow passageway.

A short time later Harry was on his way to Providence, where Felicia's father would shelter him until it was safe to return.

Pale and shaken, Felicia set to the routine chores of fixing supper. She laid a meal of stew and bread on the table. Bethany nibbled at a corner of bread but declined the stew, having no room for food in the twisting hollows of her stomach. Felicia ate with good appetite, blushing as she reached for a second helping.

"You must think me unfeeling to be eating like this after all the unpleasantness."

Bethany forced a smile. "Eat, please do. You've the babe to think of."

Felicia attacked her meal again. Bethany marveled at the slimness her sister-in-law maintained despite her appetite; not the slightest swelling betrayed pregnancy on her willowy body.

"Why would the British want to arrest Harry?" Bethany asked.

Felicia wiped her mouth on her napkin and kept her eyes fastened on the oiled linen table covering. "My husband's loyalties are a threat to them."

"But men are not arrested simply because of political disagreements."

Felicia looked up. "Where have you been these past years, Bethany? Do you not know what has been happening? The British have begun to fear the patriots. Men have been dragged from their homes on the flimsiest of charges, forced to—"

Bethany brought her fist down on the table. "For God's sake, Felicia, an innocent man is being held for something Harry has done. I would know what that is." Felicia's eyes lowered like shutters, and Bethany's anger rose. "You can trust me with the truth. I may not agree with Harry's politics, but I'd never betray my own brother."

Felicia nodded, looking relieved. "Of course. Forgive me for even hesitating. Harry's been active in the rebellion. Riding express and procuring information about the British defense."

Bethany's face sank to her cupped hands. "A spy, then," she said dully. "Harry is a spy. Oh, Lord, 'tis worse than I thought."

"'Tis no sin," Felicia declared. "He has to follow his convictions. You of all people should understand that about your brother."

"Yes," Bethany said. "Harry will do what he must, no matter what the cost." No matter, she added silently, that Ashton is being held for crimes he had not committed. No matter that Felicia had been left alone in Bristol. "What will you do?"

"I must stay here. If I go to Providence, Colonel Chason's men are sure to follow me. Harry will find a way back to me."

"I don't like to think of you here alone."

"Justice will see to my needs. He's very loyal to Harry. He's also a skilled carpenter. You should have seen this house before Justice set to work on it. The man was in dire circumstances when he arrived in Bristol."

"Justice is from a slaver, isn't he?" Bethany said.

Felicia looked away, but not before Bethany read the truth on her face. Damn Harry. Riding courier, spying, and harboring fugitive slaves. Yet the last of the three crimes met with her unabashed approval and exonerated him from the first two. Harry had a decided talent for endearing himself at the precise moment when he should be chastised.

Restlessly her thoughts moved to Ashton. Where was he now—in manacles somewhere in the jail, wondering how on earth he had landed himself in such an unenviable position, and how he could get out of it?

Frowning, she traced circles on the tablecloth with a nervous finger. Tomorrow Colonel Chason would realize his mistake and release Ashton. But Harry was still in danger. Glancing at Felicia, Bethany felt an inkling of hope. Surely Chason was not so heartless as to take the life of a man whose wife was expecting a baby.

Feeling somewhat encouraged, she decided that, should Colonel Chason ever get his hands on Harry, the baby would provide ample cause for mercy. She went to bed that night in the house on Hope Street assuring herself that the nightmare would be over, for Ashton at least, when she presented herself before Colonel Chason in the morning.

Yet when she awoke at dawn, her heart was pounding from some unremembered dream. Her first conscious thought was, what if Chason was not the fair officer she expected him to be? What if he managed to find Ashton guilty? Unlike Harry, Ashton didn't have the sentimental shield of a pregnant wife.

But Chason didn't know that. As she pulled on her rumpled riding habit, a grim smile tightened her lips.

Ashton sat stiffly on the hard wooden bench where he'd attempted to sleep the previous night. His elbows were on his knees, fingers steepled together in front of his face. The combined annoyances of a half dozen matters had robbed him of sleep and given him ample time to think. And to grow dangerously angry.

Harry Winslow was prominent in his black thoughts. The pup had no business riding express for the patriots, endangering his own life and jeopardizing the future of his wife and child as well. Damn, was he even worth what Ashton had done on his account?

Yet Harry wasn't the only object of Ashton's temper. His thoughts swung to Bethany, who, after flirting for several weeks with Dorian Tanner, had suddenly come running to tell him of some trouble. He was beginning to feel like a human handkerchief for the girl. What was it she'd been trying to tell him before Sergeant Watson had crashed into Harry's house?

Whatever outrage Dorian had committed had sent Bethany riding at breakneck speed to pour her heart out to Ashton. He was almost glad she'd not had the chance to saddle him with her worries. He'd shouldered enough of other people's problems.

Scowling into his hands, he turned his mind to his latest and most immediate annoyance: the British militia. Granted the Redcoats believed him to be Harry Winslow, guilty of sedition, but they treated him more like a condemned man than a prisoner awaiting trial. He'd been given lukewarm beer and days-old bread to eat, this abominable bench to sleep on, and not enough water even to wash his hands.

Sergeant Watson opened the door with his shoulder. "Up with you. Court's about to sit."

The guards flanked Ashton, snapping their heels smartly at Watson's commands. The corridors of the building were crowded with soldiers. Ashton paid them little heed until he heard a man speaking with a familiar cockney accent.

"Jesus blind me," said Sergeant Mansfield, peering at him.

Ashton would have been grateful to stop and explain his situation to the man who had been his superior at Fort George, but Watson's men hurried him through the corridor. He could only spread his arms helplessly as a bayonet nudged him into a receiving chamber appointed with a long table in front, benches along the back.

On the far wall was a portrait of King George III in his coronation robes. The King of England seemed a remote, abstract figure, but his legions were chillingly real. The British officers at the table supported enough brass on their uniforms to sink a whaler. The men were groomed and wigged far too grandly, Ashton thought, for the task of questioning a prisoner. In the center sat Colonel Darby Chason, the presiding officer. Ashton stood before him, meeting his gaze directly.

Chason appeared the consummate officer, sitting ramrod stiff in a thronelike wooden chair. He had a hawk nose and keen eyes, one of them enlarged by a gilt-edged monocle, and lips so severely thin that they appeared almost nonexistent. There was anger in that imperious face and a glint of cynicism in the magnified eye.

Chason studied Ashton for long moments, as if testing his prisoner's ability to withstand the pressure of his scrutiny. Then he neatened a stack of papers in front of him and nodded at the bailiff.

Before the bailiff could open his mouth, there was a scuffling sound at the door. It swung open and Bethany Winslow pushed inside, staring down the guards as if defying them to attempt to remove her.

Ashton couldn't help but admire her aplomb, her regal bearing as she crossed to the long table. She exuded an air of wealth and privilege; it was bred into her bone and character like the finest of bloodlines. Today her beauty was endearingly flawed; he noticed smudges of fatigue beneath her large eyes and a decided lack of color in her cheeks. He was not surprised she had come alone; Harry was either too wise or too selfish to appear.

As she faced the Redcoats, she reminded him of a slightly rumpled flower. His pleasure slipped away when he noticed the defiant gleam in her eyes. He realized she fully intended to complicate an already troublesome situation.

"Get her out," he snapped, jerking his head in her direction.

Bethany planted herself beside him, tossing her head. "I've a vested interest in the outcome of this proceeding."

Sergeant Watson stepped forward and whispered something to Colonel Chason, who nodded, "You may take a seat by the door, Mrs. Winslow." Then, as a concession to Ashton's fury, he added, "You will be removed at the first outburst, ma'am."

She settled herself on the bench. Ashton fixed a hard stare

on her, trying to tell her that she would jeopardize Harry's life if she insisted on speaking up. She met his gaze placidly, her face immobile, her resolve as firm as her uptilted chin.

"Shall we proceed?" Chason asked.

The bailiff pounded the floor with his staff, and the court scribe dipped his quill.

"State your name," the bailiff intoned.

Ashton sent him an ironic smile. "Just who do you think you've arrested?"

"'Tis accepted procedure," the bailiff said, nonplussed.

Chason shook his head in annoyance, raising a waft of scented pomatum that caused the lieutenant beside him to cough. "Let us get on with this, Mr. Winslow. You've been arrested for sedition. What say you?"

"I'd say, sir, that the fact that I've been arrested is undeniably true."

Chason shifted his monocle from one eye to the other. "Have you any political opinions, Mr. Winslow?"

Ashton hooked a thumb into the waist of his breeches. "None whatsoever. Sir."

"Yet you've just admitted to sedition."

"I admitted to being *arrested* for sedition."

The officer scowled. "Are you a patriot, Mr. Winslow?"

"I am a horseman, sir."

"I think you are being quite deliberately evasive."

Ashton gave a short laugh. "You *think*? I did not know soldiers knew how."

The monocle dropped from Chason's astonished eye. The scribe's quill scratched furiously.

"Would you insult an agent of your king, Mr. Winslow?"

"Ah, that would be unfair. Instead, let us speak of the king himself. The man you so loyally serve is a soft-brained Bedlamite who raids the Colonies to fill his privy purse, whose ministries are run by misguided mediocrities."

Chason's jaw dropped. "God, what has England bred in her Colonies?"

"A generation of men and women who think for themselves," Ashton shot back.

"Outlaws," Chason muttered.

Ashton shrugged. "Keep Lord North out of our pockets and we'll all be honest men."

The colonel's hand clapped down on the table. "That is treasonous in itself!"

"Is it now?" Ashton asked.

"Are you aware that you've committed a hanging offense?"

"More than one, in your estimate."

Almost reluctantly, Chason folded his hands. "Then there is nothing more to be said." The monocled eye blinked at Ashton. "There is but one way to save yourself from hanging."

Ashton smiled. "I am—dare I say it?—dying to know what that way is, sir."

"This court would show you mercy if you were to cooperate."

"You mean name names, places, that sort of thing?"

"Yes. Spare yourself, man. The lives of a few radicals aren't worth hanging for."

"Who am I to decide that, Colonel?"

They stared at each other for a long, tense moment. "So," Chason said, "you'll offer us nothing."

"Nothing." Ashton had never meant anything more sincerely in his life. Bethany clapped a hand over her mouth to stifle a sob.

The gavel descended onto the table. "By the authority of His Majesty King George the Third, I sentence you, Henry Adler Winslow, to hang at noon on this day, the eighteenth of August in the year of our Lord seventeen hundred and seventy-five."

Ashton heard a soft gasp behind him. He was as surprised as Bethany by the sentence, delivered even before the charges had been debated and borne witness to. He wondered how far he should push the officer before revealing the misunderstanding.

"About the hanging, sir," he said slowly. "Must it be so . . . expedient?"

"I've little time to spare granting last requests to wastrels like you. Besides, were we to keep you in custody, you'd likely meet a slow, tormented death aboard one of the prison ships."

Ashton considered that, then grinned. While in the army, he'd heard dreadful tales of the conditions on prison ships. Keeping his grin in place, he bowed to the colonel with mock formality. "I defer to your better judgment in this, sir. Hanging is far more merciful."

He nearly laughed aloud at the expressions on the assembled officers' faces. "There now, gentlemen," he added consolingly, "there's nothing at all to choosing a way to die. You've spared me from the harder puzzle—from choosing a way to live."

"You are either fearless or foolish, sir." Chason waved an agitated hand at the guards. "Take him away. Prepare to carry out the sentence."

"No!" Bethany's ragged objection filled the silent room. She rushed across to Colonel Chason, looking like a bedraggled, tawny-gold angel. "This man is innocent."

Chason shook his head, scattering more powder. "His actions over the course of the summer have been noted by informers. His insolent speech today only proves his lack of penitence." He nodded at the guard. "Carry on."

Bethany planted herself in front of Ashton. The sergeant took her by the arm. "Mrs. Winslow—"

"I am *not* Mrs. Winslow, you infernal fool. I am *Miss* Bethany Winslow, and this man you intend to murder is not my brother, Harry!"

A murmur rippled through the assembly as the door opened to admit several more Redcoats. Ashton expelled his breath as he recognized the officer who had just entered the room. The ruse would soon be over.

Sergeant Mansfield presented himself to Colonel Chason with a smart salute. "Permission to speak, sir."

"No one else has done me the courtesy of asking," Chason replied dryly. "You may speak."

"I saw this man being brought up from the jail and thought to point out to you that Ashton Markham performed loyal service under my command. He was wounded in the line of duty at Fort George nine months ago."

"Who the devil is Ashton Markham?"

"Why, the prisoner, sir!"

The buzz in the room swelled to a low roar. The bailiff pounded madly with his staff and shouted for silence.

Chason leaped to his feet. His monocle swung against the front of his scarlet coat. "Watson, what is the meaning of this?"

The sergeant reddened to the tips of his ears. "Blind me if I know, sir. I was only carrying out orders."

The colonel held himself stiffly. "Take your men and find Henry Winslow straightaway."

The sergeant scurried from the chamber, and Colonel Chason switched his agitated gaze to Ashton, who was trying to conceal a look of amusement.

"You've an infuriating manner, Mr. Markham." The colonel turned and addressed Mansfield. "The punishment still stands."

Bethany stepped in front of Ashton, her face deathly pale. "He's done nothing, sir!"

Chason opened and shut his mouth three times in quick succession. "Miss Winslow—or whoever you are—this man has committed treason and slander in this very room. For that he must hang. 'Tis a matter of necessity."

"He was tried without benefit of witnesses. He—"

Ashton touched her shoulder, no longer amused but too astounded to fully appreciate the severity of the sentence he'd been dealt. "Love, you waste your breath."

She whipped around fiercely, her eyes snapping. "Will you just let them hang you, then?"

He was suddenly stricken by a keen sense of his own mortality. The winds of fate were capricious, snatching a man's life away with the ease of a shifting breeze. "I don't see as I've been given any choice."

Chason barked an order and the men formed up in readiness to escort the prisoner from the chamber.

"Wait!" Bethany blocked the doorway, gripping the frame as if to fix herself there for all eternity. Ashton could almost hear the whir and click of her calculating mind. What was she up to now?

Without looking at him, she calmly addressed the colonel. "Sir, in the name of decency you cannot allow Ashton Markham to hang."

"And why not, pray?"

She moistened her lips and drew a deep, shuddering breath. "I did not want to bring up an indelicate subject, sir, but I see that I must. I need Ashton Markham, and he is of little use to me dead."

Although misguided and certainly futile, the arrogance she showed the British officer ignited a flame of tenderness with Ashton.

"Dear lady," Chason said, "this man has spoken sedition before this court of military law."

"Still," she said, an odd, strained look on her face, "I cannot believe our sovereign's army is completely heartless."

Chason groped for his monocle and raised it to his eye. "What's that? Are you a Loyalist, then, miss?"

"To my very soul," she returned primly.

"Ah. Then perhaps you can solve this mix by telling me your brother's whereabouts."

"I do not know where Harry is."

Ashton was impressed by her finesse in lying. Chason obviously believed her, for he questioned her no further.

"Colonel," she said, "I respectfully ask that you release this man."

"I'm sorry, miss, but I cannot. The man condemned himself out of his own mouth. Unless you can show me some mitigating circumstance—"

"There is one," she said faintly. She looked almost as pallid as she had on the ferry the day before.

"What's that?" Chason asked. "Speak up, girl."

She cleared her throat, and Ashton discerned a light sheen of moistness on her brow. "Colonel," she said more loudly. "Ashton Markham has compromised my honor, sir, and gotten me with child. If he is hanged, I'll be forced to bear the babe in shame and rear it in poverty."

Ashton's breath left him with a great *whoosh*. Bethany's words stunned him more than the death sentence he'd just been dealt. And felt worse than the rough hemp of a noose biting into the flesh of his neck.

As the assembly murmured and exclaimed, a great rage took hold of Ashton and squeezed hard. Things came together to form a picture with icy clarity.

So this was why Bethany had sought him out so frantically, why she had been so ill on the voyage to Bristol. Dorian Tanner had gotten his bastard on her and refused to marry her. *The most awful thing has happened. . . .* The words she had choked tearfully against his chest on the ferry swam through his mind.

The revelation seethed and swelled in Ashton's mind. He didn't hear Chason until Sergeant Mansfield nudged him in the ribs.

"I asked, Mr. Markham," the colonel repeated, "if you did, indeed, compromise Miss Winslow."

"I've no doubt the young lady has been compromised."

"Were you aware that she is, er, enceinte?"

He looked at Bethany. Their eyes met and clashed. She shuddered as if chilled by his cold stare.

"I am now," he said.

Chason waved his hand at the scribe, who had been scratching away with his quill. "That will do. This entire affair is distasteful enough. No need to make it a matter of public record." He turned back to Ashton. "What do you propose to do, Mr. Markham?"

"I seem to recall I've been sentenced to hang. Sir."

Chason cleared his throat. "Yes, well, I think not. Instead you will marry this poor girl. Perhaps the responsibilities of a wife and child will make you think twice about spouting sedition and insulting the king's men. I might even dare hope the lady will teach you some measure of loyalty." He addressed Sergeant Mansfield, who looked vastly relieved. "Is the magistrate in this morning?"

"Aye, sir, just down the hall."

Chason gave a satisfied nod. "Fetch him without delay." The monocle came up to magnify the eye that focused on Ashton. "Count yourself lucky for Miss Winslow's intervention. And if you hope to seek an annulment or desert the young lady, think again. My informants will be watching you. If I learn you've not done right by her, you will hang immediately."

Bethany gasped, then pressed her lips together, clutching the doorway for support. Ashton tried to keep the terrible rage from his voice when he said, "Colonel, I demand some sort of discretion in this matter."

"Why is it, Markham, that you are less reluctant to meet the gallows than a bride?"

Ashton set his jaw hard and looked out the window, where a picket detachment had begun constructing a gallows. Then he raked Bethany with a gaze so furious that she winced.

The wedding, such as it was, consisted of a hasty signing of papers and another stern warning from Chason. In the space of one hour, two entities had conspired to rob Ashton of his freedom: the British army and Bethany Winslow.

6

Ashton took the length of Court Street with strides so long that Bethany had to run to catch up. He didn't look back at her; he didn't say a word.

Her mind reeled with the impact of what she had done. Later there would be much to say—she dreaded to think just how much—but such was not for the ears of the seamen and soldiers and women who hurried through the busy street.

The entire morning had been a series of absurdities that would have struck her as farcical had it not been so terribly real. And final.

She could not blame Ashton for being angry. Yet the alternative to marrying her was hanging! Couldn't he see that she had only lied to save his neck?

He stopped at one of the wharves and had a word with the ferrymaster, then turned to her. "Wait here," he ordered. "I'll be back shortly."

"Where are you going?"

He sent her a cold smile. "I seem to remember a delivery

I was supposed to make." He pivoted on his boot heel and strode away.

She lifted her knuckles to her mouth. "Oh, Lord," she said, "what have I done?"

"What, indeed, Miss Bethany Winslow?" came a clipped voice behind her. She turned to see Miss Abigail Primrose, who had appeared on the dock, her tiny kid-clad foot tapping with studied precision on the wooden planks.

"We are not a fly trap," Miss Abigail intoned crisply. "Close your mouth, miss."

Responding without thought to her teacher's familiar imperative, Bethany snapped her mouth shut. Then she said, "I'm sorry, Miss Abigail. You surprised me."

The lady waved a small, immaculately gloved hand. The crisp breeze didn't dare stir a single ebony hair on that erectly held head. "I am on holiday from New York. The academy has been turned into barracks for His Majesty's soldiers." With eyes the color of gun metal, Miss Abigail took in Bethany's poorly done hair and rumpled riding habit.

Bethany drew a shaky breath, tasting the bitterness of the brine in the air. "It is so good to see you, ma'am." She found it impossible to pretend everything was normal, so she gave up and gazed out at the harbor.

"What's this?" Miss Abigail raised her tiny chin high above her stiff white collar. "My best student of elocution is at a loss for words?" She paused, leaning forward to peer closely at Bethany. "Tears, miss?" She stretched out her narrow arms. "Come here, child. You've not forgotten I am your friend as well as your teacher."

Bethany stumbled forward, drawn by Miss Abigail's kindness, the softness beneath the starched exterior. Although the lady was considerably smaller than Bethany, she had a firm embrace and a generosity of heart that made her seem much larger.

"There," she soothed, her familiar scent of barley water

enveloping Bethany. "You might as well get over your tears straightaway, for I shan't release you until you do."

Bethany nodded and stepped back. "I'm sorry."

"Stop apologizing, child. 'Tis an explanation I want."

Bethany lowered herself to an upended barrel. As Miss Abigail's penetrating gray stare appraised her, she said wonderingly, "I'm married."

Miss Abigail allowed one carefully tweezed eyebrow to lift. "I see. Was that your husband who just walked away from you?"

Bethany nodded. "His name is Ashton Markham."

"He's a fine figure of a man."

Bethany had never thought of Miss Abigail as a lady who would notice a man's looks. "Yes," she agreed, "he is that."

"Yet I sense a certain commonness about him."

"There is nothing common about Ashton," Bethany said. "If he looks somewhat unkempt, 'tis because he spent last night in the custody of Colonel Darby Chason."

Miss Abigail's other pruned eyebrow joined its partner high on her forehead. She seated herself beside Bethany and folded her gloved hands primly on her knee. "It appears we've much to discuss, child."

The entire absurd story poured from Bethany then, beginning with her fascination with Ashton upon returning to Seastone and her plot to use Dorian to make him jealous, and ending with the wrongful arrest and travesty of a trial.

"He was sentenced to hang, Miss Abigail," Bethany said. "So I simply blurted out that he—he'd gotten me with child."

"And has he?"

"Of course not!" she looked down at her hands and added, "Unfortunately, most of Bristol now thinks otherwise."

Something akin to admiration glimmered in Miss Abigail's shining eyes. Birdlike, she cocked her head to one side. "You always had a lively imagination," she commented. "And a quick wit. A bit too quick, I fear, for your own good."

A wan smile haunted Bethany's lips as she regarded her teacher. No one but Miss Abigail would accept her story so matter-of-factly.

A gloved hand smoothed back Bethany's wind-tangled hair in a gesture more maternal than any Lillian Winslow had ever bestowed on her daughter. Bethany studied her teacher for a moment, seeing her in a new light. Why had she never noticed how remarkable Miss Abigail was, with her raven hair and china-doll face? Her tiny figure was compact, as well proportioned as a Bartholomew fashion baby. With a start, Bethany realized her teacher was probably not much older than thirty.

"Thank you for listening," she said. "Ashton barely spoke to me after we left the jail."

"You saved his neck, child, but at the price of his pride. Men are fools when it comes to such things. In one morning you've managed to wrest control of his life from his own hands."

"But he would have died!"

"At least he condemned himself of his own free will."

"What shall I do, Miss Abigail?"

The tiny kid-clad foot began tapping again. "Your parents are certain to object, and Mr. Markham is furious. But you say you love him. Hold on to that. Be a good wife to him. Tread lightly on the man's pride, for it's been wounded."

"Drat Harry," Bethany said. "If it weren't for him, I wouldn't be in this fix. At least he's safe in Providence—"

"Your brother's gone to Providence?"

Bethany nodded. "To his wife's father's."

Miss Abigail glanced back at the street and stood, resting her hand firmly on Bethany's arm. "Your husband is coming," she said quickly, her other hand moving to eradicate a single wrinkle in her corded silk skirt. "Please try not to botch the introductions, child."

But botch them Bethany did, stammering as she presented Ashton to her teacher. "My hus—" she faltered, then began again. "Miss Abigail, this is Ashton Markham."

He bowed slightly, the parcel under his arm rustling with the movement.

"Your wife was always a favorite of mine," Miss Abigail said. "She is a young lady of considerable intelligence and heart."

"I agree with you about her intelligence." Ashton looked down to meet that imperious stare. "About the heart, I am not so sure."

"Then you'd best be about getting to know the girl."

He cast a cool glance at Bethany. "I daresay I know her abundantly well, Miss Primrose. Good day."

By the time the stabler at Bristol Ferry brought the horses around, Bethany's nerves were wound taut with tension. Ashton had ignored her during the short voyage across the bay, in favor of a lively discussion with a Quaker man on the merits of the hackamore over the bit.

She mounted and watched as he did likewise. He twisted in the saddle to secure his package with a leather strap.

As her eyes were drawn to the hemp-strung parcel, she remembered where she'd seen it before. There was no mistaking the significance of Harry's papers. Gusting fear added to the emotional storm that had raged in her all morning. She looked up; her gaze locked with Ashton's. Lord, why had she never noticed how cold those eyes were?

"Oh, no," she said softly, braving his icy stare. "Oh, Ashton, you cannot get involved with the rebels."

He laughed humorlessly; the bitterness in his voice stung her like a lash. "Involved? I believe I have just proven myself one of them."

"But you must not—"

"'Must not'? How quickly you take to wifely imperatives." He nudged Corsair with his heels and led the way to Newport.

She brought Calliope in step with him. "Please," she called over the sound of cantering hooves, "'tis only that I fear for you."

"You're just smothering me with your favor today, aren't you?"

She felt her throat constrict with the ache of unshed tears. "I'm sorry you were given no choice about marrying me, but I didn't know what else to do."

"I believe you knew exactly what you were doing," he returned harshly. "Still, I suppose I should sink to my knees in gratitude. You did, after all, snatch me from death's door so I may spend the rest of my life in matrimonial bliss with you."

She recoiled inwardly, lanced by his sarcasm. The girlish fantasies she had indulged in all summer suddenly took on a nightmarish quality. Miss Abigail had once warned her about wanting something too much; achieving a dream often led to disillusionment. Here she was married to the man she loved, but nothing had happened the way she'd imagined it. There had been no tender proposal on bended knee, no church bells and well-wishers, no grand ceremony to end in a loving kiss.

There was only the heaviness of sorrow over what she had done, and Ashton's bitterness over the fate she had forced on him.

For the first time in his life Ashton entered the Winslow mansion through the front door, stealing Mrs. Hastings's composure as he strode across the vestibule, Bethany following with small, hurried steps. Graceful mahogany newels and balusters flew by in a blur as he crossed to the library door and pulled it open. He stepped into a room that smelled of leather and tobacco and the less tangible but quite unmistakable tinge of money.

Sinclair Winslow raised startled eyes from his copy of the *Newport Gazette*. "Ah, there you are, Markham," he said briskly, placing his knuckles on the surface of his Goddard desk. "I've been wanting to see you about a horse trade I made in Little Rest yesterday."

Ashton took a moment to study the man who, save for a four-year hiatus in the British Army, had been his employer all his life. Sinclair Winslow was shrewd, severe, arrogant, and so brimming with blue blood that he found it hard to contend with common people. A sapphire stud of considerable size winked from his cambric stock.

"Send for your wife, Mr. Winslow," Ashton said. "I must speak to both of you." He looked back at the door. Before Mrs. Hastings could duck guiltily away, he repeated his request to her. The housekeeper hurried off to find Mrs. Winslow.

Moments later Lillian appeared, touching a pampered hand to her faintly puckered brow.

"Please sit down, Mrs. Winslow," Ashton said. His voice hardened perceptibly as he added, "Bethany and I have something to tell you."

Lillian arranged herself in the Townsend chair by the fireplace. Ashton moved to the sideboard and poured a generous dram of brandy for Sinclair and a crystal goblet of Madeira for Lillian. The Winslows were apparently too shocked by his familiar actions to protest.

"Bethany and I were married this morning," Ashton said.

Lillian's mouth formed a silent O.

"What!" Sinclair exploded.

"Bethany and I are man and wife."

Sinclair's brandy disappeared in a single gulp. "By God, this is an outrage, you greedy upstart. I'll have you flogged!"

"Father, please," Bethany said.

He turned the full force of his glare on her. "And you, young lady—how dare you defy me in this way? I told you only yesterday that matters had been satisfactorily settled with Captain Tanner."

God, Ashton thought. Was Winslow actually pleased Tanner had ruined his daughter?

"To your satisfaction, Father, not mine," Bethany retorted.

"And this"—Sinclair waved an agitated hand at Ashton— "this is satisfactory to you?"

"'Tis done," Bethany replied quietly, keeping her eyes averted from Ashton.

"Oh, Bethany," Lillian wailed, fanning herself with her hand, "think of your reputation."

"That is exactly what she was thinking of," Ashton commented dryly, unmoved by Sinclair's temper.

"I will not allow this." Sinclair's sapphire stud winked as he loosened his stock. His neck was flushed an angry red. "We'll arrange for an annulment at once."

"No!" Bethany cried. "I won't let you!"

Lillian wept into her manicured hands. Sinclair's murderous gaze climbed to Ashton's face. "How much?"

"Sir?"

"Don't play ignorant with me, Markham. 'Tis clear you wed Bethany to get your hands on her portion. I'll pay you double that—whatever price you name—if you'll consent to an annulment."

Ashton's eyes stabbed him with furious resentment. "'Tis all shillings and pence to you, isn't it?"

"I suspect a man like you is vulnerable to my brand of persuasion."

"I will not take so much as a single copper from you."

"Do you realize how much money I'm willing to part with?"

"Keep it," Ashton growled. "Every bloody penny of it."

"You drive a devilish hard bargain, Markham."

"Believe me, money was the last thing on my mind when I married your daughter."

Sinclair rose from the massive desk, taking the length of the library with angry strides. "Just how do you intend to support Bethany?"

"As I've supported myself all my life. By the sweat of my back. Her pampered life will be a thing of the past, of course, but she didn't pause to consider that this morning."

"I can't bear it," Lillian wailed. "My daughter, living in a servant's cottage—"

"Bethany may stay here," Ashton snapped. "In her own room with my sister dancing attendance on her. But not for long, I'm afraid, Mrs. Winslow. I've decided to peddle my skills elsewhere. We'll be leaving soon."

Sinclair wheeled about. "What's this?"

"I shall be leaving your employ."

"What about the races, the breeding program—"

Ashton's laughter cut a dry, humorless swath through the tension-thick air. "Have I not mortified you enough by marrying Bethany? Would you still keep me around to pander to your horse trade?"

"I am a man of business before all else," Sinclair said. "I've never made light of my admiration for your skill with horses."

"Ah. I'm good enough to raise your horses but not to marry your daughter."

"I'll become a laughingstock if my horses cease to win. Damn, but I was wrong to think you'd inherited your father's loyalty." Sinclair snapped his fingers. He rushed to a Smibert portrait of one of his horses and moved it aside to reveal a wall cache. From this he extracted a document, yellowed and crisp with age, and handed it to Ashton with a tight smile. "As a matter of fact, Roger did leave you something. A legacy, if you will. You won't be going anywhere for a long time, Markham."

"What is this?" Ashton fished his spectacles from his pocket.

"An old debt. One I'd forgotten and would have forgiven—until you brought this unpleasantness upon me."

Ashton's eyes scanned the page, narrowing behind the spectacles. His jaw grew tighter and tighter as he read.

Sinclair chuckled humorlessly. "Seems your father never told you he'd indentured himself to me, Mr. Markham. Fool that he was, he accepted a wage instead of serving out his seven years. Had some infernal idea about getting you a gentleman's education."

"What has this to do with me?"

"Read on. There's a clause stating that if Roger failed to serve out his bondage, the obligation would fall to his son."

The edges of the paper crumpled in Ashton's grip. Bethany's gasp shuddered in the silence.

"You're mine," Sinclair announced. "You belong to *me*, body and soul, and you'll breed and train my horses exclusively for the next seven years."

Ashton let the document slip from his fingers. It wafted to the floor and settled in front of Sinclair's silver-buckled shoes.

"I demand my portion!" Bethany burst out. "I intend to buy Ashton's indenture from you."

Ashton tore off his spectacles and turned to her, stifflipped with rage. "I am already your husband. Would you call me slave as well?"

"No! Ashton, I didn't mean—"

On feet made swift with fury, Ashton left the house.

Her heart in her mouth, Bethany heard the clatter of Corsair's hooves on the stone drive.

She faced her father. "How could you?" she whispered. "How *dare* you?"

"I have done nothing wrong," Sinclair said. "I am merely invoking the terms of Roger Markham's indenture. Terms he readily agreed to."

"Because he trusted you! He never would have wanted his son to be a bond servant!"

Sinclair extracted a wad of tobacco from his leather-clad humidor and tamped it into his clay pipe. "I'm sure Roger never expected his son to do so foolish a thing as to marry above himself."

"Why, Bethany?" Lillian asked. "Why did you marry him?"

Bethany turned to the French window. Nothing would be served by spilling the entire twisted tale to her parents. They would only be hurt to learn Harry was a fugitive from justice. And they would never understand the lie she had told to induce Chason to revoke Ashton's sentence.

"You had everything," Lillian persisted. "Every advantage we could give you."

Bethany smiled bitterly out the window. "You've spent a small fortune on my education and clothes. But how young was I—three? four?—when I learned not to muss your gown by crawling into your lap? By the time I was five I discovered there was more companionship to be found in the stables than at your knee."

"Bethany, I do not see what this has to do with your insane actions. You could have had any man you chose. Captain Tanner has offered for you—"

"I *chose* Ashton Markham." Foolishly, perhaps, and impetuously, she had chosen him long before this morning. She moved toward the door.

"Where are you going?" Sinclair demanded.

"To pack some things. I shall be out of the house in an hour."

"Bethany," Lillian said, "surely you don't mean to live in that—that hovel by the stables."

"I mean to live with my husband." She fixed a stare on her father. "Thanks to you, that 'hovel' is to be my home for the next seven years." She walked out and closed the door.

Only when she was safely outside the library did Bethany realize how badly she was shaking. Behind her she could hear the muffled sounds of her mother's sobs.

Regret came on tiptoe, seizing her by surprise. Never had she deliberately hurt her parents. They had done nothing to deserve such a shock. Her hand found the brass door handle. Perhaps she should speak to them again, try to explain.

"Let her go," her father was saying. "She'll come running back as soon as she gets a taste of squalor."

"I cannot bear the shame," Lillian wailed. "I shall not be able to face my friends. And the governor's reception is next week. . . ."

Bethany's hand dropped from the door handle and she walked away. Her mother's concern was social disgrace, not the fact that Bethany might have just made the most desperate mistake of her life.

"This isn't how we'd planned it at all," Carrie Markham said as she selected an assortment of smallclothes from a lowboy chest and tossed them onto the bed. "Are you sure your father won't settle your portion on you?"

"Even if he did, Ashton wouldn't accept it."

"Then he's a fool. But so am I," Carrie said, half to herself. "I should have thought of your parents. While you wooed Ashton, we should have been preparing your father and mother for this moment." She jerked the walnut armoire open, fingering the silks and velvets of the formal dresses.

"Leave those," Bethany said. "I shan't be needing them." Ruefully she shook her head. She owned perhaps two dresses that wouldn't look completely out of place in Ashton's cottage.

"What about me?" Carrie demanded.

"You shall have to stay on here in some other capacity."

"As what? A slut in the scullery?"

"Mother's maid is getting on in years. Perhaps you can take her place."

"I can't possibly please Mistress Lillian. I'd need four hands just to do her hair."

Bethany wished Carrie would stop complaining. Ashton's resentment, her father's duplicity, her mother's wailing, and now Carrie's self-pity and unconcealed disappointment at not having a portion of the new wealth she'd expected all gathered into an overwhelming wave.

Her heart was heavier than the tightly packed valise she carried down to the cottage by the stables. She wondered why she had never noticed the great distance between her father's house and the stable compound, or the sharpness of contrast between the gambrel-roofed mansion and the stone-end cottage with its split-maple shingles.

She stopped before the door and set down her valise to stare at the place that, because of her father's treachery, would be her home for the next seven years. Currant bushes, gray with years and sea air, brushed the whitewashed walls, sheltering a late summer array of sweet William and snowy phlox. Thick stems of portulaca framed the door.

She stared for a long moment at the entrance. She found herself comparing it to the door of her father's house, its panels polished to reflect the caller, its jewel-like side panes and fanlight shining above, its heavy brass knob and knocker speaking with quiet eloquence of the wealth and privilege contained within.

The door to Bethany's new home had vertical planks, roughly hewn from knot-infested pine slathered with whitewash and held together by iron tacks. The hinges whined as she pushed the door open and stepped inside, to be greeted by a hollow ring of emptiness.

*   *   *

Finley Piper didn't smile as he enveloped Ashton's package in the folds of his frock coat, but there was an unmistakable glimmer of satisfaction in his pale eyes. His son, Chapin, lank-haired, his bony knees bumping the underside of the table, displayed less reserve as he lifted his mug of beer and grinned at Ashton.

"Well done," he said. "Your countrymen are in your debt."

Ashton pulled long at his beer, raising an eyebrow over the rim of the tankard. "My countrymen?"

Finley dipped a thick, ink-stained finger into his collar and drew out a small silver amulet suspended on a length of black ribbon. Ashton recognized the insignia of the Liberty Tree.

"We need men like you," Finley said, "to keep the tree alive."

"Your tree needs pruning," Ashton replied. "What business have you with the rebels, Finley?"

Finley and Chapin exchanged looks. "I'm a member of the Committee of Safety. We're concerned with communication, sabotage, espionage." He patted his coat. "And now this. If we can't get it by free will, we get it by stealth." His eyes probed Ashton. "What brings you into our fold?"

He smiled ruefully into his mug. "If I told you, you'd never believe me. Suffice it to say I've been given a taste of British military justice and I've found the experience decidedly lacking in fairness."

Chapin nodded vehemently and leaned forward. "Can we count you as a friend, then?"

Ashton surveyed father and son for a moment. They were good men, simple men, Finley a widower who reminded Ashton of his own father, Chapin a young man eager for action. Catching Ashton's perusal, Finley said, "Chapin and I are men of the printing trade. We've been pushed to our limits by the British."

"We've no wish to be heroes," Chapin added, looking very unlike the lantern-jawed hobbledehoy he'd seemed on first impression. His eyes regarded Ashton with knifelike keenness. "But I would lay down my life for the cause of liberty."

A vague chill crept up Ashton's spine and stole across his scalp. Many a patriot had brayed out similar words at town meetings in the Brick Market. Only weeks ago, Chapin's loftiest goal had been to attract the attention of Carrie Markham.

"You're a bit young to be taking on the British Army," Ashton said.

"'Tis we who must live in the world we make for ourselves. 'Tis we who must take a hand in its shaping."

Finley rose from the table. "I take it you'd not be averse to other assignments."

Ashton steepled his fingertips. "I'll not kill or injure anyone for any reason."

"Quite so." Finley leaned forward and lowered his voice. "All summer long we've been deviled by a spy. Too smart to be regular army; too discreet to be an ordinary Tory. I'd dearly love to speak to you about this devil. Are you still working for Sinclair Winslow?"

"Aye." Ashton almost choked on the admission. "And will do so for the next seven years."

"Winslow is loyal to England. Raises horses, doesn't he?"

"He buys them, I raise them."

Finley rubbed a finger over his chin. "The Continental Army could use some good horses."

"They're not mine to give. Besides, the horses aren't battle trained." He lingered to drain two more mugs before stepping out into the fast-gathering twilight.

As he rode home, his mind filled with the one thing his thoughts had been fleeing from all day. Bethany. His wife.

Bitterness mingled with the taste of stale beer in his mouth. The laughing, guileless companion he had once trusted as a friend seemed like a dream now. Beneath that wide-eyed gaze lurked a cunning and guile that defied imagination. She had given her innocence blithely to Dorian Tanner and maneuvered Ashton into salvaging her reputation. Granted, his neck had been spared because of her treachery, but at what cost!

He hoped she had sense enough to stay in her father's house tonight.

Bethany sat gazing down at her knuckles, which had been struck raw by the flint and steel she'd used to set a spark to a bit of scorched linen from the tinder box. Pride had kept her from begging a pan full of glowing coals from her father's kitchen, and she took a certain grim satisfaction in having coaxed a fire in the hearth by her own hand.

She turned those hands over, studying the unfamiliar array of blisters at the base of her fingers. The bucket, stone, and chain of the stable well-sweep had placed the blisters there, chafing the untried flesh of her hands as she drew water and brought it to the cottage. In one afternoon she'd discovered her complete ignorance of the steps in performing the simplest of domestic chores.

Gladstone, whom she'd fetched from the kennels to keep her company, lazed on a rag rug by the hearth, oblivious to her turmoil. The fire snapped in the grate as she tried to accustom herself to the idea that this was her home. For the rest of Ashton's indenture, she would tread this rough puncheon floor and gaze out the tiny glass panes of two windows. She, who had never brought so much as a crumb to table, would learn to prepare meals and clean up afterward. Hands that had never known the harshness of lye soap would become rough from washing. A body that had been pampered and fussed over by others would now know the aches and twinges of having worked.

Bethany didn't need to invent chores with which to busy herself while she waited for Ashton to return. She stowed her belongings in the Duncan chest at the foot of the bed. The watery soup of beans and turnips and a few shreds of salt meat from the tiny larder was dismally bland, yet tasted of her success in having prepared her first meal.

Now that night had crept over the two-roomed cottage, she was restless. She added a log to the fire and, with prickling trepidation, laid her white lawn night shift on the quilt-covered bed.

She had often envisioned her wedding night, images suffused with half-formed ideas of coupling, ideas garnered from Carrie's prattle and the secretive giggles of the girls at school. Yet never in those vague imaginings had she considered that her new husband would avoid her. Where was Ashton?

Apprehension seized her as she recalled Harry's package. If Ashton was caught with the secret documents, he might never come back.

Her fingers were cold as she unbuttoned her riding habit and let it drop to the floor. She pulled on the nightrail, shivering as she drew the combs from her heavy locks. Gladstone meandered over, sniffing at the discarded riding habit.

"It's not going to get up and walk to the chest by itself," she said. For some minutes she worked at folding the garments. Carrie always made it look so easy, yet Bethany couldn't seem to smooth the sleeves and skirt at all. In the end she wadded up the clothes and stuffed them in the chest.

The August night was warm, softly breezy, redolent of late-summer flowers and the nightingale's song. Yet Bethany couldn't help the shiver that trembled through her as she slipped between the coarse muslin sheets and felt the unfamiliar and oddly comforting rustle of corn husks beneath her. Gladstone settled on the floor at her side.

Trailing a blistered hand over the dog's silky head, she closed her eyes tightly. Yet still a pair of scalding tears escaped and slipped down her temples into hair that hadn't been brushed by anyone but her maid for as long as she could remember.

* * *

A pair of hands bit into her shoulders and pulled her roughly to a sitting position, drawing her from a warm cocoon of sleep. She found herself staring into the darkened hollows of Ashton's eyes.

"What are you doing here?" His breath was warm and smelled of malt. His fingers curled deeper into her flesh.

She winced. "You're hurting me."

The grip slackened, but his voice remained harsh.

Her chin climbed a notch. "I live here now, Ashton."

"Don't be absurd. You no more belong here than a hot-house rose belongs in a weed patch."

She kept her eyes steady despite the bitterness of his voice. "I belong with my husband," she vowed, "wherever that may be."

He released her so suddenly that she dropped back onto the pillow.

"Where are you going?"

"To the stables."

She leaped from the bed, earning a splinter from the puncheons. Wincing, she placed herself in front of him. "Stay, Ashton."

She heard him hiss as he sucked in his breath. "Why?"

"Because you can't keep avoiding me."

"You might have shackled me in the eyes of the law," he returned, "but not in fact."

She touched him, laying her hands alongside that hard, angry, handsome face, and felt it tighten beneath her warm palm. "I do not wish to shackle you," she whispered. "I love you."

He flinched. "Any port in a storm, pet?"

The sting of his sarcasm knifed white-hot through her, lodging in her heart. "I speak the truth," she insisted. "I do love you, and have ever since I returned to Seastone. Before that, too, but not as I do now."

"That would account, then, for your flirtation with Captain Tanner."

She fastened her gaze on the faintly glowing fire in the grate. "Dorian is nothing to me. 'Tis you I want, Ashton."

He grasped her chin in his fingers and forced her to meet his glare. "Why can't you look at me when you say that?"

She blinked and swallowed. The firelight gave his features a stony, forbidding look. "I want you," she forced herself to say. "I want you so much I ache inside."

The smile that twisted his lips was cold. His hand snaked into her hair with an ungentle tug. "Aye, my love," he said. "'Tis a wanting with which you are intimately familiar."

7

Ashton watched her throat work as she swallowed again. "I know you're angry," she whispered, "but 'tis not in my power to release you from either the marriage or the indenture."

"I should forgive you because you cannot undo what you've done?"

"Perhaps it is too soon to expect forgiveness."

"Then what do you expect from me?"

"I . . . 'tis our wedding night, Ashton."

The log flared with a hiss, illuminating her eyes. She looked as innocent as a kitten and he almost softened . . . until he remembered that she had claws. Of course she wanted him to lie with her. Perhaps she thought to convince him that the babe Tanner had saddled her with was actually his.

"So you want me in your bed, do you?" he asked.

Her gaze fled from his. "Yes." The admission came on a nervous sigh.

His hand twined more firmly into the heavy silk of her hair. "I didn't hear you, my love."

Her eyes sought his again. "Yes," she repeated in a steadier voice. "I want you in my bed."

He disentangled his hand from her hair and tugged at the ribbon at her throat. The lawn shift gaped wide, revealing a smooth bosom that sent rivulets of desire gliding through him. Her flesh was dewy, and a maddening scent emanated from her, the warm tinge of sleep mingling with her jasmine perfume. His own need ignited anger as well as desire.

"You'll not find me gentle," he warned, and he impaled her with a challenging stare.

"You'll not make me afraid," she countered, and her chin rose defiantly.

Reason dictated that he had every right to toss her on the bed and show her the fate she had tempted in forcing him to marry her. The other was to succumb to the powerful magic of her eyes, to enjoy the enchanting offering of her scented flesh, to eradicate her memory of Dorian Tanner by driving her to mindless passion.

As he fitted one arm around her slim frame and the other behind her knees, Ashton wasn't certain which impulse would win out. When he lifted her to his chest and felt her curl against him, he found himself seized by an absurd tenderness that made sport of his anger.

After he had placed her on the bed and lowered himself beside her, the urge to bury himself thoughtlessly in her began to give way to a more tender approach. When he dropped his gaze to her luminous eyes and the fullness of her mouth, he realized anger would have no part in the love he intended to make to her.

Even as he cursed the tenderness welling within him, Ashton bent his head and took her lips with a raging thirst. Beneath his mouth, hers slackened. Under still more pressure, her lips parted. His tongue grazed her teeth and probed the yielding softness beyond. The taste of her was warm, welcoming.

"Dear God," he murmured as he felt her body shudder to life beneath his hands, "what is wrong with me that I find you so sweet? How is it that I still want you after you've run roughshod over me?"

"Perhaps . . ." Her tongue darted out as if to sample the taste he'd left on her lips. "Perhaps you'll find we've not committed such a terrible mistake."

His hands became hard and demanding on her pliant frame. "By all rights I should show you the error you've made." Inexplicably, his harsh touch became a soft caress over her lovely contours. "Yet instead, for some reason, I want to show you paradise."

Her response was a sigh and a tiny smile that held no hint of the guile he knew she possessed. Her hands crept, tentative and searching, around his neck, and she offered him her lips again. He drew her next sigh into his mouth and gloried in the dulcet cushion of her body even as he cursed the weakness that made him want her so. When the heat in his loins ignited to unmanageable warmth, he drew back, studying her lovely face, so radiant in the burnished firelight. A look of wonder shone in her eyes. Her hand moved from his neck to his face, and he was startled by its rough texture.

He removed her hand and held it before him, his brows descending as he took in the array of blisters. He questioned her with a look.

She answered him with a smile. "I've been drawing water."

"You?"

"Aye. I suppose my hands will soon become accustomed to the work."

He laid her blistered palm in his, noting the raw and broken skin of her knuckles. "And this?"

"Striking flint for the fire. I'm afraid it took several dozen attempts."

Something quivered deep inside him as an image formed in his mind of Bethany performing such menial chores.

"You'll never be happy with me," he told her brusquely, tracing the marred flesh of her hand with a finger.

"My happiness does not depend on the way I live," she countered. "It lies with you, Ashton. With us, with what the two of us can make of life."

Anger bristled within him. "Have you not already saddled me with enough responsibilities? Must you insist that it is in my power to make you happy or unhappy?" His lips drew upward in a rueful smile. "Tell me, then, Mrs. Markham, what you would have me do to ensure your contentment."

A blush crept to her cheeks, and her lashes swept downward. "It makes me happy to hear you call me that," she admitted. "And to feel you touch me."

Anger deserted him as she faced him with a bittersweet smile. He brought her hand to his lips and kissed it, giving each finger the feathery attention of his mouth before kissing the blistered palm. He folded her fingers into a fist as if to keep the kiss within.

"My touch?" he queried, watching the blush spreading downward into the gaping neckline of her shift. "That is little enough to ask."

"It is all I ask."

The fire in his loins screamed out for him to have done with inane conversation and meaningless love games and spend his mind-sapping lust without delay. But he hesitated. For reasons he refused to scrutinize, he wanted her ready, in body as well as in spirit. He steeled himself against the need that ran rampant all through him.

He drew her to her feet. Inexplicably he found himself on his knees before her, his face pressed to her thighs, his hands caressing the delicate flesh at the back of her knees. Coming slowly to his feet, he lowered her shift. The fabric glided over her breasts before pooling at her waist.

He stepped back and caught his breath, studying her like an artist admiring the work of a superior craftsman.

Her breasts were two perfect swells adorned by crests of an enticing dusky rose hue. She shivered and brought her hands up to cover herself.

He shook his head. "You shrink like a virgin," he told her harshly, drawing her hands away.

"I—I've never—"

"Did your captain never look upon you?" Ashton demanded.

"Of course not!"

Ashton laid his fingers on her lips. "Speak no more of him. You're an artful actress, Bethany. Perhaps we could play this as if it were the first time." He drank from her lips and mumbled against them. "Your first kiss . . ."

"But—"

He silenced her again with his mouth and moved his hands over her breasts. "Shall we pretend that I am the first to touch you here?" he continued, and one hand disappeared beneath the shift. "And here . . . ?" As he caressed her trembling body, he could almost believe he *was* the first. Her responses were so startled, so unguarded. She seemed clean, unsullied, despite what he knew of her. God, he wanted to forget that, beneath his very hand, the evidence of Tanner's predominance grew in her still flat belly.

He paused to peel off his shirt and drop it on the floor. He felt her eyes on him, a shy caress from beneath a thick skirting of dark honey lashes. When she lifted her eyes to his, he saw astonishment on her face.

"You act as if you've never looked upon a man before."

Her gaze moved over his shoulders and down to the patch of burnished chestnut hair on his chest. "I have not," was her soft admission.

Ashton stood and shed the rest of his clothing. Either she lied with incredible virtuosity or Tanner knew nothing of making love to a woman. Bethany kept her eyes on his face as he lowered himself beside her.

"You are free to look on me, Mrs. Markham."

She swallowed hard. Her blush was furious now, visible even in the dim light.

"You said I'd not find you fearful."

She fingered the scar on his left side. Her touch felt hotter than the musket ball that had made the wound. Her hand trailed upward, finding places he had never realized were so damnably sensitive.

He circled her waist with his hands, loosening the shift until it drifted to the floor. Then he untied the ribbon at the top of her pantalettes. These he lowered slowly, his desire mounting as the thin fabric descended.

"And you," he said grudgingly, "are nearly perfect." He glanced for a moment at her midsection, which would soon swell with a child not of his making. "Nearly," he repeated, and saw her flinch at the anger of his tone. "I think we both settled for something less than perfection in this marriage."

She caught her lower lip with her teeth, and her eyes filled. Ashton brushed away a tear; it seemed to scald his finger.

"I want no weeping girl in my bed." Then he relented, kissing her. "We've talked much tonight and said little. I think perhaps the time for conversation is past." He laid her on the bed. His kiss deepened and his hand played downward, paying court to her unresisting body.

His mouth left hers to follow the path his hand had taken. A pulse leaped in her pale throat, its rhythm matching the racing of his own heart. She tasted of feminine dew and flowers, a combination far more heady than the spirits he had quaffed at the White Horse. His tongue licked her breast, evoking a small whimper of wanting. He took the crest into his mouth, nearly bursting with desire when his teeth and tongue encircled it.

Beneath his ever-lowering hand she quivered; he sensed her desire in the faint lifting of her hips. He indulged in teasing then, barely brushing her flesh, sharpening her appetite with gossamer touches. When the movement of her hips became more pronounced, he slid his hand downward, to touch and caress the soft female flesh of her.

She stiffened and tried to pull away. "Ashton!"

He raised his head and gave her a questioning look.

"Not . . ." Her voice trailed off as his hand filled itself with her.

". . . there," she finished weakly, but her passion-drenched eyes told him otherwise.

"Especially there," he assured her, and lowered his mouth to her other breast. She relaxed with a sigh of capitulation.

Ashton found her utter trust in him inordinately exciting. The joy he took in pleasuring her was as compelling as the most intimate caress she could have bestowed on him. When he felt her rapture crest and spill beneath his hand, he experienced her shudder as if it were his own. And as if it were completely new for both of them.

Her eyes glowed with wonder as she recovered from his touch and raised herself to press a kiss on his shoulder. "Is there not something I should do to . . . ?" She let her voice trail off.

God, he thought, had she really taught herself to blush at will? Did she know how beautiful those spots of color looked in her cheeks?

"To what?" he asked, his fingers leaving her ready moistness to trail upward over her midsection.

"To please you?"

"I shall leave it to you to discover that," he told her, dropping a kiss on her nose.

"Oh," she murmured. Then, shyly, her hands and lips found him, moving with gathering confidence over his shoulders and neck, his chest and then his hips. Those hands worked magic on a body that had long since grown tired of artful wenches and tavern bawds; Bethany touched him as he'd never been touched before. When one hand brushed him intimately, he nearly cried out at the searing sensation that ravaged him.

His desire breached the wall of bitter resentment he'd spent hours erecting, driving him mindless with wanting. She was alternately brazen and bold, shy and shrinking as her hands and mouth explored and tasted him, drinking from his lips and flesh until boundless urgency hammered at his resistance.

"Bethany," he whispered.

She paused and lifted her eyes to his. "Have I done something wrong?"

He tried to smile through the fog of desire enveloping him. "I daresay you've not made a single false move."

"You look as if you're in pain."

"Aye, painful it is to want you so badly."

"Then . . . ?"

He answered her with a swift movement of his body, bracing himself above her to look into her lovely confused face. "Then," he replied, "we stop these games."

Her arms wound about his neck. The look of astonishment on her face raised a glimmer of hope in him. Could it be that he was mistaken about Tanner, that the Redcoat hadn't taken her innocence after all?

His every muscle strained as he poised over her, waiting, wanting to know, yet dreading to find her sullied by another.

"Ashton?" she whispered. She shifted her thigh; the satin-smooth limb brushed him in a way that banished all hesitation. He moved inexorably downward.

"Rise your hips to me," he instructed.

Sweetly she complied and he lowered himself to her in one great caressing movement, praying he'd encounter the evidence of her innocence.

But her flesh didn't resist him; her body welcomed him. Her sigh of delight seared his cheek.

Surrounded by the moist silk of her, he found he no longer cared that he was not the first. With long, slow strokes he reveled in her warmth and filled her with the passion that, he now admitted, had hammered away at him for weeks.

Her breathy cries reached his ears and he knew it was good for her, that he'd answered her need. She was all dewy satin and feminine softness and seemed—incredibly—surprised to feel the rhythm of his lovemaking.

Through a burgeoning rush of desire, he felt he was touching her in places she'd never been touched before, pleasing her in ways no man had ever pleased her.

Because she told him so in a soft whisper that reached his ear like an intimate caress. Her hands spoke her pleasure, feathering across his shoulders and sliding down his sides, then rising again to thread into his hair. While he moved above her, she blossomed beneath, taking deep, startled breaths. Her scent was all the perfume of a summer garden, wave upon wave of heady, sensuous sweetness.

Nothing in Ashton's past experience could have prepared him for the intensity of her response as she spiraled to ecstasy beneath him. When she whispered that she loved him, he came so close to believing her that his passion crested and he joined her in the dark, sweeping pleasure of utter completion.

He left her with slow reluctance and settled at her side, shifting to find room on the narrow bed.

She settled her tousled head into the crook of his neck and warmed his flesh with a sigh. Ashton found himself wishing she weren't so agreeable, so infernally accommodating. Even the jasmine scent of her hair was enough to ignite his passion anew. A muttered oath, directed at his own weakness, escaped him.

He felt her stiffen and she lifted troubled eyes to search his face. "Ashton, did I not behave correctly? If I've failed you in some way—"

His fingers crept to her lips, silencing her. "Hush." How could she not know what she did to him? "In the space of one day you've saved me from the hangman, married me against my will, and goaded your father into making me a bond servant." His fingers left her lips and wandered leisurely downward. "But tonight, ah, tonight, you've made me forget all that." He punctuated his statement with a teasing touch to her thigh and felt her quicken in response.

"I have?"

"Aye. Most exquisitely."

She was more bold after that, full of newfound confidence and insatiable youth. As Ashton came to her a second time, he reflected that, although Dorian Tanner had taken her, he hadn't taken the best of her.

The first of Bethany's faculties to come to life the next morning was not her reason. Nothing so coherent as thought disturbed the quiet shifting of her mind; she was aware only of the warm cradle of Ashton's arms, the unfamiliar and fascinating scent of his body, the hardness of his sinews as, in a luxurious stretch, she ran her feet up and down his legs.

Her gaze slid over the dawn-lit expanse of his chest, the muscles rising and falling in a rhythm of deep slumber. His hand lay on her shoulder, slack-fingered and tan against her paler flesh.

Memories returned, memories of what that great blunt-fingered hand had done to her last night, teaching her things about herself she'd never known, igniting feelings of a power she'd never imagined. His lovemaking had left a sweet ache within her that stirred again now, and the ache became a nest of need. Fingers hungry to explore crept from beneath the covers and trailed up the length of his torso, encountering firm planes and ridges shaped by hard muscle, a texture so compelling that she caught her breath.

He stirred beneath her touch and she raised herself on an elbow in time to see his eyelids lift. She smiled.

His hand moved beneath her chin. "Could you parcel

out and sell that smile," he told her in a sleep-rough voice, "you'd be a wealthy woman."

"I *am* a wealthy woman."

A tremor passed through him. "I can't dispute that you're a woman." The statement was punctuated by a kiss that seemed to envelop all of her, awakening urgent clamorings and an unabashed greed for fulfillment. She returned his caress with hands that knew, despite her inexperience, how to touch him. His body sprang to life with a speed that filled her with a heady sense of power.

A sigh seeped from her lips as he soothed her ache with the heat of his desire. She wondered if her soft cries could be heard in the stable compound outside. And then she ceased to think at all.

Afterward she wanted to bask for hours in his embrace. But the kiss he dropped upon her lips before sliding from the bed was distracted, as if his mind had wandered to other things.

"Stay with me," she begged, her body already lonely for his touch. "It's not yet full light."

He pulled on his breeches and threw an unreadable look over his shoulder. "A working man has no time to lie abed."

The statement fell hard on her ears, hammering home the notion that she was married to a man who lacked the leisure to rise when he would. She hastened into her shift.

He sluiced water from the basin over his face and neck, furrowing droplets through his hair before tying the chestnut locks in place with a leather thong. She watched furtively as he drew a shirt over his head, his muscles rippling with the movement. He eased into stockings and boots, then drew a woven hemp belt around his waist.

His routine act of washing and dressing looked, to her, like an intricate and fascinating dance. Glancing at her, he seemed amused by her expression. "You're staring, Mrs. Markham."

Color stung her cheeks. "This is all quite new to me."

His mouth grew hard above the endearing cleft in his chin. "You'll soon find marriage tiresome enough."

"You're determined to make me regret what I did," she shot back in sudden annoyance. "I will not. I mean to be a good wife to you."

His lip curled, but not into a smile. "You do, eh? Very well, then. I've a long day's work ahead of me. I should like to start it with breakfast."

She caught a challenging gleam in his eye and squared her shoulders, marching past him to the kitchen. Feeling his eyes on her, she set the kettle she'd filled the day before onto its crane in the hearth and bent to add fuel and stir the fire to life. Ashes rose and smudged the pristine sleeve of her shift; still more tickled her nostrils, and she stifled a sneeze. Her nerves tingled as she went to the larder and stood peering into gloomy shadows, finding herself at a loss.

He laughed harshly at her look of confusion. "Are you surprised to discover that breakfast isn't a meal that magically appears on a silver tray at your bedside?"

A chilly tremor scuttled through her. Finding her voice, she said, "I'm surprised by only one thing, Ashton. How is it that last night you were so considerate of me, yet this morning you seek to wound me?"

Eyes narrowing, he said, "Some aspects of marriage are pleasant, but all is not kisses and sighs in the dark. There's a lot more to living together than the marriage bed."

She veiled her hurt with lowered lashes. "I'm determined to be a good wife to you. But I shall need your help."

He took in his breath with a hiss. "I've little time to train you in housewifery." Taking his cocked hat from a hook, he jammed it on his head and went to the door. "Don't bother with breakfast this morning."

He left with the cool breeze of dawn, taking the spaniel with him. Bethany stood at the doorway, listening to the thud of his boots on the path and watching as his broad form was swallowed up by gray light.

She leaned against the frame, her nostrils filled with the morning scents of bay and ribbon-grass, her heart filled with the glory of loving Ashton, and the pain of not knowing where to begin with him.

But begin she did, sparing not a moment for worry or regret. The kitchen clock at the manor house was marking the hour of six when she appeared, hair flying and apron askew. Dudley, the cook, twitched his mustache in surprise at her appearance. Two maids peered from the pantry, whispering behind their hands.

"Miss Bethany?" Dudley asked. "What's your pleasure this morning?"

"I'd like you to teach me to cook, Dudley."

The mustache worked agitatedly in the cook's sharp, thin face. She forced a smile. "'Tis no jest." Her eyes flicked to the whispering maids. "My capacity here has changed. I have to learn my way about a kitchen."

"I hardly know where to begin, Miss—"

"It's Mrs. Markham now. Surely the gossip has reached you." Her smile took on genuine amusement. "Actually, you ought to start calling me Bethany; I'm afraid there can be no formality between us now. And then you may teach me to prepare supper for my husband." She found an odd sense of delight in the idea.

And so Bethany, who had once contemplated Euclid's axioms, now contemplated a lump of bread dough. A mind once occupied with Berkeley's idealism was now absorbed in the proper way to dress a chicken for roasting.

Her studies had never exhausted her like Dudley's tutelage. That afternoon when she made her way back to the cottage and set about preparing her first meal, she didn't allow herself to consider failure.

*   *   *

Ashton hesitated on the path to the cottage, frowning at the unexpected aroma of roasting chicken that wafted from the window. His stomach, groaning for want of food, made him quicken his step as he entered the dooryard. Gladstone waited, ears perked and tail quivering, on the newly swept stoop.

He pulled the door open and the dog darted inside. Dumbfounded, he contemplated the scene before him. Years of clutter had been cleared from the keeping room. A quilt concealed the scars and gouges on the wooden settle; the mantel was free of dust, its few ornaments polished to a reflective shine. Mary-bud and sweet William and primroses graced a corner shelf. The rag rugs had been beaten, the floor swept, and the betty lamps wiped clean of soot and grease.

Then his eyes were drawn to the kitchen. In contrast to the spotless keeping room, the area was a place of unrelieved chaos. Every surface, from sideboard to floor, was dusted with flour and cornmeal. His amazed eyes moved to the hearth, where every pot he owned seethed and spluttered, then to the table, piled high with utensils. A crock of molasses oozed dark stickiness over the table and down one leg, pooling in the flour coating the floor.

His gaze jolted to Bethany, chopping onions at the sideboard. She wielded the knife like an ax, reducing the onion to chunks. Her hair hung, carelessly tied, down her narrow back. Every so often a flour-coated hand came up, whitening the honey-gold strands around her face as she brushed them aside.

He cleared his throat. Bethany pivoted, knife pointed outward. He swallowed mirth at the unlikely sight of her startled, flour-smudged face.

"Hello, pet," he said, unable to keep the warmth from suffusing his voice. "I see you've been busy."

"Aye." She set the knife aside and wiped her hands on an impossibly soiled apron. "Supper is nearly ready." She whipped into action again, scooping up the onions and hurrying to the hearth. Before he could give warning, she seized the lid of a pot, then yelped as the lid fell from her burned hand and clattered to the floor. The onions dropped into the fire and her seared fingers flew to her mouth.

"Do you," she said around her fingers, "mind your chicken without onions?"

"Don't give it a thought."

She sent him a grateful look. "Shall we eat?"

He washed his hands, brushed flour from the bench, and sat down. She lowered herself opposite him, and for a moment they gave thanks. Then her brow furrowed at the molasses crock. "I haven't set a very good table, have I?"

"Never mind."

She looked blank, then shook her head. "Here I am sitting like a lackwit, waiting for someone to serve me." She climbed to her feet again. This time she remembered to cloak her hands with a linen towel before lifting the iron roasting pan. She set the meal on the table.

"I did it all myself," she said, "save plucking the bird with my own hand." With equal pride she produced a pot of Indian pudding and went to the brick oven, removing a loaf of bread.

At least he thought it was a loaf of bread. His eyebrows rose as her face fell. The loaf was hoecake-flat, charred on one side and pasty raw on the other.

"I don't understand it," she said. "I did everything Dudley told me."

"It doesn't matter," Ashton said quickly, his stomach clamoring now. "We'll do without."

But his appetite shrank in revulsion when he sampled the chicken. Like the bread, it was half raw; her aggressive seasoning of sea salt and white pepper caused his mouth to scream for a draft to chase away the evil taste.

He braced his hands on the table, about to bolt for the cider keg when she smiled expectantly at him.

"Well?" she asked.

His knuckles paled as he gripped the table. The morsel of near-raw chicken mingled with the sting of salt and the burn of pepper in his mouth. She was looking at him so eagerly.

Summoning the armor of a palate made hardy by four years of poor soldier's fare, Ashton swallowed. His eyes stewed in tears with the pain of having ingested a volatile substance.

"Ashton?" she leaned forward, her knife poised daintily, her round eyes bright.

He found his voice in the burned, stung, and tortured recesses of his mouth. "It is highly seasoned," he remarked, wishing his voice didn't sound so raspy and broken.

"It is," she said, and the smile that blossomed on her lips suddenly made the torture all worthwhile. "But perhaps I should have sprinkled it around a bit. It all seems to be concentrated on your portion."

He tried to be nonchalant as he moved to the sideboard and drew a mug of cider from the keg. Soothed by the cool drink, he tried not to look too suspicious as he took another bite of chicken.

Bethany, he saw, barely sampled her food, so intent was she on watching him. He braved the Indian pudding, finding the molasses-spiced corn mush as heavy as chalk ballast, but digestible after he drowned it with cream. Somehow the food on his plate disappeared and he wiped his mouth with a napkin. Napkins. Fancy that. He couldn't help but smile at Bethany.

Her eyes swam with tears. "How can you look so pleased with me?" she asked, "when I've nearly poisoned you?"

Tenderness curled deep within him—unbidden, unwelcome, but so much a part of his feelings for her that he couldn't help himself. "My smile has little to do with the fare," he admitted, "but everything to do with your efforts." His hand crept across the flour-dusted table and closed over hers.

"Why is it," she wondered, "that you are kindest to me when I least deserve it—and when I most need it?"

His grin broadened and lingered. "Let me help you clear up." He avoided her question as he began picking up soiled pans and utensils. Gladstone's less discerning appetite made short work of the chicken.

Ashton left Bethany elbow-deep in wash water and went behind the house to bring in the small wooden tub from its hook. Setting it before the hearth, he filled it with water from the red cedar bucket by the door. She swiveled around, eyeing him questioningly.

"I think we could both do with a bath," he explained. "I've the grit and sweat of a day in the stables." He snared a dewy droplet of perspiration from her brow with his thumb. "And you have not had a moment's relaxation all day, from the looks of you." He caught her watching him as he warmed the bath with a kettleful of boiling water. A mocking grin tugged at the corners of his mouth. "Aye, this is how one draws a bath when one lacks servants to do so."

She finished in the kitchen and stood looking at the small wooden tub, the steam rising from it misting her face. "I know so little about being a wife."

He came and stood before her, searching deep for the anger, finding instead that he plumbed a well of tenderness and understanding. Could he really blame her for what she had done? She was young, alone, rejected by the man who had replaced her innocence with the scourge of an illegitimate child, a notion frightening enough to make a woman go to desperate lengths.

His hand crept behind her waist and he plucked at her apron strings. "I am no lady's maid," he told her, "but I, too, am willing to learn." She gasped and shivered as his fingers climbed from her waist to the nape of her neck, leaving a row of unfastened buttons in their wake.

By God, but her beauty stirred him. He dealt uncomfortably with the hungry ache in his loins as he finished divesting her of her clothing and held her hand at a dainty angle to steady her as she stepped into the tub.

She drew her knees up to accommodate the tub's smallness. He found himself wishing the tub were large enough for the two of them, that his hands could join the warm sluicing water that trickled in a liquid caress over her shoulders, arms, breasts, and thighs, which trembled beneath his stare as if he'd actually touched her.

Bethany was maiden-shy as she bathed. He had to remind himself that she was far from the innocent child she seemed. Not so very far, though. He busied himself with sweeping the kitchen as she washed her hair and rinsed its dark honey length, her back curving like a willow bough as she bent to dip the strands into the water.

She finished bathing and wrapped a linen towel around her slim form. Only with concentrated effort did he keep himself from following her wet trail into the bedroom.

He hurried through his own bath. Desire flared high as a droplet of water trickled into his mouth and he imagined it tasted of Bethany. By the time he hastened to the bedroom, as ready as he had never been ready before, he nearly shook with wanting her.

He approached the bed, his eyes moving over the delicate slimness and enticing fullness of her supine form. The flames of hunger leaped higher. He lowered himself beside her, his mouth exploring, his hand rising to the undercurve her lawn-clad breast.

She sighed and curled near. It was not a sigh of desire but one of deep, exhausted sleep. His smile was rueful as he gritted his teeth and stilled the clamoring in his loins, battling his hunger until at last he joined his wife in sleep.

8

Bethany had been married six weeks. She lay staring in terror and wonder at the rough-beamed ceiling over the bed, alternately smiling and shivering at the thought that she was pregnant.

She was not at all surprised. In the fourth week of marriage she had become aware of an inexplicable breathlessness, a tenderness of breast that put suspicion in her head. In the fifth week, queasiness began visiting her on tiptoe each morning. And now this. The monthly bleeding, by which she could have marked a calendar, had not come.

No, not a single surprise in that, she decided as she came gingerly to her feet and washed her face and neck with water from the basin. Although the days of their marriage were riddled by hard work, tense moments, and Ashton's moodiness, the nights were swathed in splendor. Lovemaking, frequent and intense, had become their refuge from Ashton's bitterness, her parents' disapproval, and her own uneasiness at having forced him into marriage.

By day there were petty annoyances and uncertainties; by night there was mindless passion and fulfillment of needs they dared not voice aloud. Mornings were tense with apprehension about what the day would bring; evenings were soft with anticipation of comfort and release. Ashton had said on their wedding night that their union was less than perfect, and that was true. But the compatibility they found in the creaky rope-framed bed banished, if only temporarily, their other problems.

She dressed in a cotton gown, running her hands over her still slim waist. The bodice hugged a bosom that was, perhaps, slightly fuller, although the change could be due to the face that she had discarded her corsets and stays, finding them a hindrance as she worked in the kitchen.

She fed a ravenous appetite on the cornbread and bacon Ashton had fried for his breakfast, and promptly lost her meal into the basin. Her stomach felt wretched; her heart soared. She ran down the path to find Ashton.

Instead she was intercepted by Dorian Tanner, coming from the opposite direction, splendid in his scarlet uniform, tight-lipped with anger. For the first time since she had known him, he gripped her with a touch that hurt.

"I returned from my tour of duty thinking to find a fiancée," he said. "Instead I find you the bride of another man."

She fixed a glare on the manicured fingers that curled into the flesh of her wrist. "Let me go."

"Not until I have an explanation. We were inseparable for weeks, Bethany."

She cast her eyes downward. "I'm sorry I misled you. I never meant for you to read a deeper meaning into our friendship."

"How could I not?" he demanded. "You foreswore other men—"

"Aye," she admitted, "but my heart was always in another's keeping." Her lashes brushed her cheeks. Never had she considered that Dorian's feelings would be hurt. She had been so intent on flaunting him before Ashton that she had not considered the possibility that Dorian would come to care for her.

Her hand crept to his cheek, lying lightly upon that too-perfect face. She stared into eyes that looked not hurt, but angry. "Forgive me, Dorian. I've been so selfish."

"I've forgiven you, my dear," he told her, "if you will forgive this." An insinuating hand wrapped her against him and his sculpted lips insulted hers with a punishing kiss. She gave a frightened squeak of protest and arched back, fighting with no hope of besting his unyielding strength. He tasted of bayberry pomatum, heavy and sweet, a scent that tickled her already churning stomach until it threatened to erupt a second time.

The soft thud of a footstep parted them as if two great hands had torn them asunder. She stumbled back, aghast to see Ashton mounting the path, Gladstone trotting at his heels. His gaze impaled first Dorian, then her, driving needles of ice into her heart.

"When you're through with my wife," he said, his voice lashing like a rapier, "I'd like a word with her." Then he was gone, leaving a wake of shivery cold behind him despite the warmth of the autumn day.

Bethany fled after her husband, nearly stumbling in her haste. She reached him in the dooryard in front of the cottage. When she called his name, he spun, and she found herself facing a cold wall of anger.

"I want you to go back to your parents." He spoke very quietly. "I'll not have you entertaining your lover here."

Her breath left her as if a blow had landed in her stomach. "He is not my lover."

"Would you call me a liar after what I just saw?"

"That was not what it seemed. Dorian and I had a . . . misunderstanding and he grew angry."

His laugh sliced the air. "Ah, yes, I could see his wrath in the way he kissed you."

"I—he was hurt that I'd married you."

A curtain of fury dropped over his face. "It was an unfortunate mistake you made, for he would have made a far better husband than I."

"I won't be seeing him again."

"Your promises mean nothing to me."

Her throat and eyes ached with unshed tears. "And I, Ashton? Do I mean nothing to you?"

His eyes narrowed to cold blue crystals. "You mean a great deal to me. You mean seven years in bondage to your father. You mean an impediment to what I had hoped to do with my life. You mean not one, but two extra mouths to feed, and neither of them of my making."

She felt all color slide from her cheeks. "*What*?" Her hand trailed to her belly. "How did you know about the baby?"

"Do you think me blind and deaf? You followed me to Bristol, ill with pregnancy and clamoring to unburden your troubles to me. You announced before the military court that you were with child!"

She stumbled back, clutching at the vine-covered pickets of the fence. Her mouth worked; no sound save a small sob of protest came out. He believed that she had been pregnant at his trial. Carrying another man's child.

Hope flared within her. Once she explained, he was sure to forgive her. And his forgiveness would mark a fresh beginning for them. She caught his gaze and held it. "Ashton, listen to me. I was not pregnant at your trial. That was a lie I invented to induce Colonel Chason to set you free. He wouldn't waver until I told him of a mitigating circumstance. I was certain you didn't believe the falsehood, or I'd have explained long ago."

Something flickered in his eyes. Not a softening, not a weakening, but a vague lessening of distrust. The hope blossoming within her chest unfurled its petals further.

But his eyes narrowed again. "If what you say is true, then how is it you didn't come to your marriage bed a virgin?"

Her mouth dropped open. "You presume to tell me I was not a virgin?"

He shifted uncomfortably from one foot to the other. "You weren't intact the first night we lay together."

She felt the heat rise in her cheeks. "I know very little of such things. If I was not . . . what you expected, it wasn't because I'd been with someone else." She dragged her eyes back up to his.

Again that flicker, that waver in his cold blue depths. But it was gone even more quickly than the first. "There are some things," he informed her, "that you cannot falsify."

"God! I could hate you, truly I could," she yelled. Anger reared up from humiliation and held her in a relentless grip. "You presume to know much of women. You presume it is a necessary thing for a woman to come to her husband a virgin. What if I made the same requirement? What if I thought less of you because you were not a virgin on our wedding night?"

"It is hardly the same for a man," he muttered.

"Can a woman not have the gratification of knowing she was the first, the only? Or is that a fantasy reserved exclusively for men?"

He looked away, as if he could not bear the sight of her. "I never pondered such questions when I was a ready youth."

She studied his profile and all anger drained from her. "I've turned your prejudice back on you, haven't I? But I'm not so petty that I would even care, or hold it against you." She chanced a step closer and placed her hand on his sweat-slick forearm. "I was chaste until our wedding night, despite what you say. I was not pregnant at your trial . . ." She drew a deep, steadying breath. "But I am now."

He flinched. "How many lies have you told me, Bethany? How many more will you put before me with your limpid doe-eyed stare and your soft, cultured voice?" A sigh shuddered from him. "You claim the child is mine.

Very well, claim it if you like. I trust only time to give me the truth."

She swallowed hard. "Nine months is a long time to wait for your trust, Ashton. A long time for me to ponder your insulting accusations. Suppose I do carry the baby to May. What then?"

His eyes returned to her, no longer angry. "Then I hope you'll humble me properly."

A tang of winter sharpened the December air as Ashton crossed Marlborough Street, heading toward the White Horse Tavern. Newport was different, the change having been brought about as much by the winds of rebellion as by the cold of winter. The town had closed in on itself, windows and doors shuttered against the Redcoats who strode with surly contempt among the wharves and billeted themselves in the citizens' houses. Captain James Wallace of the HMS *Rose* had earned the title of scourge of Narragansett Bay. Only friends of the Crown remained unmolested by his fleet.

Ashton hoped Newport would weather the invasion. As for him, his work went on at the stables as usual. His marriage to Bethany followed an uneven course of peaks and valleys, the unborn child a constant thorn between them. As if by mutual agreement, they spoke little of the babe. But sometimes, when he saw Bethany rest her hands on the gentle swell of her middle, bitterness and confusion and undeniable tenderness stabbed at him. She was so steadfast in her contention that Tanner had nothing to do with her pregnancy.

He hated himself for needing proof.

Still, there were times when she touched him so intimately that he felt she had branded his soul. Times like that almost made him forget his distrust. Almost.

The wind scuttled a torn broadside across the street in front of him, and he caught a fragment of the message the printed scrap of paper bore: "To Arms! Rise, all ye lovers of freedom, ye patriot sons . . ." Shaking his head, he set his foot upon the broadside and walked on. Finley Piper's press had spat sedition all through the autumn of 1775, flirting with the royal officials' patience, courting reprisal from wealthy Tories.

That Finley had requested today's meeting with such urgency boded ill. Ashton entered the tavern on a cold gust of wind that swirled his greatcoat about his knees. A few of the patrons looked up, gave him a cursory glance, and went back to their idling.

The arrival of British ships had slowed the commerce that had been the lifeblood of Newport. The city's business partner—the vast Atlantic—had been cut off by Wallace's menace. There were no sailors with thirst to slake, no ships to unload, no tea to brew, no rum to distill, no accounts to copy, no barrels to build. . . . At Madame Juniper's brothel, the girls had resorted to taking in laundry.

Ashton spied Finley and his son Chapin and joined them at their table. The aleman provided a noggin of mulled berry wine, warmly spiced and steaming.

"Your broadsides are not to be avoided," Ashton said. "They blow about the streets like carrion birds."

Finley grinned. "I wonder when you'll take refuge beneath the branches of the Liberty Tree."

"Refuge? It's more like running into a raging inferno to warm myself against the cold."

"But surely you've a patriot's heart," Chapin said.

"I've a common man's distaste for the British ministry, and a coward's fear of bloodshed."

"You? A coward?" Finley shook his head. "I seem to recall a story about a Newport man putting his head in a noose to protect another."

"How did you find out about that?"

"There's no such thing as a quiet act of heroism. The news was all over the colony by summer's end."

Despite the tales, he knew better than to consider himself a hero. No hero would allow himself to be saved by a woman's lies.

"We've something to discuss with you." Finley grew serious and brisk. "It concerns your wife's brother."

"Harry Winslow?"

"He's been found. Arrested."

Ashton clenched his fists. All he had done on Harry's account had come to naught. "No more than four people knew of his whereabouts, and none of us would have divulged it."

"I don't know how it happened. I suspect the same British sympathizer who tried to foil our commerce with Hortalez et Cie."

"Damn," Ashton muttered. "So the lad's doomed after all."

"Not necessarily," Chapin said. "Curiously enough, the informant has a heart. He betrayed Winslow's whereabouts only after an assurance that the young man wouldn't be put to death."

Finley nodded. "There's a good chance we can gain his release by means of a prisoner exchange. Problem is, we don't hold a prisoner the Redcoats want badly enough to release Winslow."

Sudden comprehension added a bitter tang to the drink Ashton sipped. "You want me to procure one."

"Aye." Finley raised his cup. "And you'll be thrilled to learn who we have selected."

Bethany quickly composed her face when she heard Ashton lift the latch and enter the cottage. The tiny bunting she was embroidering for the baby lay neglected in her quilt-covered lap, several stitches knotted by her nervous hands. The hearth fire flared as wind gusted in the open door. Gladstone whined a greeting.

"You should have gone to bed." Ashton shrugged off his greatcoat. The sharpness of cold sea air wafted from him. The wind had placed color high in his cheeks, accentuating the rugged bones of his face.

"It's late," she said. "Where have you been?"

"You needn't concern yourself with my whereabouts."

She glanced away. For four months she had endured his distrust. She had grown accustomed to the hurt, but not so accustomed that she did not feel it anymore.

"Am I not permitted to worry about my husband?"

He leaned his forearm on the mantelpiece and studied the gray stones of the chimney, stones that had once been black with soot but were now clean due to Bethany's whisking. She saw a tightness in his shoulders and a slight droop to his head as he said, "Aye, worry if you will, but spare me your questions."

Always he hid the better part of himself from her, as if afraid of what would happen if he returned her feelings. She rose from the chair and went to him, running her hands up the back of the woolsey shirt defined by the taut sinews beneath. He tensed beneath her touch.

"Talk to me," she said softly. "Don't wall yourself off from me. I'm your wife."

He turned and froze her with his stare. "A marriage should be forged by trust, wrought by love. We were thrust together by happenstance."

"I love you, Ashton. I do."

"You love a girl's fantasies, some image you've built up and carried around with you." He encompassed the keeping room with a sweep of his arm. "Is this what you wanted? Seven years as a bondsman's wife in a house so small you can barely turn around? Being snubbed by people who used to polish your shoes? Shunned by those who used to wait with bated breath to see if you would accept an invitation to tea? Has that made you happy?"

Tears sparkled on her lashes and blurred her vision. "I

don't care where I live or whose soirée I've been excluded
from. I just want your trust. I want us to build a life together."

"You commend your heart into my keeping and expect
me to know what to do with it."

"You know. I've felt it." Her hand reached for him,
encountering the warmth and hardness of a chest that rose
and fell too quickly. "I've felt it each time you forget yourself and smile at me. I've felt it when you draw water for
my bath or spare me from doing the laundry on cold days.
I've felt it when you hold me in your arms at night and
make love to me."

At first the softening of his face was so slight that she
thought she had imagined it, and turned away. He brought
her back to him with a hand on her shoulder, and then she
knew; she knew some of what she'd said had breached his
indifference and touched him in the place her guarded so
jealously. There was no bitterness in his eyes as he wrapped
her against him, winnowing his fingers into her hair and
clasping her to him as if he never wanted to let go.

Bethany shivered and hugged her brown wool cloak around
her, shielding herself from the biting December wind. The
windows of Peleg Thurston's shop were fogged and
frosted, the display within rather dusty and haphazard, but
her eyes fastened hungrily on one object, which drew her
attention like a beacon.

"Lordy, and will you look at that!" exclaimed a voice
beside her.

The woman's rouged and powdered face and the garish
gown peeping from beneath a threadbare cloak marked her
as one of the fancy women from Madame Juniper's. She
sent Bethany a wide, brazen smile and pointed at the window. "Them ostrich feathers must be a full yard high.
Lordy, but wouldn't I like to have 'em for a bit of extra
plumage."

"They're rather striking," Bethany said.

The woman laughed in a gin-rough voice. "Not exactly to your liking, eh? So what're you looking at here?"

Bethany indicated a small calf-bound volume, its pages edged in gold.

The woman squinted at it. "I ain't much for reading."

"The pages are blank. It's a journal."

"Ah. For writing down your thoughts and such."

Bethany nodded, feeling more comfortable talking to this painted stranger than her own mother. "I thought to give it to my husband for Christmas."

"Well now, that's just fine, missus. That man of yours must be something special. Wouldn't mind getting my hands on a man like that myself."

Bethany smiled. Ashton hardly had to pay for what she adored giving him, night after night.

"I'm off, then." The woman wrapped a frayed scarf around her frizzy red hair. "I've a big night ahead. Good Christmas to you, missus, and many happy returns of the day."

Bethany lowered her head into the wind and plunged into the warmth of Peleg's. She dropped back her hood to inhale the fragrance of spices and coffee.

"Well, well," said a crystal-hard voice. "'Tis our own Bethany."

Bethany's hackles were already up by the time she saw Mabel Pierce and Keith Cranwick standing near the big central stove. Her friends had deserted her last August, so swiftly they might never had existed. Her marriage had been fodder for the gossip mongers; now that her pregnancy was evident, she was aware of finger counting and speculation as to why she had, so hastily, married beneath herself.

A tart retort leaped to mind, but she reeled it in. Nothing disinfects like sunshine, Miss Abigail used to say, and so she forced herself to smile.

"Hello, Mabel, Keith. Monstrous cold, is it not?"

"Indeed." Mabel tossed her ringlets over the fur collar of

her cloak. "If I had a smidgen of sense, I'd have stayed home today, but I simply had to do some errands before your parents' reception tonight." Her hand fluttered to Keith's sleeve. "Mr. Cranwick was kind enough to accompany me. I do find shopping so tedious." She fingered a frieze of green and scarlet, then nodded at her maid, a skinny girl who staggered beneath the bulk of a half dozen parcels.

"I'm sure the chore is very hard on you," Bethany murmured.

"Will you be at the reception tonight?" Keith asked. "Your former teacher, Miss Abigail Primrose, is over from Bristol for the season, I hear."

Bethany eyed the journal, which the proprietor had already removed from the window. Mr. Thurston had seen her coming and was well aware that she had longed to buy the book for weeks. Ashton would love it. He kept copious notes in his breeder's journals, but she wanted him to have a place to put his own private thoughts.

"I'm sure I'll see Miss Abigail while she's in Newport, but not at the reception. Ashton and I will be celebrating at home."

"A pity," he said smoothly. "I cannot imagine you living in that rude cottage with a stable hand."

Her smile wavered. "If you'll excuse me, I've come to buy my husband his Christmas present."

Mr. Thurston wrapped the journal and accepted her coins, painstakingly hoarded over the weeks. She turned to see Keith and Mabel still looking at her. Mabel was muttering something behind her kid-gloved hand. Both their faces held such smug pity that her temper snapped.

"Pardon me," she said. "I'm sorry I can't stay around to entertain you any longer."

"Bethany," Keith said, "we're concerned about you. 'Tis a crime you're married to an unwashed commoner, and a rebel to boot."

She chewed her lip. Ashton had had nothing to do with

the patriots since the day they'd married. "Why do you say he's a rebel?"

"I've seen him hanging about the White Horse Tavern."

"He's free to go where he will."

"More than ale is served at the White Horse. A man can get a generous helping of sedition there as well. I saw him slip into the taproom not an hour ago, as a matter of fact."

"You needn't inform me of my husband's whereabouts."

Mabel said, "Bethany, dear, we don't want to see you shamed."

She brushed past them, pausing only to borrow Mr. Thurston's quill and pen a message on her manila-wrapped package: *Merry Christmas, my dearest love.*

Stepping onto the street, she drew up her hood and started toward the little pony-driven trap she'd brought into town. The wind had gathered strength, pushing a bank of heavy clouds over the harbor, turning the bay waters into a frothy tempest the color of raw iron. Flurries of snow swirled through the air, filling the cracks in the brick street and stinging her face. The bell of Trinity Church tolled, its rich sound reverberating through the snow-laden twilight.

Possessed of a sudden impatience to be home, she climbed to the hard bench of the trap and chucked the pony into a slow walk. Snowflakes swirled in a vigorous, wind-tossed dance as she drove up Marlborough Street. Red brick and pastel-painted buildings wavered uncertainly through an ever-thickening curtain of whiteness. In the distance a figure appeared, emerging from the White Horse Tavern in a whirl of dark wool. A queue of chestnut hair hung over the collar of the greatcoat, sending a stab of pleasure through her as she recognized her husband.

She called his name, but the wind stopped her voice short and curled it back to her. Heedless and seemingly distracted, he hurried off in the opposite direction. She urged the pony after him, but the animal refused to quicken its pace beyond a reluctant plod. Anxious and frustrated, she kept her eyes fastened on Ashton as he passed Vernon's silverworks and the Brick Market and slowed when he reached a tall, narrow town house with a pink façade and a welcoming glow in its front windows. Madame Juniper's!

She hauled on the reins, bringing the trap to a stop as dead as her heart had suddenly become. Even as her mind screamed a denial, she stared, knifed by dread, as he cast a swift look right and left and went inside the brothel.

Comprehension crashed through her mind, sliding icy fingers through her heart. So this was where he had been last night, and Lord knew how many other nights. What was it, revenge or lust, that sent him into the arms of Madame Juniper's ready courtesans?

She could not weep, for tears were not enough to warm the ice that froze her heart. She could not curse Ashton, for she knew no words to describe the shattering disillusionment that roiled within her.

"Why?" she whispered brokenly, and the wind picked up her voice and swirled it away. Why did he seek the skilled, impersonal arms of a whore when Bethany's willing love awaited him at home? Did he find her so repellent that he needed the solace of another woman? Did he think her so tarnished that one of the painted birds at the bawdy house looked more savory to him?

An image pushed its way into her mind, of Ashton enfolded in the plump white arms of a woman like the redhead who had admired the ostrich feathers in the shop window. Revulsion welled in her throat as she turned the pony northward and plodded to the place she no longer wanted to call home.

Snow crunched beneath Ashton's boots as he stepped up the path toward the cottage. It had been snowing ceaselessly since late afternoon. The box hedge and yew trees lining the path formed vague, drifting shapes. At least the wind had settled.

Captain Dorian Tanner, locked in a salt lick shed in the eastern meadows, had ample clothing and covers to avoid freezing to death. Although no sound disturbed the snow-cushioned silence of the cottage garden, the Redcoat's bellows of rage and fear still rang in Ashton's mind.

The abduction had gone smoothly. A sack of gold slipped into Madame Juniper's hands, another to the shapely octoroon who entertained Tanner, and the hapless captain had fallen like a ripe apple into the patriots' hands. Unsteady with rum punch and blinded by the sudden dark when the courtesan had doused her lamp, the Redcoat was an easy mark.

Tanner had not awakened from the blow Ashton had laid to the vulnerable spot below and behind his ear until they had reached the stout rubble-built shed.

Ashton told himself he was entitled to feel a certain grim satisfaction that the lordly Captain Tanner had become a prisoner of the rebellion. But all he felt was grim. Things would be tense until tomorrow night, when he would transport his furious prisoner to Butt's Hill Fort.

Blowing out a sigh that froze in the air before his face, he quietly lifted the latch and stepped into the cottage.

Something was different, and he couldn't quite mark it. All was in place; the keeping room was snug and warmed by fireglow. Sprigs of holly and yew surrounded bayberry candles on the mantelpiece; the scents of the candles and greenery lingered in the air, adding a bit of holiday cheer. All the small comforts and homey niceties Bethany had brought to this house were in place: the bright quilts on the settle, the basket of pine cones on the hearth, the sprays of drying herbs hanging above the sideboard.

An inexplicable shiver of apprehension gripped him. Spying a small parcel on a settle, he went to inspect it.

Merry Christmas, my dearest love was written on the manila parchment in Bethany's neat, apothecary-like script.

"Ah, Christ," he murmured as the wrapping unfurled. "I've forgotten Christmas."

He looked at the gift—a handsome journal. How perceptive of her to give him a journal. And how pointed a statement. He spoke little to her; perhaps she had guessed he might like to record his thoughts and dreams on paper. How had she known?

His mouth thinned into a smile. How, indeed? A foolish question. She had an uncanny gift for anticipating his every need, his smallest desire, sometimes even procuring what he wanted before he was aware he wanted it.

He slipped the book into his pocket, full of warmth at her generosity, full of regret at his own thoughtlessness.

Hard-pressed to select a gift for Bethany, who had once had servants dancing attendance on her and more clothes and jewels than a half dozen ordinary girls, he had planned to give her his mother's wedding ring. But Harry's emergency had driven away all thoughts of keeping Christmas. Until now. He wondered if she would accept the gift, if she would appreciate its significance. She asked for little, yet she craved the impossible.

She did want something from him. She wanted him to believe she had been a virgin on her wedding night, that the child swelling her middle was his. She wanted his faith in her, his trust.

She wanted his love.

He moved restlessly to the hearth and laid a pine log on the embers, hearing the hiss of the sap, smelling resin. The feeling that something was out of kilter nagged at him once again.

And then realization came. Never had he entered the cottage to this misleading silence, this false peace. Gladstone, ever ready with his big, clumsy paws and wet tongue, was nowhere in sight. No matter how late it was, he could always be sure of a low whine of greeting or the thumping of the spaniel's tail on the puncheon floor.

With a hand gone suddenly cold, he pushed the bedroom

door open and peered unseeing into the gloom. He listened. And heard nothing, not Gladstone's whine, not Bethany's soft breathing, not the rustle of the cornhusk mattress.

He swung the door wide to let the glow of the hearth fire fall in an elongated triangle across the room. The light told him what he already knew, what he had been dreading since the moment he had stepped into the cottage.

Bethany had left him.

9

The wind numbed his ears and snow dusted his hat and shoulders as Ashton ran through the mile-long maze of paths to the main house. Let her be there, he thought over and over again until the words were a tattoo in his head. Let her be there. Let her be safe.

He had often urged Bethany to return to her parents, to live the life she was accustomed to and remain his wife in name only. He had suggested the idea in anger over the bitter futility of his situation, in concern when he saw Bethany struggle with some unfamiliar task, in annoyance when he saw how unsuited she was as a bondsman's wife.

But she had never wavered in her determination to be a wife to him in the fullest sense of the word. With stubbornness and fierce pride she declared that her place was with him.

So why now? Why, after all the months of enduring his silence, the bursts of temper that outnumbered the bursts of passion, would she at last succumb to his suggestion?

Winter-bare willows loomed over the path; naked branches clacked in the wind like dry bones.

The answer was obvious. It was Christmas Eve and he had not come home to her. Guilt writhed through him as a picture formed in his mind of Bethany waiting for him so she could place her gift in his hands. No matter that his task was to save her brother; she could not know that. All she knew was that it was Christmas Eve and he had not come home.

He sprinted across snow-blanketed gardens to the manor house. The ballroom windows glowed golden. Music spilled out across the snow-wrapped silence. He could hear the laughter of footmen and drivers who waited in the carriage house and guest stables. The Winslows always celebrated Christmas in grand style, opening their home to scores of visitors who drank and danced until the wee hours.

He stepped up to the veranda. The French doors, rimed by frost, framed a flurry of color and motion. He looked past a pinwheel of gold-shot gowns and scarlet uniforms, through a mass of powdered hair and black-patched faces, and his gaze found a bright head of honey-gold hair framing a pale oval face and two large, solemn eyes.

She wore a dress he had never seen before, curiously old-fashioned and maddeningly becoming. The gown was of some shimmering dusky rose fabric, high in the neck and falling loosely below her full breasts to cloak her swelling middle. A black velvet ribbon with a scrimshaw brooch circled her throat. Bathed in candlelight and framed by the frost-clad windows, she looked as beautiful as a goddess.

Nearby, a cluster of women cast scandalized looks at her and whispered behind their hands, no doubt speculating as to why, after having married a commoner, she was in their elegant fold once again. His heart ached for her when he saw the way she was smiling. It was a haunted smile.

He recognized the two people with whom she was talking. One was that birdlike teacher he had met briefly in Bristol. Abigail Primrose was on the arm of a monocled officer in a braided wig—Colonel Darby Chason.

Ashton wondered what Bethany had told the colonel about the marriage. Had she fed the man's male pride by declaring that he had done the right thing in forcing them to marry, or was she confessing that she was desperately unhappy?

He did not know. An ironic thought, for he knew Bethany's routine, the way her newly capable hands kneaded bread dough or wielded a birch broom. He knew her warm responses and sighs of passion when he made love to her, the way she awakened each morning like a flower unfurling its petals to the sun. But, to his profound regret, he realized he did not know what his beautiful, intelligent wife thought about from day to day.

He was certain of only one thing. It was Christmas Eve, and Bethany had left him.

On Christmas day Bethany sat in the summerhouse with winter all around her, the gardens stark and barren and the sea below the cliffs shifting, gray as a headstone. Wind slid icy fingers through the open windows, seeming to reach in and curl around her heart. Her hand cupped the burgeoning swell of her middle.

There was only this one warm spot within her, where even the bitter wind could not reach. For the first time she had felt a quickening as she lay alone in the beautiful pink and white room of her girlhood. The sensation had begun as a vague fluttering, then the stirring became more apparent.

Ashton Markham had taken her heart and torn it asunder. He had taken her faith and trust and the wealth of energy she had expended in pleasing him. He had taken her very soul and turned it black and bitter with his betrayal.

But he had not taken this from her. No matter what he did, he could not spoil her love for this child.

She wrapped her brown cloak more tightly about her. The wind caught her sigh, and the air chilled it to icy vapors.

"Young lady," said a curt female voice behind her, "just why are you mooning about on Christmas day?"

She snapped to attention. "Good morning, Miss Abigail," she said. "Many happy returns of the day."

Miss Abigail negotiated the snow-clad steps of the summerhouse with dainty precision. Her hair was covered by a voluminous rabbit-lined hood, and the cold had placed spots of color high in her fine-skinned cheeks. A hint of redness even dared show itself on the tip of her tiny nose, looking incongruous in an otherwise elegant face.

Miss Abigail perched like a chickadee on the seat Bethany had brushed off for her and fixed a keen stare on her former pupil. "So. You've not answered my question. You evaded me last night as well. How is it you arrived, quite late, quite unattached, and quite . . . enceinte, at your parents' party?"

Bethany looked away, reluctant to share her troubles even with Miss Abigail. "'Tis Harry," she said quickly. Even her radical brother was a less painful topic than Ashton. "I've not heard from him in some weeks, and I'm beginning to fear something went wrong in Providence."

"Don't worry about Harry," Miss Abigail said. "He's fine . . . er, I'm sure you'll soon find he's quite well. By the way," she added quickly, "the gown you wore last night was stunning. 'Tis a shame your husband wasn't present to enjoy it."

Bethany winced.

Miss Abigail nodded sagely. "I thought as much. What sort of rift drove you back to your family?"

"I can't talk about it. Ashton betrayed me and I had to get away."

"I must remember to thank your husband for allowing you and me to meet again at the reception," Miss Abigail said wryly. "Colonel Chason certainly asked you a lot of questions."

"He wanted to make sure Ashton had done right by me."

"And you told him he had."

"Of course. Colonel Chason has promised to hang Ashton if his orders are violated."

"And you don't want your husband to hang."

"Never." The admission was dragged from her on a sob. Then Miss Abigail's arms were around her. Perfectly tailored merino-clad shoulders absorbed Bethany's tears until her sobbing dissolved to bitter hiccups.

"Will you go back to him?" Miss Abigail gently inquired.

"He never wanted me in the first place. Now I don't know if I want to be with him."

"But you're not certain."

"I'm not certain of anything, Miss Abigail."

"Neither is your husband." Miss Abigail pointed over the balustrade of the summerhouse, indicating a snowy ribbon of sand below the cliffs. A figure stood on the beach, very still, hands secreted in his pockets, facing out to sea. Waves played hide-and-seek between jagged ice-capped rocks, and curlews braved the wind in the gray sky overhead, their sharp cries cutting through the song of the wind and the roar of the dark sea.

"That is Ashton, is it not?" Miss Abigail inquired.

Bethany nodded.

The wind lifted a rich chestnut strand of hair and curled it skyward. He made a lonely picture, standing pensively, surrounded by wind and water. His shoulders seemed somehow weighted.

"He's troubled," Miss Abigail commented.

Bethany shivered. "Perhaps," she murmured. But why? Was he regretting that he'd spent Christmas Eve at a brothel rather than home with his wife? Or was he only sorry that she had found out, as he must have realized by now?

"I must go," Miss Abigail announced. "Colonel Chason has offered to escort me to Little Rest. I'll be spending the remainder of my holiday with the Bryce family." She gave

Bethany a quick hug and moved to the steps. "Talk to him, child. Whatever it is between you two must be discussed. Nothing will be served by feeding your hurt with silence."

"But I can't—"

"Can't? Do you not recall that I banished that word from your vocabulary? You can overcome your problems with your husband. You will."

"Yes, ma'am," she replied softly. She watched Miss Abigail leave, her dainty steps sure as she picked her way through the bare fingers of the Persian lilacs framing the path. The lady looked back and sent Bethany an encouraging smile. Bethany returned the gesture half-heartedly. Then she turned her sorrow-heavy gaze back to Ashton.

The wind bit at Ashton's face, but he did not turn from it. His mind seethed with worries more discomforting than the winter cold. Tonight, Finley had told him. Tonight, under cover of cold and dark, he would deliver Captain Tanner to the small fort ten miles to the north. And that, he hoped, would be the last time he would have to concern himself with Harry Winslow.

He thought bitterly of Bethany's defection. It's exactly what you wanted, he told himself angrily. So why do you dwell on it?

It was the manner in which she had complied that bothered him. In order to get her to leave, he'd had to hurt her. She must remain in protective ignorance of his patriot activities at any cost. Would he have to explain about last night?

Perhaps his gift would soothe her pain. The thin band of rose gold would look lovely on her finger.

The idea of giving her a wedding ring gave him pause. In so doing, he would be giving credence to the fact that, however reluctantly, he recognized her as his wife. At one time he could have been sure of her delight; now he did not know whether or not she would accept his gift.

At last he turned from his contemplation of the cold, shifting bay waters. He glanced up, his gaze moving between a great cleft in the rocks. At the top stood the summerhouse. He remembered kissing Bethany as they sat there once, long ago, when kisses were easy to give.

As he watched, a figure appeared at the balustrade. Bethany. She looked curiously small in her brown cloak, her face a pale oval too distant to read the expression.

On feet made swift by sudden urgency, he climbed the rocks to his wife.

Bethany stifled an urge to flee as she watched him approach. Remembering Miss Abigail's insistence that she face her problems rather than run from them, Bethany stayed where she was.

Ashton scaled the last steep crag and, placing his hand on the railing, vaulted over the balustrade in a single lithe movement.

His hair, wind-tossed and in a state of appealing disarray, framed a face made ruddy by cold.

"Hello, pet," he said. He reached into his pocket and produced a small velvet bag. "Merry Christmas to you."

She backed against the rail. "No, Ashton," she said. "I couldn't accept a gift from you, not now."

"Wear the ring. Please." Before she could object again, he slipped the ring on her finger.

She stared down and the new, cold presence on her hand and said, "Thank you." How absurdly formal they were being. Did all married people face major disasters with such impersonal formality?

"Bethany." His voice, low and grating, called to her. She dragged her eyes to his. "Bethany," he said, "I'm sorry."

"You're sorry," she echoed. "Is that all? No explanation?"

"There is one."

"Such as . . . ?" Please don't lie to me, she prayed silently. I couldn't stand it if you lied to me. Silence stretched between them, punctuated by the roar of the sea and the mournful whine of the curlews. Suddenly she cast her reticence to the winter wind and faced him squarely.

"Shall I spare you the trouble of inventing excuses, Ashton? I know perfectly well where you were last night, and exactly what you were doing. I was in town buying your journal and I saw you."

Alarm leaped to his eyes, more damning than any denial. "I had no choice."

"I suppose I truly am naive about men, then. Exactly what imperative compelled you to seek the company of one of Madame Juniper's whores?"

Confusion, surprise, annoyance, and finally relief passed over his expression. "Is that what you thought I was doing?"

"I am not so thickheaded that I don't know what goes on at a brothel."

"But . . ." He snapped his mouth shut and narrowed his eyes.

"Ashton, why? Why did you seek the arms of a stranger when I never denied you my bed?"

"Don't carry on like this," he said quickly. "I never— Bethany? Bethany, don't cry."

"I understand at last. For months I've been denying that our marriage is a sham. You told me from the start that we don't belong together. Time and time again you've tried to drive me away with your cold, silent indifference. But I ignored the signs of your discontent, even when they were staring me in the face." She choked back a sob. "You must be grateful I've finally fallen back to earth."

He ached to gather her into his arms and soothe away the hurt etched on her face. It's not what you think, he longed to say. Never would I desire a stranger when I have your willing warmth.

But he kept this mouth pressed into an implacable line. The belief that he had spent Christmas Eve with a courtesan broke her heart. But far more damage would be done if he succumbed to the clamoring instinct to explain everything to her, to soothe her pain by admitting he had only gone to the brothel to secure a prisoner to exchange for her brother.

He had committed an act punishable by death if he was caught. If she knew about his activities, she would be in danger as well.

"Bethany," he said, feeling the tear that slipped down her cheek as if it were his own, "I never meant to hurt you." His eyes moved to the distant manor house, starkly grand in its setting of pristine white. "I understand why you returned to your home, but I'll miss you."

Anger drove away the hurt in her eyes; a violent swipe of her hand dried her tears. "But not at night, Ashton," she accused. "You have other women to fill those needs."

She stared at her reflection in the gilt-framed looking glass on her dressing table. The flesh beneath her eyes was swollen and dull red, but her eyes were dry now. She had no more tears to spare for Ashton Markham.

A figure came into view in the looking glass. The bright red hair and blue eyes of Carrie Markham had once been a familiar sight; now Bethany felt surprise at seeing her former maid.

"I've come to help you dress for supper," Carrie announced, crossing the room. "Lord, but I'm glad you're back, miss. Your mother can't make up her mind about anything. Has me running in circles trying to gather things for her toilette every morning. I still don't know pomatum from ceruse, rouge from carmine. Sometimes I think the Lord made women imperfect just to confuse me with all those cosmetic remedies."

"I don't need any help, Carrie. I've learned a lot about doing for myself lately."

"Thanks to that mule-witted brother of mine," Carrie grumbled. "Honestly, the man's a fool. Only Ashton would manage to get himself in such a fix, marrying quality and finding himself a bondsman the same day. I just wonder that it took you so long to tire of playing house with him and come back where you belong."

"I don't belong here," Bethany said. "Nor do I belong with Ashton." But she didn't object when Carrie took out a loosely cut *robe à l'anglaise*. It was one of the few garments she owned that would accommodate her growing figure.

As Carrie fastened the loop catch at the back neckline, Bethany said, "I'm going for a walk. A long, solitary walk."

"Oh, no, miss, you mustn't go out in the cold. Think of the babe."

"Tell my mother I'm not feeling well and not to expect me at supper."

Half an hour later, dressed warmly against the cold, she walked away from the manor, away from the family that pitied and misunderstood her, away from the husband who had betrayed her. Evening was stealing softly over the island. The westering sun glowed pink and amber over soft waves of snow, cushioning the sounds of her footsteps.

With feet clad in riding boots, she stepped high through drifts and clambered over a rubble-built stone fence, making for a broad eastern meadow. All was silence and solitude; she felt at home in the bleak surroundings. The wind had gentled to a chilly breeze, stirring up tiny tempests of powdery snow.

She had taken this walk to escape, to relieve herself of the bothersome thoughts that nagged her. But instead of relieving her, the scenery made her even more wistful. All around her were stabbing reminders of happy times long past. To her left was the stock pond, frozen over as it did each year.

Memories crept out of a corner of her mind—memories of the blithe girl she had once been. She recalled tagging after Ashton, begging him to wait for her, the laces of her ice skates dragging. She remembered how he had taken her around the waist and guided her until she could skate on her own. Harry always rushed past, far more interested in speed than in form; inevitably he ended up in a snowdrift, laughing. William always played the gallant, trying to impress the girls with his smooth style on the ice.

Those days of innocence were so long past that they might have been a dream. Now Harry was a rebel and a fugitive, unwelcome in his family and unable to support the wife and child he had taken in defiance of his father's wishes. William's reports from the army post in Connecticut hinted that he had not changed his habits of drinking, gambling, and entertaining the ladies. And Bethany was the unwanted wife of a man shackled in bondage to her father, big with a child he would not claim.

Never in their youth could they have anticipated that the rebellion would tear the family apart. Never had Bethany realized she could feel so much, love so piercingly, hurt so deeply.

Her eyes made a restless survey of the surroundings. Straight ahead, some yards distant, was the salt lick shed where she and Harry had often hidden from overbearing nurses and exacting tutors. To her right was the trail to the cove Ashton had showed her, when she had first felt the magic of his kiss.

The wind moaned across the meadow. She stopped, frowning. The wind wasn't blowing hard enough to raise an eerie sound like that. She heard the noise again and realized it was not the wind at all. A pair of stable cats embarking on their evening prowl, perhaps? No; the sound held a distinctly human quality. And it was coming from somewhere in front of her, perhaps in the salt lick shed.

Apprehension tingled down her spine. She glanced skyward, noting that the pink and amber sunset had melted into the deep, secret purples and indigos of twilight. A few stars winked like cold white eyes in the sky. It would be dark soon. She should go back.

But she heard the moaning again and thought she detected a note of pleading. Gathering up the hem of her cloak, she plunged through the snow toward the shed. The moaning grew louder and was punctuated by inelegant curses, sounding curiously like the speech of one of the cockney sailors who haunted Long Wharf. Then curses gave way to disjointed pleas for mercy.

"Hello!" Bethany called, her voice shaky with apprehension. "Hello!"

"Who goes there?" The voice became clipped and alert.

Cautiously she approached the shed, surprised to see a latch on the door made of new wood, fitted into the wooden handle. The door was locked from the outside. She pressed her lips to a crack in the wood, wondering who in heaven was being held in this crude prison, and why. "Who are you?" she inquired.

"Bethany?" The whisper was hoarse, incredulous, full of gratitude. "Open the door, Bethany."

She stumbled back. The voice that had been uttering cockney curses now became Dorian Tanner's familiar, precise speech.

"Dorian?" she asked, "what are you doing here?"

"Let me out, and I shall try to explain before I freeze to death."

Her fingers were clumsy as she dislodged the wooden latch from the door handle. The latch fell and the door swung open on its wooden hinges.

A disheveled and shivering Dorian Tanner tumbled from the shed. "Where the devil am I?"

"Why, at Seastone. What happened?"

"I was set upon by rebel scum," he said, stamping his booted feet to warm himself. He grew still and measured her with reddened eyes. "Bread and brandy were my only fare." His look softened to gratitude. "Thank God you happened by."

She found herself straining against his weight. At first she thought the ordeal had weakened him so much that he had swooned, but then she felt his hands plunge into the warm folds of her cloak. "'Twas ungodly cold in there," he murmured. "So cold. And you're so warm, Bethany."

His kiss was wet and brandy-sweet. Though she struggled to free herself from his embrace, she was pinned between his warmth-hungry body and the shed, and could not escape.

Breathless from struggling and from the shock of discovering the officer in such an unlikely place, she could not give warning as, suddenly, a shadow loomed behind Dorian, broad and black against the deepening twilight. An arm rose and then descended with blinding swiftness.

She heard a dull thud like a muffled musket shot and watched, aghast, as Dorian moaned and slid to the ground.

10

Bethany shrank against the building, squeezing her eyes shut in anticipation of a second blow. All she felt was the stinging lash of Ashton's harsh chuckle. "Don't think I'm not tempted," he told her. "But no, I won't strike you."

Her eyes flew open and widened in horror. "Ashton!"

"If I'd known you were so frantic to find your lover," he bit out, "I wouldn't have detained you at the summerhouse this morning." His gaze settled disparagingly on the ring he had placed on her finger. Turning away, he lifted Dorian, staggering momentarily beneath the weight. He barely looked at Bethany as he crossed the meadow, his strides swift despite his burden. He dumped the captain into the bed of a cart.

Bethany ran up behind him. "What was Dorian doing locked in that shed?"

"Swilling brandy, by the smell of him."

"That is not an answer," she retorted. But she didn't wait for one before firing off another question. "Where are you taking him?"

Ashton slid a cold glance at her. "You need not wonder about that. To her horror, he bound Dorian's wrists and wound a length of torn wool over his mouth before covering him with a Tattersall blanket.

"But he's a British officer. His superiors must be notified."

Ashton drove his icy stare at her. "You'd do that, wouldn't you?"

She was allowed no time to respond. Her speech dissipated into a squeak of surprise when she felt him position himself behind her. Hands like iron vises lifted her up and plopped her unceremoniously into the cart. Before she could react, he leaped in beside her and hauled on the reins. The horse surged into a smart canter. In minutes they were on a dark and lonely road, heading northward at a brisk rate.

"I can't risk leaving you behind," he said between clenched teeth. "You're too much the avid Tory to be trusted."

She felt dizzy with all the new and scathing things she had discovered about her husband. Once, she had thought him decent; now she knew him to be a libertine who rejected his wife in favor of a courtesan. She had thought him wise to moderate his political views; now she realized he was thick with the rebels. She had believed him to be honest and aboveboard; yet he was abducting a British officer. Rage rendered her speechless; she was bitter beyond words, beyond tears.

The miles flew past, twilight sinking into night, cold and cavernously dark. Frozen bogs and marshes that yielded bayberries and wildflowers in the warmer months were now stark and draped in winter white. The moon crept skyward, sending long fingers of pale light over the blanketed meadows with their small clusters of mulberry trees.

At length she forced herself to look at Ashton. He stared straight ahead, his square jaw grim, his eyes narrowed against the oncoming stream of cold wind.

"Why have you done this?" she demanded.

"It certainly wasn't to procure him for a convenient lovers' tryst."

"I came upon him by accident. Was I to pretend I didn't hear his cries for help?"

Ashton was the guilty one now, she thought. "You're wrong about Dorian and me," she said. "But I was not, was I, when I saw you go into Madame Juniper's?"

He sent her a sharp glance, and she thought for an incredulous moment that he would deny it. But he only looked over the gelding's bobbing rump and said nothing.

They veered eastward, climbing the gentle slope of Butt's Hill where a crude fort had been erected. Palisades of pine jutted upward, creating a jagged silhouette against the night sky, a dark monument to the rising tide of rebellion.

They came to a halt in the shadows. A gust of wind came scurrying up from the fields, sighing coldly. The gelding laid its ears back and turned a baleful eye backward; she saw its nostrils flare and emit puffs of vapor. He dropped to the ground with a soft thud.

Out of the corner of her eye she noticed a ripple of movement. For the first time, she realized they were surrounded by men. Apprehension crawled up her spine.

Keeping the blanket over Dorian's head, Ashton set the Redcoat on his feet. Dorian moaned and swayed. Ashton shoved him forward. The secretive movements of the surrounding men stilled as Redcoat and rebel approached the fort. The movements started again when Ashton and Dorian disappeared inside.

Bethany's teeth savaged her lower lip as she waited. The fabric of her cloak crumpled within her nervously twisting hands during the interminable wait. Finally, when her composure was in shreds, she saw two figures walking down from the fort. She recognized Ashton's long, purposeful stride. The other man was tall and thin, moving with a vigorous step. They reached the cart and alighted.

She drew back with gasp. Ashton was driving away from the fort before she found her voice.

"Harry?"

His arm slipped around her. "Aye, 'tis your brother, back among his own again."

He looked different. Thinner, his clothes shabbier. The lines made by his grin were deeper, and there was a world-weary dullness in his eyes that was new to Bethany. "What is this all about, Harry?"

"Didn't Ashton tell you? No, he wouldn't boast. The British found me in Providence. Came right to me, they did. Somehow our secret got out." He brightened. "But they decided not to hang me after all; they agreed to a prisoner exchange."

Realization dawned with a leaden thud in her heart. "Tanner," she said.

"Aye. No doubt it took the good captain down a peg when Ashton snatched him from the arms of one of Madame Juniper's girls on Christmas Eve."

Bethany expelled a shaky breath and looked at Ashton. He sat stiffly, his face expressionless. Suddenly all the scathing revelations she'd had about him dispersed like snow flurries in the wind. She moved closer to him. "I was wrong, Ashton. I'm sorry."

"You made a logical assumption. I can't fault you for that." But he spoke coldly and would not meet her gaze.

They took her brother to Bristol Ferry. He frowned. "I'd like to get my hands on the bloody informant who gave me away to the British." He sent an inquiring glance at Ashton. "Will Tanner be a problem?"

Ashton shook his head. "He knows nothing, not even that Bethany witnessed the exchange."

Reassured, Harry disappeared into the night, whistling as he ambled down to wake the ferryman.

*　　　*　　　*

Ashton dressed hurriedly in the predawn chill of the cottage, his teeth chattering. The water in the pitcher had a skin of ice on it that he had to break with his knuckles before enduring the torture of washing.

Once he was dressed, he looked back at the bed where Bethany slept beneath a mound of quilts, only the gold silk of her hair and one hand and cheek visible.

He felt a familiar and unwelcome lurch at the sight of that hand. She had come to this marriage untried in the ways of keeping house, her hands as soft and tender as the skin of her flawless cheek. Her cheek was flawless still, but her hand had grown rough and chilblained with the day-to-day chores. She never complained about the work; each new task she mastered became a source of pride to her.

Lately she had taken to visiting Goody Haas, the midwife, exchanging women's talk and recipes. Bethany had proven herself an able tutor in that house, helping Goody's grandnieces and grandnephews with their lessons.

She could be happy, he thought. She could be happy if he would give her what she wanted. His trust. His love.

Troubled, he did not leave for the stables immediately. Almost without thinking, he stoked the fire and filled the kettle so she would have a warm cottage and warm water when she awoke.

It was little enough to do for her, he told himself. She did work hard for his comfort, mastering the cooking of johnnycakes and chowder, washing his clothes and keeping his house. He returned to the bedroom to pour warm water into the pitcher. She was sitting up in bed, regarding him solemnly.

"I fell asleep before I had a chance to thank you for getting Harry released."

"I'm used to getting your brother out of scrapes," he told her, then grew angry at his own gruffness.

She looked terribly fragile to him. Her eyes were wide and pleading; her lower lip trembled with a vulnerability that stabbed at him. He tore his gaze from her, wishing he were not responsible for her happiness—and her lack of it.

"Why didn't you tell me?" she asked. "Why did you let me believe you went to Madame Juniper's for . . ." Her voice trailed off and she looked away, flustered and lovely.

"I didn't want you involved. You're a Loyalist, remember?"

"I'm Harry's sister first. I wouldn't have stood in your way." She twisted a loose lock of hair around her finger. "I'm sorry for the things I said yesterday. I'm sorry I left you."

"Are you?" he asked. "You seemed to be enjoying yourself at your parents' reception."

"It was dreadful," she said. "Only the fact that Miss Primrose was there made the reception bearable." She climbed from the bed and approached him, placing a sleep-warm hand on his sleeve. "I'm back now. Nothing can be solved by running away."

He tried to put aside a feeling relief, just as he tried to put aside the fact that he had missed her—missed the heady scent of jasmine that clung to her, the warmth of her body sweetly pressed against his. But, like the wide hazel eyes studying him, the feeling would not leave him alone. His arms went around her, pulling her close.

"You're not one to run away," he murmured against her hair.

"No, Ashton. I'm home. And home is here, right here in your arms."

He felt a stir against him, a fluttering upon his middle. He stiffened and pulled back, filled with alarm. "What was that?"

There was mystery in the smile that tugged at her lips. "Did you feel it, too?" Her hand crept upward, lying in the hollow between his shoulder and neck. "'Twas our baby."

Wonder and excitement, suspicion and resentment all jumbled through him. Who had made the tiny life that stirred so delicately against him?

He wanted to be sure. And damn it, he was not.

But did it really matter?

He brought his hands up, cradling her face while his thumbs brushed circles through the silky hair at her temples. Aye, he admitted to himself. It did matter. Not that he would resent an innocent babe, but if she had knowingly lied to him—aye, that was the part that mattered.

"Ashton?" Her breath was soft on his face. "I should have trusted you, even when all I saw and all you said condemned you."

She raised herself on tiptoe and found the corner of his mouth with her questing lips. He groaned with frustration and desire. As he received her kiss, he found himself envying her the ability to trust.

A tenuous peace settled over the cottage through the month of January. Outside, all was bleakness: white-gray skies and snow growing stale and crusty on the moors and meadows, the lonely cries of curlews and kestrels as they braved the wind in search of herrings and quahogs. But within, the abode was snug and golden with the hearth fire and the smells of Bethany's baking.

The horses required less attention during this quiet waiting season. Often Ashton was present, insulating Bethany against the cold, against the barbs of her former friends, against the onslaught of her parents, who sent frequent missives requesting her at tea, pointedly omitting him from the invitations.

He liked to sit in his father's old armchair, spectacles perched on his nose, keeping his journal while the ever-present Gladstone lounged nearby.

The British still held Boston, but the rebels hemmed them in and snapped at them like feisty terriers. General Washington's Eight Months' Army had used up their commissions, yet many remained to fight, and still more trickled in from all over the Colonies. Farmers traded their rakes for entrenching shovels to help dig in the assault. Jacob

Dupuy, who had been Ashton's schoolmaster some twenty years earlier, gave up his chalk for a musket. Even prissy Sylvester Fine, the dancing master, had joined a regiment. These men were untrained as soldiers, yet they believed deeply in the cause that underlay the call to arms.

News filtered to Newport of a fat bookseller named Henry Knox, who was said to be bringing Fort Ticonderoga's heavy artillery to Boston. Few thought Knox would manage in the dead of winter to cover three hundred miles of roadless wilderness and killing mountain climbs. But the unlikely had happened in this rebellion. Had not General Richard Montgomery pushed up into Canada and occupied Montreal in December?

Ashton never seemed surprised at the news that appeared in the *Newport Gazette*; Bethany suspected his cronies at the White Horse, many of them members of the Committee of Safety, advised him of events well before the news saw print.

There was a new wag-on-the-wall clock in the cottage from Miss Abigail Primrose, the only person to mark Bethany's marriage with a gift. One cold day, Bethany checked the hour as she looked over a tattered *Cocker's Arithmetick*, which she intended to present to the Haas children on her next visit. It was five o'clock. Ashton would be up from the stables soon, hungry for the warmth of the kitchen and for a taste of her buttery oyster stew.

Her brow wrinkled at the sound of a knock; she was expecting no one but her husband. Setting the book aside, she lifted the thumb latch.

She stepped back, moving her eyes down and then upward again, from polished jackboots topped by white gaiters to the handsome, impatient face of Dorian Tanner.

He seemed to sense her reluctance to invite him in, so he merely insinuated himself into the keeping room and closed the door. "You know why I'm here," he stated, carefully lifting his cocked hat from his wig.

She darted a quick look at the door.

"Afraid your husband might find us together . . . again? I say, he seems a rather jealous sort. Then I'll be quick. I want you to tell me who my abductor was."

She managed to summon a wide-eyed, guileless look. "I do not know."

"You do. You were there, Bethany."

"I saw nothing." Her voice rang sharp with anger.

"Abetting the rebels is a serious crime, my dear."

"Ignorance is not. I swear to you I know nothing of what happened." It was so easy to lie when the truth was so damning.

"You must have seen something," he snapped out.

She looked down at her hands. "It all happened so fast. I was startled and ran off. It was too dark to see anything."

He captured those nervous hands in his own. "I wonder if you know how you blundered in flouting my favor for that bondsman. Instead of toiling over a kitchen hearth, you'd be gracing Newport's finest salons on my arm."

She extracted her hands from his. "I'll never regret what I've done," she told him firmly. Dorian was so enamored of wealth and social position that he simply didn't understand her feelings for Ashton. She swung the door open, but Dorian did not move.

"Bethany!"

She froze, seeing Ashton coming up the path.

"Hello, pet," he called. "Barnaby said we had a visitor." He entered the cottage, smiling. His face was ruddy, and the fresh smell of outdoors clung to his greatcoat.

The smile became a scowl when he saw Dorian. His nod was curt.

"Captain Tanner was just leaving," she explained.

The Redcoat spent a moment in silent assessment of Ashton. Apparently—and wisely—he chose not to brave Ashton's greater size and temper, for he placed his hat on his head.

"This business is far from over," he told Bethany. "I'll have the truth from you one day." The door slammed behind him.

"He was asking me about the abduction," she said.

Ashton turned away, removing his hat and greatcoat and hanging them on pegs beside the door with unusual meticulousness. Always he arrived with a smile and a kiss for her. Always.

Not this time. She swallowed. "I told him nothing. He thinks I ran from the scene the moment he was knocked unconscious."

Without looking at her, Ashton said, "I thought you were the consummate Loyalist."

"My first loyalty is to you."

She watched his shoulders relax slightly. When he turned back to face her, he was smiling.

Bethany's eyes softened as she looked out the cottage window into the dooryard, now crowded with springtime abundance. Her hands worked idly over a batch of early peas in a half-full piggin, her attention caught by the scene outside.

Ashton had finished his chores for the day and was playing with Gladstone, flinging a well-chewed crook of driftwood for the dog to fetch. His low murmurs of approval and the spaniel's whines of excitement mingled with the buzzing of catbirds and the steady hum of bees.

Winter had lingered through March, but mid-April had given way to the new season. She was only too happy to bid the cold and dark farewell, to shed her woolen shawl and scratchy stockings for voluminous dresses of cotton and linsey.

Goody Haas arrived, startling Bethany. The plump, apple-cheeked midwife was never wont to announce her presence by knocking. She moved into the kitchen, rattling as she walked. Her many-pocketed apron contained a mystifying assortment of herbs and remedies, metal fleams for bleeding, flasks and beakers, the strange devices of folk healing.

"Peas look mighty fine." Goody spoke around the iron-maple burl pipe perpetually clamped between her teeth. Her small, bright eyes roved in frank assessment over Bethany. "Ye look fine, too, girl. How're ye feeling?"

"Very well." She hung the cedar piggin on a nail above the sideboard and began fixing tea. Although Goody sat at the table, her face impassive, Bethany could feel the woman's approval as she warmed the teapot with a small amount of water from the kettle before infusing the vessel with a fragrant mixture of lemon balm and chamomile.

"You've come a long way, girl," Goody said as Bethany set the pot on the table to steep. "And I don't just mean the babe."

Bethany grinned. "Eight months ago I couldn't even boil water."

"You been taking the Venice treacle I left?"

"Every day." She tried not to grimace as she remembered the foul taste of the concoction. She added a dollop of honey to her tea; Goody added a dollop of something stronger to her own from the flask she kept in her apron pocket.

"It's done you a world of good," the midwife said. "Your cheeks're blooming and the babe's already a healthy size." She chuckled and drew on her pipe, sending blue-gray smoke to the rafters. "Wouldn't be surprised if the child came early."

Bethany nearly choked on her sip of tea. She clutched her cup to still the trembling of her hands. "The babe is not due for five more weeks."

Goody's brown hand settled on Bethany's arm. "There now, don't get yourself all in a snit. Such has happened before."

"It can't happen to me."

Goody leaned back and puffed thoughtfully. "Ah. I see the way things are. You been married but eight months, eh, and to a man who used to oil your harness. Worried about the month counters, eh?"

"No." Bethany studied the knotty pine of the tabletop. In

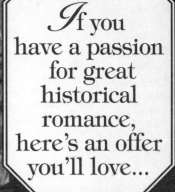

If you have a passion for great historical romance, here's an offer you'll love...

Introducing
The Timeless Romance

Passion rising from the ashes of the Civil War...

Love blossoming against the harsh landscape of the primitive Australian outback...

Romance melting the cold walls of an 18th-century English castle —— and the heart of the handsome Earl who lives there...

Since the beginning of time, great love has held the power to change the course of history. And in Harper Monogram historical novels, you can experience that power again and again.

Free introductory offer. To introduce you to this exclusive new service, we'd like to send you the four newest Harper Monogram titles absolutely free. They're yours to keep without obligation, no matter what you decide.

Free 10-day previews. Enjoy automatic free delivery of four new titles each month —— up to four weeks before they appear in bookstores. You're never obligated to keep a book you don't want, and you can return any book, for a full credit.

Save up to 32% off the publisher's price on any shipment you choose to keep.

Don't pass up this opportunity to enjoy great romance as you have never experienced before.

Reader Service.

Receive **4 FREE HISTORICAL NOVELS** ($20.49 VALUE)

Yes! I want to join the Timeless Romance Reader Service. Please send me my 4 FREE HarperMonogram historical romances. Then each month send me 4 new historical romances to preview without obligation for 10 days. I'll pay the low subscription price of $4.00 for every book I choose to keep--a total savings of at least $2.00 each month--and home delivery is free! I understand that I may return any title within 10 days and receive a full credit. I may cancel this subscription at any time without obligation by simply writing "Canceled" on any invoice and mailing it to Timeless Romance. There is no minimum number of books to purchase.

NAME

ADDRESS

CITY   STATE   ZIP

TELEPHONE

SIGNATURE

(If under 18, parent or guardian must sign. Program, price, terms, and conditions subject to cancellation and change. Orders subject to acceptance by HarperMonogram.)

truth, she was not. The parlor gossips and whispering biddies in church bothered her not at all. There was only one person whose opinion mattered.

She knew Ashton was counting the months as closely as any fencepost gossip, but he had a much greater stake in the outcome. If the baby was born too soon, he would still doubt her.

"Then what's hectoring you?" Goody fixed her with a probing stare.

She looked away. Her eyes found the window, where Ashton was still tossing the piece of driftwood for Gladstone.

"There 'tis, then," Goody said. "'S him you're worried about."

Bethany nodded a mute admission.

"Were you with another before him, then?" The dark eyes never wavered, nor did they accuse.

"No," Bethany said quickly. "But Ashton thinks . . ." Her voice faded and her cheeks grew hotter.

"Lordy, girl, 'tis Goody Haas you're talking to, not the parson's wife. You can tell me what's got you all aflutter."

"He doesn't believe I came to our marriage a virgin." Her voice was a shamed whisper. She dropped her gaze. "I know little of such things, but there was no . . . difficulty, no pain on our wedding night."

"You think the Lord made all women the same? Why should a big, healthy girl like you, who's spent her life riding astride same as any man, be afflicted with a maiden's pain, eh?"

Bethany brightened. "He'll have no more doubts once the baby is born. In five weeks." She stood and moved restlessly about the kitchen, aware that the midwife's keen eyes followed her.

"I don't know about the five weeks," Goody said. "Babe seems to've dropped some."

Bethany clutched protectively at her midsection.

"Aye, you'll need faith from your man, not counting."

11

A sheaf of broadsides, smelling of fresh ink, dropped in front of the kid-clad feet of Miss Abigail Primrose as she and Bethany negotiated the busy walk along Thames Street.

"Excuse me." A gray-haired, middle-aged man, hatless and coatless, stooped to retrieve the papers.

Miss Abigail fixed him with her most severe stare. "Sir, you have soiled the hem of my gown."

The look that had made Bethany squirm many times at school only made Finley Piper grin sheepishly. "Well now, I'd brush it off for you, ma'am, but . . ." He held out a big ink-smeared hand.

Miss Abigail's eyes flicked over the broadsides. Her nostrils thinned in disapproval as she took in the headlines.

"Never mind, sir," she told him with quiet, controlled annoyance. "My gown is not so soiled as people's minds will be by your seditious broadsides."

He sank into an exaggerated bow, toe pointed. "Pardon me, your ladyship. I'd no idea I had the pleasure of staining a highborn Tory."

He moved on with a casual, ambling gait. Bethany wondered if Miss Abigail had ever been treated so. Apparently not. The starched front of her dress rose and fell rapidly, and twin smudges of color appeared in her flawless cheeks.

"Who *was* that man?" she demanded.

Bethany bit the insides of her cheeks in an effort not to smile. "Mr. Finley Piper," she explained. "A printer by trade."

"And a rebel by design, I gather."

Bethany took Miss Primroses's arm and propelled her along the walk. "Let's have our tea at Haskel House. I'm delighted to see you back in Newport again."

"I may be here for some time. 'Tis a comfort to know Admiral Howe's fleet is bound for New York, but all that digging the rebels have been doing about Long Island and Manhattan has me worried. They seem to be putting in for a long stay."

They were seated at a table set with Houplan crystal and Wedgwood jasperware. A single white rosebud arched from a finger-slim vase, quivering slightly as a servant came to pour. Only the finest East India tea was purveyed at Haskel House. A murmur of female conversation lowered to a whisper as Bethany and Miss Abigail sipped their tea.

Bethany ignored the stares of Mabel Pierce and Mrs. Joseph Wanton and pretended not to hear the scandalized whispers of Julia Cranwick and Mercy Thompson.

Miss Abigail did not ignore the ladies in the salon. She systematically sought out each pair of eyes, holding them with an unwavering stare until the inquisitive tea room denizens were forced to look away in chagrin.

"Most unmannerly," she pronounced, and made short work of a comfit from a Vernon silver plate. "Perhaps I shall not find Newport society so agreeable after all."

"You must admit," Bethany said, "they've good reason to stare." She glanced with rueful fondness at her enormous belly.

"I've always thought confinement of expectant mothers quite a lot of poppycock," Miss Abigail said. "'Tis not as if you need to be quarantined for some disease. There is no person so aglow with loveliness as a woman awaiting her first child. How much longer, Bethany?"

"Four weeks." *And not a day less.*

"Things are . . . better between you and your husband?"

"Better, yes."

"But not how you want them to be."

"Perhaps I want too much. Perhaps what I want doesn't exist."

"More poppycock."

Bethany found both humor and encouragement in Miss Abigail's stern fondness. "I'll make things good between us," she vowed.

"The child won't solve everything, Bethany." She dropped her voice to a whisper. "What of the rebellion, of your divided loyalties?"

She regarded her teacher in alarm. "Ashton has never done anything out of rebellion." She, too, was whispering. "There have been circumstances that have required him to act in concert with the patriots."

"I see. I hope your brother has learned his lesson."

"My . . . Miss Abigail, how did you know about Harry?"

The lady's hand was too quick as she reached for another comfit. Her teacup spilled, amber liquid soaking into the crisp white linen of the table cloth. With an expression of concentrated annoyance she daubed at the cloth with her napkin. "Yes, well, things do get around. I heard, for example, that you became an aunt last month."

"Felicia had a little girl; they named her Margaret. Harry told me in a letter that Felicia's travail was difficult. She probably should not have any more children."

"Your brother is a young fool. He should know better than to say such things to an expectant mother."

Bethany wondered how Miss Abigail knew so much

about Harry, but there was no time for further questions. The sounds of shouting and running feet broke the quiet of the elegant tea room. She and Miss Abigail exchanged glances, then hurried to the door.

A mob of angry, fist-shaking men surged down Thames Street, cursing and singing songs of defiance. In the middle of the mob, straddling a length of pine, was the terrified Mr. George Tweedy, a royal customs official. Wig askew, face pale, he bobbed helplessly over the shoulders of the surging rabble. Bethany saw resentment on the men's faces. In better times such men would be away at sea; now they were idle and restless, looking for someone to blame, and easily manipulated by sly leaders.

The leader of this mob was a man called Bug Willy. Sometimes a sailor, more often a wharfside idler, he had a reputation for inciting violence and an unfortunate flare for the dramatic.

"Lord above," Miss Abigail said. "They're riding him on a rail." Both women left the tea room, following the rebels' unruly parade, which ended at Long Wharf.

The unmistakable acrid burn of hot tar pervaded the wharf area. "Why Mr. Tweedy? He seems so harmless."

Miss Abigail's lips thinned into a line of concern. "Just this morning he admitted the *Eastern Star* into port, bringing three hundred crates of tea."

The customs official was hoisted high on a lading platform. His periwig was yanked from his head to reveal a bristly pate. His frock coat was stripped from him, then his waistcoat, stock, and shirt, the garments flung to the howling masses.

"Can't something be done?" Bethany turned away from the scene in time to see Miss Abigail placing a shilling into the hand of a youth, who sprinted off in the direction of British headquarters.

"I've sent for help," she said. "All we can do now is hope Mr. Tweedy endures the wait."

A vat of steaming tar was brought forth. Bug Willy leaped to the platform brandishing a brush. He plunged the brush into the tar and anointed Tweedy until the victim's howls rose even higher than the curses and catcalls of the mob.

The rebels flung handfuls of goose feathers at Tweedy, who soon resembled a macabre scarecrow. A lighted candle was held to the feathers, but the feathers failed to catch fire. Bug Willy put a halter around Tweedy's neck.

"Before we cart you the rounds, sir," he mocked, doffing a rumpled hat, "we'd like to offer you a drink."

"Aye," someone shouted, "Give him a taste of his own poison."

Mr. Tweedy was presented with a large bowl of strong tea and told to drink to the king's health. With some confusion he complied, draining the bowl. Immediately the vessel was refilled and he was made to drink to Queen Charlotte, then to the Prince of Wales.

Having been forced to gulp three big bowls of tea, Tweedy staggered. "Please, no more," he begged.

But the bowl was thrust at him again. "Make haste, sir," Bug Willy said. "You've nine more healths to drink." A quantity of tea was forced down the victim's throat as he was made to toast the others, beginning with the Bishop of Osnaburg and continuing until each of George III's offspring had been honored.

At the last toast Tweedy went deathly pale beneath his coating of tar and feathers. Instantly he filled the bowl he had just emptied.

"What!" Bug Willy boomed. "Are you sick of the royal family already?"

"No," Tweedy wheezed. "'Tis the tea."

"And yet," Bug Willy shouted, "you damned infernal rogue, you would drench us to the skin with this overtaxed poison."

Jeers rippled from the crowd. "Hang him! Hang the scoundrel!"

Bethany was sure that, in this murderous frenzy, the deed would be done. But the rebels satisfied their thirst for vengeance by using the halter to baste the victim's neck until his ears bled. He was made to repeat various humiliating oaths until, weak, sick, and defeated, Mr. Tweedy resigned his commission.

He was seated on the rail once again in readiness to cart the rounds. But as the rail was shouldered by the jubilant rebels, three shots rang out, stilling the crowd.

The British militia appeared. Dorian Tanner was among them, barking orders. In minutes the crowd dispersed, the rebels scurrying to the anonymity of local taverns and private homes. Tweedy was carried off to his house.

Ashton came striding across the wharf. The fury of his pace touched off a shiver of apprehension in Bethany, but the concern on his face warmed her. He acknowledged Miss Abigail with a nod, then spoke to Bethany. "What are you doing here? For God's sake, you could have been hurt."

"I'm fine. Which is more than I can say for Mr. Tweedy."

He took Bethany's elbow. "We're going home."

"I'm not ready to go home." She felt obstinate, angry that her husband was in sympathy with the rebels who had just committed such a cruel act.

Miss Abigail started walking away. "I've things to do," she said. "We'll have tea again soon."

As soon as Ashton delivered Bethany to the cottage, he muttered something about going back into town. She was too proud and angry to ask him to stay.

"This afternoon's display didn't endear your cause to me," Ashton said to Finley and Chapin Piper, who were priming their Franklin press in readiness to print up a batch of handbills.

"We had nothing to do with Tweedy's tarring and feathering." Chapin's Adam's apple bobbed as he stifled a sneeze caused by a puff of dry ink.

"People tend to lump all patriots together." Ashton turned to Finley. "You've got to do something to control them. People want liberty, not lawlessness."

"I know, I know." Finley sighed in exasperation. He shot a treenail into the shank of the press to secure it. "By the way, I ran into your wife this afternoon. Quite literally, I fear. Dropped a sheaf of broadsides right at her companion's feet. Who was that dragon with her?"

"Miss Abigail Primrose, Bethany's teacher from New York."

"A teacher, eh? A redoubtable example of female independence and accomplishment, I'm sure." Finley's face soured. "She ought to go back to whatever lair she crawled out of."

"Sounds like you got singed." Ashton chuckled. "Miss Primrose can have that effect on people. Bethany regards her highly."

"Maybe your wife shouldn't make her Tory leanings so apparent," Chapin suggested. "After what happened to Tweedy today, I'm beginning to think things could get uncomfortable for Loyalists."

"It'll be the other way around," Ashton said. "I wouldn't be surprised if we were treated to full British occupation if the rebels keep this up."

Chapin looked glum. "We need to get rid of that infernal British sympathizer who's been reporting our every move."

"We'll catch him," Finley stated.

"How?" Ashton asked.

"We'll set a trap."

"'Tis a spy we're after, not a lobster."

"The *Rose* is in the bay. Wallace sends longboats to the Purgatory Rocks to leave messages for his informants. If the water's calm, there should be an exchange tomorrow night." He rubbed an ink-stained finger over his chin. "Are you with us, Ashton?"

He looked away. "No."

"No violence, nothing like you saw today. You have my promise."

"I've things to do besides chase after a spy who's probably too smart to take your bait anyway."

"I don't understand you, Ashton. You weren't so hesitant before."

"Someone I care about was involved, Finley."

"And you care less for liberty?"

"I care less for involving myself in something I'm not sure of."

"Will you at least think about it?" Finley snapped his fingers. "I have something for you to read. Chapin, fetch one of those pamphlets from the shelf."

Ashton hesitated when he stepped into the cottage, standing quietly in the doorway to study his wife. It was uncanny, he reflected, her ability to move with such lithe grace despite her now cumbersome profile. As she turned to stir a pot of bubbling chowder, bending delicately forward, it struck him that her beauty had suffered nothing because of her pregnancy. Her hair was caught in a heavy coil at the nape of her neck, small wisps escaping to frame her sweet and earnest face.

She turned her head at the sound of his footsteps. Her spoon swirled nervously in the chowder.

"Hello, Ashton."

He reminded himself of the argument this afternoon. On the way home he had decided to inform her that he did not care to have his wife attending public mob scenes, and that he would tell her so in no uncertain terms. But when he opened his mouth to speak, all he said was, "Come here, pet."

Her lack of hesitation told him that she, too, had lost

her anger. She moved into his outstretched arms and laid her cheek against his chest, her hands creeping around his middle.

He laid his lips on her forehead; her skin was warm from the fire, damp from exertion. He loved the taste of her, the spicy-sweet scent of her hair and skin. She was very much a woman now, and yet a child, too, evoking both passion and protectiveness.

His kisses made a slow path toward her mouth. "You shouldn't have followed that mob today," he murmured. "It was dangerous, my love." Hardly the reproof he had planned for her.

"I never felt I was in any danger," she whispered beneath his lips. "The rage was directed at Mr. Tweedy. Capt—the soldiers weren't long in coming."

He drew away from her. "How studiously you avoid speaking his name."

"We always quarrel when Dorian comes up."

"And we've better things to do than quarrel." He captured her lips again, firmly, as if to wipe Tanner's name from them. Soon, though, he forgot the Englishman. He savored the soft openness of her lips and discovered, as if for the first time, the silk of her inner mouth with his tongue.

After a while, with a reluctant and concerted effort, he set her away from him. "I'm hungry," he told her.

"So am I." He was certain she did not mean the chowder. He moved toward the kitchen; she laid a hand on his arm and he saw a blush rise becomingly to her cheeks.

"Ashton, Goody Haas told me it was all right to—"

"Goody Haas is full of nonsense. If she'd lived a hundred years ago, she'd be tried for witchcraft." What he didn't say was that he was afraid of intimacy in her advanced stage of pregnancy. He was afraid of hurting her, of perhaps bringing on early labor, which was the last thing he wanted to do.

After supper, they shared the chores of cleaning up.

Then they retired to the keeping room. Bethany had grown weary of knitting and mending weeks ago; lately she had preferred going over the Haas children's lessons in the evenings.

Ashton watched, feeling reluctant fondness as she twisted a tendril of hair by her cheek with an idle finger and smiled in amusement at a penciled drawing. Catching himself, he lent his attention to the slim pamphlet Finley had given him—"Common Sense; Addressed to the Inhabitants of America," by an English immigrant named Thomas Paine.

He put on his spectacles. At first his gaze meandered over the pages; then he thought about the author's message. The treatise was a hot tirade against ministry and monarchy, aye, but the stark phrases were used to good effect. "Oh! ye that love mankind, stand forth . . ."

Ashton blinked as an unfamiliar feeling gripped him. Rightness. Devotion. Purpose.

Shaken, he stared at the final page. It carried a single stark black phrase: THE FREE AND INDEPENDENT STATES OF AMERICA.

Free, not bonded. Independent, not bound to another's will.

The pamphlet slipped to the floor, its message burned into his mind. He walked to the window of the keeping room, spectacles dangling forgotten from his fingers. From this point he could see beyond the bounds of Seastone, past gardens aflame with peony bushes and mourning bride blossoms, past the stone-rimmed stable compound . . . to the meadows of swaying seagrass in the distance.

Freedom beckoned.

Bethany frowned when Ashton didn't answer her. He looked so oddly intent as he stood there by the window. He held himself in an expectant stance, knuckles pressed hard on the windowsill.

He seemed to be in the grip of some private awakening. Drawing a deep breath, she repeated his name more loudly.

This time he turned. His eyes had never looked so deep or clear. "Yes?" His voice was quiet and rich.

"I've invited Miss Abigail to supper tomorrow evening."

Regret and impatience showed on his face. "I won't be able to attend. I've an engagement."

She left him alone with his thoughts; he turned back to the window. Bracing her hands on the edge of the settle, she brought her cumbersome form to her feet. Quietly she crossed the room to his chair and picked up the pamphlet he had left on the floor.

She read swiftly, caught by the power of the prose, frightened by the effect it had on her husband. Everything came suddenly into sharp focus: Ashton's strange, quiet mood, his claim of an engagement.

She supposed this had been building for months, beginning, perhaps, with his disenchantment with the British army, revived by his erroneous arrest and indenture to her father. The transition from indifference to commitment was complete.

Her husband had become a patriot.

Bethany jumped up at the sound of scratching. Although it was suppertime and she was expecting Miss Abigail, she knew her teacher would never scratch at the door, but would announce herself with a sharp, imperative rap. Gladstone whined and sniffed impatiently.

Her suppertime visitor was young Jimmy Milliken, whose mother ran the boarding house where Miss Abigail was staying. Bethany smiled at the eight-year-old's spiky brown hair, his sprinkling of freckles.

"Come in, Jimmy." She stepped aside. He hesitated; she pressed on his shoulder. "You're welcome here, lad."

His face blossomed into a wide, gap-toothed grin. He

walked to the kitchen table and began digging in his pockets. "I've a message for you." His dusty brown homespun breeches seemed to hold more than Goody's apron. His tongue stuck out and one eye was narrowed in concentration as he placed his treasures on the table, searching for the message.

There was a wrist rocket, a single copper for games of huzzlecap, a wooden top missing its spinning knob, the skeletal remains of some small animal, a blue jay feather, a half dozen seashells, and . . . last of all, crumpled by the weight of his treasure and limp with boyish sweat, a small scrap of paper.

He held it up with a triumphant flourish. "There you go, missus. Just like the lady said."

Bethany added another copper to the items he was scooping back into his pockets. Then she unfolded the message, recognizing Miss Abigail's script: "To my dismay, I shall be unable to visit this evening due to an unforeseen engagement. Do accept my sincere regrets. . . ."

Bethany put the note aside with a sigh. So she would be alone after all. She glanced at the kitchen hearth, where a small feast of codfish, potatoes, and pudding was in preparation.

Jimmy Milliken was looking at the hearth, too.

Impulsively she invited him to supper and watched fondly as he devoured his meal. She pretended not to notice when he slipped a crust of bread to Gladstone, who lolled at the boy's feet.

"You a friend of Miss Primrose?" Jimmy asked around a mouthful of potatoes.

"I am indeed. She used to be my teacher."

He rolled his eyes. "Miss Primrose thinks she's everybody's teacher. Has me minding my manners even when I go out to fetch water. Lately I go to bed reading my letters off a battledore."

Bethany smiled. "That's just her way, Jimmy."

"You know what?" He cast a furtive glance left and right. "I think she's a—an adventuress in disguise."

Bethany laughed. "Why do you say that?"

He dropped his voice lower still. "Just as I was leaving to come here, I heard this noise in the shed back of the house. Thought one of the chickens had gotten out, but then I saw it was Miss Primrose." The lad sipped his cider. "At first I didn't think it was her, 'cause she was all got up like a boy, but before she put her hat on I saw that hair of hers, all knotty on top of her head. She covered up with an old hat and slipped right out of the yard."

Bethany shook her head, bewildered. Either the boy spun an extremely plausible yarn, or he was telling the truth. "Where do you think she was going, Jimmy?"

"I don't know. But I'll bet my best huzzlecap copper she has a secret iden—identity. She headed off toward Purgatory Rocks."

"Jimmy, how many others have you told this story to?"

"No one, missus, honest."

"Maybe we had better keep it just between us."

The wag-on-the-wall clock chimed softly. Jimmy's lips moved silently as he counted the chimes. "Seven o'clock!" He jumped up. "Mama'll have my skin where it counts if I don't get home."

Bemused, Bethany watched him flee down the garden path. She was unable to decide whether his tale was fanciful or if it held a grain of truth. Absurd, she thought, shaking her head. Miss Abigail Primrose, disguised as a boy.

And yet, only yesterday she had mentioned Harry, alluding to something few people could possibly know. Then there was tonight's engagement, sudden, unexplained . . . just like Ashton's.

The spoon she was holding slipped from her fingers and clattered to the floor. Snatching her shawl from a hook, she left the cottage and ran to the stables.

12

Cloaked in darkness, three figures approached Purgatory by means of a dusty road that ran from Easton's Beach to Sachuest Beach. Soundless footfalls made small indentations on a broad stretch of sand. Keeping to the shadows of a high bluff, the men moved silently among a tumble of dark gray soft-slate rocks at the foot of the bluff. Thready salt grass and broom stirred in the night breeze.

A distant light winked on the waters of the Middle Passage. Finley gestured toward it. "The *Rose*. In rendezvous position."

"I don't see anyone," Ashton said.

"You will. Just be patient."

Above them rose a vast ledge of rock piled up in a most singular formation, remarkable for the size and position of the stones. At one point the escarpment reached out in a line, rising at the extreme outer edge on a bluff and then suddenly plunging down into the sea.

High upon a spur was a great boulder known as Negro Head, for the rock formation resembled an African profile.

Fissures divided the rock as though tons upon tons of slate had been neatly cleaved by a knife.

Ashton, Finley, and Chapin climbed to a vantage point at the lip of the largest of the fissures, which plumbed fully one hundred sixty feet. Long ago the dangerous cleft had earned the name Purgatory and a reputation for swallowing drunken sailors. At the base of the forbidding chasm the sea broke ceaselessly with deep basso crashing sounds.

Ashton recalled playing games of nerve here with Chapin and other childhood playmates. But never, even when as a youth convinced of his own invincibility, had he approached the huge, deadly cleft without giving heed to his footing.

Once, just once, he had leaped the chasm. Not willingly, not out of any sense of bravery, but at the bidding of a girl. He had been fifteen at the time and helplessly in love. Here at the sharp ledge, on a day sweet with the smells of wild chicory and sorrel thorn, he and Peggy Lillibridge had pledged their hearts to each other.

"Leap Purgatory for me, Ashton," Peggy had said. "As a test of your love for me. Jump, if you would claim me as yours."

He heard her words now on the wind as if a soft voice had just whispered them in his ear. He recalled the bitterness that had welled in him at Peggy's command: his first discovery that love was not so much a matter of faith, but one of manipulation.

He remembered her shining face and felt again the sizzling sense of danger. He had run forward, closed his eyes, and launched himself in a wild leap. He recalled perfectly the sensation of soaring, the breathless brush of time in which he was not certain he would live or die. And finally, the bone-crushing sense of relief when he landed on the opposite bank.

He had dusted off his hat and stood looking across the abyss at her flushed and delighted face. He had raised his hat, bowed sharply from the waist, then turned and strode away, leaving Peggy Lillibridge forever.

Ever since, he had heeded the lesson in the destructiveness of romantic love. Never again had he allowed himself to be manipulated into foolishness by a woman. But would the cause of independence be an equally demanding mistress?

Probably so, and the rewards were not nearly so tangible.

Forcing his thoughts to the task at hand, he peered at Finley and Chapin through the misty gloom of the spring night. Fog swirled in from the bay, rime-scented and pudding-thick. The moon was a haze of white light, casting shadows down into the depths of the chasm.

Chapin took out his pocket knife and began flipping the blade in and out with small, rhythmic clicks that set Ashton's teeth on edge.

Fog dampened and chilled his outer coat; his own sweat moistened his clothing from within. The phrases of Thomas Paine's pamphlet still lingered in his mind, although he had begun to wonder if this was what was meant by "Common Sense."

He wondered, too about Bethany. The worried look she'd fixed on him when he last left the house told him she was aware of his new commitment.

His jaw tightened in annoyance. Couldn't she see what independence might mean to him? To them? Freedom from England meant freedom from Sinclair Winslow, for he could not hold Ashton to the indenture governed by British law.

A year ago the idea of a new nation had been tossed out by radicals and ignored by the populace. Now the assembly of Rhode Island was about to formally declare itself an independent state. Surely others would follow until at last every one of Britain's thirteen unruly children had severed the umbilical cord of dependency.

Chapin suddenly stopped clicking his pocket knife.

Finley's nudge sent Ashton's gaze downward to the breaking waves. At first he discerned nothing. Shadows within shadows, the whisper of the wind through birch trees. Then a moving shape, small and fleet and of a darker and more substantial quality than the shadows, flitted into view.

"'Tis him," Finley whispered. "Not a big man; could the Redcoats be using children?" Chapin started to edge toward the bluff, but Finley pulled him back by the sleeve. "Wait, lad," the older man cautioned. "We had best make certain there are no others."

They waited and watched. The figure darted in and out of the shadows, then went to the foot of the bluff. A ship's boat slipped back out into the bay, toward the bobbing lights of the *Rose.* The figure gained the bluff and scrambled up to the road.

"Let's go," Finley said at length. "We don't want to lose him now." Moist salt grass cushioned their footfalls as they closed in on the spy. He was just a few yards ahead of them when his head snapped up.

The spy sprinted away. As Chapin gave chase, Ashton became aware of hoofbeats. Too late, he realized a rider was heading toward them from the beach road.

Chapin dove for the fleeing figure, catching an ankle and sending them both sprawling. At the same moment, the horse jerked to a stop in front of the struggling pair.

"Leave her alone!"

Bethany's frightened command reached through the gloom, delivering a shock of recognition to Ashton's ears. Chapin seemed equally surprised; he held his quarry fast but gaped at the angry rider on the lathered, agitated horse.

"Let her go!" Bethany cried again.

Finley reached them first. "Here now, what's this?" He glowered at Ashton. "The plans have been hitched. I'll have a word with you later."

Ashton came to Bethany's side, his hand reaching to quiet the snorting mare. Calliope settled down immediately at his touch and scent. Looking up at Bethany's furious face, he knew his wife would not prove so tractable.

"What are you doing here?" he asked.

Before she could answer, Chapin muttered, "Christ. I don't believe this." His struggling prisoner's hat had dropped to the ground to reveal a perfectly neat, shining topknot and a small but livid—and distinctly feminine—face. Ashton's surprise gave way to a leaden feeling of disappointment, tinged with deep chagrin.

"I know you." Finley stared at her. "You—you're—"

"Miss Abigail Primrose," came the clipped reply. She slid an offended glance at Chapin. "Unhand me, young man." Chain dropped her wrist as if it had burned him.

Bethany slipped from the mare's back and went to Miss Abigail, walking a little unsteadily and resting her hand on her belly. "Are you all right, Miss Abigail?'

The lady was inspecting her wrist. "Quite. But you, my dear, should not be out riding. Whatever possessed you?" Her gaze flicked to Ashton, and her lips thinned. "Oh. I see. You've guessed."

"And so we have," said Finley. "You've impeded the rebellion for the last time." He offered her his arm with exaggerated politeness. "Shall we go?"

"I'd sooner seek the company of the devil himself."

Finley chuckled. "You don't understand, ma'am. You have no choice. Now, you can walk with me to my house like the lady you are, or I'll shoulder you like a sack of potatoes."

Bethany stepped forward. "You're not taking her anywhere."

Ashton touched her shoulder. "She won't be harmed."

"Like Mr. Tweedy wasn't harmed yesterday?"

He drew in his breath slowly, despising the position he was in. He was faced with an impossible choice. His loyalty to the cause he had recently embraced ran at direct odds with his loyalty to his wife.

"You're awfully protective of the woman who betrayed your brother," Chapin snapped.

Her eyes blazed with bewilderment. "Harry?"

"Chapin, that's enough." Ashton wanted him to stop, wanted to protect Bethany from the truth.

"Aye," Chapin went on, ignoring Ashton, "'twas your dear lady friend here who sent the Redcoats to seize Harry in Providence."

Ashton watched Bethany's agonized gaze seek Miss Primrose. He saw deep disappointment in those wide, wondering depths. She wanted to deny it, yet Miss Primrose herself took matters in hand.

"He's correct, Bethany," Miss Primrose said.

"Miss Abigail, when I spoke to you that morning in Bristol, I believed you would hold my confidence."

"I agonized over the information you gave me about your brother. If I had left things to chance, Harry might have been caught by others and sentenced to death. So I struck a bargain with . . . my military contacts. I agreed to tell them where to find your brother in exchange for their promise he'd not be harmed, only traded in a prisoner exchange." Miss Primrose's voice quavered. "I'm sorry, Bethany." She turned back to Finley. "I shall not fight you, sir." Docilely she held her hand out to him; reluctantly he led her away.

Finley and Chapin flanked the small form in boy's clothing as they started toward town. Ashton hung back, wishing there was some way to erase the hurt etched on Bethany's features.

"I'll walk you home," he offered. "You look like you could do with a rest."

"I'm going with Miss Abigail."

"Bethany, there's nothing you can do—"

"I want to be sure she isn't harmed." He saw a sparkle of defiance in her moonlit eyes. "Not that you would care about her."

He drew a shuddering breath. Far in a corner of his

heart, feelings for her waged a silent, relentless battle with reason and honor.

"Very well," he said and reached for her arm.

For the first time since he had known her, Bethany pulled away from him.

The smells of Finley's print shop tingled in Bethany's nose. The sweetish scent of ink mingled with stale tobacco to create a singularly nauseating aroma. As Chapin worked with flint from a tinderbox, she found herself swallowing bile.

"Bethany?" Ashton was at her elbow, his breath warm in her ear. "You don't look well."

As she had back at the bluffs, she sidled away. "Perhaps I'm not well, Ashton," she snapped. "This whole incredible situation repulses me. What are you going to do to Miss Abigail, try her in some barbaric drumhead court?"

Scowling, he said, "Would you rather we gave her a medal for arranging your brother's capture?"

"You heard Miss Abigail's explanation. I can forgive what she did."

"But you won't forgive me."

"You and the Pipers have mishandled a lady."

"She ought to count herself lucky we found her, rather than the mob that got George Tweedy."

Bethany turned away. Rubbing at a sharp twinge deep in her lower back, she stood in the shadows and waited for Chapin's spark to set fire to a candle. At last a long yellow flame appeared, casting mysterious patterns over the cumbersome shape of the printing press with its wooden frame braced against floor and ceiling, iron type forms stacked on a table, and a collection of stuffed leather ink daubers.

Bethany saw a shadow move in one of the corners. That shadow was joined by several other shapes. Human shapes. "Ashton," she whispered, her anger forgotten as she clung to his arm.

Out of the gloom appeared the triumphantly grinning face of Bug Willy and eight of his cohorts, the same men who had brutalized Mr. Tweedy the day before.

She brought her hand to her mouth. She saw Finley move in front of Miss Abigail. Turning to Ashton, she exclaimed, "You said she wouldn't be harmed!"

Bug Willy's evil snicker resounded with chilling glee. "So he might've. You always were a bit too soft for my tastes. Now, hand over the lady. We're going to hold a trial."

"A trial!" Anger exploded from Bethany. What sort of justice will Miss Abigail get from you?"

"Don't worry, little mama," Bug Willy said. "We'll be sure our Tory meets with a proper punishment."

He was armed, as were his companions. The steel of knife blades and spontoons glinted dully in the candle glow. A wicked-looking spurlike instrument clanked against Bug Willy's paste belt buckle.

"This is not business of yours," Ashton said to the man in a low, careful voice.

"Come now, did you really think I'd not hear of your spy hunt tonight? I knew the *Rose* was skulking about the Middle Passage." The grizzled and scarred head moved from side to side. "Can't hide much from Bug Willy, can you now?" He fixed a small-eyed glare on Miss Abigail, who stared unflinchingly back.

"Bold little piece, eh? Let's see just how bold."

Bethany's horrified eyes weren't quick enough to take in all that happened next. The intruders rushed forward, seizing Ashton, Chapin, and Finley, thrusting them against the wall. Two of the attackers howled, suffering the speed and anger of Ashton's resistance, but finally the point of a deadly honed spontoon, pressing into the exposed flesh of his throat, subdued him.

Bug Willy wasted no niceties with Miss Abigail. Whiplike, his arm shot out and grabbed her. Bethany moved forward with a cry of outrage, only to find herself detained by a sailor. Ashton spat a curse between his clenched teeth. She looked back to see the spontoon pressing into his neck, almost breaking the skin. As fear pounded through her, the odd pain in her back bit again, sharply.

"Let's see what the lady has for us tonight." Bug Willy plunged his hand into her jacket pocket. Miss Abigail was quicker. Her fingers darted into the opposite pocket. She snatched out a silver bullet and popped it into her mouth, swallowing as calmly as if she had just enjoyed a comfit.

Willy's roar of outrage reverberated through the shop. "You goddamned high-and-mighty bitch! I ought to slit your belly and sift through your innards for that message."

"No need to soil your hands," came a smooth voice from behind them. Bethany recognized Isaac Sewell, a young, bandy-legged apothecary's apprentice who had been guarding the door. He dropped a cloth bag into Willy's hand. "Tartar emetic," he explained. "'Twill bring forth the ball— and anything else the lady's hiding in her Tory guts."

Bethany was nearly overcome by wave after wave of nausea as the purge was roughly administered to Miss Abigail. Never could she have imagined her teacher to suffer such humiliation, to be transformed by this wharfside scum into the pathetic, retching creature who crouched miserably over the basin held by an exultant Bug Willy. Miss Abigail knelt on the floor, pale and mortified beyond speech. The apprentice covered his hand with a handkerchief and extracted the ball from the basin.

He opened the small silver object and painstakingly unfurled a tiny scrap of paper. Holding it to the light, he frowned at characters as tiny as flea tracks.

"What's this? French? Can anyone read French?"

Bug Willy jerked Miss Abigail to her feet. "You! Tell us what that message says."

"I neither speak nor read French," Miss Abigail told him with remarkable steadiness. Bethany prayed Bug Willy would not discern the lie; Miss Abigail was fluent in French as well as three other languages.

Apparently Bug Willy bought the ruse. He ground a keen look at Bethany. "What about you, little mother?"

"Leave her out of it," Ashton said, still with the blade to his neck.

Bethany shook her head mutely and battled another sharp pain in her back, not trusting herself to speak. French had been one of her better subjects in school, but she would never betray England to a scoundrel like Bug Willy.

He took the message and pocketed it. "We'll get someone to translate it later." He dragged Miss Abigail toward the door. "Hold the rest of them here. My lady friend and I are going out for a little sail in the bay."

The captors closed around Ashton, who clearly posed the greatest threat. When his hand broke free of the two-handed grip of another, the spontoon bit into his neck.

The sight of his blood soaking the opening of his shirt caused something within Bethany to burst with sheer terror. She felt as if a great hand had wrapped around her and squeezed.

Liquid warmth crept down her legs. She gasped, mortified, and struggled with the man guarding her. "The baby," she said. "Please."

"Didn't you hear the lady, you bogtrotter?" Finley demanded. "Her time is near."

Goody Haas had told her of the water and the back pain. But the midwife had not given words to the cold clamp that seized Bethany, sending her to the floor in mindless agony.

Warmth and pain . . . pain and warmth . . . The excruciating rhythm of Bethany's suffering melded with the surge and rise of the sea, with the rapid thud of something firm and familiar, close to her ear.

Dragging herself slowly from the comfortable stupor of pain, she took stock of what was happening.

Beyond the hot twinges clawing at her was awareness of Ashton. The stubbly texture of his homespun shirt covered his chest; the unyielding corded strength in his arms circled her secretly. His scent, that unique mingling of leather and sweat and salt air, enveloped her.

He was carrying her through the mist-shrouded night, cradling her like a child as he sat Calliope. Through a fog of anguish Bethany heard him admonish the mare to move slowly. She tried to speak, to give voice to her worries about Miss Abigail, and to tell him of the awesome power of her own pain, but her voice failed her. All she could manage was a desperate strangled cry as she felt Ashton bring her down from the horse and take her into the stone-end cottage.

The familiarity of her bed did nothing to ease her pain. She could not appreciate the gentleness of his hand on her brow or the tenderness in his voice when he said, "Chapin's gone for Goody Haas, love. Let me help you into bed."

She squinted at Ashton. His face, illumined by a flare from the betty lamp, was drawn and pale; beads of sweat stood out on his furrowed brow, and the blood was drying on his neck. She held weak arms out to him in supplication, aware that tonight she had lost faith in him, aware that this night what little trust he had in her would be destroyed.

But he was still Ashton, to whom she had run with her troubles since she was old enough to run. Buried deep inside her was a longing for the simple whimsy of the life they had led as children, gigging frogs in the millpond, staging mock battles with spear grass, eating warm sugar together when the maple trees ran in February. Her troubles then were trifling enough that he could dispense with them by showing her a new card trick or spending hours with her in lazy conversation as he worked his hands over a length of harness.

But now . . . there was nothing trifling about giving birth. The pain she felt was not so inconsequential that it could be soothed by kindness or softened by old memories. Fear sent sharp arrows through her body. She had little reason to suppose Ashton would even want to help her.

And yet his hands were gentle, grappling with the hooks of her dress and slipping off her shoes. "There you are," he said in a soothing voice. "We'll get you comfortable."

A huge contraction pressed giant fingers around her body and she stiffened, arching her back and clutching at Ashton's hand until she felt every detail of bone and sinew beneath his flesh.

"Comfortable," she whispered once the pain had subsided to throbbing dullness. "I'm afraid"—her tongue flicked out to moisten dry lips—"that I'm dying. And I'm not dying comfortably at all."

For a moment he held his breath; then he gave her a smile that looked only slightly forced. "Goody will be here soon. She'll know what to do."

But "soon" was not soon enough. Bethany endured eternal moments of wracking shivers and harrowing pains. Each one came faster, gripped longer, and left her more breathless than the last. She found herself mesmerized by the wag-on-the-wall clock, visible through the bedroom door. The long pendulum measured the moments of her agony with such regularity that, oddly, she felt an inner quieting.

During a rare lull in the contractions she dragged her eyes from the swinging pendulum and focused on Ashton.

"Miss Abigail."

"Hush, love, she'll be all right. Finley's gone after her."

"Why, Ashton? Why did you seize her tonight?"

"I had no idea who we were looking for. I was as shocked as you were when I saw who we'd captured."

"And—Bug Willy?"

"We didn't know he'd be waiting at the print shop."

But words could not erase what he had done. He had delivered Miss Abigail into the hands of dangerous radicals. The thought put a sharp edge of bitterness on the birth pains.

Further comment was impossible as a new convulsion roared through her. Her eyes sought the clock and her hands sought Ashton's. Deep beneath the pain was the knowledge of bitterness to come. Perhaps it was the baby's uncommon size, as Goody had said; perhaps it was the fast, heedless night ride and the shock of seeing Miss Abigail abused. . . . Reasons didn't matter. The cold fact was that the child was coming early. Too early to convince Ashton he was its sire.

"Where're the women?" demanded a rasping voice. Bethany felt Ashton's grip slacken with relief at the arrival of Goody Haas. The contents of the midwife's apron stirred as she crossed to the bed.

"There's no one here but me," Ashton said.

"Can't very well have a birthin' without women," Goody grumbled. "Fetch the girl's mother. And didn't you say you had a sister?"

"No." Bethany's voice was firm despite her pain. "'Twould only make things worse."

"Her mother faints when she pricks her finger on a sewing needle," Ashton explained. "And my sister is . . . she wouldn't be of any use."

"And you suppose you will, eh?" As she spoke, Goody moved her hands over Bethany.

"I've attended countless foalings," Ashton said.

"Your wife's not made like a mare," Goody snapped. "But I'll let you stay if you can make yourself useful. Get me some basins of water and a goodly pile of linens."

"That's all?"

"Ain't much to a birthing. Only a lot of pain and sweat."

Pain and sweat . . . sweat and pain. Seconds melted into minutes and then hours until even the relentlessly wagging pendulum failed to mark the passage of time for Bethany. She was in a stupor of agony and exhaustion.

Just when she was certain she could not go on any longer, she was tackled by a monstrous pressure building within her. Through hot flickers of pain she saw Goody's face light up.

"'Tis time," the midwife announced. "Now the real work begins."

Bethany felt an inward deflation; hadn't she been laboring for hours with all her might? But the urge within her was strong, irresistible. She clamped her eyes shut and strained.

"You've the idea," Goody said. "But it'll take more'n that to bring the child forth."

Clutching desperately at Ashton's arm, Bethany struggled, sure she would burst with the effort. Suddenly Goody gave an exclamation of satisfaction. "Come here," she said to Ashton. "Since you insisted on being present, you might's well be the first to hold your babe."

Bethany's focus changed for a moment from the mounting pressure within her to Ashton. Oh, God, she thought, watching his indecision. Oh, God, he's going to leave rather than witness the birth of the child he believes to be Dorian's.

But Ashton did not leave. He squeezed her hand reassuringly, dropped it, and went to the end of the bed. And in moments found his trembling hands filled with what the midwife declared to be a good half stone of wet and squalling infant.

Thunderstruck, Ashton stared down at the baby in his arms. Emotions too fleeting and too intense to name pounded through his mind: awe at this tiny, perfect child that had been delivered into his hands; relief that Bethany's agony was over; and a deep pride that she had borne her nightlong labor so bravely.

Wasting neither time nor words, Goody Haas tied off the cord and severed it. She held a clean length of linen across her outstretched hands and Ashton gave her the child.

"A boy," Goody said. "Fine as any I've ever seen."

Bethany was smiling as she received the squirming bundle. Ashton saw something in that smile he'd never seen before: a softness, a serenity, a supreme contentment that caused a tender stirring in some forgotten corner of his heart.

The baby quieted as Bethany held him to her. She moved a hand reverently over the tiny reddened brow, the tight fists that waved at her. Goody cleared her throat and Ashton noticed a suspicious gleam in her eye as she set about the business of tidying up.

Finally Bethany looked at Ashton. "We have a son," she told him quietly. In her eyes he recognized a silent supplication. She wanted him to claim the baby.

He wanted to. God's blood, but he wanted to make an everlasting bond with the child. But all he could bring himself to say was, "Congratulations, pet. You were braver than an entire army." He dropped a kiss on her damp brow. "What will you name him?"

She looked up at him tentatively. Her teeth chewed a barely trembling lip; then she drew a deep breath. "I thought . . . we could name him for your father."

Ashton felt the breath leave him as if he had just been sucked beneath a cold sea. Under different circumstances he would have been fiercely proud to name his son for the father he had loved. But now . . . his conscience would not allow him to give Roger's name to a child who might have been sired by Dorian Tanner.

Bethany was looking at him expectantly, waiting for an answer.

"I think not," he said, his voice quiet and full of regret. He made himself smile, made himself move the covers aside to peer at the wizened face, the tiny red mouth that worked silently like a little bird's maw. "Looks a mite like you and Harry, don't you think?"

That was true. The child had a fine nose and bow lips

and a chin that promised the obstinance that was the hall-mark of the Winslow twins.

"Henry Markham," she said, not looking at Ashton. "I suppose 'tis fitting, since Felicia can have no more children."

"Your brother will be proud, love."

"And you, Ashton? Are you proud?"

Once again his lips were drawn to the fine, damp skin of her brow as he eyed the tiny bundle in her arms. The boy would be raised as his own no matter who had sired him. "Aye, love," he said sincerely. "I'm proud of you, and of this perfectly beautiful child."

He watched her exhale visibly with relief. And then, overcome with feelings he preferred not to explore, he sat and stroked her temples until exhausted sleep claimed her. Carefully he extracted the baby from her arms. The child, too, seemed wearied by his travails, and the dark, slitted eyes closed against the bright light of the world he had just joined.

Ashton carried the bundle into the kitchen, where Goody Haas was working, pipe clamped between her yellowed teeth.

"They're both asleep," he told her.

She eyed him through a thready haze of smoke. "'Tis well," she declared.

"She named the boy Henry, for her brother."

The penetrating gaze never wavered. "I heard."

He sucked in his breath. "I trust you'll say nothing."

"You trust me right enough." Goody jerked her head toward the quiet bedroom. "But you don't trust her."

He swallowed. "We've been married but eight months." His gaze dropped to the sleeping child in his arms. "This fellow is as big and hale as a nine-month babe." He sought the midwife's eyes again. "Is there any way to be sure?"

She regarded him for a long moment, sucking on her pipe and scraping her hobnail boot idly on the puncheon floor. "Aye," she said at last. "Aye, there is." The bright eyes enfolded in aging flesh drilled into him. "There is such a thing known as faith. You believe the child is yours because that woman in there loves you enough to be truthful about it."

13

Bethany held court on the rope-frame bed all through the first day of her son's life, sitting with him in the sun-washed bedroom that now bloomed with jars of Persian lilac and gillyflowers and blue hyacinth. The light scent of the flowers mingled with the unfamiliar and irresistible odor of baby. Not once did she regret missing out on the formal, luxurious lying-in that would have been hers had she married according to her parents' wishes. There was no room to spare in her mind for such thoughts because her son's new presence filled her so completely.

The people who came to call were not the polite, murmuring highborn of Newport. They were Dudley, the cook, who bore the traditional fare of groaning cakes and caudle; Barnaby Ames, who shuffled his feet and gawked, promising that the newly foaled Indian pony would be ready for little Henry by the boy's third summer; and Finley and Chapin Piper, who brought a small printed card which read, "Welcome, little stranger, tho' the Port is closed."

"Very witty." Bethany narrowed her eyes. "Where is Miss Abigail?"

The printer started to speak but was interrupted by the arrival of the stable hands and Moses Gibbs, the gardener.

"Congratulations," Gibbs boomed, pounding Ashton on the back. He lifted a mug of caudle. "To Ashton Markham's firstborn son!"

She watched in uncomfortable silence as the others loudly bestowed their good wishes on her husband.

"How does it feel, having a boy of your own?" one man asked.

She bit her lip. She hoped others would not notice the strained edges of Ashton's smile when he said, "I'm overwhelmed."

Moses Gibbs began expounding on his views of childrearing. Ashton, Finley, and Chapin slipped out of the cottage.

Then Carrie arrived, and for once the girl's hard cynicism was replaced by open admiration for her nephew. Bethany had to leave her query about Miss Abigail unanswered.

Henry bore up well under the scrutiny of the callers, waiting until they had gone before setting up a squall for his first meal. In her matter-of-fact way, Goody Haas showed Bethany how to suckle him. The baby's instincts made up for the mother's inexperience, and soon both mother and son were content.

Some soft feeling too new to name eddied through her as she stared at the baby nursing sweetly at her breast. "And to think," she mused, "that most women insist on wet nurses."

Goody gave a satisfied grunt. "The bond you're forming with that child is worth a hundred times the loss of a few vain inches on your figure."

"Did Ashton leave?"

Goody nodded. "Off on some errand. He didn't say what. I told him you'd be in good hands all day."

Disappointment pushed through the brightness of the day like a thunderhead. Most men would have hurried to the nearest tavern to toast the arrival of a firstborn son. Ashton was likely drinking as thirstily as any new papa, but not out of exultation. He would more probably be seeking forgetfulness in the bottom of his tankard.

Little Henry was sleeping in infantile fits and starts in his willow wicker cradle and Goody Haas was snoring on a truckle bed in the keeping room when Bethany heard Ashton return. He seemed unaware of her scrutiny as he banked the fire, then entered the darkened bedroom and disrobed, shrugging into a clean nightshirt she had not even realized he owned. He normally slept less modestly clad.

There was something odd in his movements as he washed himself at the basin. She peered hard at him. He did not seem unsteady with drink, as she had anticipated; rather he bore himself stiffly and moved almost gingerly. He hesitated over the wicker cradle, then supported himself with its hood as he bent to touch the sleeping baby.

The gratification she felt over that gesture soon gave way to concern. When Ashton slid carefully into the bed, she was certain she felt him wince.

"Ashton?"

"Bethany. I didn't realize you were awake." What was it she heard in his voice? Some rasping threadiness as if he fought pain.

"What time is it?"

"I don't know. Past midnight."

"You were gone so long, Ashton."

"Goody said you'd be taken care of."

"I was." *But it was you I needed today.*

"Can I get you anything?"

"No . . . yes. Kiss me, Ashton." She needed his touch, needed some confirmation that their relationship was not in ruins.

He complied with a haste that did nothing to allay her worries. The brief contact confirmed that something was amiss. She felt the sheen of perspiration on his upper lip, but not the odor of stale beer and smoke from a taproom.

Strangely, his hair was damp with seawater, and another smell mingled with the salt, sharp and distinctly unsettling.

She shifted on the bed. He drew in a harsh breath.

"You're bleeding," she said. "You've been hurt, haven't you?" He said nothing, and she knew she had guessed the truth. "What happened?"

"Nothing, pet. Don't worry about it. Just a bit of a scuffle with some rowdies. I took a nick or two."

"A scuffle? You've never been a fighting man."

"And you've never been a prying wife." His hand crept to her chin, and this time he kissed her more tenderly. "We had best get some rest while we can. Goody says babies entertain absolutely no regard for their parents' sleep."

His abrupt dismissal rankled. She remembered that while they lay in the security of their bed, Miss Abigail was in the hands of Bug Willy because of what Ashton and the Pipers had done.

"'Tis not so easy for me to drift off into peaceful sleep." Her voice was sharp.

Ashton's response, by contrast, was rough, as if he had been on the edge of sleep. "What's that?"

"How quickly you've forgotten Miss Abigail," she snapped. "While you were out drinking and fighting all night, she is still in the hands of that barbarian."

"She . . ." He coughed and winced. "Bethany, listen—"

"I don't want to hear your excuses. I want—"

The baby began to cry and she flounced from the bed. He muttered something about letting her temper sour her milk, but was asleep before she returned to the bed.

Morning's light, coming too soon after the baby's last feeding, showed Bethany what an understatement Ashton had made about the "nicks" he had sustained. His face was bruised and lacerated; there was a crude gauze bandage on his shoulder.

Goody Haas clicked her tongue and plunged a gnarled hand into her apron for a salve, then peeled the bandage away to reveal a deep and jagged cut.

"This promises a scar even more ugly than that one," the midwife said, indicating the depression in Ashton's side where he had taken the patriot musket ball.

Bethany shivered as Goody deftly applied the herbal salve and dressed the wound. Ashton made no comment, but his face was visibly paler when he bent to kiss Bethany and then the brow of the infant she held.

"About last night—"

"Never mind," she said, trying to discount the exquisite warmth his kiss had left on her lips. She darted a glance at Goody. His eyes narrowed, but he merely shrugged and turned away.

After he departed, she sat wrapped in silence and confusion. Then, to her amazement, she heard the clipped, precise tones of Miss Abigail Primrose greeting Goody Haas.

Not a trace of her ordeal with the patriots marred Miss Abigail's meticulously groomed countenance. Beneath a neat little tippet, every dark hair was in place. A gray cloak, perfectly clean and free of the slightest pucker or wrinkle, wrapped her poised figure.

She smiled a greeting at Bethany, but her eyes were entrapped by the sleeping child. The sharp gray of those eyes suddenly turned to the misty softness of pussy willows.

"It seems we've both been busy," Miss Abigail said, holding out her arms. "And who have we here?"

"Henry Markham." Bethany placed the baby in Miss Abigail's arms.

"He is lovely. No, that is not the word I want. " Miss Abigail spent a moment in grave contemplation of the small round face and the tiny balled fist that waved at her from the folds of a knitted shawl. "Superior in every way. Absolute perfection, my dear." She took out a rattle made of silver and sea coral and dangled it in front of Henry's face.

Then Miss Abigail did a strange thing. Her eyes never leaving the child, her disciplined face melted into a mask of foolish adoration. "There now, here's our little man." The clipped voice dissolved into a string of the most outrageous, sugary baby talk Bethany had ever heard. "Come, nestling, a smile for Auntie Primrose. . . ."

Goody Haas's aptly timed entrance covered the giggle that burst from Bethany's lips. The sound of her hobnail boots and clanking apron seemed to bring Miss Abigail back to herself and she straightened, looking like a schoolgirl caught in the larder after hours.

"Fine little piece, ain't he?' Goody remarked.

"He is divine," Miss Abigail agreed, gently laying the baby in the cradle and hanging the rattle on its hood.

Bethany smiled at the two women. It was impossible not to see the contrast they made. Goody's earthy appearance struck oddly but not discordantly against Miss Abigail's stylish grooming. The two had nothing in common, yet they were united in their admiration of Henry and their concern for Bethany. For a moment an unpleasant feeling wriggled through her. There should be another woman here, offering love and congratulations along with the midwife and the teacher.

But Lillian Winslow had been mortified by her daughter's crashing social descent and doubtless did not want any connection with the grandson she would consider shockingly lowborn.

Goody hurried away to get tea; then, sensing Miss Abigail's desire for privacy, retired to the dooryard to sit among the lilacs and smoke her pipe.

"So you're the spy." Bethany peered at Miss Abigail, trying to reconcile the image of the proper lady with that of a ruthless informer who committed perilous acts of espionage.

"Yes," came the prim reply.

"But why, Miss Abigail?"

The lady perched on the edge of a chair and sipped daintily from her teacup, wrinkling her nose at the "Yankee brew" Ashton insisted on. "I really happened into it quite by accident," she explained. "Last summer one of the girls at the academy became ill. She had no kin other than her father, a lieutenant colonel in the army, who was defending Boston from the rebels. I was told there was no way to get word to him."

Miss Abigail added a large dollop of honey to her tea. "I decided to take matters into my own hands. People had been saying it was impossible to cross the Neck into Boston, but none of the rebel patrols thought to stop me."

Bethany had no trouble believing that. How could anyone suspect Miss Abigail Primrose of subterfuge? "When the girl's father learned how easily I'd slipped across the Neck," Miss Abigail continued, "he asked me to carry a letter to a gentleman in Bristol. After the success of that, there were a number of requests." Slowly she stirred her tea, gazing out the window at a bobwhite perched on a pink-blooming branch of a cherry tree. "One thing, as they say, led to another."

"To Harry." Bethany pressed her lips together. "Perhaps, in the end, it was for the best. He did get back to his family, just as you intended. But what will you do now?"

"I expect I'll be subjected to some sort of inquiry and asked to sign the Association."

"What is that?"

"Some document stating I've renounced my allegiance to the kind, et cetera, et cetera."

"Will you sign it?"

Miss Abigail set her cup in its saucer with a loud clatter. "Certainly not."

"Will they punish you?"

She gave a thin smile. "Of course. It's become a point of

honor with Mr. Finley Piper. Now, don't look at me like that. Most probably I'll be required to remain in Newport under Mr. Piper's eye. But enough about me." Her eyes focused on the sleeping child. "Is Ashton as pleased as you are?"

Bethany glanced away. "He would not let me name him for his father."

Miss Abigail's mouth tightened. "I see."

She nodded. "After the birth, he left and didn't return until well past midnight. He'd been brawling."

The perfect arches of Miss Abigail's brows lifted high. "Brawling!"

Bethany cringed at her teacher's tone. She knew Miss Abigail had disapproved of Ashton from the start. Now, it seemed, he was bearing out the lady's image of him.

"Brawling!" Miss Abigail repeated. "Is that what he told you?"

"Aye," Bethany admitted.

Miss Abigail's hand reached for her, stroking her shoulder. "The man lies."

"What?"

"My dear, your husband was not out brawling last night. He took a dory into the bay to get me away from Bug Willy. He wasn't brawling with the men; he was fighting for me!"

Bethany stared in shock. That explained the scent of seawater in his hair last night, the savagery of his wounds. "Oh, Lord," she whispered. "I didn't know."

"I can't think why he didn't tell you."

"I never gave him a chance."

"I think you had both learn to listen to one another, my girl."

She nodded, wondering how on earth she and Ashton would ever find peace. When one was ready to trust, the other was ready to accuse, and she could see no end to the cycle.

*   *   *

Nearly six weeks passed before Miss Abigail was brought before the Committee of Safety in the house of Jarred Kilburn on Broad Street. To Ashton's irritation, Bethany insisted on attending.

"I've taken pains to arrange for the trip into town," she said. "Carrie will look after little Henry. And this is my favorite gown."

His eyes were drawn to her newly voluptuous bosom. "Aye." He felt a familiar heat in his loins. One of his favorite sights was watching her nurse the baby, her breasts full, the child content. "Carrie doesn't know the first thing about taking care of a baby. I think you should stay home."

"I don't understand you at all, Ashton Markham," she snapped. "While you loftily declare the rights of man, you demand absolute power over your wife."

His mood changed from annoyance to amusement. It had been some weeks since he had glimpsed this side of her, this pert and oddly pleasing obstinance.

"You have me there, wife," he conceded, and offered her his arm.

The house in Broad Street was crowded with members of the Committee of Safety. Finley Piper arrived with Miss Abigail, who was dressed in Union Jack colors—a gown of blue overlaid with a short jacket of red superfine, decorated with a white Mechlin lace fichu.

"'Tis the fourth of June, our king's birthday," she announced. "Let us dispense with matters quickly, Mr. Piper." She cast a disdainful eye about the room. Jarred Kilburn looked away, clearly ill at ease. The rest were a nervous, impotent-looking lot who wrung their hands and gaped in slack-jawed awe at the prisoner.

Miss Abigail sniffed. "Clearly this entire business is a mockery. Can't you gentlemen see that? Before long your rebellion will be put down by His Majesty's forces and you'll all be declared outlaws."

Finley planted himself in front of her and lifted a sheaf of papers. "Madam, I'm chairman of this committee."

She gave a sage nod. "The scum rises to the top in patriot circles." Her nostrils narrowed in a sniff as she reached out and selected a biscuit from a tray on the gate-leg table at her side.

"What!" Finley snorted. "My God, does it eat biscuits! I thought it ate only raw meat!"

Bethany stifled a sharp intake of breath. Ashton felt her tremors of silent mirth. Miss Abigail had been in Finley's company for some weeks. During that time they had sniped at each other ceaselessly.

Her look was a steel-gray dagger as Finley proceeded with the inquiry. He made much of her position as headmistress of the academy in New York, wondering aloud how a woman born to no particular means or title had achieved a reputation that drew the very cream of Tory society.

Miss Abigail cleared her throat and faced the assembly with an elaborate flaring of her nostrils. "Gentlemen, I owe my position to hard work, discipline, and intelligence."

Finley set his face into a dark scowl. "How charmingly modest you are, madam."

"I am neither charming nor modest, but it doesn't really matter, does it? Unless those issues are at stake today—"

"Perhaps you'd like to tell the committee how it is you have a fortune amounting to" —he consulted his notes with a dramatic pause— "two thousand seven hundred pounds sterling."

"I have never accepted money for performing my duty to the Empire."

Finley spent the better part of two hours trying to wring details of those duties out of Miss Abigail. Nail-hard, she refused to tell him anything he didn't already know. She sat like a sparrow wrought of iron and denied knowing anything of the communications she carried, the people she contacted, the sources of her information.

Finley looked exhausted and the committee looked bored when at last he left off his line of questioning.

"Miss Primrose," he said in an elaborately patient voice. "There is but one thing left to offer you that might spare you a severe sentence." He laid a piece of paper in front of her.

She recoiled as if the document were a hissing viper. "Never," she stated. "I will not sign the Association." Her gaze swept the dismayed faces of the committeemen. "I am an Englishwoman to the marrow of my bones. To my death, if need be." She picked up the paper by one corner, holding it at arm's length as if it were something foul, and let it drift to the floor.

Finley turned to the committee. "There you have it." He sighed. "We've no choice but to sentence her."

At last the committeemen stirred into animated discussion. Their suggestions ranged from a public ducking in the millpond to hanging. Bethany braced her arms on the chair, rising.

Ashton touched her hand. "Don't, my love."

"There is no justice here," she said. "This is a drumhead tribunal with no authority over this woman."

"Ah, and we're both aware of the superiority of English justice," he said reminded her.

That brought her back to her seat.

Finley brushed back the lapels of his frock coat and hooked his thumbs into the plackets of his waistcoat. He rocked back and forth on his heels. "I've been a widower nigh on fifteen years. Haven't had a lady about the place in all that time. Might be nice to have a female touch here and there, have my socks darned properly and a decent meal now and then."

Miss Abigail gasped. "I am a prisoner of war, not a bond servant."

"You prefer the pillory?"

"I prefer being roasted alive by the devil himself to darning your socks, Mr. Piper."

Over the laughter of her listeners, Miss Abigail argued frantically. But in the end, she agreed to submit to the custody of Finley Piper. Bethany suspected she meant to make him regret his sentence.

14

Crouched between two brick warehouses in Bristol's wharf area, Ashton held Bethany until the cannonade ceased. The baby in her arms wailed as the big guns of the HMS *Rose* belched a deadly threat on the town of Bristol.

In the cramped space, she had her first taste of the acrid bite of sulphur, her first stinging smell of burning saltpeter. Ears accustomed to sounds no more threatening than the roar of the ocean crashing against rocks were now assaulted by the thunder of cannon fire. Her eyes smarted in a nefarious fog of black smoke and she closed them, snuggling herself and the baby closer to Ashton.

"There, love, hang on to me." His murmur rumbled comfortingly against her ear. "The shooting will be over soon."

The guns from the British fleet grew quiet. Little Henry's cries subsided to soft whimpers. The ensuing hush was eerie, uncertain, a nervous settling of smashed brickwork and plaster from the ruined façades of waterfront buildings.

Then the human sounds began: Voices rose into cries of agony; shouts escalated to bellows of rage. A mortified town greeted Captain James Wallace as he emerged from a ship's boat accompanied by red-frocked and gold-bedecked subalterns.

"Damn the bastard," Ashton muttered.

Bethany withdrew shakily from his arms and quieted the baby. Her eyes were wide with confusion and watery from the smoke. Her head throbbed and her legs felt weak, as if she had been a victim of the heartless assault on Bristol.

Slowly she shook her head, trying to make sense of the turn events had taken. What had begun as a family outing on a glorious summer day had turned into a nightmare. They had gone to visit Harry and Felicia, to admire Margaret, their infant niece, and to show off little Henry. The day had been filled with congenial talk in the tiny parlor on Hope Street and games of piquet in the quiet garden.

They had not spoken of the war. Instead they had reminisced over childhood afternoons spent paddling and swimming in the bay, collecting mussel shells and turtles, digging clams. Summers were sweet freedom then, innocent irresponsibility, a time for riding horses and inviting the imagination to wander.

For a few hours she had found affection and release in the cooing over the babies and the trading of nonsensical jokes. Spirits renewed, and feeling closer than they had in weeks, Ashton and Bethany had made their way back to the ferry.

Six British frigates had loomed like dark birds in the harbor.

She would always remember that moment—Ashton's stone-hard face and the look of fury seething in his stormy eyes. Harsh curses had issued from his lips as he hastened her and the baby to shelter. From beneath a slanting door, they had witnessed the cannonade.

She looked at him now and saw the anger still lingering in his eyes.

"Ashton, why would Captain Wallace do such a thing?"

His jaw worked as if he were fighting to prevent the emission of yet another string of oaths. "Would you believe he's hungry?"

"What?"

"Just listen."

They moved in among a loose ring of angry townspeople circling the soldiers, who wielded evil-looking bayoneted muskets.

Captain James Wallace, the scourge of Narragansett Bay, flicked eyes ugly with anger over the citizenry and lifted his long, arrogant nose. "Fifty sheep!" His voice belled out to touch every ear. "I demand fifty head of sheep from the town of Bristol. The King's Navy is in want of meat."

Amid grumbling both fearful and defiant, several farmers pledged sheep to forestall further bombardment.

Bethany hugged the baby closer and sagged against Ashton. "Ah, the world is going mad. He bombarded a whole town for meat."

Ashton's fingers ran gently through the feathery, honey-gold waves at her nape, beginning a tender rhythm designed to ease the tension from her knotted muscles.

"Civil war is the bitterest kind, love."

A month later Bethany found herself among another group of citizens. But shouts of joy rather than gunfire filled the air.

"This mob is no place for an infant," she said with a worried frown. Her eyes traveled over the throng gathered in the parade in front of the Colony House. All Newport had come to hear Major John Handy's announcement from the lime-washed balustrade of the building. The people were hemmed against the edge of a park shaded by Dutch elms and poplars. A company of British regulars lounged indolently against hitch rails and gateposts. Their easy pose belied a readiness to subdue any mischief a gathering so large might produce.

Someone jostled Bethany from behind and the baby whimpered a protest. "Ashton," she said, "I think we had best go home."

"Hand the lad to me." He took the shawl-wrapped bundle from her. He smiled down at the baby, who favored him with a wide, toothless grin. "I don't want you to miss this moment, little one."

She instantly relented when she saw the look on his face. The hard, handsome lines of his profile became soft with the emotion that always seemed to touch him when he held the child. A lesser man, doubting the parentage of the child, might have turned his back on little Henry. But not Ashton. With tender pride he supported the small, golden head to turn Henry's blinking gaze on the scene at the Colony House.

"Your mother's not quite sure I won't drop you, lad." Ashton chuckled. "But we know better, don't we?" In the cradle of those big, gentle hands it appeared no harm could befall the child.

"Watch now, lad," Ashton said. "A page of history is being written before our eyes. You'll tell your grandbabes of this one day."

A lull of silence settled over the throng at the appearance of several men at the balustrade high above them. Major Handy, smartly clad in the blue and buff of the Continental Army, produced a large document with a ceremonial flourish.

"'When in the course of human events it becomes necessary for one people to dissolve the political bonds . . .'" The voice rang clear, cutting through salt-tinged air and falling on ears rapt with astonished attention. On the reading went, dealing out hard, powerful words like cannon shot that shook the convictions of even the most radical of listeners.

Bethany frowned. Independence! What else could the defiant words mean but all-out war? How in heaven's name could the infant nation prevail over the vast empire of England?

Long moments of silence followed the reading. Then, with a rumble like a gathering storm, people wept and laughed and cheered in jubilation. Hats were flung into the air and ladies were swung around in joyous salute to the Declaration. Bethany watched Ashton, and her throat began to ache.

He celebrated quietly, clasping his son against him as the majesty of the day washed over him. She had lost him; she could see that.

They reached the end of the commons, passing in front of a tight-knit group of Newport Loyalists. Bethany saw angry outrage in the darkened brow of Keith Cranwick. On his arm, Mabel Pierce fluttered a silk fan emblazoned with the king's arms and declared in a high-pitched voice, "Imagine that! A ragged mob challenging England!"

"They haven't enough guns or boats to sink a child's dory, much less the Royal Navy," Keith added.

Ashton kept walking. He had not seemed to notice that her hand had turned ice cold.

On July 25, 1776, at the age of fifty-five, Sinclair Winslow fell in love.

He had been in his library when a small sound disturbed him. A sound he hadn't heard in some nineteen years. The singularly stirring cry of a baby.

Leaving his bills and trading certificates scattered on his Goddard desk, he went to investigate.

At the top of the narrow back stairs he paused, covered the tightness in his chest with a hand gone suddenly cold, and frowned in annoyance at this evidence of physical frailty. Catching his breath, he lowered his head and walked to the maid's room at the end of the hallway.

The baby on the red-haired maid's bed was not merely crying. The child was in the throes of a full-blown, red-faced squall.

An imperious brow dropped to a scowl. "Miss Markham! What is the meaning of this?"

The maid stared in horror at her employer. "Mr. Winslow! Sir, I'm sorry you were disturbed." Hastily she rose and dipped a deferent curtsey. "I offered to look after little Henry for Miss Bethany this afternoon, and I can't seem to get him quiet. Truly, sir, I—"

"Enough!" Sinclair stopped her short. "Miss Markham, I have looked the other way at all your various escapades over time, but *this*" —he cast a stern eye at the howling baby— "is inexcusable."

She swallowed visibly. "Yes. Yes, sir, I quite agree. I never should have brought the baby to the big house."

"Pipe down," he snapped. "Do you know nothing of caring for an infant?"

"Not very much, sir."

He shook his head in disgust and crossed to the bed. "By God, the child is soaking wet."

The maid drew a swath of cotton from the supply Bethany had provided. Her hands fumbled as she tried to fold the square of cloth.

Sinclair snatched it from her. "Give me that." With quick deftness that filled him with absurd pride, he folded the napkin and soon had the infant changed. Without looking at the maid, he held out his hand. "The shawl." He spread the knitted garment at an angle, placed the baby on it, and wrapped the tiny body as securely as a parcel of herring from market. Still awash with pride at his own competence, he lifted the baby into his arms. The squalls dissipated to sobs, then tentative hiccups, then blissful silence.

Sinclair looked smug. "And that, young lady, is how one cares for a baby. Don't forget it. And close your mouth. You look like a codfish."

"Uh, yes, sir."

Sinclair turned abruptly and walked to the end of the narrow room. A dormer window gave a view of the gardens below and the vast reaches of meadows leading to the surf-battered coastline.

But he wasn't looking at the view. He was gaping with unabashed wonder at his grandson.

"Henry, is it?" he asked. The baby gazed up at him with a steady blue stare. "Had one of those myself once. Both my sons, alas, have proven useless. William's courting a case of the gout at his army post, and Harry's a rebel. I pray you'll become a better man than your namesake. Ah, but I do miss your mother, lad. She was the best of the lot."

The baby cuddled a flawless milky cheek against the worsted silk of Sinclair's frock coat. And then the miracle of a moist, toothless smile spread across the baby's face.

That was the moment Sinclair lost his heart. Love for this tiny, beautiful child blossomed in his old man.

He brushed his lips over the smooth, downy head, inhaling the aroma of purity unique to babies. While Sinclair slowly gained control over his astonished emotions, Henry Markham tucked a tiny thumb into his mouth and fell asleep in his grandfather's arms.

Sinclair turned and laid the baby on the narrow bed, securing a corner of the shawl beneath the sleeping form. "You see," he whispered to the dumbstruck maid, "there is nothing to this business of babies."

Leaving her to gape, he descended the backstairs and returned to the library. He bellowed for his day clerk, who came scurrying with ink salver, quill, and paper.

In a voice firm with conviction yet oddly thin with emotion, Sinclair Winslow dictated a new version of his last will and testament.

*   *   *

Bethany hid a smile behind her hand when Finley Piper, his apron dusted with flour instead of printer's ink, set a tray of scones on the table in his narrow parlor above the shop. Although at Miss Abigail's hearing he had vowed she would serve him while living in his house, Miss Abigail had quickly taken the upper hand.

With singular and completely unfeigned incompetence, she had created utter disaster in Finley's kitchen. After weeks of undercooked meat, charred toast, and slimy porridge, he had relented and taken over the cooking chores himself. Although Miss Abigail claimed her eyes were too poor to wield a darning needle, she appeared to have no trouble poring over his impressive library of books and pamphlets.

"Oh, my," she exclaimed in a too sweet voice, "you've outdone yourself with these scones, Mr. Piper. They are delicious." Making no pretense of a dainty appetite, she helped herself to three of them.

"Don't know where she puts all that food," he grumbled, casting a doleful eye on the tiny silk-clad figure. "Eats more than Chapin."

Miss Abigail sniffed and turned away, pretending to ignore him. Finley removed his apron and sat down beside Ashton, who held Henry, vigorous and inquisitive at seven months of age, in his lap.

Bethany loved the sight of her husband thus occupied. While many men would consider caring for a baby emasculating, the task suited Ashton perfectly. The diminutive and delicate child only made her husband's handsome largeness more striking.

"Seems we're both doing women's work," Finley grumbled. Then he narrowed his eyes. "I understand Sinclair Winslow has a distinguished guest."

Ashton nodded. "Governor Joseph Wanton."

"An excellent gentleman," Miss Abigail remarked, slathering a scone with butter. "Such an honor for the Winslows."

"He's a damned sorry excuse for a governor," Finley

countered. "'Tis well the General Assembly replaced him with Governor Cooke."

"Illegally," Bethany pointed out. "Governor Wanton still retains the colony charter."

"We'll see about that."

Chapin called up the stairs from the print shop, needing help with a fresh run of broadsides. As Ashton handed the baby to Bethany, their hands met and their gazes locked for an instant. She felt a familiar stab of frustrated longing and tore her eyes from his. Lately, most touching outside the bedchamber had been accidental.

He and Finley excused themselves and went to help Chapin.

"They're planning something," Miss Abigail said.

"Do you think they'll try to retrieve the charter?"

"The new governor can hardly run things without our set of laws."

Bethany slumped against the back of her chair with a dispirited sigh. "I hate Ashton's involvement with the patriots. We argue about it endlessly." She shuddered. Often those arguments were so heated that they spent their nights with their backs turned to one another. The war was tearing them apart, and each was too stubborn to accede to the beliefs of the other.

Miss Abigail's pristine hand rested lightly on Bethany's arm. "Perhaps, my dear, you should think about moderating your views."

Bethany's eyes narrowed. "I'm surprised to hear you speak so."

"My loyalty to England has cost me my personal freedom," the lady admitted. "But that is all. You, however, have lost something infinitely more precious: the bond with your husband."

"I'll not pretend to embrace the patriot cause just to get Ashton back into my arms. Nor would I expect him to do the same, as if he ever would."

"But the two of you are suffering so."

"I try, Miss Abigail, really I do. But when he starts talking of self-government and free markets, I simply cannot keep myself from pointing out everything we stand to lose. I cannot lie to him or to myself."

"Both of you are too stubborn to give even a little."

"Like you and Finley?" She could not resist the comparison, nor could she help smiling at the pair of pink spots that leaped to her friend's cheeks. The two of them seemed to thrive on a constant state of adversity.

"Mr. Piper and I are sworn enemies," Miss Abigail insisted.

Henry began to fuss, clinging to the hem of her skirts. Scooping him up, she said, "We must be going. This little one needs his nap."

Miss Abigail dissipated into the ridiculous baby talk she reserved for Henry alone. "Come back and see your auntie Primrose soon." She placed kisses on his little face. "Tell your grandpapa to let Governor Wanton hold fast to that charter." She looked up at Bethany. "We'll make a proper Loyalist of this child yet."

Bethany started down the stairs to the print shop. "Not if Ashton has anything to say about it."

Ashton experienced a ripple of displeasure at the task entrusted to him. Standing in the grand arched front hall of the manor house, he scowled down at an official commission from the Committee of Safety. The paper was poorly covered with hastily scratched writing, still gritty with blotting sand. He and Bethany had argued bitterly over what he was about to do. He could still hear the slam of the cottage door she had whipped closed after he had left.

"What the devil are you doing here?" Carrie's voice came from beneath the main stair.

"I'm here to see Mr. Winslow. And his guest. Where are they?"

She stepped back. "No, Ashton. I know you. You'll only make trouble. Mr. Winslow hasn't been well lately."

"I'll only be a few minutes."

"Fool! Do you realize what you're throwing away by siding with the patriots? Mr. Winslow is mad about your son. Hasn't he made the lad his sole heir? He'd place all Seastone in your lap if only you'd give up this madness about independence."

He fixed a hard look on his sister. What she said was true. Taking everyone by surprise, Sinclair had willed the major part of his estate to little Henry, naming Ashton as trustee until the boy reached his majority. Ashton wondered if Sinclair appreciated the irony he had created. The possibility existed for Henry Markham to one day hold his own father's indenture.

He dismissed Carrie with a curt nod and climbed the wide staircase to the upper parlor. Sinclair and Joseph Wanton were smoking clay pipes and having their morning tea. As yet not wigged and dressed for the day, their heads were wrapped in turbans. Sinclair wore an India silk paduasoy gown, and Wanton sported a bright red Genoa robe.

Ashton's greeting was a perfunctory nod as he strode into the richly furnished room. "I'm here for the charter, gentlemen."

He held out his commission. "I have orders to deliver the document to Governor Cooke."

Scowling, Sinclair snatched the paper and scanned it before handing it to Wanton. The ex-governor's jowls puffed out, but he remained calm. "Tell the Commissioner I've refused to cede the charter."

With a rakish grin, Ashton said, "I'll tell the committee. They might also be interested in passing on some facts about you to the General Assembly."

The jowls worked agitatedly. "Do go on."

"As things stand, most people are unaware of your part in closing the customs house."

"But I—"

"And wasn't there something about your association with the Master of Rolls in England? Ah, *that* would endear you to the populace."

Wanton's face drained of color.

"Shall I go on?" Ashton asked. "Perhaps the Assembly would like to know the bounty you accepted from Captain Wallace's raid on—"

"Enough!" Wanton cried.

Sinclair caught his breath in astonishment. Wanton turned his back on Ashton. "I'll never hand over the charter. However, were you to fetch the document from that coffer on the side table, I doubt we would be able to stop you."

Ashton tried not to smile as he found the charter and slid the long, rolled document into his pocket.

"This will cost you dearly, Markham," Sinclair muttered.

"Dearly? In terms of what, sir?"

"'Twill cost you your son, damn your eyes."

Fear sliced a cold blade through Ashton, although he made certain his face stayed impassive. "You've no hold on the boy, Mr. Winslow."

Beneath a flush of outrage, Sinclair's face seemed pale; there were taut lines about his mouth as if he were staving off pain. "We'll see about that, Markham. Just take the damned charter and get out."

Captain Dorian Tanner caught sight of himself in a gilt-framed Fauquiers mirror in the upstairs parlor of the manor house of Seastone. His obsidian eyes narrowed at the image, finding the brass gorget at his throat askew. A perfectly manicured hand straightened the ornament, then lightly patted the powdered tie-wig, which sprinkled a discreet puff of whiteness into the air. Dorian made a half turn, admiring the severe cut of his knee-length coat and the gleam of polished brightwork crisscrossing his profile.

Ten years earlier even Dorian himself could not have imagined he would ever cut so fine a figure. He had dared to dream only after a certain member of the House of Lords had happened upon him as he performed horse tricks at a fair. Carnival life was preferable to spending his days up to his elbows in muck at his father's stinking tannery in St. Giles. But the titled gentleman had offered Dorian an even more appealing career.

Dorian made a delicate grimace, recalling the darker aspects of Lord Mawdsley's tutelage. The price of becoming a gentleman had been dear, but worthwhile. Eventually the enamored nobleman had bought Dorian a commission, little suspecting his protégé would be shipped thousands of miles away.

Yet even this post was not enough for Dorian. The black eyes kindled like hot coals when he recalled how close he had come to marrying Bethany. She would have brought his fondest ambitions to full flower; she had beauty, wealth, and the one asset he coveted above all else: respectability.

Finding her married to the lout of a stable hand had been a staggering blow. He meant to exact revenge against her for the slight, and against Markham for putting him through the humiliation of the prisoner exchange. Aye, Markham had been involved in that affair; Dorian was sure of it. Unfortunately, months of investigation had given him not a scrap of evidence. Perhaps Dorian would need to resort to less conventional means of exacting vengeance.

A few minutes later he was shaking hands with Sinclair Winslow. They relaxed in Townsend chairs as a discreet servant poured cognac into crystal snifters. Dorian adored the elegance of this setting so much, he had to work at seeming nonchalant.

"I'm delighted to see you again, Mr. Winslow," he said.

"I hope you still feel that way when I tell you why I asked you to come." Sinclair sipped his brandy.

"As an officer of the Crown, sir, I am at your service."

"Yes, well, this is not a military matter." His hand crept to his chest. "My life has been a fruitful one." He waved his free hand about the room. "As you can see."

"Quite so, sir."

"I have no wish to see what I've spent years building fall to ruin."

"Perfectly understandable, sir."

"To which of my sons do you suggest I leave my estate? To Harry, an undisciplined rebel, or to William, who was captured, stone-drunk, by patriots and is now mining copper in a prison camp in Connecticut?"

"If I'm not mistaken, sir, you've decided neither son is fit to care for your estate, and you've willed the bulk of it to your grandson."

"Aye, but I've decided Henry's father is unfit to serve as the boy's trustee."

"I quite agree, sir." Dorian hoped he had not spoken too quickly in his eagerness. "You're wise to be so selective."

Sinclair cleared his throat. "I'd hoped to have you as a son-in-law."

"Your daughter's impetuous marriage to a commoner was a great disappointment to me, sir."

Sinclair leaned forward. "May I be so bold, Captain, as to ask you to be the boy's trustee?"

Dorian's every muscle tensed. Careful, he reminded himself. Slowly. He schooled his face into a mask of sincerity. "Mr. Winslow, I should be honored to allay your concerns by serving the lad."

"Very well." Sinclair took a document from a portfolio on a nearby gateleg table. "'Tis done, then."

With that, Dorian realized, his fondest dream came within reach once again. Fortune was beaming down on him this day, and he basked in its warmth.

*   *   *

Bethany glared through midnight shadows at the wagging pendulum of the clock on the keeping room wall. The rhythmic ticking, usually so soothing in the night quiet of the cottage, irritated her now. Although she was staring at the clock, what she was seeing was Ashton when he had returned from her father's house with the charter.

A grimly satisfied smile had curled his lips as he had entered the details of the day's activities in his journal. Lately that journal, which she had hoped would become a home for his tender thoughts, had become a frighteningly long list of subversive acts, of espionage and sabotage, of things she did not want to know about. He seemed compelled to write it all down, as if to preserve it for some future use.

After finishing his writing, he had at least had the decency to flinch when she had practically flung his supper at him.

She moved to the bedroom door, earning a disgruntled huff from Gladstone. An orange shaft of firelight illuminated two sleeping faces, so alike in form, so alike in dearness to her. Henry, on his railed truckle bed, poked a tiny thumb into his mouth. Ashton's sleep was equally untroubled, his face a disquieting vision of almost boyish innocence.

A strong urge welled up in her to brush a hand across a lock of hair curling endearingly toward the cleft in his chin. She clenched her hand against the impulse, turning away. How long had it been since she had felt free to touch him, to give vent to the desire that clamored through her whenever he was near?

They were husband and wife, yet they lived like strangers.

Damn you, she told him silently. Damn you and your bloody patriot cause and your high-sounding principles. Don't you see what you're doing to us? Don't you care?

For months he had flouted her loyalty to England while committing acts of treason before her very eyes, blithely certain she would not betray him. For months she had resisted the urge to sabotage his efforts in the name of loyalty.

But until tonight the urge had been weaker than her need to turn a blind eye to his activities.

His latest act caused her conviction to flare like a flame in a quickening breeze. She'd had enough of his subterfuge; it was time to act on her principle just as he acted on his.

Her fingers felt like ice as she stood on tiptoe at the corner shelf and groped for his strongbox. Her hand trembled as she raised the leather-hinged lid. She nearly dropped the charter in her nervousness. Forcing her hands to remain steady, she closed the box and stowed it away.

She slid the document into her pocket. The charter must be kept from the rebel governor at all costs. There was only one person she could think of who had the means to safeguard the document: Miss Abigail Primrose.

Bethany threw a shawl around her shoulders to stave off the chill of the November night and carefully laid her hand on the door latch. She depressed the lever with her thumb, eliciting a quiet metallic click. Apprehension pounded through her and she drew a deep, steadying breath.

The vaguest prickle on the back of her neck was her only warning. Dread thudded through her veins as she turned slowly.

To confront her husband's shadowed face.

"Going for a midnight stroll, love?" he inquired.

15

His easy pose in the bedroom doorway, the splendor of his masculine nudity, and the knifelike sharpness of his stare turned Bethany's insides to churning liquid.

"I . . ." Her mouth had gone dry. She moistened her lips with her tongue and summoned conviction. "Yes, I am, Ashton. Do you object?" Despite her apprehension, the sight of his magnificent body as he crossed the room with a fluid motion made a traitorous part of her long to stay.

"Object, pet?" Long fingers, deceptively gentle, flicked at a stray tendril of hair at her temple and began a languorous descent. She caught her breath as he traced a burning path over the leaping pulse in her throat, across her upthrust chin, rising to her trembling lower lip. "Why would I object?" he queried mildly. Slowly, very slowly, he closed the door against the cold. Then his hands returned to the tense contours of her body.

There was something taunting in the gentleness of his touch. Taunting, because he was aware of the compelling effect his unclad, aroused body had on her and no doubt aware she'd been hungering for him for weeks. She pulled sharply away, only to find herself hauled against the fascinating expanse of his chest, her determined thoughts scattering like snow flurries.

The arm around her was gentle and his voice teased. "You cut me to the quick, wife, slipping off by yourself as if to escape my company." He gave a soft laugh. "And to think I fancied myself capable of keeping you home at night."

The scent and texture of him assailed her senses. Eyes heedless of the barrage of inner warnings she was sending herself remained fastened on the sensual curl of his lips and the lids of his glinting eyes, which played over her bosom like a caress.

There was power in the touch that feathered across her cheekbone and dipped to the rounded neckline of her dress. Not the insistent power of a heavy-handed grasp, but a more insidious pull that drew her inexorably to him.

His smile was darkly sweet as his fingers left her bosom and traveled upward again, this time over her lips, expertly parting them. An inner voice warned her to flee, but she was hopelessly trapped by the arm that circled her waist and by her own undisciplined need.

His lips were a whisper against her own, gossamer-soft yet so explicitly suggestive that a slow burn of desire found a home deep within her, radiating out to limbs gone pliant with wanting.

"Ashton." His name trembled from her lips.

His tongue found hers and his teeth grazed her inner lip with cunning acuity. A slight motion of his hips sent her a frank message of temptation. As if she had willed them there, his hands began to massage the tender ache of her breasts and then played over the supple column of her spine.

Even as she succumbed to his clever love play, she felt small tingles like warning bells of alarm going off in her head. There was something different about him, a sort of bloodless expertise in the movement of his hands and mouth.

His touch was too studied, too emotionless, to manipulative. When he lifted his mouth from hers, she sought his eyes and saw chilling glints like ice crystals dancing in their depths.

The anger glaring down at her now was cold, as sharp and pure as a blast of arctic wind. The controlled gentleness of his rage terrified her.

She dragged herself up from the heavy fog of desire drenching her senses and forced her eyes to remain locked with his.

His hand, which had been curling tenderly through the waves of hair at the nape of her neck, kept up a soft, circular motion.

"Ashton, please." She was shamed by the tremor in her voice.

"Please," he mocked softly. "Please what, darling?" Her response was an incoherent whimper. "What do you mean, Bethany? Please don't touch me . . ." His hand burned a trail over her heat-flushed cheek. "Or please do?"

With a swift motion he unfastened her apron and dress and skimmed the garments to the floor. Her shift and pantalettes met a similar fate. She tried to protest and pull away, but her mouth would not form a denial; her limbs would not heed the warning of her mind. Apprehension mingled with rampant desire as he swept her into his arms and carried her to the rug before the hearth, wrapping her legs against his hard, sinewed form.

"You haven't answered me, love," he murmured. His tongue curled wickedly into her ear. "Say you want me." His hands rode the ripe curves of her body, warming her flesh and raising a tempest of longing within her.

"I can't deny it. I hate it that we haven't been close these past weeks. I want you so much that I hurt."

His hand found a place of searing intimacy, and his touch left her breathless with wanting. "At least," he said, brushing his lips back and forth over hers, "you're honest about that."

He laid her back on the rug, teasing her to readiness until tears sprang to her eyes. He took her swiftly, urgently, thoroughly.

Riding a soaring crest of passion, she was engulfed by a tumult of emotion. Their conflicting loyalties made them enemies, yet she adored him. With a heart so full that it ached. His touch was angry, yet she found that anger wildly exciting. The task of delivering the charter was pressing, yet she forgot it in her ardor.

"Ashton . . ." Her feelings brimmed and overflowed. "Ashton, please . . ." She let her voice trail off, unable to say all that was in her heart.

He tumbled away from her, looking both replete and still dangerously angry. He cocked his head to one side. "You repeat yourself. Please what? Perhaps you mean please let me go and hand the charter to my Tory friends."

Surging to his feet, he snatched up her apron and seized the document from its pocket.

Chilly gusts of reality chased away the warm afterglow of their love. Feeling suddenly vulnerable and afraid, she grabbed her shift and pulled it over her head.

"Who were you taking this to?" he demanded, shaking the charter at her. "Straight to Captain Tanner? My, my, you're getting as wily as your friend Miss Primrose."

Bethany went cold in every cell of her body when he disappeared into the bedroom, then emerged a few moments later fully dressed, the document protruding from an inner pocket of his jacket. He jammed on his hat and moved to the door.

In that instant her rage mounted to match her husband's. "How dare you." She planted herself in front of him. "How dare you condemn me for doing exactly as you've done all these months!"

"Move aside," he said wearily. "Obviously I can't trust the charter in the same house as you."

"I'm no more a thief than you are."

"There's a difference, love. You steal from your husband. All these months you've talked of trusting one another, so convincingly that I saw no danger in being open with you about my convictions." Each word was a dagger thrust to her heart. "It was all a lie, wasn't it? While you begged me to lay myself open to you, you planned on betraying me at the first opportunity."

"Do you think," she said, "that I never felt betrayed? My God, every time you walk out that door to ride express or commit some act of sabotage, you betray everything I hold dear. I am an Englishwoman. I feel the same loyalty to my country as you do to this—this Independent States of America or whatever you're calling it these days. All this time I've said nothing. I've kept my own counsel when you warned the farmers on Prudence Island about Wallace's raid. I sat and watched the *Sartoris* burn in dry dock, knowing one of your friends had set it off. When the Brentons' barn was burned, I never let on that I knew the name of the person involved—your companion, Chapin Piper! I've held my silence long enough."

His eyebrows rose in astonishment at the vehemence of her tirade. "So the battle lines are drawn. What will you do now, Bethany? Match me blow for blow?"

"Don't be ridiculous," she spat. "But count on this. I'll no longer keep my convictions to myself. I intend to help the British to keep law and order here."

"Do you think," he wondered, elaborately casual as he lounged against the door frame, "that we two will manage to live together under such conditions?"

Her head snapped up. "What are you saying?"

"That I'm through pretending. This marriage was never meant to be in the first place. Lately it's become a sorry joke."

"Are—are you leaving?"

His laughter lashed out, stinging her. "There's the irony in it. I'm forbidden to leave. I belong to your father because of the indenture and to you because of Colonel Chason's mandate. Unless, of course, one of two things happens. I could simply steal off in the night like a runaway slave, or the Americans could win this war and your father would be forced to give me up along with everything else he's gained by exploiting people."

His statement found a region of her mind that such reasoning had never touched before. How was it that in all the hours she'd spent trying to understand Ashton's commitment, she had never considered that his motives had to do with more than the independence of a new nation?

"Did you never think about that, Bethany?" He must have seen the transformation from anger to confusion in her face, for his voice had lost its harsh edge. "Did you never consider what independence from England would mean to us?"

"No." The faint whisper shuddered from her.

"You might consider it, then. You might consider your son, and his sons to come. And decide whether 'tis worth the price of your loyalty."

He left her leaning her forehead on the door, her teeth biting her lip to hold in a flood of weeping.

The Liberty Tree ornament was a cold presence against Ashton's chest as he rode homeward. The Committee members, startled out of their sleep, had made much of his recovery of the charter. He had accepted the silver amulet, which Samuel Ward of Westerly had promised to the man who recovered the document.

Ashton thrust the incident from his mind as he stabled Corsair and trudged up to the cottage. His reputation for subversive activities was growing, but he took no pride in that fact. Instead he thought of Bethany. And wondered anew at the murderous rage that had seized him on discovering her attempt to take back the charter.

That piece of paper had nothing to do with his reaction. No, his anger had sprung from the gut-twisting sensation of a trust betrayed. He had been a fool to hope she might someday support his cause. Instead, she clung to her Loyalist ideals. She was helping strengthen the ties that bound Ashton to her father.

Heaving a discontented sigh, he stepped inside the house, which smelled of wood smoke and the herbs and apple slices Bethany had hung to dry from the rafters. As he stood at the bedside and stared down at her beautiful face, the smooth cheeks marred by the salty ghosts of tears, he wondered how she always managed to appear so innocent, so guileless. Even when lying, she managed to sound earnest.

Despite all that had happened, the sight of her, softly sleeping, lips parted to invite the attention of his mouth in a way he found hard to resist, made him long to pluck a single perfect star from the dawn sky and lay it at her feet.

Why? he wondered feverishly. Why did he feel this way about a woman who had maneuvered him into a marriage he did not want and fought his efforts to break free of the empire he did not support? Sifting through a confusion of disquieting emotions, he discovered one sentiment he could understand.

He respected Bethany. Respected her stubborn pride, her misplaced but dogged loyalty.

When he lowered himself beside her, cupping her body against his, she turned to him in sleep in a way that pride prevented her from doing when awake.

The flame of patriot fervor ignited by the Declaration of Independence burned unsteadily as the year drew to a close.

The fire of rebellion wavered when Pieter Haas, Goody's nephew, limped home to Newport to announce that the beaten Continental Army was evacuating Long Island. Admiral Richard "Black Dick" Howe's transport decks were thick with the blue uniforms and miter-shaped brass helmets of regiments hired by the Crown from the Duchy of Brunswick in Germany.

The flame of liberty weakened still further when Peggy Lillibridge had a letter from her brother in Fort Ticonderoga reporting that the American flotilla on Lake Champlain had been smashed down to the last bateau.

Slowly, inexorably, the British were pounding away at the brash American resistance, sending foraging parties out into the countryside, radiating like a deadly web, gobbling up American depots and supplies.

Although Bethany nurtured a quiet hope of the British getting matters in hand, she was chilled by the evidence of conflict trickling into Newport. Men returned wounded, sick, near to starving, with tales of wartime atrocities. Yet these ordinary-men-turned-soldiers remained steadfast in their commitment to independence.

For, despite the crushing defeats, the heartless marches, the endless discomfort of any army on the run, changes were taking place. Rhode Island's hero, Nathaniel Greene, led a Virginia division into action. Britain's "quarreling children" no longer balked at marching under the flag of a man from another town.

When he was not riding to some secret assignation or tending the horses, Ashton was a quiet, thoughtful presence in the cottage. The eyes behind his spectacles were expressionless as he wrote in his journal. Although he and Bethany reached a shaky truce over the matter of the charter, his silences grew longer, his smiles became less frequent. He ate less and worried more; tension filled every moment.

One evening in December she had just finished steaming the best pudding she had ever prepared. Henry, who moved at will in his two-wheeled standing stool, was by turns deviling the infinitely patient Gladstone and studying the fire screen as if weighing the possibilities of what might happen should he explore the forbidden wonder.

Using a pair of iron tongs, she lifted the pudding from the Dutch oven, where it had been steaming for hours. Setting it on a tin plate, she peeled away the gauze wrapping, inhaling curls of fragrant steam. A slow smile crept across her face. The pudding was a masterpiece of molasses and egg and flour and currants, redolent of ginger root from Goody Haas's collection.

"Not a bad piece of work at all," she remarked cheerfully. Ashton, absorbed by his writing, seemed not to hear. She crossed the keeping room and scooped up Henry, who began to wail at being interrupted in his gleeful tugging of Gladstone's ears.

The noise startled Ashton into crushing the point of his quill. "God's blood." He snatched the spectacles from his face. "Must you make that child fret so?"

She pursed her lips and began methodically securing the howling baby onto his mammy board and tucking a bib beneath his chin in readiness for feeding. "'Tis time for him to eat," she called over the wailing of the child.

Ashton glowered. "Doesn't appear to have much of an appetite."

She bit back a retort. "Come to the table, Ashton. The pudding's getting cold."

He stood, but he didn't come to the table. Instead, he yanked his greatcoat from a peg by the door. "I don't feel so hungry either. I'm going to check on the horses. Lately Barnaby has made a habit of leaving stalls unlatched."

He was gone in a swirl of wool and cold wind, his exit leaving a void of angry silence. Bethany glared at the door for a long moment, shivered in the lingering chill, and turned to the baby, who watched her with wide, milk-blue eyes.

Seating herself in front of Henry, she took up a pewter porringer and began spooning rye cereal into the tiny red mouth.

"Papa doesn't know what he's missing," she told the child. "I worked all day on that infernal pudding and he refuses even to taste it."

Henry responded by puffing up his cheeks and ejecting the last mouthful of porridge. She wiped it from his chin and poked in another bite.

"One would think each failure of the patriots was his personal defeat," she went on, "for all he's been slogging around like Atlas beneath the weight of the world." A spoonful of porridge plopped onto the floor en route to Henry's mouth.

"Drat," she said. The baby made an impatient noise, so she didn't pause to clean it; Gladstone ambled over and gamely made short work of the spill.

"Honestly," she said, offering another spoonful to Henry, "your papa seems to have decided to take on the entire British Empire. . . ."

Outside the cottage, Ashton paused. Through the window, divided into four glowing and frosted squares, he could see Bethany feeding the baby. Her hands worked methodically, but her face was animated as she spoke. He doubted her conversation had anything to do with the merits of rye cereal. Unlike Carrie and that harpy Miss Primrose, Bethany didn't indulge in meaningless baby talk.

Tension, which had found a knotty home in his shoulders, seemed to flow away as he stood in the cold, surrounded by the sharp, barren smells of the dying year, and continued to watch as if mesmerized. He felt the unexpected tug of a grin at the corners of his mouth. Lately she had made little Henry her confidant, heedless of the absurdity of pouring her heart out to the child. At the moment she was probably giving Ashton a verbal flaying on the matter of his shortness of temper.

A flaying richly deserved, he conceded. Little heartening news had sped to the Committee of late. And the last bit, like a frigid roar of wind, was the most chilling of all.

The British were coming to Newport. They were coming, and there were not enough fighting men in the area to mount even a puny resistance.

His sigh was a small drifting cloud against the window. The next few days would be trying. As hopeless as the situation seemed, he and the other patriots could not sit still and let Newport fall. In the morning he and Chapin were sailing to Point Judith to reconnoitre the occupying force. Bethany would ask all the usual questions. He would have to tell her all the usual lies.

He went back inside, his spirits no higher that when he had left, but all the anger gone from him. As he removed his greatcoat, he saw Bethany's narrow back stiffen and recalled how he had stalked out on her as if she were the one responsible for all his troubles.

Remorse gripped him and held fast. Nothing could be further from the truth. Despite their political differences, Bethany worked hard to make life agreeable for him. The rich gingery smell of her pudding hung in the air, and he remembered how proud she was of her cooking.

He walked to the table and sat down, discerning pain and anger in her face. Gently he pried the baby's spoon from her hand.

"Let me, love."

Although her surprised gaze flew to him, she said nothing, only sat back and watched as he spooned the last bites of porridge into Henry's mouth. Then he lifted the baby from the mammy board and cradled him in the crook of his arm, taking him to the settle in front of the hearth.

He had put the baby to sleep countless times before. He enjoyed the quiet moments, enjoyed watching the child's eyes grow heavy-lidded. Yet tonight he studied Henry more closely than usual, gazing into the clear eyes, emotion shuddered through him. The bond between them was strong, their two souls knit in some forceful, mystical way. Sinclair Winslow's vague threat made Henry, blinking slowly with contentment, all the more precious to Ashton.

Something in that wide blue gaze stirred Ashton, knocking on a door of his mind until he could resist no more. He allowed the door to open, slightly at first and then cracking wide.

He felt himself begin to shake. He knew this child's blue eyes. He knew the shape of the mouth and the motion of the tiny fingers curling into the wispy golden hair. He knew the form of the ears, the set of the chin.

He saw them every time he looked into a mirror.

Against everything he had heard and seen since the day he had married Bethany, he finally admitted the truth. He sat pale and shaking with a hard lump of emotion in his throat until his son—*his son*—drifted into a secure cocoon of sleep. Gently he put the baby to bed.

His legs felt wooden as he came to stand before Bethany, laying his hand along her cheek and staring into eyes that searched his soul like a barber's probe.

"He's mine." Ashton's voice cracked on the admission.

A smile trembled at the corners of her mouth as she stood up. "So I've said."

He tried then to imagine the depths of the suffering he had inflicted on her. She had said so; she had sworn in anger and tears and frustration that she had come to this marriage a virgin, only to encounter the cold wall of his disbelief. She had lied, but to the military court, not to him.

"Bethany, can you forgive me for doubting you?"

"I'm not sure what you mean by that. If you mean I should simply say, 'Of course I forgive you, darling, think nothing of it,' then the answer is no."

He drew in a breath that seared his throat. What he had put her through was not so trivial a thing as a forgotten birthday or tracking mud on her clean floor. He had doubted everything she had ever said to him.

"But," she went on softly, breaking in on his thoughts, "if you're asking me to accept you, to live with what has gone before, then the answer is yes."

Relief burst within him, sending warmth to every cell of his body and soul. He kissed her long and hard and gratefully.

She warmed to him, her lips softening beneath his, her hands gliding over his back. In a single grand sweep, he lifted her, carried her to the bed, and made love to her. His every touch on her silken flesh was a reverence; his every kiss held the healing balm of understanding.

An act that had been sheer physical splendor now became a celebration of emotional release. Hands that formerly gave pleasure now gave something more precious, the tender understanding that had, until this moment, eluded their lovemaking.

Bethany was filled with a completeness she had never felt with Ashton before. All he had taught her of physical love paled against the panorama of color and sensation she experienced in his arms now.

She did not ask why he had realized the truth now, long after she had ceased trying to convince him Henry was his son. That didn't matter. A new world opened up to her that night, a world that before had only existed in her imagination. It was a universe of texture and light and exquisite, scorching intimacy.

Only when she felt herself so full of him that she was on the brink of tears did she realize how much bitterness she had harbored. Now the bitterness was gone with a sigh, replaced by shuddering splendor.

He smiled down at her astonished face as she lay recovering from a sensual assault that left her breathless. "I take it," he murmured, nuzzling her earlobe, "you have decided to accept me, love."

She blinked slowly, dragging her lashes over her flushed cheeks. "You were so sure I was telling the truth at your trial."

"I was. Woman, you rushed to me at the ferry, babbling in distress about Tanner, and you were ill—"

"Seasick. If you had given me half a chance, I would have told you the reason I was so upset that morning. Father had just informed me I was to marry Dorian."

A look of pain twisted his mouth. "Then you should have run to him."

"I wanted nothing to do with him. I've always run to you, Ashton. Haven't you noticed that about me?"

"You'd been keeping company with Tanner for weeks. A proposal was inevitable under those circumstances."

The blush began to smart her cheeks. "The only reason I entertained him at all was to get your attention, Ashton." She could barely meet his eyes. "I never knew where my foolishness would lead."

"Why the devil would you want to do a thing like that?" He nipped at the flesh below her ear. "Didn't you realize you were very much in my attention?"

"You made a point of avoiding me."

"'Twas easier to sidestep you in the stables than it was to drive you from my thoughts."

She sat up, gripping the quilts to her chest. "Really?"

"Aye. Day and night." His hand dipped inside the quilt. "Especially at night."

A smile of deep satisfaction curved her lips, and the sensation of feminine power rippling through her made her feel mature beyond her years. "I see," she drawled, her voice low.

Laughter rumbled from him. "Brat," he said, plucking the quilt away from her. "Come here."

She sighed as she found herself gathered into his arms, her heart enfolded at last into his safekeeping.

As the chill fingers of dawn slid into the dimness of the cottage through the frost-clouded window, Ashton smiled down at his sleeping son. Unbidden, Sinclair's angry promise to take the boy crept into his thoughts. Winslow's influence was not to be scoffed at, but did he possess the power to wrest the boy from his own father? Or did Winslow mean a more insidious revenge, using his wealth and the indenture to one day seduce Henry into his influence?

Ashton didn't know, and he disliked the dark feeling of apprehension that gripped him. The dangerous protector within him was roused. He feared not for himself, nor even for the boy, but for Sinclair Winslow, if Sinclair was foolish enough to try to make good his threat.

Beside him Bethany stirred. She gave off a sweet, sleepy fragrance of jasmine and warmth and the less tangible scent of their love. Trying to shrug the black thoughts away, he leaned down and awakened her with a kiss.

"I have to go away for a few days, love." Although he spoke gently, he felt the jolt of her dismay like a physical pain. Hazel eyes that had gone soft at his kiss grew troubled.

"Where?" she whispered.

"Don't ask, pet. Please."

She looked away. "Last night I thought we had reached an understanding. Apparently I was wrong."

"We're closer now than we've ever been. But there are some things I can't share with you."

"Because you don't trust me."

He smoothed a lock of hair that had drifted over her brow. "If the British suspected you were privy to the things I do, both you and our son would be in danger."

She was troubled still, but when she lifted her arms and twined them sweetly around his neck, he felt her capitulation.

Their farewell was a brutal wrench after the new intimacy they had discovered. He held his son, kissing the soft down of the baby's head and the cheek sweet with milk.

Then he took Bethany in his arms, laying his mouth upon hers with a probing intimacy as if to memorize the shape of her lips. Awash with regret at leaving them, he shouldered a well-provisioned knapsack and trudged down to the wharf to meet Chapin and embark on a desperate errand.

16

Frigid dawn crept over the ice-capped rocks of Point Judith on the second day of the vigil. The jut of land, covered with dead salt grass and wild mulberry, was in the far southern corner of the mainland, affording a view of the roiling Atlantic. Ashton crouched in the frost-rimed grasses at the shore, set his back against a vertical upthrust of rock, and flexed his fingers to remind the blood to flow to their tips. Wordlessly he passed a flask of rum to Chapin, who took a long draw and passed it back.

"What's that?" Chapin's breath puffed white as it mingled with the chill air.

Ashton squinted at the horizon, not really expecting to see anything. If nothing else, his experience as a patriot agent had schooled him in patience. Younger, and newer to the task, Chapin was given to restlessness.

But this time the young man's keen eyes had served him well. A line of ships, their dark hulls riding the swells beneath full sails, was approaching. As they watched the flotilla, Ashton and Chapin shared a few biscuits and a wedge of cheese and warmed themselves with more rum. The ships moved ever closer, but still not close enough to discern their colors. Hardy seabirds dove into the sinfully cold ocean after their prey, the winter wind soughed through the salt grass, and the moments wore tensely on.

Finally the first tall frigate swept close enough to see. British colors flew from the mainmast, snapping arrogantly in the wind. Behind the flagship glided the rest of the fleet, pushing relentlessly toward Aquidneck Island.

Betrayal and frustration engulfed Ashton. It was not enough that Wallace had choked off Newport's trade and stolen the better part of the town's wealth; now the British meant to make their possession of the city complete.

He jumped up and stretched the stiffness from his limbs. "Can we outrun them?"

"Must you ask?" Chapin led the way to his sloop.

Ashton grinned at Chapin's pride in his sailsmanship. The pride was well-founded; as a lifelong island resident, Chapin was an adept pilot. Yet as they cast off into the curling gray surf, the youth sent a troubled glance at the oncoming fleet.

"Plenty of Redcoats there," he remarked.

"If we make it back in time, there's a chance we can mount a resistance."

"And if we don't?"

"The British will occupy Newport."

Although Dorian Tanner's experienced eye wandered over the red-haired wench with lusty appreciation as they spoke together in the main hall of Seastone, he found her transparent admiration of his rank and figure almost laughable. The half-starved look she laid on him evoked pity more than preening. And the way she devoured the rare chocolates he plied her with told him she would be as malleable as lead in his expert hand.

"So you are Ashton Markham's sister," he ventured. "Pity the man doesn't share your comeliness and common sense."

Carrie's blush was not genuine, but Dorian didn't care. "Can you imagine? He's married to one of the wealthiest girls in Newport and won't lift a finger to claim her portion. Instead he thinks to better his lot by fooling with codes and invisible ink and riding courier for the rebels."

"It all sounds terrifically exciting."

She wrinkled her nose. "He's probably freezing to death by now."

"What do you mean, dear?" Dorian slipped a coin into her apron pocket.

She beamed. "Yesterday he sailed off with that no-account Chapin Piper. Said he was going fishing, but I know better."

God, he thought, the chit was a veritable fountain of information. He smiled charmingly. Trapping the scoundrel was going to be easy. "Miss Markham, your brother is flirting too closely with danger. You had best let me help before he gets in real trouble with the authorities." Aye, that was it, play the local militia, growing friendly with the populace.

She frowned and was silent for a long time. Dorian smiled and tipped her chin up with a gentle finger. With his other hand, he dropped another coin into her apron pocket, where it clinked against the first. "I prize loyalty in a lady, my dear."

"He . . . keeps a journal," she said at last.

Dorian deflated. "I don't imagine his wife would be inclined to show it to me."

"Bethany's taken the baby to call on Miss Primrose. Do you think, Captain Tanner, that we would be terribly improper to—"

"Say no more, my dear. 'Tis for the greater good, you might say."

*   *   *

"Your sails had wings," Ashton declared to Chapin. "I'll wager we made the crossing from Point Judith in record time."

"We've plenty of time to carry the news to the Committee. The Redcoats won't find Newport such an easy mark after all."

They stood on the dock, their backs turned from the harbor as they bent over the sloop, busily mooring the boat at a wharf that had been deserted due to Wallace's incessant pilfering.

Ashton lifted a dripping creel of fish. "Here's a bonus for our trouble." He laughed, feeling confident and eager to get home to Bethany.

But when he turned, his smile faded. Before him stood Captain Dorian Tanner, flanked by six armed military guards.

"In the name of the king, I arrest you." Tanner's words were a chilling echo of Colonel Chason's men in Bristol. "Come along, both of you." As he spoke, one of the guards deftly sliced through the mooring of the sloop with a sword, setting the craft adrift.

Chapin hurled himself at the soldiers, trying to break through the wall they had formed. Steel flashed and Chapin yelped in pain.

His blood pounding with rage, Ashton swung the creel in a vicious arc at the officer, catching him on the side of the head. The force of the blow sent Tanner sprawling to the dock.

Ashton had little time to savor his satisfaction at the sight of the Redcoat's fish-slimed face. As Chapin sank, moaning and clutching at a blossom of blood below his ear, Ashton's consciousness splintered into a thousand bright lights of agony beneath the crushing blow of a rifle butt.

And on December seventh, in the folds of a dark gray

dusk, the British fleet slid unresisted into Newport, and eight thousand red-frocked troops settled in for a long occupation.

William Bugston closed the drapes of his room in the Newport town house and sent his manservant away. As he sat down to await his guest, his sharp eyes took in the new furnishings with satisfaction.

The antique French desk with its tooled leather top was a handsome addition, as was the delicate matching fruitwood chair. Over the mantel hung a whimsical Watteau painting, handily obtained from a failing Newport shipper. A tall wood and glass case from London boasted a priceless collection of Limoges china.

William smiled. People used to call Bug Willy a ne'er-do-well, a wharfside idler, but he had proven them all wrong. Months ago he had abandoned his leadership of the patriot mob, finding no profit in harassing the Tories. Now, with a complete absence of scruples, Willy straddled the fence between the two factions. Wartime shortages had made profiteering extremely lucrative.

A discreet knock stirred the silence of the illegally elegant room. Willy rose, crossed to the door, and drew his guest inside. In civilian clothes and a modest wig, Tanner hardly resembled a decorated British officer. The garb lent him anonymity; Willy knew well why he sought that trait.

Tanner accepted a crystal goblet of Madeira. "Are we quite alone?"

"Aye, Cap—er, Mr. Tanner. Just like you asked."

"Then let us get to the business at hand. I went through no little amount of searching to find someone who could provide me with the service I require."

"You got the right man. But I hope you know that if I hadn't wanted you to find me, you wouldn't have."

Tanner took a drink of his Madeira and narrowed his

gaze at his host. They were two of a kind, Willy thought, both willing to set aside scruples for the sake of advancing their own interests.

Tanner said, "I want you to stage a profiteer raid."

"Christ, Mr. Tanner, the British are in complete authority here, as of yesterday. They're not buying from the profiteers now. They've no need."

"You don't understand, Mr. Bugston. I mean for this to look like a *patriot* raid. On Thursday next, General Clinton will reduce his forces by half. It will seem natural for the patriots to grow bold."

Willy lifted a black eyebrow. "I'm surprised to hear the request from a British officer."

"I have my reasons."

Willy rubbed a hand over his chin. "It's risky. And it'll cost you. Just what do you want, Tanner?"

"A raid on the Winslow property called Seastone. Take the usual valuables and livestock, whatever else you can sell. And make it vicious, Bugston. That's your specialty. Leave the main house intact, but burn some of the outbuildings. I want the rebels to look like the savages they are." He smiled coldly. "I've even arranged for a pair of culprits to take the blame."

Bethany hummed as she worked in the kitchen, setting a pot of dried apples to stew beneath a sprinkling of cinnamon and maple sugar. Wiping her hands on her apron, she looked into the keeping room. Henry and Gladstone lay on the braided rug, a tangle of sweater-clad limbs and silky fur, fast asleep.

Smiling, she shook her head. "Fat lot of company you two are," she told them. "I'll be glad when your father gets home." Her smile softened and her eyes grew wistful. Ashton had been gone for four days. When had an eternity ever stretched so long?

She hugged herself, barely able to wait. Never had she looked forward to his return as she did now. Everything would be different now. At last Ashton understood why she had lied at his trial. Soon, very soon, he would know that she loved him.

The thought sang through her veins, and her feet traced a little dance of joy on the puncheon floor. Of course she had told him so, right from the start, on the very night of their ill-fated marriage. But he had not believed her.

In truth, what she had felt then had none of the depth and complexity of her emotions now. A year and a half ago she had been a naive girl, her head so full of romantic notions there had not been room for serious thought.

Back then she had seen Ashton as a storybook prince, the epitome of masculine perfection. In the darker moments of their marriage she had realized her husband was stubborn and temperamental, a far cry from the girlish fantasy she had created. Now she knew him as he was: human and fallible and endearingly flawed. And she loved him with the heart of a mature woman. She had drawn a mantle of love over his imperfections.

This new love burned like a bright star within her. It burned so brightly that Ashton could not fail to see it now.

She glanced out the window at the winter-white day. Hurry, love, she silently urged. Hurry home to me.

As she looked out, a figure came into view on the path to the cottage. Her smile became rueful. She did not begrudge her father his visits to see Henry, but they never managed more than a few minutes together without arguing about Ashton.

As she opened the door for him, Sinclair placed a fatherly kiss on her brow. Seeing Henry asleep, he smiled indulgently.

"Worn himself out, has he?" He looked askance at Gladstone. "Must you let him loll about on the floor with that disreputable creature, Bethany?"

"They're the best of friends."

"Aye, I suppose so. The lad's in more danger from his father than from the dog."

She drew a cup of cider from the keg at the sideboard and handed the drink to Sinclair. "Don't start. I'll not listen to you criticize Ashton."

"By God, the man's in thick with the rebels! Lawless pirates! Smuggling and defrauding the king of his rightful duties."

"Captain Wallace has chased every vessel from the bay, Father. If anyone is defrauding the Crown, 'tis he."

"Patriots." Sinclair glowered into his cider mug. "Drabbing little knot of thieves and transports. What business have they in Newport?"

"Loyalists are fewer than you imagine," she said patiently.

He touched his chest, then gestured around the cottage. "Can you not see what Ashton Markham has made you?"

"He has made me happy." *As I never was with you, Father.* "But you" —she loosed a bitter laugh— "ah, you have made me a bondsman's wife."

"I couldn't stand to lose you, daughter." There was a curious catch in his voice.

"Let Ashton go, Father," she pleaded. "You know he was never meant to be a servant."

He glanced at the sleeping child on the rug. "Don't you see, Bethany? Were he free to leave Seastone, he would take you and Henry God knows where. The frontier, perhaps. Here, at least, I know you're safe."

"Do you realize how selfish that sounds, Father?"

"I'm a selfish old man." His hand sought his chest again, and he made a massaging motion with his fingers. "Old and stubborn," he said.

The baby awoke and crowed with delight at the sight of his grandfather. In moments the lad was being dandled on Sinclair's knee and toying with his brass buttons.

Watching them, Bethany felt a surge of bittersweet love. Her father remained immovable on the point of Ashton's indenture, but the adoration he showered on little Henry endeared him to her.

"Don't hate Ashton," she said as Sinclair made ready to leave. "Would you think more of him if he had no ambition?"

"There is much to admire in your husband," Sinclair admitted. "Unfortunately, there is much to despise. Damn it, girl, the man is a menace!"

"As are all opposing men in wartime."

Sinclair grabbed his greatcoat. "I can only hope the presence of General Clinton's forces will curtail Ashton's activities." He paused and, in a rare gesture of affection, touched her cheek. "I can see one thing, my daughter. I can see that you love him."

She nuzzled her cheek against the warmth of her father's palm. There had been too few of such touches between them.

"Good-bye, Father."

The urgent whine of a dog brought Bethany awake to the chill gloom of the December night. She pushed herself up on her elbows, her eyes automatically seeking Henry. Finding him asleep, she scowled irritably at Gladstone. The spaniel crossed to the door, nails clicking over the puncheons, and whined again, sniffing at a crack at the bottom of the door.

With a longing glance at her warm bed, she slipped her arms into the sleeves of her wrapper and pushed her feet into her shoes. She moved the frantic dog aside and opened the door.

And saw, high above the winter-bare tops of the Dutch elms surrounding the summerhouse, a faint orange glow shimmering with ghostly translucence against the night sky.

Gladstone scampered outside. Bethany fled back to the bedroom and scooped little Henry up from his bed, tucking a shawl around him and tethering another around herself. The baby whimpered, then settled onto her shoulder. Outside, Gladstone's yelps had risen to furious barking.

At the door, Bethany was greeted by four men smelling of rum, their faces concealed by scarves.

"Who are you?" Her voice faltered over the words, and the distant fire sounded like thunder.

"As if we'd tell you, you bleeding Tory." The man stepped into the cottage.

Her scream streaked through the night air. Hauling the baby closer, she hooked her foot around the edge of the door and tried to slam it shut. She tried to scream again. A hand that reeked of pine tar choked off the sound. The baby, now wailing, prevented her from fighting off her attackers. She heard distant shouts, horses whinnying, the thud of running feet, the low rumble of the fire. In some unseen part of the yard Gladstone growled and snapped, then fell abruptly silent.

Bethany flung her head from side to side in frantic denial, but the brutal hands held her face. Amid a scuffle of laughing, cursing, rank-smelling men, she was dragged outside.

"Comely little piece," one of the ruffians grunted as his hands traced the outline of her form. "Let's have a go at her before—"

"None of that, now," another said, shoving her down the path. "We've orders not to harm this one, nor the brat."

She twisted and struggled and wrenched her head around in time to see two dark shapes circling the cottage. A smoking torch touched the shingles, igniting a flame. She made a desperate sound against her captor's hand, but the man only grinned.

"Shut the brat up," he ordered, removing his hand, "or I'll do it myself."

She jiggled the baby and nestled him against her bosom. His screams dissipated into distressed sobs.

Ahead loomed the granary, its door yawning wide and dark. Rough hands pushed her inside.

"Please." Her voice was ragged, and her breath came in sharp, throat-searing gasps. The door slammed shut. She heard the latch rattling into place. She stumbled back against a hayrick, surrounded by unrelieved darkness and the pungent-sweet aroma of dry oats and hay.

Clutching Henry close until he quieted, she leaned, dazed, against the hayrick and listened as the nightmare outside continued. Ugly curses, the squeals of panicked horses, the crackle of fire . . . and the scent of woodsmoke.

Sinking to the packed-earth floor of the granary, Bethany cradled the baby, seeking comfort in the warmth of her son. She tried to make sense of the nightmare, but the shock had numbed her. The shock of war.

War was upon the colonies. Tonight war had touched her.

17

With a chill of terror Bethany gathered the sleeping baby closer.

A loud thunk hit the door to the granary and she pressed herself against the far wall, wondering if the raiders, having despoiled the manor and stables, would now turn their attention to her.

The door swung open. The gray forebear of dawn outlined a large shape in cocked hat and jutting epaulets.

"Bethany?"

"Dorian!" Her voice cracked; her throat was raw from the hours she had spent calling desperately for help. "Thank God you've come. Is everyone all right?"

He took her by the shoulders and brought her to her feet. She wobbled on legs that felt like calf's foot jelly and leaned against him.

He cradled her hand in his. "You're cold as ice," he murmured, leading her out of the granary.

"But the others . . ." Her heart froze at the sight that greeted her. To her right were the stables—every door ajar, every stall empty. Straight ahead was the stone-end cottage that had been her home.

Blackened stonework stood a bleak vigil over the charred remains of the cottage. Here and there, thready wisps of smoke reached to the dawn sky, climbing above the burned rubble of all she and Ashton had possessed.

Gladstone's body lay lifeless and blood-soaked in the yard. Bethany cried out and tried to break away from Dorian, but he held her fast.

"Who did this monstrous thing?" she whispered.

"Patriots." His voice was hard with outrage. "I've sent out patrol; already most of the livestock was found awaiting transport to Warwick Neck."

She shuddered. A killing rage seized her. Patriots! No doubt the very scum responsible for Miss Abigail's drumhead trial.

As if he had read the ire in her face, Dorian gave her shoulders a squeeze. "You'll have your retribution, dear. I promise you that."

She gazed at Gladstone. "That's not what I want."

"Ah, Bethany, there's nothing you can do for the poor little beast now. Come away, dear. Your mother needs you."

The raiders had ransacked the manor house. Dorian led her through a confusion of overturned furniture and shattered glass. In the main hall, the servants were crying and clutching at each other and wringing their hands.

"The damage looks worse than it actually is," Dorian explained. "My men arrived in time to scare off the cursed rebels before they had a chance to set fire to the main house." He glanced at Carrie Markham, who was blowing her nose into a limp handkerchief. "Where is Mrs. Winslow?"

"Taken to her bed, sir." Carrie sniffed. "Your surgeon gave her a dose of laudanum to help her sleep."

"Where is my father?" Bethany asked.

Dorian turned her to face him, his features drawn taut. "My dear, I'm afraid the greatest shock is yet to come." He swallowed, and for a moment he did not look quite so handsome—only human. "Bethany, my dearest girl, your father's heart failed him last night. The shock of the raid was too much for him."

Woodenly, she placed Henry in Carrie's arms and trudged upstairs to her father's bedchamber. Here, too, furniture had been overturned, drawers rifled. Dudley, the cook, was clearing debris from around the big four-poster bed. His thin, mustached face pale, he picked up a well-oiled fowling piece, which had been smashed beyond repair.

"He tried, ma'am," Dudley said. "But there were too many of the rascals. In the end your father broke his gun, declaring no damned rebel would ever burn powder in it."

She forced herself to look at her father. Death had erased the irascible lines of his aristocratic face. His stock hung open; the usual sapphire stud he wore there was gone.

She sank to the bedside, her mind a turmoil of disjointed images and painful regrets. She and her father had never been close, but she had loved him. Henry had loved him. She squeezed her eyes shut and groped for words to express her grief.

A hand touched her lightly on the shoulder. She turned to see Carrie. "You'd best go down," the girl said. "They've caught the culprits. I'll take little Henry to my room."

Dashing the tears from her cheeks, Bethany walked to the top of the stairs. Icy hatred filled her. She paused to look at the men who had brought about her father's death.

In the dawn shadows below, Dorian and his three men struggled in the foyer with two rag-clad men. The reek of rum and unwashed bodies assaulted her senses as she descended. Curses filled the air. One of the captives wrenched away from the soldiers and lunged for freedom. Steel flashed; the man bellowed a final curse and fell against the door, his hands squeaking on its polished mahogany surface.

Bethany forced herself to look at the dead man. Lank hair framed a thin, lantern-jawed face—the face of Chapin Piper.

"No!" The other rebel's bellow tore through the tension-thick atmosphere. Recognition exploded within Bethany, The furious denial hit her like an arrow aimed dead at her heart.

Ashton.

Gripping the banister, she swayed, then stumbled down the stairs to her husband. "Deny it," she whispered, falling to her knees to beg him. "Deny that you are responsible for what happened here tonight. Speak, my love! Tell me you had nothing to do with this."

He looked at her for a moment, then raised burning eyes to Dorian. "I deny it," he said through his teeth, "but what good will that do?"

She struggled to her feet. "I have to know you are telling the truth, Ashton. Please—"

With a roar, he lunged at Dorian. It took all the men to subdue him, and he only quieted when the butt of a rifle knocked him unconscious.

The sound of boot heels clicking together in salute awakened Ashton.

"That will be all, private."

He sat up and his eyes sought the damp surface of his cell wall. Squinting through the gloom, he silently counted the marks he had dug on the brick with the edge of the manacle on his wrist. One, two, three . . . this was his fourth day in captivity.

Dorian Tanner entered the cell and closed the door behind him. Even the fact that he was manacled to the wall did not prevent Ashton from straining forward, filled with a rage so poisonous it shook him to the depths of his hate-blackened soul.

The chains stopped him short, biting into the abraded flesh of his wrists. The force of his movement snapped him back. His breath left him with a hiss as his back smashed against the wall.

Tanner's chuckle was as smooth as rich cream. "Patience, my friend." With a grimace he plucked a silk handkerchief from his sleeve and breathed discreetly into the fabric, showing his distaste for the rank odor of the cell.

"You supercilious son of a bitch," Ashton said.

Tanner shook his elaborately wigged head. "My, my, I was hoping a few days in the cold and wet down here would dampen your temper. Apparently the heat of rage has been keeping you warm. I should have dispensed with you as I did your friend."

Ashton's mind shrank from the image of Chapin Piper, dead at the hands of the Redcoats. Dead, before his youth had flowered into manhood. Dead, before he could savor the taste of liberty for which he had fought.

"So." Ashton expelled the word with disgusted loathing. "You can add murder to your list of accomplishments, Captain."

"Death to an enemy in wartime is not murder. He'd have hanged, anyway. He was a dangerous spy."

The only dangerous thing about Chapin was the lad's devotion to the cause of independence. Ashton felt a tearing pain in his gut. Finley . . . Now, Finley was a different turn altogether. How could he bear the death of his only son?

"Everything," Ashton vowed, his voice trembling with fury, "every single thing Chapin Piper suffered will be visited on you tenfold."

Dark laughter eddied from Tanner. "By whose hand, Markham? Certainly not yours. You see, you're about to hang."

This was no revelation to Ashton. He had never doubted his fate. From the moment he had turned on the wharf and seen Tanner standing there, he had known he would die. "Even a British military court won't be taken in by your idiotic scheme to implicate me in the raid on Seastone," he said.

Dorian drew forth a small packet with a flourish. "Every single act of treason you've ever committed is documented right here by your own hand. Also the treasonous acts of . . . let's see . . . ah, Samuel Ward, Benjamin Tallmadge, other operatives. . . ."

Ashton felt the color leave his face, and a chill crawled up his spine. "Where did you get that?"

Tanner's smile was a bright glitter of triumph in the gloom. "Where do you think?" He placed the journal and other materials back in the packet and patted it. "From your wife."

Ashton froze. Doggedly he contained his wild fury and forced logic to take hold. Somehow his private papers had found their way into Tanner's hands. But Bethany had not placed them there. She could not have.

He almost smiled at the idea that Tanner, for whatever cruel purpose, wished him to believe Bethany had betrayed him. She would never do that.

Because she loved him.

True, she had nearly gone mad with fury on seeing him the morning after the raid. But doubtless she had since realized that he had been gudgeoned by Tanner. The thought had sustained Ashton through the days of inhuman cold and gnawing hunger.

She had declared her love many times, but only on their last night together had the words penetrated his wall of distrust. She loved him, and now that he understood all she had done for him, he was free to love her.

A rueful smile turned up the corners of his mouth. There was still the small matter of his impending execution.

"No doubt, Captain, you thought your lie would reduce me to despair," Ashton said coolly, leaning against the wall.

"'Tis no lie. Why wouldn't your wife—an avowed Loyalist—wish death on the man who caused her father's death?"

"I'm sure she's realized the truth by now. Her first loyalty is to me." He remembered how bravely—if misguidedly—she had come to his aid at the trial in Bristol.

"She hates you now," Tanner said. "She's convinced you led the raid."

His insides grew as cold as the rest of him. "She'll know that for the goddamned lie it is."

Tanner's pruned eyebrows drifted upward. "She's not a fool, Markham. You have every motive to wish Sinclair Winslow dead. The man owned you. The two of you clashed over the colony charter. Sinclair threatened you with the loss of your son. And no one knows about your excursion to Point Judith. You have no possible alibi." The Redcoat laughed. "You look surprised, my friend. Sinclair told me all about the charter business. Just before he named me in his will as your son's trustee."

Two bodies were given up to their Maker at the Common Burying Ground at the end of Farewell Street. Bethany stood shivering with cold and grief and rage at the edge of her father's grave, her thoughts scattered due to a liberal dose of laudanum. She was surrounded by few people, for many had fled the increasingly dismal atmosphere of the war-ravaged city. Only days earlier, Newport's Loyalists had presented General Clinton with an oath of allegiance. Now they clustered around the grave site, murmuring their outrage at what Bethany's husband had done to her father.

She wanted to scream at them, to hurl a demand that they leave her alone with her ravaged heart and broken dreams. But she stood quiet and dry-eyed and becalmed by the opiate as she accepted condolences from all those who had scorned her for marrying Ashton Markham.

The Pierces and the Malbones and the Cranwicks consoled her with empty words. Keith Cranwick, with a simpering and scandalized Mabel Pierce on his arm, paused to speak. "The scoundrel hasn't but a day left to make his lame denials before the royal commission. After that he'll be sent to the devil, where he belongs."

Bethany blinked, her drugged mind unable to dredge up a response. She drew her face farther into her black mourning veil while her eyes sought her mother through its folds.

Lillian Winslow was, predictably, in her glory as the center of bereaved attention. She knew every subtle facet of funeral etiquette and played her role to perfection, her smile tremulous and beatific, her black-gloved hand daubing daintily at a tear.

Bethany turned away, scolding herself for her uncharitable thoughts. But she could not escape the realization that Lillian mourned not so much the death of her husband as the loss of a secure and lavish way of life.

Backing away from the scene, Bethany nearly collided with a cloaked figure behind her. "Careful there, sister," murmured a familiar voice.

She turned, awash with relief. "Harry!"

"Hush. There're enough Redcoats around to rig out a man-of-war. I can't risk being recognized." He took her by the elbow and steered her away from the mourners toward the black-wreathed coaches and chaises lining Farewell Street. They stopped beneath the sodden and dripping branches of an elm tree. Bethany's laudanum induced numbness began to give way to dull pain.

"Where's my little namesake?" Harry inquired.

"I left him with Carrie. How did you know to come, Harry?"

"I had an urgent message from Miss Primrose. Where is our intrepid schoolmistress now?"

Bethany nodded at a group of mourners at the far end of the burying ground, this one even smaller and less grandly turned out. "She's with Finley Piper."

"Tell me, Bethany." Harry's eyes probed hers through the dark veil.

"Patriots raided Seastone."

"That much I heard."

"Ashton led the raid."

Harry laughed, startling her. "You can't possibly believe that."

"I saw him, Harry. Don't you see? It all fits. He and Father were at loggerheads. Then Ashton left without explanation and was gone for several days. And who but he would instruct the raiders to leave Henry and me unharmed?" The tears came, burning and bitter on the pale skin of her cheeks. Harry held her briefly, then set her aside.

"I have to go, Bethany. We're attracting stares." He gave her hand a squeeze. She looked at him—really looked at him. He seemed tired. His hands were callused and rough in a way that told her he was not just keeping Mr. Hodgekiss's books in Bristol.

"Harry, are you well? And what of Felicia and little Margaret?"

"We're all fine. Don't worry."

"Father's will has already been read." She looked away.

He seemed to know what her silence meant. "He left me nothing."

"If you need anything, I'll be at home. At Seastone."

He looked left and right. "Yes, well . . ." Again he squeezed her hand. "You'll be all right, Bethany. You always are."

As she watched him walk away, she whispered, "No. Not ever again."

*   *   *

Bethany lingered at the burying ground after Sinclair's mourners had left. She approached the knot of silent, dark-clad people around Chapin's grave. In contrast to the gorgeous coffin Mr. Townsend had furnished for her father, Chapin was buried in a box of knotty pine.

Finley stood watching, his face vacant, his eyes shot through with the redness of drink. Strands of graying hair whipped unheeded around his face. Miss Abigail was a discreet and sympathetic presence at his side, solemn and resplendent in black velvet. Her tiny gloved hand held Finley's. To Bethany the gesture seemed the very essence of comfort.

Spying Bethany, Miss Abigail murmured something to Finley, who nodded distractedly. She hurried to Bethany and embraced her. "My dear girl, I'm so very sorry."

Bethany swallowed. "I find it hard to believe I'll bear this without losing my mind."

"I know, dear."

"Miss Abigail, how could he?"

"Are you so very sure the raid was Ashton's doing?"

Bethany nodded and, in a voice thready with pain, related all that had happened that night. "He is certain to be hanged." She shivered at her own words.

"You went to great lengths to save him from hanging once."

"But how can I live with the man responsible for my father's death? Besides, 'tis out of my hands. Ashton is to be tried tomorrow. Dorian says the sentence won't be delayed long after that."

"Bethany—" Miss Abigail's voice rose as if a thought had occurred to her, but then she stopped herself. "My dear, I must go. There is something I must do."

Dorian Tanner stood at the top of Easton's Beach, armed with golf clubs and genuine Caledonian balls generously given him by one of General Clinton's officers. He wanted to shout and dance through the streets of Newport, proclaiming his triumph before all the town's miserable inhabitants. But he held the impulse in check.

Instead he indulged in the quiet, gentlemanly pursuit of golf, lining up his drives with studied precision. But, oh, how sweet was his private celebration. As he mulled over his triumphs, he applied his exultant energy to the leather-clad balls near his feet.

His first drive was short, but he could not stop smiling. He now held all Seastone in trust for a puling infant who would not reach his majority for many years—if he did so at all. True, Sinclair had surprised him by entrusting Bethany with a good portion of the horse interests.

His second shot sliced to the right. But even that would soon cease to matter. In just days, the delectable Mrs. Markham would be a widow.

The third drive hooked to the left. By implicating her husband in the raid, he had left her vulnerable, searching for something stable in her life. Dorian had already won her trust by returning the "stolen" livestock to the stables. Bugston had commanded exorbitant rates, but the money was trifling compared to what Dorian stood to reap from Seastone.

By summer he intended to win her hand in marriage. And then Seastone would be wholly and undisputedly his.

The final shot was perfect, straight and true, finding the very heart of the distant green, a tribute to Dorian Tanner's skill.

Miss Abigail Primrose smiled grimly as she heard the lock on Captain Tanner's desk succumb to her skillful probing with the middling pin she wielded. The drawer slid open. Beneath its false bottom she found what she was looking for. A stack of evidence against the prisoner, Ashton Markham.

No qualms possessed the lady as, one by one, she tore the journal pages from the book and fed them to the fire. She hesitated at a particularly charming description of little Henry's first attempt at crawling, but doggedly burned that innocuous entry along with the rest. No trace of the journal must remain. She then burned the letters and pocketed the Liberty Tree medallion.

She checked the drawer again to see that she had left nothing behind. Deep in one corner, a small object glinted at her, a stud such as gentlemen sported in their cravats. The stone was a good-sized sapphire.

Ashton owned nothing so dear. Yet in the back of her mind she recalled seeing the object somewhere. Try as she might, Miss Abigail could not place it. Still, since Captain Tanner had seen fit to hide the jewel, there might be some significance to it. She tucked the stud into her apron pocket.

She frowned at the papers in the grate. The glowing embers burned the journal at a sluggish rate. To stave off her nervousness, she reviewed the steps she had taken to ensure Ashton's safety. General Clinton, in her debt for quartering his junior officers at the academy in New York, had been happy to oblige her request to disallow the testimony of Tanner on grounds of his interest in the estate of Seastone. Mortified by the violent murder of Chapin Piper, Clinton was preparing a stern reprimand for Tanner.

Ashton would not be hanged now that no evidence remained. He would be released, and then it was up to him to prove to Bethany that he'd had nothing to do with the raid.

Burning the documents was a crime against the empire Miss Abigail had served faithfully, but what was at stake was far more important. Bethany and Ashton needed another chance to live and love and forgive.

Miss Abigail prayed her actions would give them that chance. She stepped from the office in Banister House, suddenly eager to get back to Finley. He might be comforted when he heard what she had done for Ashton and for Chapin's memory. But when she reached the print shop, she found him too deep in his cups to appreciate her exploits.

"Ah, Finley." She went to him with outstretched arms. "Look at you. You're covered with ink."

"Recruiting broadsides," he said, then fell against her. "Abigail. God, Abby, I hurt."

She did not move away when he lurched against her, his hands soiling the bib and skirt of her apron with ink. She helped him to the stairs and into bed, then took off her ruined apron, forgetting the contents of her pockets as she added the garment to the rag pile.

Ashton spent a pain-filled moment surveying the charred rubble of the stone-end cottage that had been his home. Days in the frigid cell beneath the Colony House had reduced his clothing to mildewed tatters. A diet of stale beer and a gill of rice per day had robbed him of half a stone. Inactivity imposed by the chains shackling him to the wall had made his muscles slack from disuse. And the idea that Bethany had handed his letters and journals to Tanner had almost doused the tiny glimmer of hope within him that they might one day come to understand and forgive.

That was the bitterest blow of all. No matter that the evidence had mysteriously disappeared, much to the foul rage of Dorian Tanner. No matter that Sinclair Winslow had willed Ashton his freedom. There was no heady triumph in having cheated the hangman, because the new life that had been granted Ashton stretched like a bleak, endless winter before him.

Turning his ragged collar against the bitter wind, he trudged to the main house to confront his wife.

Bethany looked fragile and lovely as she sat in the downstairs parlor, her father's account ledgers lying forgotten in her lap. She was staring at the fire in the grate, which winked at her from behind an iron embossed with the king's arms. Her head was bowed. Neglected honey-gold hair spilled over her shoulders and caught the morning light glinting through the window.

Sweet Jesus, he thought, had the devil really contrived such an adorable guise?

She looked up, startled, at the sound of his footsteps on the parquet floor. Her eyes sent him a message of loathing so clear that Ashton imagined he could taste hatred in the tense air that hung between them.

"So they've set you free." Her voice was low and husky, much as it was when he inflamed her passion, but the hard edge of bitterness lent the sound a sharp bite.

"No thanks to you, pet. Your captain managed to lose the evidence you gave him."

"I?" The ledgers fell as she surged to her feet with a rustle of black silk, stirring a maddeningly familiar scent of jasmine and a wealth of unwelcome emotions in him. "I gave Dorian nothing."

He turned his filthy hands to her and applauded in a haughty imitation of an aristocratic theater patron. "Brava, love. A virtuoso performance. You're a superlative liar."

"I have no reason to lie to you. I no longer seek your favor." Her laugh sliced through the hatred-thick air. "Ah, I did squander a lot of tender emotion on you, trying to be a good wife even when you mistrusted me, thought I carried another man's babe in my belly. That starry-eyed girl is no more. You taught me to love, aye, and then you taught me to hate. They are two lessons I shall never, ever forget."

He felt something inside him grow very cold. She was right, the bit about the girl she had been and was no more. Standing before him was a woman he no longer knew, a woman who had been hurt, a woman who knew how to hate and inflict pain.

An overwhelming sense of loss enveloped him and propelled him across the room to her.

Arms in rank-smelling tatters enclosed the elegant silk-clad shape; lips that had tasted nothing but prisoner's fare for days now sampled the clean essence of her lips. He was compelled to search for what had existed between them, to probe until he found the sweet, sharp passion and that other deeper, sweeter thing he had fought against since the day he had married her.

For a brief moment her mouth was soft and open to his, sending pure desire rocketing through him. Then she wrenched away, her face a pale oval in the curtain of her unkempt hair.

"Don't touch me," she said.

"Bethany, you can't believe I had anything to do with the raid."

She pivoted sharply away from him. "The royal commission hasn't enough evidence to convict you, but I know what I saw. You may not have meant to do so much damage, but 'twas done. You may not have meant for my father to die, but he did."

"You would believe Tanner's lies over what I'm telling you?" His voice was rough with astonishment.

She turned back to level a bitter gaze at him. "'Twas you who taught me to doubt, to question. You believe only that which can be proven. I am that way now. I no longer have faith to accept your word."

Her speech was like a blow, leaving him breathless. "I take it you intend to stay here."

"I have no other home. And you?"

"I'll be boarding with Mrs. Milliken in town."

"To carry out more of your treasonous schemes."

He drilled a hard stare at her. "To be near my son. You can push me out of your life, Bethany, but not Henry's."

18

In London the year began on a hopeful note. A betting-book was opened at Brooks Club; the first wager was penned by Handsome Jack Burgoyne and Mr. Charles Fox. General Burgoyne bet fifty guineas that he would be home victorious from America by Christmas. Parlor strategists of the fashionable set envisioned the united forces of British, Hessian, and Tory setting themselves down as an anvil for the hammerblow of Sir William Howe, soon to launch an assault from New York.

In Newport the year began on a bleak note. Tory and patriot alike fled the besieged city. Long Wharf, once the scene of frenzied commerce, became the site of boarded-up storefronts and empty warehouses. Citizens scuttled to avoid the domineering red-frocked occupying force.

Churches and public buildings became crowded barracks; private homes and riding academies were commandeered by garrison troops. The mansions at the Point were overrun by soldiers. Corrupt commissaries and barrack masters robbed drovers and bilked farmers on requisitions of wagons, teams, and livestock.

Some citizens lacked the means to flee. The poor of the city remained—widows and their children, slaves manumitted because their owners could no longer afford to feed them, unemployed dockworkers, and their kin. These unfortunates huddled against the privations of war, burning furniture and even houses for fuel because the wood purveyors' boats had left the bay to seek less hostile marketplaces. Children took to begging in the streets and pandering to the swaggering, well-fed soldiers in hopes of garnering a bread crust or soup bone.

These were the children Bethany invited into her home, to warm themselves in front of the big library fire while she guided them in their lessons and filled their bellies with Dudley's cooking. The charity school was as much a product of the turmoil she had suffered as it was of her desire to succor the victims of war.

Her new endeavor sparked controversy in the household. Carrie Markham fussed and worried that the urchins would pilfer the valuables, most of which Captain Tanner had recovered. Lillian was appalled at the idea of opening her home to the poor, and wrung her hands, despairing of her reputation. Dorian, who as Henry's trustee had set himself up as master of the household, stopped just short of ordering Bethany to cease her tutelage.

But she would not be swayed, not by the scandalized gossip circulating about her and the husband she had shut out of her life, nor by the wagging tongues wondering about her devotion to the children.

Teaching gave direction to her shattered life. When a child blessed her with a smile after reading a passage from the *New England Primer* she forgot just for a moment her own unhappiness. When small, grubby fingers clasped her hand, she forgot just for a moment how much she missed Ashton's touch. Childish laughter chased away, if only for a moment, the mournful stillness of the household.

One bleak January day she was sending her small class

back to town, bending to tie Hittie Slocum's muffler more snugly, helping Jimmy Milliken to button his coat, giving them both a parcel of food to take home. Beaming, Jimmy clutched under his arm a brand-new edition of *Enteck's New Spelling Dictionary*. Miss Abigail had procured the book, and Bethany had not dared to ask what the lady had gone through to get it. Aware only that new books were rare in these lean times, Jimmy grinned from ear to ear, then scampered off after his schoolmates.

Bethany looked up to see Ashton's broad form filling the doorway. Very briefly an indulgent light shone in his eyes as he watched the boy leave. But just as quickly indulgence gave way to searing anger.

Now what? she wondered, trying to effect a calmness she did not feel. She stepped behind the desk and brought her hands to her bosom in an unconscious protective gesture. The hurt and anger flying between them were as fresh and sharp and new wounds.

Despite the icy fury in Ashton's eyes, he exuded a powerful magic as he strode into the room and snatched off his hat, looking as lean and fit as a wolf on the hunt. He dug into his pocket and produced a newspaper, slamming it down on the Goddard desk so hard that Bethany jumped.

"No doubt you'll soon have your little charges reading this," he snapped.

Forcing her hands to remain steady, she opened the paper. It was the first copy of the *Gazette*, a journal put out by the Loyalist, John Howe. She should have been glad to see the seditious *Mercury* replaced by a Tory mouthpiece, but she was not.

"'Tis well known," Ashton said, his voice dangerously low, "that the *Mercury* press was commandeered to crank out this rot." He circled her like a cat about to spring upon a mouse. "But where did he get the type? See the *n*, pet?" His finger jabbed at the character. "The letter is missing a serif. Finley Piper's type has the same flaw."

Bethany swallowed a knot of fear in her throat. "What an extraordinary coincidence."

"The extraordinary part, my love, is that Finley dismantled his press and buried his type. Only one person knew it had been buried behind Kilburn House. Miss Abigail Primrose."

Bethany's heart began to thud against her rib cage. Despite the nobility of her intentions, she simply was not made for subterfuge. "Miss Abigail didn't dig up the type."

"True. Finley hasn't let her out of his sight. But she did receive you for tea not long ago."

"She did," Bethany burst out in exasperation. "And yes, I was the one who showed Mr. Howe where the type was hidden."

Ashton's curse made her ears smart. He snatched the newspaper from her hands and flung it into the fire. "It's not enough that you gave my private papers to Tanner. Now you must take your petty revenge on Finley as well. Hasn't he lost enough?"

"The papers were not my doing," she told him in a low, shaking voice.

"So you've said. But why should I trust your word now?"

"Because it's the truth." She dropped her gaze to the blackened and curling pages of the *Gazette*. "But in the whole of our marriage you never trusted anything I said, so why should you start snow?" She had meant to sound angry, but a curiously wistful note had crept into her voice.

"Bethany—" His hand came up and for a wild moment she thought he was reaching for her. But he only picked up his hat from the desk. "I'd like to see Henry now."

Her first impulse was to deny him, but she checked herself. No matter what enmity existed between her and Ashton, Henry should not have to suffer the loss of a father's love.

"I'll see if he's up from his nap."

Ten minutes later she descended to the hall with the baby. Both were dressed warmly against the January chill. Henry's delighted crowing at the sight of Ashton tore at her heart. They should be together, the three of them. She turned away, hiding her pain as she gathered her brown cloak about her.

Ashton felt his anger ebb as he took the baby, holding him against his cheek, closing his eyes and inhaling his sweet scent and the warmth of the squirming body. Nothing but the soft ache of yearning filled him now. "There," he murmured, "off we go." He darted a look at Bethany, who was tying her hood beneath her chin.

"You needn't worry," he told her. "I'm not going to abscond with the child."

A maddeningly becoming flush rose in her cheeks. "'Tis not that. I just thought I'd join you on your walk."

Every moment in her presence was a hot needle of pain, but he could not bring himself to refuse her. "Come along, then." He held the door open for her. She passed close in front of him and left him dizzy with the jasmine scent that wafted from her hair.

Everything had changed, and yet everything was the same. Somewhere in the turmoil of betrayal and distrust was a tiny glimmer of some other feeling. Years ago, that feeling had made him pause during a busy day in the stables to help an overprivileged and underloved little girl look for her lost kitten or to listen to some hilarious tale of a prank she and Harry had played on the dancing master. Buried deep beneath the drifts of bitterness lay the tenderness he had always felt for that vulnerable girl. She had grown up indulged by him. He could not help himself. He indulged her still.

They walked through the winter silence of the gardens. Nearly all traces of the raid had been erased. Benches had been righted; hedges trodden by hobnail boots had been pruned to their usual geometric precision. But when they reached the summerhouse, he saw that one ugly scar remained.

The structure loomed like a winter ghost on the precipice of gray slate overlooking the bay. Soot-blackened walls supported a charred roof, and the wind soughed through the unglazed windows.

He slid a look at Bethany and found her staring at him with an expression of deep dismay. Anger prickled within him. "You're still convinced the raid was my doing."

"Convince me otherwise, Ashton."

He hesitated, then decided to tell her about the mission he and Chapin had set out on last December. No harm would come of an admission now; Chapin was well beyond needing protection, and the British were dug deeply into their occupation. Ashton drew a deep breath, feeling weary.

"Chapin and I sailed to Point Judith to observe the British fleet. When we arrived back at the wharves, your good friend Dorian seized us."

"Did no one else see you?"

"Not anyone who would admit it."

She lifted her chin and fixed a stare on him. "The British army does not simply arrest a man for mooring a boat."

He gave her a thin smile. "How conveniently you forget your own part in this. Tanner had my journals."

"He didn't get them from me."

God, he thought, but she's stubborn. "And who else, pray, knew where I kept my private papers?"

He watched her anger diffuse on a troubled sigh. "I can't answer that. You'll just have to—"

"Trust you?" His laugh was a bitter bark that startled the baby, who whimpered until Ashton stooped down and tickled him under the chin. "As you trust me, love?"

The clouds parted momentarily and a single shaft of sunlight found a glinting home in her eyes. There was a look of such profound sadness in those hazel depths that he had to look away. He, too, felt that loss but was powerless to bridge the rift between them.

Discomfited, he turned his attention to the baby. The cold salt air nipped at the child's plump cheeks, causing them to blossom with healthy ruddiness.

Bethany, too, seemed eager to leave the subject of their estrangement. She walked to the steps of the summerhouse and peered at the gloom within.

"I'm going to have this place restored," she said over her shoulder. "I think it will make a perfect schoolroom."

Ashton caught himself smiling. War had visited every corner of Aquidneck Island. Most people had no worries beyond wondering where their next meal was coming from or whether they would survive another freezing night without fuel. And yet, with a vision that was not quite so naive as it seemed on the surface, Bethany was planning on erecting a school.

She glared. "I see nothing amusing in trying to do a little good for the townspeople."

"Nor do I, but I'm afraid these days most people are more concerned with keeping their bellies full."

"Just because a lot of unreasonable men keep trying to kill each other doesn't mean children shouldn't learn to read and write."

For reasons Ashton didn't quite understand, he found himself listening with unwavering attention to her plans for her school. Already she had decided on a name: the Primrose Academy.

Miss Primrose had promised to acquire copies of *Bailey's English Dictionary* and *Bluckstone's Commentaries* and paper through the black market. Ashton had to admit to a grudging admiration for the hardheaded schoolmistress. Miss Primrose had taught Bethany well, had given her a set of convictions which would transform a girl into a dedicated teacher. She could have idled in the protection of Dorian Tanner, yet instead she maintained her independence and dignity by pursuing a worthy calling.

"I like your ideas," he said after she had finished.

Her eyes widened. "I intend to be a smashing success."

A maddening urge welled up in him, an urge to take that earnest, beautiful face between his hands and sample those moist lips. He pulled her against him swiftly, giving her no chance to protest. The sweetness of the kiss was deep and sharp, almost painful. Only after long moments had passed did she attempt to pull away.

"Ashton, we must not do this."

"Damn it, Bethany, you are my wife."

"But there's so much keeping us apart."

He laid his hungry mouth over her protesting one, filling his starved senses with the taste and smell and feel of her. The satisfaction of that preliminary hunger only gave him a deeper, more disquieting appetite. One that could not be assuaged here in the cold winter garden with their son crawling about their feet.

When Bethany dragged herself away, he noticed tears sparkling like dewdrops on the ends of her lashes.

"Bethany." His voice was husky with desire. "Don't fight me, love. Don't deny me." He lifted his finger to trace the trembling outline of her jaw and the pliant moistness of her lips. Desire roared through him with the force of a storm. "Let me in, pet."

Fierce anger took the place of tearful uncertainty in her eyes. "Let you in? And what am I to do, forget all you've done and invite you to my bed, in my father's house?" She flounced away, rending him to pieces with a furious glare. "You weren't welcome there when he was alive. Do you think you're welcome now that you and your raiders have brought about his death?"

Her scathing speech, uttered through the thickness of tears, sent sparks of pain straight to his heart. He was so stunned by her loathing that he made no move to stop her when she scooped up little Henry and hurried back to the house.

*　　*　　*

Spring burst into full blossom over Aquidneck Island, bringing tidings from the mainland that Handsome Jack Burgoyne had arrived in Quebec, ready to smash down through New York and finish the rebels. Curled on the settee in the library one Saturday, Bethany read the news in the *Gazette*.

Feeling restive and at odds with the world, partly because Ashton was at this moment in the garden with Henry, she put the journal aside and walked over to the paper-strewn desk where Dorian sat frowning at an account ledger. The frown disappeared when he looked up, giving way to a smile of frank appreciation. His dark eyes drifted over her dusky pink *robe à l'anglaise*.

"How fresh you look, my dear. I don't know how you manage when the rest of us are fairly melting in this unseasonable heat." He glanced at the paper she had left on the settee. "Anything of interest?"

"Just the news of General Burgoyne's arrival."

"Ah. The rebels will be put down before the year is out. Can I get you some Madeira?"

"Yes, please." She watched him move to the sideboard, handling the crystal decanter and Waterford goblets with studied precision. Since he had taken over managing Henry's trust, he had behaved with impeccable manners. Lillian Winslow could not speak highly enough of the captain. And Bethany . . . she could find nothing in him to fault, although it was not for lack of trying. Somehow he made her uneasy. And she could not help comparing him to Ashton. Dorian's smile was polite; Ashton's was genuine. And Dorian's touch—his hand at her waist when he escorted her to supper—was distant.

Driving away the thought, she went around the desk and glanced at some papers. Her attention was drawn to a letter penned in Dorian's tight, painstaking script.

"What is this?" she asked.

He set down the goblets and snatched the paper away. "Some correspondence. Here, drink your Madeira."

She took a sip. "That letter is to the Bank of England. Does Seastone have business with that institution?"

"'Tis personal, dear."

"I didn't mean to pry. So tell me, how are the finances getting on?"

His frown told her he did not approve of a lady being interested in business matters. Her direct gaze made it equally clear that she intended to involve herself in anything having to do with her son's legacy.

Dorian sighed elaborately. "I let Barnaby Ames go."

Her face fell. "He's worked here for years. He was so good with the horses, almost as good as—" She stopped herself and raised the glass to her lips. Ashton was a sore point with Dorian; nothing would be served by mentioning her husband's name.

"I suspected Ames of consorting with rebel trash," Dorian said. "I won't tolerate disloyalty on my—at Seastone."

"I should think you'd hire a man for his skill, not for his political convictions."

His smile was indulgent. "You are so charmingly naive, my dear. Never mind, 'tis done. I've already acquired another stockman down in Spring Street."

"And what is his name?"

"I suppose it shall be Winslow now that the man is Seastone property."

Her eyes flashed as comprehension dawned. A slave market was located at the corner of Mill and Spring Streets. She gripped the edge of the desk, leaning across stacks of paper and calf-bound ledgers. "He's an African?"

"Aye, and quite a good worker. The man was a runaway, caught skulking around Bristol some weeks ago. I'll keep him in line." Dorian buffed his nails on his sleeve. "I intend to engage more Negro help around here."

She slammed her fist down on the desktop, scattering papers, sloshing the wine in her glass. "You shall not. I forbid it. The Winslows have never owned slaves and we never will."

His smile stiffened around the edges. "Bethany, do be practical. We'll save a fortune in wages. Your son's fortune."

"I will not have Henry grow up a slave owner. I want my boy to learn that a man has no right to hold another in bondage. I shall give the man you purchased his free papers and pay him a regular wage."

"What about the sum I spent acquiring him?"

"Consider it the price of learning the strength of my convictions." She set down her wine glass and left the room.

Still in a rage later that afternoon, Bethany marched down to the stable offices to find the man Dorian had purchased. Freeing the bolt, she flung the door wide. Evening light poured over a slim, erect figure and a darkly handsome face. A face she knew.

"Justice Richmond!"

His hot brown eyes narrowed. "So you be my new mistress."

Bethany frowned. His rich, musical West Indies accent was a thick drawl. Then she realized he was mocking her with a falsely subservient attitude.

"I am your mistress only if you choose to work for me, Justice." Smiling, she handed him the certificate she'd had drawn up that afternoon. "I've manumitted you. You're a free man. If you stay here and work for me, I'll pay you a wage. If you choose to go back to Harry, I'll understand."

Astonishment lit his dark, angular features. "What sort of work?"

She thought for a moment. "Didn't Felicia say you were a carpenter?"

"I've been known to wield a hammer a time or two."

"I'll pay you extra if you'll rebuild the summerhouse that was burned in the raid." Dorian had fixed all the other damage from that December night, but his reluctance to tackle the summerhouse demonstrated his opinion of her charity school. She gestured at the charred building, which hugged a distant cliff. "I want it converted to a schoolroom. I've been holding classes for some of the children of Newport."

Justice Richmond glanced down at the manumission papers aswirl with a solicitor's artful script, then back at Bethany. "I won't build you a schoolhouse for money."

She deflated. The British had employed all the carpenters in Newport building garrisons and earthworks. She would never be able to find someone to work for her.

Justice grinned at her. "Not for money, missus. But for something I want more. I want you to teach me to read."

Happiness warmed her from head to foot. "Done," she declared, setting her hands on her hips.

She was still smiling when she turned and saw Ashton standing in the doorway. Henry clung to his father's finger, chortling and toddling about his father's booted feet. Ashton nodded a greeting to Justice, who started up the path toward the summerhouse.

In the stables outside the office, Corsair blew a salute to Ashton, nodding his great black head. But Ashton wasn't looking at the horse. He stared intently at Bethany.

She flushed. "Hello, Ashton."

"Hello, pet." He had not given the endearment such a fond inflection in a long time. And he had not touched her as he was doing now in a long time, running a gentle, exploratory finger over the surface of her hand in a motion that never failed to set fire to her blood.

"I heard what you said to Richmond."

What was it she saw in his eyes? It was not the cool distrust she had become accustomed to.

"You know," he said softly, "there is much about you a man could love."

Could love. So conditional. So dependent on a trust neither of them could give.

She took her hand from his and bent to pick up the baby. Ashton moved to Corsair's stall. He whistled a soft echo of the sound he had trained Corsair to recognize as his alone. The horse's ears pricked forward and Bethany heard his hooves stamp eagerly. She glanced away, feeling suddenly guilty. Despite her protests, Dorian had commandeered the stallion in the name of supplying a king's man with a suitable mount.

Knowing how that fact galled Ashton, Bethany felt a softening. But her thoughts were interrupted by Dorian's arrival at the gate. Settling the baby on her hip, she walked across the yard to meet him.

Dorian spared a brief scowl at Ashton, then put his hand on Bethany's shoulder. She stiffened, wondering what Ashton would think.

"My dear," Dorian murmured, "we've gotten some bad news."

She clutched the baby closer. "William?"

He nodded. "Your brother died of the smallpox in that disease-infested Yankee prison in Connecticut." He moved to draw her closer, but she stumbled away, unthinkingly seeking Ashton as she always had in times of trouble. He covered the distance between them in three long strides.

Her husband's arms were warm and welcoming as he enfolded both her and the baby. "I'm sorry," he whispered against her hair. "So sorry."

"You lying bastard." Dorian's voice was a snarl of rage. "'Twas at the patriots' hands that William Winslow died. Is it not your objective to murder all those loyal to England?"

"William was my friend," Ashton said, "and the brother of my wife."

"Yet the hatred you show toward all men of the Crown is the same hatred that killed him."

"I was not the one who convinced William to enlist, knowing he wasn't suited to soldiering."

Bethany stepped away from them, surveying them with tear-drenched eyes. "Stop it, both of you. Can I not even grieve for my brother without being subjected to a political discussion?" Brushing past them, she clutched the baby and ran up to the house.

After that day a pattern developed in their relationship, a pattern of mutual avoidance. When Ashton came to visit Henry, he chose a time when Bethany was busy in her new schoolroom. When she went to visit Miss Abigail, she went at the pub hour, when Ashton and Finley were sure to be swapping grievances with their cronies at the White Horse.

At times she ached to explore the possibilities of a reconciliation, for she longed for his touch, his smile, the warm things he used to whisper in her ear. Yet even if she could discount the raid, even if he could believe she had not informed on him, the world itself seemed to tear them apart.

She saw him once in May, when Dorian took her to town for a victory celebration. Captain Esek Hopkins of the fledgling Continental Navy, a man distinguished for his disregard of authority, had sailed into the bay to liberate Newport. Royal vessels bottled the brash little fleet and then handily repulsed them.

Amid the noise of artillery salutes in front of the Colony House the celebrants raised toasts of "Tory roosters," quaffs of rum and fruit juice decked in feathers. When Bethany spied Ashton walking toward her from the foot of the parade, she wished she had not imbibed so much of the potent drink. She would need all her faculties to face the blazing fury she saw in his forbiddingly handsome face.

She had no chance to respond to his temper. Their eyes held for a moment, exchanging a bitter message. He swept off his hat and sketched a bow, then pivoted and stalked away.

Late in the summer they met again. Major General Richard Prescott, the bad-tempered commander of the occupying force, had suddenly become a hero. While the officer was spending the night in Overing House on King's Highway, a party of rebels led by Colonel Barton had slipped across the bay from Warwick Neck and kidnapped Prescott, forcing him to accompany them clad only in his nightshirt.

The humiliating act could only have been accomplished if the invaders were guided by someone familiar with Prescott's comings and goings.

The day after the kidnapping Bethany saw Ashton at Hammersmith Farm, which the British were using for a military hospital. She was bringing quilts and bandages to the wounded. Ashton, no doubt, had contrived some pretext to circulate among the Redcoats. With a stab of resentment Bethany realized he was probably trying to extract secrets from the patients. When he slipped out to the orchard, she followed him.

His dazzling smile flashed in the sunlight. "Hello, love," he called jovially. Snatching a green apple from a tree, he tossed it to her. Unthinkingly, she caught it. "Hungry?" he asked.

She thrust the apple into her pocket. "Hardly." She could not help but notice he looked as if he had not slept.

Unable to stop herself, she approached him, hands on hips and chin high. "You led Colonel Barton to General Prescott," she accused.

"Are you so certain of my guilt?" He spread his arms wide, and his blue eyes laughed at her.

Her gaze moved meaningfully over his rumpled clothing, fastening on a tar-smudged pant leg. He had probably soiled his clothing shinnying down a wharf piling to help moor the party from Warwick Neck.

"I'm sure," she said.

"No harm done. General Washington needed a bargaining chip to exchange for Charles Lee."

"So you took it upon yourself to procure one."

"The only wound Prescott sustained was to his pride. Such injuries are long in healing, but painless." He abandoned the subject with a grin. "How is my son?"

"Henry is fine, of course."

"I've been wondering how Justice is coming along with that Indian pony. The boy'll be ready to sit a horse before too long."

She felt a prickle of discomfort. He was determined that Henry would one day be as good a horseman as himself. But Dorian, it seemed, had other ambitions for the boy. Already the captain had begun sending inquiries to England for tutors.

"The pony has been sold, Ashton. Dorian felt it would be wise to wait several more years before allowing Henry to ride."

Anger kindled in his eyes. "Damn it, Bethany, who is raising the boy, anyway?"

"You and I. But you must understand, as Henry's trustee, Dorian—"

"Can give him everything I cannot."

She flinched. "I didn't say that."

"But the message is clear each time you parade the lad about town in his Manchester velvet finery purchased from a Tory profiteer. Or when you effuse to Miss Primrose about the shiny new lead soldiers Dorian bought. Has Dorian informed the boy that his father is a pauper?"

She recoiled from his temper. "You forfeited all, Ashton, when you became a rebel."

"Don't push me, Bethany. I'm sure you try to forget, but you are my wife and Henry is my son. I've every right to take him if I so choose."

"You might have stopped caring about me, Ashton, but I know you wouldn't force Henry to live in poverty."

His glare held her for a long, deliberating moment. She glanced down, saw his fist clenching and unclenching at his side.

"Just don't push me too far." He stalked away.

She stared after him, fingering the apple in her pocket and casting about for the resentful anger she had every right to feel. But the only thought that came to her as she watched his broad shoulders disappearing among the branches sagging with abundance was an unbidden and completely illogical notion.

Oh God, I love him still.

19

The summer of 1777 died on a wistful, lingering note. Petals fell from the wild roses tangled in fringes at the beachheads, leaving ugly bald rosehips to weather the cold season. More people fled the occupied island of Aquidneck, yet a few returned. Goody Haas's nephew, Pieter, who had recovered from his first wounds only to reenlist and return to the fighting, limped home a second time with a wooden peg where a healthy limb used to be. Bleakly he reported that the British had trounced the rebels at the Battle of Brandywine Creek. Congress fled Philadelphia. York, Pennsylvania, became the temporary and uneasy capital of the United States.

October brought new hope to the rebels. Jimmy Milliken burst, breathless, into Bethany's schoolroom, puffed up with importance as he handed her a crumpled newspaper.

"My Uncle Thad brung—brought—this all the way from New York. We beat the Redcoats! Smashed them all the way down the Hudson!"

Bethany rumpled the lad's sandy hair and smiled as

Jimmy swiped the air with an imaginary sword. From the outset she had kept politics out of her teaching, leaving that aspect of training to parents.

She set the children to work in their copybooks and looked at the newspaper from Albany. General John Burgoyne, Britain's golden hero, had been defeated. Fleeing the rebels, his army dug in on the heights of Saratoga, only to find itself surrounded by patriots barring an escape route to Fort Ticonderoga.

Bethany envisioned the humiliating scene of British men reduced to prisoners, marching past American companies of old men, young boys, Negroes who bore arms as free men, and wounded and war weary officers. Their faces would resemble the faces of Pieter Haas and Thaddeus Milliken—intense and rangy, hungry for victory, uncaring of the cost.

She closed her eyes, let a sigh escape her, and called the children to their arithmetic lesson.

By year's end the British had given up Fort Ticonderoga, Crown Point, and all hope of a route through Hudson and Champlain upcountry. Their only strongholds were New York, Philadelphia . . . and Newport.

The occupation was wearing on the city. As winter swept in on salt-scented windheads across the island, still more residents fled. Making her way to Finley's house to bring Miss Abigail a batch of Dudley's mince tarts, Bethany barely recognized the city whose golden age had abruptly died.

Much of the wharf area had been reduced to rubble by British guns and looters. The ruins had a sinister look because they were inhabited. People lived in barren rooms with rags stuffed in the windows because glass was no longer available. Girls who in better times would have been reading Scripture or doing needlework at the fireside now received lusty soldiers at regular intervals to earn money for food. Children in tatters clawed in the gutters for table scraps cast off by their British hosts. Bethany gave most of the tarts to a waif and emptied the pennies in her reticule into the skeletal hand of an old man.

Revulsion threatened to erupt in her throat. She swallowed it back. Catching her cloak about her, she pressed on through the windswept squalor of the wharves.

She averted her gaze from the empty print shop below Finley's house. The few tools John Howe had not pilfered for his *Gazette* hung like dusty ghosts on the walls. When Miss Abigail invited Bethany to stay for a game of whist, she accepted, eager to delay the return trip through the desolate town.

Finley and Bethany were cordial, although threads of tension spun between them. Only Miss Abigail's skillful and relentlessly witty conversation drew Finley from his black thoughts and Bethany from her disconsolate mood.

"Are you ready to be thoroughly trounced at whist, Finley?" Miss Abigail asked.

"Wishful thinking, Abby." He gallantly held out chairs for the ladies.

"Since we are only three, I shall have to deal a dummy hand. Ah, I didn't mean you, Finley." She winked. "I feel lucky today."

Bethany glanced at the meager glimmer of coals in the grate. "Shall we build up the fire a bit?"

"Sorry, dear," Miss Abigail said lightly, holding out her hands to show her fingerless gloves. "Shortages, you know."

Bethany felt gauche and ill informed, living in comfort at Seastone while others suffered from cold and hunger. "I'm sorry," she said. "I could bring some lamp oil and wood if you—"

"I can do without Tanner's charity," Finley said.

Miss Abigail captured him with a hard stare. "Are you certain you're up to being humiliated today?"

He snatched the cards from her. "Just pipe down. I'll deal."

Miss Abigail kept up a steady stream of chatter, her sharp eyes watching Finley's hands. She nibbled daintily at a tart. "Heaven," she proclaimed. "Finley, you really should learn to make mince tarts."

"Tory fare," he grumbled, although he had already devoured one. "Too much cinnamon."

"I thought you liked everything highly spiced."

Bethany watched the two of them with amusement. The barbed remarks flew between them like shrapnel. And yet a subtle playfulness flirted about their conversation, and the underlying tension was charged, Bethany realized to her surprise, with sexual attraction.

Long ago Miss Abigail had ceased to be a prisoner in the tidy chamber behind Finley's parlor. The pairing was incongruous: Miss Abigail, the perfect lady, the epitome of English loyalism, and Finley, blustering yet sensitive, the most passionate of patriots. Unlikely as it seemed, the two had turned their fiery conflict into a mutual warm glow.

Bethany's hand shook as she laid a trump card on the green baize table. Sweet Lord, but she missed Ashton.

As if summoned by her ache of longing, he entered the dimly lit parlor. The smell of cold salt air clung to him as he shook a mist of sleet from the shoulders of his greatcoat and hung the garment and his cocked hat on a hook. Tendrils of chestnut hair, damp with moisture, spilled over his brow. Bethany's fingers itched to comb through those wayward curls.

He was flashing that open, comradely smile as he said, "I've got it, Finley. At last—" He looked up and spied Bethany for the first time. His smile died along with his next words.

Her heart sank with a resounding thud that send tremors all through her body. She knew from the sudden dark veil of anger dropping over his face that her presence spoiled the visit he had been anticipating.

"We were just having a game of whist," Miss Abigail explained. "Join us."

Ashton's eyes flicked from Miss Abigail to Bethany and then to Finley. The older man nodded at an empty chair. His lips tightening with impatience, Ashton took a seat. Briefly his knee brushed Bethany's leg. They both recoiled from the accidental touch.

"How is my son?" he inquired.

"Henry is fine. Your sister is keeping him for the day."

Ashton's look was long and measuring, touching her in places that ached for the caress of his hands. He seemed to be considering whether or not to rise to the bait. "So I see," he said at last.

"How neatly done," Miss Abigail said. "You've managed to avoid apologizing for not asking after your wife's health, and she hasn't even struck you yet."

Ashton's mouth stiffened; then his sensual lips lost the battle and his teeth flashed in a grin. "Bethany will have to practice for years to achieve your piquancy, Miss Primrose."

"To become a royal pain," Finley said. "But sometimes I find her shrill conversation rather endearing."

"Is Finley always this annoying?" Bethany asked Miss Abigail.

"Usually more so," Miss Abigail replied. "Still, he's a passable cook. And he's rather handsome in an elderly sort of way, don't you think?"

Oddly, the insults had a relaxing effect, and the game resumed. Ashton played with nonchalance, pausing to lay a packet of newspapers in foreign languages on the table. "Finally, the world is taking note of our rebellion. The Comte de Vergennes is working with the American Commissioners in Paris."

Bethany started. His French pronunciation was flawless. She had almost forgotten his education, which he had paid for in bondage to her father. She felt a prickle of alarm. If the French joined the rebels, there would be no hope of a swift end to the hostilities. And no hope of a reconciliation with Ashton.

"I think we should look to Lord North's Conciliatory Propositions rather than putting our fate in the hands of a foreign power," she said.

Ashton gave a bark of mirthless laughter as he laid a trump over her queen of hearts. "Since when has it been safe to trust Parliament?"

Trust again. Always, the lack of it stood between them.

As Ashton proceeded to win the game, she noticed his restlessness and the way his eyes kept darting to the stairs leading down to the print shop. She did not mistake the looks he kept sending her, either. He wanted her gone. Stubbornly she laid down her cards, cupped her chin in her hands, and acted as if she intended to stay all day.

Ashton asked, "Finley, do you think we could go down to the shop for a while?"

"Why don't we all go down to the shop," Bethany suggested. She imagined she could see the steam of temper rising from her husband.

Miss Abigail rose from the table. "I, for one, am anxious to see how Dr. Jay's ink works."

Stunned silence filled the moment. Then Ashton's hand slammed down on the table, scattering playing cards and pastry crumbs. "Damn it, Finley, how could you let her know?"

Miss Abigail sniffed. "Finley's been a perfect clam. I learned about the disappearing ink from someone else a week ago." She made her way toward the shop.

"Don't worry," Finley muttered to Ashton. "She's got enough evidence to hang us a dozen times over, but she never seems to use what she knows."

Bethany felt Ashton's eyes on her like the touch of a knife point. She paused at the bottom of the steps and turned. "You needn't worry about me, either. For some unknown reason I happen to value your lives."

In the shop, Finley demonstrated the wondrous fluid. Dr. James Jay, brother of the statesman John Jay, had perfected the invisible ink and its developing agent. It would prove exceedingly useful in sensitive communications.

Ashton tore the endpaper from an old almanac and was demonstrating the ink when thuds and shouts sounded outside.

"Damn." Finley wiped the frosty glass of the window with the side of his fist. "Another lottery. I'd best go, since my name's in the hat."

"I'll go with you," Miss Abigail said.

Bethany stared after them in confusion. "Lottery?"

"I suppose you wouldn't know," Ashton said, "off at Seastone with Tanner seeing to your every need and whim."

She bristled. "I asked a simple question."

"The answer's not agreeable. In case you haven't noticed, there's a serious fuel shortage. The wood purveyors have been scared out of the bay by the British patrol. In order to keep from freezing, the people have been dismantling whole houses to use as fuel. They've agreed to draw lots to see whose house will be the next to burn."

She gasped. "I didn't know."

"Tanner's kept you insulated. I suppose I should thank him for that. Henry won't know what most people suffer." He studied her for a long, thoughtful moment, then scratched a quill across the paper in front of him. Bethany's attention was arrested by the large, firm hand gripping the quill, her senses snared by the warmth emanating from his body and the scent she recognized as uniquely his. The pen left no mark.

He handed her the paper. "See if the developing agent works."

Slowly the message appeared. At first she was too fascinated by the process to take in the words, but after a moment she read: *Love, why do we do this to each other?*

She raised her eyes to Ashton, his written question filling her with pain, regret, longing. He stared at her intently, waiting for an answer. She forced her gaze not to waver.

"Because you've ceased to care about anything but the rebel cause," she said. "Because you can't convince me you had nothing to do with the raid on Seastone."

"God," he said, his voice gruff with anger and something else that made her feel suddenly hot. "God. How can you look so beautiful even as you accuse me of murder?"

They moved toward each other. His mouth was so close she could almost taste the warm honey of his kiss. His hands were but a hair's breadth from her own. But the distance might as well have been a furlong. For folded within physical desire were hurdles of distrust and misunderstanding, of stubborn pride and misplaced loyalty. The moment of hesitation stretched long, and then they moved apart.

"I'm going out to see how the lottery's coming," Ashton said.

Her stomach in knots, Bethany followed him. He paused in the yard, setting his hands on his hips and staring at Miss Abigail's laundry, which hung in geometric precision on a line stretched between two trees.

Bethany prayed Ashton didn't know the significance of the laundry. Next to a black petticoat were pinned four handkerchiefs, letting the British know which bay inlet a patriot courier would use that night.

"Odd," Ashton said, "that such a meticulous person as Miss Abigail would hang out the wash in the sleet." He yanked two of the handkerchiefs from the line and tossed them into a wicker basket. "Finley ought to be more careful," he grumbled, leaving the yard.

Bethany considered restoring the handkerchiefs, but held back. She did not want to give the British a chance to capture another spy.

Two blocks away they found a little group pressed around a barrel set on end. The drab garments of citizens contrasted with the bright scarlet coats of soldiers. Bethany stopped short behind Ashton. They didn't have to ask whose home was to be sacrificed for firewood. Goody Haas's rusty, distressed cry rose sharply above the babble of the crowd.

Incensed, Bethany pushed her way toward Goody, aware of disapproving eyes. Peggy Lillibridge pointedly swept her skirts aside to give Bethany a wide berth. The message was clear. Bethany was a Tory and not welcome here.

"You can come to Seastone, Goody," she said. "You and all your kin. I've plenty of room."

Goody shook her head. "I can't, girl. Nothing against you, of course, but . . ." Her voice trailed off and her gaze drifted to Pieter, who leaned on his good leg and held his wife gently while she wept into his shirt.

A hard lump formed in Bethany's throat. These people would sooner freeze than cast their lots with a Loyalist who housed a British officer.

Finley pushed forward. "I've just spoken with the chairman of the lottery. They'll be taking my house and the print shop instead. Go on home, Goody." Already the relieved crowd was beginning to disperse.

"Now, Finley, you can't do that," Goody said.

"'Tis done. There's nothing here for me anymore. I've a widowed brother in Tiverton who'll put me up at his farm." He waved his hand. "I'm through with Newport. The town's spent and so am I. The press is shut down." He glanced at Miss Abigail. "I imagine you'll want to move to Seastone to be with your own kind."

"Nonsense," Miss Abigail said briskly. "I'll not let this be your excuse to unburden yourself of me. I demand that you take me to Tiverton with you."

Bethany watched as Finley's astonishment changed to pure pleasure. Miss Abigail grinned as if aware of a joke no one else understood.

Miss Abigail and Finley walked away, arguing heatedly.

"I don't know why you're so hell-bent on coming with me," he yelled.

She pointed her nose high in the air. "I'll tell you on the way to Tiverton, you beef-witted old man."

Bethany raised wonder-filled eyes to Ashton. "They're in love, aren't they?"

He simply nodded his head, tamped on his hat more snugly, and ambled away.

The send-off to Tiverton by way of a ferry across the Sakonnet River was a tribute to Finley's popularity. Only as she stood holding the baby, Ashton silent and brooding beside her, did Bethany realize how many friends the printer had.

A sharp wind ruffled the winter-gray waters between Aquidneck's eastern shore and Tiverton on the mainland. Bethany rubbed her chin thoughtfully over Henry's forehead.

"I'll miss them both. Truly."

She expected sarcastic and smug agreement from Ashton. Instead, astoundingly, he rested his arm across her shoulders. His touch felt warm and good and right, and she wondered how she had managed so long without his affection. And then she wondered how she would survive without his touch through the weeks and months and—oh, God,—the years to come.

Mentally recoiling from the painful thoughts, she said, "Finley was well beloved."

The printer was doing his best to grin, accepting the funny-sad comments about learning to farm. But his eyes, the eyes of a man who had lost everything, kept straying to the white and brick spires of Newport. Just when Bethany was certain he would break down and weep, Miss Abigail placed her hand on his arm and whispered something in his ear. He smiled and patted her hand.

"They've lost everything save that which truly matters," Bethany whispered.

Miss Abigail took the baby from her. "We should say our good-byes."

Nothing could have prepared Bethany for the wrench of losing Miss Abigail. "You've given me so much more than an education, Miss Abigail," she said.

"Have I?" The sea-gray eyes narrowed. "Then why, pray, have I not charged you a *sou* of tuition? Tut, tut." She blinked against a suspicious sheen of brightness. "Look at you, my dear. My awkward, outspoken student has become a woman. A wife—"

"A sometimes wife." Her eyes shifted to Ashton, who was talking with Finley and jiggling the baby on his hip.

"—and a mother," Miss Abigail continued. "Love is a very fragile and precious thing. Find your way back into his heart, Bethany, but remember, a man's heart is a dangerous place for a woman to dwell." She glanced at Finley. "Now, kiss me quickly and let me go, or I shall never forgive you for causing me to disgrace myself by weeping in public."

Bethany embraced Miss Abigail and watched her friend hug Henry, jabbering as she always did in the baby talk only the child understood. Finally, while Miss Abigail and Ashton exchanged a few words, Bethany hugged Finley, the man she had once misunderstood, once disliked, and now respected. Over his shoulder she watched Miss Abigail and Ashton. The lady said something that brought a thunderstruck look to Ashton's face. He responded—or protested— but Miss Abigail spoke again. Ashton looked as if the lady had driven an iron fist into his stomach. His expression did not change as he walked to Bethany. Henry yawned and rested his head on his father's chest.

Bethany sagged against Ashton and watched the ferry push off for Tiverton. Breakers scooped the small craft out to sea, and the winter wind puffed the sails taut.

"Ready to go?" Ashton murmured, his breath stirring the hair close to her ear.

She nodded, and they drove southward in her chaise.

The baby, lulled by the clip-clop of hooves and the creak of the cart, slept on the board behind them.

"Ashton?"

He turned to her. "What is it?"

"What was it Miss Abigail said to you before they left? You looked so strange just after she spoke to you."

Guiltily, Ashton darted his gaze back to the rutted, muddy road. Miss Abigail's words were stamped on his brain. *Let yourself love her, Ashton. She needs you so.*

He could not tell Bethany that. Could not tell her, because he dared not bare his heart like that. And because it would be so easy, to let himself love her.

20

On Henry Winslow Markham's second birthday, Bethany felt as nervous as a new bride. Surveying the east garden with its springtime decor of Persian lilacs, freckled foxglove, and bright cascades of yellow forsythia, she shook her head, suddenly realizing the irony of the comparison.

There had not been time for nerves at her wedding. The ceremony, such as it was, had consisted of a hasty signing of papers at Bristol.

But she'd had days to ponder the present celebration. She had wanted to keep the party small, comprised only of Henry's family and perhaps Goody Haas and some of the children from the school. But Dorian and her mother had insisted on a full-blown fete destined to impress the ranking British officers and socially prominent Tories rather than a two-year-old boy.

The thought of the placid garden overrun with brass-encrusted Redcoats and Tories was not the cause of her nervousness. Bethany had faced enough scorn and scandal to harden her sensibilities to the prying looks and finely honed remarks she was sure to garner from such company.

Only one person's presence could ignite her nerves so that her hands shook and her throat went dry and her stomach disdained all save a sip of weak tea made from the stale leaves her mother insisted on hoarding.

Ashton would be at the party.

Dorian had thought of every excuse to keep him away, but to no avail. Patriot or not, she had argued, Ashton was the boy's father and had a right to be present.

"You look," said a pleasant male voice, "like you're about to stand trial."

Startled, she jumped, then turned as a broad grin spread across her face. She stretched out her arms. "Harry." They embraced. Her own troubles fled as her hands encountered the worn fabric of her brother's coat and her eyes took in his thinness. He was her brother, yet she had the odd sensation of being in the company of a stranger, someone she used to know but no longer recognized.

"I wasn't sure you'd be able to come."

"Alas, I considered the crossing too dangerous for Felicia and Margaret, but I managed to find a ferryman willing to slip the British patrol and the *chevaux de frise* in the bay." He grinned. "Imagine that. Having to sneak through enemy lines just to attend a birthday party."

In a nearby lilac bush a warbler raised its voice in trills of song.

"Go on, Harry," Bethany said, "the patrol isn't that bad. The ships are in the bay to protect, not to harass innocent people."

He clicked his tongue. "Still the tenacious little Tory, aren't you, Beth?"

She sighed, worried by her brother's world-weary air. "The war is almost three years old. I'm so tired of it that some days I don't care who wins. But," she added stubbornly, "I should like to remain an Englishwoman."

Harry regarded her with critical fondness. "I daresay there's little about you that resembles an Englishwoman.

Here you are living independently, conducting a school for the common folk."

"I've done only what circumstances have forced me to do. When the British quell the rebellion, I expect my life to return to normal."

"Not likely," he said cheerfully. "A French fleet is due to set sail any day. I'd lay odds they'll visit Newport first."

She took a moment to assimilate the news. But she had little time to ponder the French alliance. Carrie Markham came running into the garden, her ripe figure clad in a provocatively cut dress. "You'd best get to the house," Carrie said, sparing only a nod for Harry. "Henry is putting up a fuss about getting dressed, and the guests have begun to arrive."

Nervousness beat anew within Bethany like the relentless flicker of a bee's wings. "Is Ashton among them?"

"Not yet." Carrie went back to the house, patting her bright red ringlets.

Harry leveled a sad look at Bethany. "You still insist he planned the raid, don't you?"

"I suppose I'll never know. But it was the work of rebels, and he openly supports the rebels."

"So do I," Harry reminded her.

She dragged in a shaking breath. "I cannot blindly accept his views simply because he is my husband." With that, she hurried to the house.

And yet some errant, undisciplined sentiment seized her when, a short time later, Ashton strode into the garden. His unsmiling face was as rugged and elemental as the craggy shores of Aquidneck. A light breeze tossed his chestnut hair that seemed to beg for her fingers to twine themselves into the gleaming strands. In spite of herself, Bethany let her eyes caress the lean, strong body her arms longed to embrace.

Their gazes collided and held for a tense moment. Bethany managed to catch her gasp of yearning before the sound escaped her lips. He turned away as if eager to seek the less volatile company of his son.

Lillian's friends flitted here and there, ears cocked and eyes darting for morsels of gossip. British officers in dress uniform availed themselves of contraband Jamaica water. They raised toasts to the king and the Empire, making certain Ashton or Harry was in earshot. The schoolchildren wreaked havoc in the garden and attacked the array of delectable foods spread on tables on the veranda.

Dressed like a fashion baby in figured blue Manchester velvet and at least half his weight in lace, Henry Winslow Markham toddled after the children, soiling his finery with berry stains and sticky sweetmeats.

When Bethany brought him to the veranda to receive his gifts, he protested until he understood the purpose of leaving his play. The supply of gifts ran out, and the lad screwed up his face to howl, when Ashton approached. His somewhat worn morning coat was muddy and covered in threads of white fur. In his arms he held an unruly brown and white puppy.

Ignoring the disdainful audience assembled on the veranda, Ashton hunkered down beside his son. "I've been calling the spaniel Liberty, but you can pick a different name if you like." The boy shrieked with delight and scrambled off after the dog.

"Just like Gladstone," Bethany whispered.

Ashton grinned with pleasure at Henry's delight. "Not quite. He's a she."

The puppy was tearing the lace at Henry's sleeve.

"Bethany, can't you see the boy's clothes are going to be ruined?" Dorian's question held an unspoken command.

"Let him have a little fun, Tanner," Ashton said. Bethany heard a thread of anger in his voice and silently prayed the men would not indulge the suddenly interested audience with a scene.

"My guests are not interested in seeing that disagreeable

little beast destroy the child's garments." Dorian stalked away and found Justice Richmond, who had been serving rum punch to the visitors. "You! Take the dog down to the kennels."

Henry set up a resounding wail as Justice took the puppy away. Glancing at Ashton's clenched fists, Bethany said, "Dorian would love for you to hit him, don't you see? Then he'd have a perfect excuse to arrest you."

"She's right," Harry murmured, joining them. "Why don't you best him in a way no one can fault—on the racing green? The contests are about to begin."

Ashton's hands relaxed. With a final bitter look at Bethany, he turned and led the way down to the racing green, a track bordered by a sandy beach. She scooped up her howling son and followed the eager company.

No celebration in Newport was complete without a horse race. Even in these lean times, Seastone's stables remained populated with champions.

Gentlemen who had been Sinclair Winslow's rivals during better days were eager to see if Bethany and a manumitted slave had been able to sustain the quality of the stables.

The British officers were in their glory on the beach-edged racing green. Most were landed gentlemen disgruntled at having been uprooted to endure the barbaric conditions in the Colonies. Their buff-clad legs enclosed the flanks of their horses.

Captain Tanner began the festivities with a display on Corsair. The midnight stallion had become his favorite mount.

Ashton drew his mouth into a line of repressed anger. Then he said, "He's ruining Corsair's mouth, sawing on the reins to get the poor beast to do carnival tricks."

Bethany had a sudden image of Ashton as he had been ten years earlier. A vibrant youth, awestruck as everyone at Seastone had been on the occasion of Corsair's birth. They had hoped for a stallion; they had hoped the Thoroughbred would be black like his sire and spirited like its dam. Corsair's subsequent triumphs had surpassed their ambitions.

Much of the stallion's greatness was due to Ashton's handling. Now Corsair, at the end of his triumphant career, was being forced to perform like a circus pony, doing sly tricks far beneath his blooded dignity. She ached for the man who had trained him.

"Dorian doesn't do this often," she said.

"If I hadn't trained the beast to be so damned obedient, perhaps Tanner would break his fool neck." Ashton sat down on a bench, taking Henry into his lap.

Dorian finished his display, dismounted, then fixed an imperious gaze on Ashton, who eyed him back unflinchingly. "Care to race me, Markham? We could place a wager on the outcome."

Ashton handed the baby to Bethany and walked to Dorian. Together, the pair made a vivid contrast. The officer was resplendent in dress uniform, his wig sculptured, his face a handsome mask. Standing inches taller, Ashton looked raffish and unkempt in his simple garb. A spring breeze tossed his careless hairstyle. No pretended civility dwelled in his features.

"What sort of wager?" he asked.

"'Tis obvious you lack the means for a monetary bet. Perhaps a forfeit, then? Should you lose, you'll agree to stay away from Bethany and boy. Permanently."

Gasps rose from the listeners. Bethany pressed her fingers to her mouth, straining against the urge to beg Ashton not to be goaded into the cold-blooded proposal.

"And if I best you?" he asked.

"Name your price, Markham."

"You give me the horse of my choice."

"The horses aren't mine to give. They belong to your son."

"Not Corsair. Bethany told me you'd commandeered the stallion for your own mount."

The Redcoat's head snapped up. He glanced over at a beautiful sorrel stallion called Blunderbuss. The horse pawed the ground and arched his neck. Dorian smiled, and Bethany knew exactly what he was thinking. At four years of age, Blunderbuss was the new champion of Aquidneck Island.

"Done," Dorian said. "Have you settled on a mount?"

"I'll ride Corsair."

Bethany surged to her feet and hastened to his side. "Corsair is over ten years old. He can't possibly win."

"Is it really the horse you doubt, or is it me?" Ashton gave a brittle laugh. "If I lose, you'll get what you've been wanting all along."

"Ashton." She lowered her voice. "I want you to take part in raising Henry." *Ah, God, in spite of everything, I still want you in my life.*

The crowd buzzed madly as Ashton tossed his coat to the grass and approached Corsair. The stallion whickered softly as he stroked the muscled arch of his neck and murmured like a lover against the buffed velvet muzzle. The bond between stallion and master was still strong.

Yet while Corsair stood calmly at the starting line, Blunderbuss pawed the ground and strained at the bit. Bethany went to the finish line at the end of the green.

One of the officers set off the competition with a single thunderous pistol shot.

The two riders sat low on their mounts, leaning over straining necks as the horses ran. Bethany thought she saw Ashton's lips moving and imagined him speaking to the horse with gentle urging. The animals ran abreast, heads and flattened ears even. Bethany nearly forgot to breathe as she watched.

The sorrel nosed ahead. Then its entire head pushed past the black's. Bethany started to turn away, loath to witness the defeat of Ashton and the magnificent stallion.

But as she turned, incredulous murmurs rose from the onlookers. She whirled back.

There were two things she had underestimated in this contest—Ashton's and Corsair's hearts. Years ago, Ashton had explained it to her. Racing hurts, he told her, but Corsair had the ability to move past the pain and temptation to slow down. He would win even if he must suffer in the process.

In a blur of movement, horse and rider seemed to meld and become one awesome force of unearthly speed. Defying nature and logic, Corsair's hooves seemed to leave the ground. The long, strong body with its skillful burden stretched to its limit, surged a head, then half a length past the sorrel, crossing the finish line with the grace of a mythical beast.

The cheering was sparse. Bethany's laughter mingled only with Harry's clapping and Justice's basso shout of approval. "There be magic in that horse," the stockman said, going off to cool out the lathered, triumphant stallion.

Bethany Winslow Markham, long admired for favoring her Loyalist principles over sentiment for her patriot husband, ran like a girl across the end of the green. In a swirl of skirts and musical laughter, she hurled herself headlong into her husband's arms. The couple embraced in the shadow of the dark horse that had, in the space of moments, become a legend.

Ashton sat surrounded by June sunshine, swishing sea grasses, and hissing waves. The gulls were out in force, screaming and diving for prey amid the frothy blue waves. The cove had been a place of wonder and solitude for the boy he had been. Now it was a place of safety. The inquisitive British patrol had not yet discovered the hideaway.

With relief and wistfulness, he readied a communiqué in French from the subterfuge firm of Hortalez et Cie.

Now that the alliance was in place, he would no longer be involved in supplying the patriots with Lavoisier's powerful explosives. The company had been dissolved, for the French could now supply the rebels openly.

He would miss dealing with his cherubic French contact. Lamoral, as Ashton knew him, accepted requisitions for gunpowder with the nonchalance of a baker taking an order for bread.

Now Ashton had another project to occupy him. Since winning Corsair two months earlier, he decided to acquire and train horses for the Continental Cavalry. Preposterous, the committeemen had told him. Certain suicide. He would be conducting his subversive business right under the noses of the Redcoats, stealing their horses and training farm nags and shipping animals off on a dangerous crossing to rebel-held Providence.

He worked at Gaylord Parson's Middletown farm, so degenerated by neglect that the British had not bothered to occupy the place. Behind him, corralled in a pen thrown together of driftwood, were the first four cavalry horses.

One was a plump country dobbin and the next a mongrel bay with long, mulish ears and muzzle. The third was a swaybacked nag with a sweet temper and a fondness for Russian thistle. The last illicit mount had been the most dangerous to acquire and showed the most promise. He had stolen an officer's gelding from the yard behind Banister House. Corsair lorded over the motley herd.

Ashton's throat tightened as he recalled the moment Bethany had leaped into his arms after the race. Her pliant body and sunwarmed hair had filled him with a longing so intense it took his breath away. It was a moment of healing. The wall of animosity had developed a chink.

But then, as if by mutual agreement, they had broken the embrace. Reality became a stiff mortar in the wall. Her guard went up and his spirits went down, and he had not seen his wife since.

The thought froze within him as he noticed a figure on a precipice high above the beach.

Bethany. Sitting beautifully on a dun-colored mare, she angled the horse down the narrow path. The afternoon light streaked through her hair, gilding tresses worn loose, like a girl's.

A cold stone of bitterness formed in his gut.

"You look as if the world is chasing at your heels, Ashton," she said with a wistful smile. "You said those very words to me. Three years ago it was, on a summer day just like this." She slipped from the saddle and tossed the reins around a low bush. She plucked a wild rose and approached him, her hips swaying gently with unpracticed seductiveness. His fingers contracted, forming fists at his sides. She touched him lightly on the chest with the rose.

"You were right. The world was chasing at my heels that day. My parents were urging me to find a proper husband and all I wanted was you. Was that foolish of me?"

"I can't answer that." He barely recognized his own voice in that rasping, emotion-laden query.

Her eyes swam with melancholy. "I have learned much. Of love and betrayal."

Her words tore at his heart. He wished he could peel back the years, the layers of hurt. "I danced with you that day."

"I don't think our troubles can be danced away any longer."

"I also kissed you."

"And I fell in love with you."

The next moment she was in his arms. He kissed her face and hair, reveling in her nearness. The delicate petals of the wild rose were crushed between their straining bodies. Then both the flower and their clothing fell to the sand, and in the next hour he forgot everything as he made love to his wife. He was amazed at how imperfect his memory was. He had forgotten the softness, the fragrance of her skin, the silky texture of her hair, the tide of emotions created by her consuming embrace. Her breath came in short gasps that sounded like sobs.

"God," he whispered, "What happened to us, Bethany?"

Trembling, she extracted herself from his hold. Slowly, they both dressed. She looked at the horses, ignoring his question to ask one of her own. "Are they bound for the Continental Cavalry, then?"

"How did you know?" he demanded.

"Is that Lieutenant Yarrow's gelding? Really, Ashton, Michael Yarrow has a poisonous temper. He nearly throttled a subaltern when he discovered the theft." She gazed out at the bay. "I expect you're waiting for dark so the transports can slip past the frigates. Nine o'clock would be an opportune time. You *have* memorized the patrol's schedule, haven't you?"

He grabbed her by the arms. "What sort of game are you playing?"

She looked pointedly at his fingers. "Yarrow's horse isn't worth your life to me. I have no intention of informing on you."

His grip relaxed. "Then why did you come here?"

"I've been coming every day since I learned of your plan to supply the rebels with horses. I knew you'd choose this place because it's so private." She walked a few steps away. "This is madness, Ashton. You're sure to be caught."

"Your concern is touching."

"My main concern is for Henry. With the things you do, he's likely to grow up never knowing you."

"Would you rather he knew a father who was too weak to act on his convictions? A father who turned his back on the cause of freedom?"

"A father who mocks his king and turns against his neighbors?" she shot back.

"There's no settling this," he snapped. "Not so long as you play hostess to Dorian Tanner. Or do you do more than play hostess to the dashing captain?"

Stubborn blue eyes locked with furious hazel ones. He wanted to shake her until her teeth rattled and she begged for mercy. Yet at the same time he longed to snatch her into his arms as they rediscovered all the reasons why they had once loved each other.

He knew she had too much honor to take solace in another man's arms. "I shouldn't have said that," he told her in a low voice. "I'm sorry."

Her head came up sharply. "Do you know, Ashton, that is the first time I've ever heard you say you're sorry for anything?"

"Doubtless it will not be the last."

21

Through the heavy, hot air of late July Ashton wended his way among the Seastone gardens to Bethany's schoolhouse. Unease crowded in on his feeling of exultation like an uninvited guest. Charles Hector Theodat, the Comte d'Estaing, was bringing his fleet northward from the Delaware capes to liberate Newport from the British. General John Sullivan headed the Continentals by land. By all reckoning, the double-pronged assault should whisk the Redcoats from their island stronghold in a matter of hours.

And yet Ashton's unease persisted. The plan, formed by the Marquis de Lafayette and General Washington, seemed catch-proof. Still, d'Estaing had a reputation for being overly cautious, and Sullivan's Gaelic temper and penchant for ill luck were legendary.

The retreating light of the late afternoon sun gilded the schoolhouse in warm shades of summer. The ineffable fragrance of roses and Canterbury bells wafted to him, and a sentimental memory stole into his mind. He recalled sitting in the summerhouse with Bethany three years earlier, remarking in his practical way that the place ought to be put to better use than mere ornament. He could not have known back then that she would find such a noble purpose.

Yet while the building itself had been transformed, the outside bore signs of neglect. Unclipped grass and unpruned bushes of lad's love attested to Dorian Tanner's disdain for Bethany's mission. In contrast, the stables and restored carriage house were immaculate.

Ashton hesitated at the door, squaring his shoulders and flexing his fingers as if in preparation for a fight. A tight smile curved his lips. He expected no less than a full blown battle with his wife when she found out why he had come.

Slapping at a lazy fly, he prepared to step into the schoolroom. He was about to make his presence known when Bethany's voice lifted in anger.

"That is the most preposterous idea I've ever heard!"

Ashton paused to listen.

Boots thumped on the plank floor. "The plan is perfectly logical."

Dorian Tanner. His cultured voice rang irritatingly through the schoolroom.

"'Tis never too soon to begin thinking about Henry's education," Tanner went on. "In a few years he'll be old enough to enroll at Eton."

"I shall not send my son to England for his schooling at any age." Her voice crackled like fire.

"You're being damned unreasonable about this," Tanner said. "All people of quality send their sons away to school. Both your brothers attended Eton."

"Aye, and Father spent a year trying to re-civilize Harry when he returned home. William was plagued by nightmares for months by the forcing-house system. Henry will receive a perfectly fine education right here in this schoolroom."

Tanner's dry bark of a laugh sounded like chalk scraping across a slate. "I see. So you'd have the future master of

Seastone reciting treason alongside gypsy poor and former slaves?"

"Just because my students don't happen to be to the manner born does not mean they don't deserve an education. A boy struggling over his books works just as hard whether he's the son of a slave or a nobleman."

Tanner made a choking sound. "You speak of equality and the rights of commoners like the most radical of patriots."

"Do I? Then it seems the rebels and I agree on something."

Grinning, Ashton folded his arms and leaned against the building.

"I'll not have Henry lumped in with the displaced scum of a dying nation," Tanner said.

"Ah, but who displaced them, Dorian?"

He blew out his breath audibly. "I care deeply for the boy. Had you not impetuously surrendered yourself in marriage to Markham despite my respectful suit for your hand, Henry could have been mine."

And would have been, Ashton thought, his grin disappearing, but for his mistaken arrest in Bristol.

"Ashton is the boy's father. He has final say in Henry's schooling," Bethany stated.

"You're constantly pointing that out to me," Tanner said. "My solicitors tell me a divorcement is possible in your case. The man abandoned you, pure and simple. And don't forget, he's the scoundrel who brought about the death of your father."

Ashton braced himself against the wall, feeling sick as he awaited her response.

"How I feel about my husband," she said, "is none of your affair."

"My dear, it is very much my affair," Dorian rejoined smoothly. "I want you to be rid of the traitor. My feelings for you have grown quite tender."

She made a muffled sound of dismay. A piece of furniture scraped the wooden floor.

Ashton stepped swiftly into the schoolroom. Bethany and Tanner stood facing each other. She had placed a bench in front of her. The Redcoat wheeled around, his face a mask of fury. "What the devil are you doing here, Markham?"

"I'd like a word with my wife," Ashton said. "In private."

Tanner snatched his hat from a low table and strode out of the room.

Ashton glanced around the schoolroom. It was tidy and inviting, with child-sized furniture and neat stacks of hornbooks on paddles and foolscap practice paper, used and re-used. Ink horns and Faber pencils stood in a row on a table. Glancing up at the big slate in the front of the room, he saw in Bethany's artful script: "First say what you would be, then do what you have to do.—Epictetus."

"Yes?" Bethany asked, "what is it, Ashton?" She sounded weary. He noted with surprise that she had dark crescents beneath her eyes, and her frame seemed thin in its loose-fitting lavender dress. With a jolt, he realized that Bethany was not only tired; she looked desperately unhappy. Yet even in her haggard state, she appeared lovely to him.

"I've brought you some copybooks," he said awkwardly, handing them to her.

Her smile touched his heart like a shaft of sunlight. "Thank you. Paper is so dear these days." She flipped through one of the pamphlets. "'Queens and Kings Are Gaudy Things,'" she read, then looked up at him in mock disapproval.

He grinned. "It was all I could find."

"I'll give them out tomorrow," she said.

"No." Before she could protest, he went on. "D'Estaing's fleet is due to arrive any day now. That's no secret. I've arranged to have you, Henry, Carrie, and your mother transported to Bristol. You'll be safer there with your brother and Felicia."

"I'll not abandon my home!"

He took both her hands. Her fingers were curled into fists. "Bethany, Seastone is a target for Continentals, especially since Tanner has seen fit to store ordnance in some of the buildings. I'm for the patriots, but I must warn you. Atrocities have been committed on both sides."

"Indeed they have," she said hotly.

He gritted his teeth. She would not leave that old wound alone. "You're going to Bristol," he said.

"Never!"

He glared at her. "You will seek a place of safety for the sake of our son, or live to regret it."

Wearily, she moved toward the door. "You force me to agree with you." She lifted troubled eyes to him. "I don't suppose there's any point in asking you what you'll be doing during the siege."

He wondered what she would do if he took her in his arms and kissed the lines of weariness from her pale face. Feeling bleak, he said, "You can be sure I'll be busy." He looked at a display of the children's drawings. One of them depicted a stick-figure soldier standing duty beside a half burnt building. Another showed a headstone beneath a leafless tree while a family warmed themselves around a fire of burning furniture.

"I hate it that they suffer from a war not of their making," Bethany said softly. "Will they be all right during the siege?"

"Pieter Haas has made provisions for the families in town."

She nodded and started down the steps. Ashton gripped her shoulders and brushed his lips over her brow. She smelled of sunshine and jasmine; she felt like love and forever. The dark shadow of a thought hung its wings over him. This could be the last time he ever held her in his arms.

"Godspeed, love," he told her quietly. "Harry will bring you home when the fighting is over."

She stared at him, her sun-shot eyes riveted on his face. She seemed about to speak, then closed her mouth and moved away. He watched her walk toward the house beneath an arching canopy of lilac and evergreen yew.

Godspeed, love.

"Good God Almighty!" Standing on the doorstep of the Tiverton farmhouse, Harry Winslow fixed a wondering look on a decidedly bulging stomach.

"Close your mouth, young man," Abigail commanded. "And mind the mud on your boots. Finley spent hours cleaning the floor."

Harry removed the mud on the iron scraper outside the door. Then he entered the house, nearly falling over himself to help Abigail to a chair in the keeping room.

"See here, Harry Winslow," she scolded, "I'm a woman who happens to be with child, not some dangerous explosive."

"Sorry, Miss Primrose."

"Young man, I am *Mrs.* Finley Piper. But you, despite your ill manners, my call me Abigail, or even Abby, if you feel the need. You Americans seem fond of overfamiliarity anyway."

"You *married* Finley?"

"Yes, indeed, for all that he's an old scoundrel and a card cheat. There was no help for it. I lost my heart." She glanced around the tidy and charming keeping room of the farmhouse. "Anyway, I would be hard-pressed to find a man who cooks and keeps house as well as Finley."

She looked away, swallowing hard against the sudden knot of fear in her throat. "He's gone to meet the French flotilla. He'll be boarding the flagship *Languedoc* this evening."

Harry let loose with a low whistle. "I knew he'd never be content with farming. What about his brother?"

"Stephen has gone to town where the patriots are mustering troops. Our nephew, Douglas, is out finishing his chores. What brings you here?"

"I came to enlist."

She nodded with inexpressible sadness. How many young men like him had died in this war? How many more would die? "Have you been in contact with Bethany?" she asked.

"Ashton tried to send her to Bristol. He doesn't know she disobeyed him. At least she had the sense to get her son and Carrie Markham out of Newport. But Bethany's still housing Redcoats at Seastone."

"She's doing her patriotic duty."

"I wish she'd think of her wifely duties for a change," he snapped.

"I'm afraid I agree," Abigail conceded.

"If only she could be persuaded that Ashton had nothing to do with that damned—that cursed—raid."

Abigail sat thinking for a moment. A faint memory nagged at her, then burst into her awareness. She hurried to a corner of the kitchen and searched through a sack of rags. Turning, she showed Harry an ink-smudged apron.

"I was wearing this the night I went through Dorian Tanner's office. I completely forgot about it because Finley was in such a state about Chapin." She dropped two small objects into Harry's hand. "Ashton's Liberty Tree ornament, but what is this other?"

Harry picked up the sapphire stud and held it to the light. "This belonged to my father," he said, his voice choked with emotion. "Tanner had this, you say? Then that can only mean . . ."

Abigail felt cold all over. "The whole thing was planned by Tanner himself!"

Harry was already striding toward the door. "I'm going

to Seastone to get Bethany away from that double-dealing Redcoat."

He leaped into his sail-rigged sloop and pushed off. The wind had risen, coaxing stiff peaks on the surface of the water. Harry turned and waved his hat, looking boyish and golden and impetuous and heartachingly brave.

Abigail turned and went back into the house.

The top deck of the flagship *Languedoc,* at the head of a fleet of eleven vessels, shifted beneath Ashton's feet.

"She is a grand dame, eh?" asked Gaston, the helmsman. "With her ninety guns and a little luck, she will blow *les Anglais* all the way to Canada." A gamin smile animated the aging face as Gaston shook hands with each American: Ashton, Finley, and five other members of the Committee of Safety.

Finley nudged Ashton and gestured astern. "Never saw so much brass in all my life."

"The conquering heroes," Ashton said wryly. "Why do we consider men about to kill other men heroes?"

Charles Hector Theodat, the Comte d'Estaing, arrived at the head of a group of officers. All wore splendid white coats and waistcoats studded with gilded buttons. Gorgets of silver flashed at their throats. Hats adorned with goat hair topped their heads.

The Americans, who had boarded the flagship at Point Judith to guide the fleet into battle position, gaped at the finery.

"Ashton Markham." The comte bowed slightly. "I was told by Monsieur Talmadge to expect a huge, angry lion of a man, and that is precisely what I see."

Ashton grinned. "Ben probably didn't mean that as a compliment."

"Eh, *bien.* Your associate also said you have an extraordinary talent with horses." He led the way to the admiral's stateroom to go over the details of the plan. "*Tiens*. I have instructed Admiral Suffren to open an east passage." He pointed to a chart.

"That would be Sakonnet," Ashton said.

"Sakonnet. Ah, *les peaux-rouges*, they give everything such impossible names."

Finley took a large gulp of French wine. One of the officers sniffed and took a delicate sip from his own goblet. Finley drained his cup and set it on the sideboard with a resounding bang; then he belched.

D'Estaing cleared his throat. "Suffren has taken hostages."

"Is that necessary?" Ashton asked quickly.

"*Assurément*. The hostages will be held on the *Languedoc* to discourage the English from bombarding us. If the flagship goes, the attack will fall apart—*pouf!*"

Ashton was glad he'd had the foresight to pack Bethany and Henry off to Bristol.

As the fleet waited off the point for word that the Middle Passage had been cleared, Ashton fell into a pensive mood, aided by the wine freely shared by the French sailors. Newport would soon be liberated. And once that happened, he intended to liberate his heart.

For too long, he had denied his true feelings for Bethany. His love was the only thing she had ever wanted from him. At last he knew he could give it to her.

Mellowed by plenty of wine, he told Gaston of his Tory wife. "I've known her since she was a girl. I remember her as a gawky filly, leggy and clumsy and full of mischief. After she came back from four years of schooling, I practically had to peel myself off the rafters when I saw how she had been transformed."

"*Très belle*, eh?" Gaston lifted an eyebrow. He refilled Ashton's cup. "Enchanting and habit-forming, like good wine."

*　　　*　　　*

The next day a small boatload of aides approached the *Languedoc* with good news. Suffren had cleared the Middle Passage. Troops under Sullivan and Lafayette had begun crossing to Aquidneck Island.

Suffren's hostages were brought aboard the flagship. One by one the unfortunate Tories were helped up the ladder: Mr. Simon Pease, a slave trader; Mr. Evan Hunt, a distiller; Mr. Keith Cranwick, whose curses rang across the bay.

Before the fourth hostage could be brought up, something happened to cast a pall on the entire expedition. Mr. Pease, looking ashen and bewildered, clutched at his chest and fell over dead on the deck at d'Estaing's feet.

In the flurry of concern over Pease's death, the fourth hostage was momentarily forgotten. Ashton heard a sound behind him and looked back in time to see a small and decidedly feminine hand appear on the rail, followed by a bright mane of tousled curls, then an angel's face set in an expression better suited to one of the Furies.

"Oh, God," Ashton said. "Bethany."

22

"*Pas de question,*" d'Estaing said to Ashton, straining the many fastenings of his coat. "What you ask is out of the question." The officer poked his face into the broad mouth of a cone while a servant sent a great cloud of powder over his wife.

Ashton stifled a sneeze. "But she's a woman."

The aristocratic face withdrew from the cone. "One needn't be a Frenchman to discern that."

"You can't keep my wife on this ship during a battle."

"*Ecoutez, mon ami.* Keeping a female hostage is irregular, but this is a far safer place to ride out the battle than Newport, eh?"

Ashton nodded grimly as he left the stateroom. "My wife will require more convincing."

"Dinner is formal tonight," the Frenchman called to his retreating form. "I trust you brought proper dress."

"Proper dress," Ashton muttered under his breath.

Finley joined him in the common seamen's quarters. "Have you spoken to Bethany?"

"Only long enough to have my character compared to that of a snake."

"Surely the girl's not blaming you for this. Why didn't she go to Bristol as you'd arranged?"

"Lillian wouldn't hear of leaving Seastone. Bethany decided to stay with her, although she did send Carrie and Henry to safety. But Bethany has a habit of blaming me for things I didn't do."

"Don't look so hopeless," Finley said. "A year ago, Abby would have cheerfully set fire to me. Now she's carrying my child." With a sheepish grin he added, "And I'm still doing her laundry."

Ashton bent to take out the formal dress he had brought, his one good set of clothing. The white ruffled shirt was an annoying froth on his torso, spilling from the confines of a winestone-fabric waistcoat. The tight buff knee breeches hugged his thighs. He grimaced at the delicacy of the silken hose, but he donned them and fumbled with the garters. At least his tall ebony leather boots hid the stockings. A navy frock coat, embroidered with far too much gold needlework, sported miles of braid.

"Dashing," Finley commented wryly, preening like a popinjay in his own finery. "All you need now is a wig."

Ashton sent him a frown and tied his hair back in its usual inelegant tail. Then, along with the other Americans, he strode astern, heading for the stateroom.

Bethany reluctantly followed a ship's boy across the darkened main deck of the *Languedoc,* stepping gingerly through a maze of low-beamed alleyways. They emerged onto an upper deck where seamen were finishing their chores for the evening.

A broad silence fell over the men. A salacious whisper drifted across the deck. "*La belle . . . mon dieu, ayez merci!*"

She ducked her head, hiding a scalding blush within the

loose waves of her hair. It was not enough that she had been seized from the Cranwicks' stables and deposited on this French ship like so much baggage. She was also forced to endure the leers of these foreign sailors. And Ashton, damn the man, seemed to think the entire episode was perfectly all right.

Admiral d'Estaing greeted her at the door to his stateroom. She looked past him at a handful of silent servants moving around an elaborately appointed mahogany table. A knot of men conferred in a corner. "Are you quite well, madame?" the admiral asked.

"I have had better days, I assure you, monsieur."

He lifted his shoulders in a Gallic shrug. *"C'est la guerre.* I am certain that in a time of peace, you and I would be the best of friends." He took her hand and raised it to his lips.

Ashton was a sudden angry shadow in the doorway. She felt his presence before she actually saw him; it was like knowing the scent of a storm before the tempest descended. She stared at him, her gaze moving from his neatly groomed hair to the gleaming tops of his boots. The elegant clothing gave him a distinct air of breeding. He was regarding her with a look she had never seen before. That softness, that gentle yearning, might have melted her heart had circumstances been different.

"Hello, love." Pointedly he took her hand from d'Estaing and bowed low, pressing his lips to the rapid pulse at her wrist. "You seem quite excited to be here tonight."

Stunned by his formal greeting, she snatched her hand away. "I hardly think excited is the proper word. If I seem agitated, 'tis because I've just spent half the day being abducted and forced aboard an enemy ship."

Ashton propelled her to the long table, his hands firm as he held out a chair for her. She refused to look at him during the meal. She gave her attention to Hunt and Cranwick, who ate too little and drank too much. Although Bethany barely knew Mr. Hunt and bore no liking for Keith, she batted her eyes at them.

"How terribly unfortunate that you chose to show me your new Narragansett pacers this afternoon. Had we stayed in your drawing room with Mabel and Mother, perhaps Admiral Suffren's villains would have passed us by."

Keith scowled into his wine cup. "Newport's been plagued by horse thieves all summer. But I never suspected the scoundrels would stoop to abducting private citizens."

The Frenchmen seemed intrigued by her, vying for her attention, trying to entertain her in poor but flowery English.

"You are collecting admirers tonight," Ashton whispered, leaning across the table. "Myself included." He trailed a finger lightly over her upper arm.

She sat back, stung. "I would like to retire now," she announced, pushing back from the table. All around, chairs scraped as the gentlemen rose. She went to the door, ignoring the chorus of goodnights behind her.

Then Ashton was at her side, his grip firm on her elbow as he propelled her into the alleyway.

She pulled her arm away. "I can find my own way to my cabin."

He seemed not to hear her. He glanced out at the sky. "There's to be a moon tonight."

Her gaze followed his and for a moment she forgot her anger. The night air was still and heavy with the tang of salt. The sky was velvety and festooned with stars that seemed very close and in constant motion due to the rocking of the ship.

"How long am I to be kept a prisoner?" she asked.

"Until Newport is ours. Look around you, Bethany." He pointed to the lights of the other eleven warships. "The Redcoats will never be able to repulse this force."

She was silent for a moment. Suddenly the prospect of a British-free Newport did not seem so awful. She just wanted the fighting to be over.

He brushed the underside of her jaw with his knuckles,

his gaze oddly tender in the way it had been before dinner. She shivered. She would have better understood anger.

"I have something to tell you," he said. "Something about myself. About us."

"There is no 'us.' Perhaps there never was. I have no interest in what you have to say."

"Then maybe you'll pay heed to this."

A sharp gasp escaped her as he hauled her against him in a tight, uncompromising embrace.

"Let me be," she said.

His mouth closed over hers. Bethany battled the heady feeling of his lips working compellingly, urging her to open. She felt herself slipping into languor. Ah, how easy it would be to plunge into his silken web, to forget all that she stood for, all that she was.

She pressed her hands against the lace adorning his shirt and forced herself to speak in a harsh, panic-edged voice. "These clothes make you look the gentleman, Ashton, but I know you for a traitor who takes what he wants by force. Force me, husband, for I'll not willingly give in to you."

He let her go abruptly. She stumbled back against the rail. His mouth was a taut line of anger, yet in his eyes she saw something else, a flicker that made him look, just for a moment, inexpressibly sad.

Bethany slept badly on the narrow bunk, awoke to a cool August morning, then thumbed in boredom through a volume of *chansons de geste*. Through a single portal in the cabin she could see the rolling blue waves as the deep-draft *Languedoc* cut a path into Narragansett Bay.

She could not tear her thoughts from the previous night. Her anger had cooled. She was not ready to forgive Ashton yet, but she was ready to talk to him.

She left the cabin and climbed a steep ladder, emerging into the light of a hot afternoon sun.

The bay islands rose on the horizon. The French fleet bobbed along like a string of wine corks. Ahead, through a web of shrouds and stout rigging, she saw their destination: Conanicut Island.

Buzzing and murmuring among the sailors alerted Ashton to Bethany's presence. In her soft dress of pale yellow silk, she stood out like a primrose against the muted colors of ship and sea and sky.

He crossed the decks, jumping over coils of hemp rope and crates. "You should stay below."

She shook her head. "Why are we headed for Conanicut?"

"That's where the four thousand French troops will land for the crossing to Aquidneck."

She shuddered. "All the drills, the intricate plans, the rolling out of powder kegs—it all seemed like a complicated game. But it's real. People will die. Families will lose everything."

He nodded. With her native Newport in the distance and the wreckage of a few British ships shifting helplessly in the bay, she finally saw the face of war. He moved to take her hand, then stopped himself. Her words of the previous night stood between them.

Standing close, they watched the debarkment of troops. Colonial regulars and their French allies poured out of the ships of the line.

The British had formed double lines across the island, with the pond in front of them. The stronghold at Tomminy Hill rose behind them.

"Who is this?" Bethany pointed to a man who had just boarded from a ship's boat.

"The Chevalier de Pontgibaud," Ashton said. "Aide-de-camp to the Marquis de Lafayette."

The rotund man breathed in impatient huffs. "Nothing is working," he raged. "The men behave like schoolboys at play. They—" He broke off, spying Bethany over d'Estaing's shoulder. "Ah, *la belle. Qui est-ce?*"

Jealousy flared inside Ashton as his wife stepped forward. "I am Bethany Markham," she said in a silken voice. "Sir, Newport is my home." She flinched as flashes and puffs of smoke appeared on the island.

"Merely a skirmish," Pontgibaud said.

"Even a mere skirmish is more fighting than I would care to see."

With obvious effort, the chevalier tore his gaze from her. "Foul news," he said to the comte. "The marquis has the patience of a saint with these Colonials. The cavalry looks like a flock of ducks in crossbelts on nags. And the infantry! They are deaf to the drumbeat and wear homespun clothing. I fear they are more eager to fill their bellies with our supplies than to fill their horns with powder."

Above the snapping of sails and the groaning of timbers, she heard a panicked shout. A party of Colonials scrambled aboard and raced across the deck to the officers.

"There's a squadron of His Majesty's ships approaching Point Judith," a man shouted. "Black Dick Howe's *Renown* and seven other vessels with ketches and fireships."

Silence fell over the decks. The waves lapped at her sides and a rising wind whistled through the rigging. D'Estaing issued a string of orders in French. Men raced to the sheets. Others grabbed the halyards, and the sails were set and made fast.

Ashton began propelling Bethany toward a hatch. "Get to your quarters and stay there. Howe doesn't know about the hostages. He'll show no mercy to the flagship."

A roiling bank of coal-gray clouds rolled in, obscuring the sun. The high wind was useless to the French fleet. The *Languedoc* headed south on the port tack, its crew hoping for a wind shift. The southwesterly breeze moved only two points to the east, then dropped to nothing. The fleet was becalmed.

Ashton went below to find Bethany. She glared at him when he entered the tiny cabin. "I can barely stretch my legs in these cramped quarters," she said.

He sent a meaningful look at the narrow bunk. "You could lie down."

"I want to go above. I'll die of heat down here." Perspiration had moistened the seams of her yellow gown, outlining a slim waist and the rise of her breasts. Tendrils of topaz hair clung to her brow and neck. His mouth went dry as hemp as he imagined how her damp skin would taste and smell.

He swallowed. His arms ached to hold her. His heart cried out for her to cast off her bitterness. "Talk to me, love," he said. You might as well. We're becalmed."

"What shall I say?" she demanded. "We've not had a civil conversation in months."

"Maybe it's not talking that we need." He gave her a flask of fresh water. She drank, looking languorous and artlessly sensuous. She lay back on the bunk, looking hardly comfortable.

With gentle hands Ashton removed first one shoe, then the other. He peeled away the gossamer silk of her stockings, feeling the even smoother texture of her legs. "Better?" he asked.

"I'm still too warm."

"Then you should take off your gown."

She stared at him.

"For God's sake," he said, "I'm your husband."

She said nothing, but presented her back. He unfastened the gown to reveal a filmy chemise and light petticoat. She lay back down and closed her eyes. A pair of tears squeezed out from beneath her eyelids.

The years peeled back, and suddenly she was a girl again, seeking his comfort, needing him. "Don't cry," he whispered against the damp tangle of her hair. "Please don't cry anymore."

Pressing her cheek against his chest, Bethany felt a sudden urgent desire for Ashton. She turned in his embrace, forgetting all the enmity that divided them, kissing him deeply.

His fingers tugged at the ribbons of her chemise and petticoat, freeing warm flesh that ached for his touch. She arched upward to invite the caresses of his hands. He seemed to cherish every inch of her.

Unable to endure the barrier of his clothing, she peeled the white linen shirt from him and put her shaking fingers to the buttons of his breeches.

"Sweet Christ, Bethany," he muttered. Slowly, relishing each second, they made love in the airless cabin, the becalmed ship a gently shifting cradle. Long moments quickened to burning urgency like tiny wavelets curling to huge surging breakers. She cried his name aloud and clutched at him. He moved over her welcoming body.

At last, at long last, Ashton felt his wife blossom beneath him with a burst of passionate sound.

The ship's creaking was loud in the silence of their afterlove. He held her and said, "Bethany."

"Mmm?"

"The words seem so inane after what we've shared, but it's time I told you, I—"

A deafening crash drowned out his next words. "—love you."

"You what?" she mouthed, gripping the side of the bunk as the ship listed.

"I love you," he yelled. "I love you." He called the words again and again, knowing she must think he had lost his wits, but knowing from the rapt look on her face that she understood. Wind and waves might drown his words, but not the fiery sentiment of his fierce embrace just before he left her to scramble into his clothing.

Bending, he kissed her one last time. And then a roar and a thunder seemed to rend the ship's timbers. A wave rose to spray the cabin portal.

The storm, which had been hovering on the horizon for hours, barreled into the bay.

23

Ashton was half thrown from the cabin by a sudden lurch. He climbed a wall of waves only to drop with a bone-jarring thud on the other side. Bethany gasped. By the time he reached her side, Ashton saw that fear had chased away the love-warm look of her.

"Ashton!" Finley Piper's voice sounded in the alleyway. "Come quickly! If we don't do something to stop him, d'Estaing's going to reembark all his troops!"

"I've got to go above," Ashton told Bethany. "Stay here." He ducked inside to kiss her swiftly, then hurried after Finley. At the top deck, the Americans were complaining bitterly about the time lost because of d'Estaing's indecision.

Finley quickly added his own opinion. "He could've bombarded Newport while Sullivan took over. But now, he thinks only of his own precious ships. And that stuffy little Pontgibaud—"

The howling tempest drowned out the rest of his tirade. All thought of battle fled. For now, the wind and the sea were more deadly enemies than a whole battalion of His

Majesty's ships. The *Languedoc* heeled wildly, buffeted by fierce, soot-gray waves which gained steadily in height throughout the day.

Every beam and plank groaned and protested. Even after the crew had taken in the badly fished sails, the vessel continued to roll and pitch. Ashton wanted to go to Bethany. He ought to have whispered his love on bended knee instead of bellowing it like a madman. But rather than retreating to the cabin, he pitched in to help. Slipping along the treacherous topsides, he clutched at the rigging as he helped clear the decks and batten the openings.

In reaching for some loose shrouds, he let up his grasp on the spars and nearly fell from the heaving deck. For a moment he clutched the spars, shaken by a vision of himself being swept away on the crest of a yawning wave or blown aside by the awesome force of the wind.

Doggedly he moved down the decks, fastening canvas and stowing cargo. The day crept by, dark as twilight. By evening his fatigued muscles ached, but the work was far from over.

At the tiller Gaston and several others strained to steer the ship. The helmsman called for help. Sweat mingled with rain and seawater, streaming down Ashton's face as he gritted his teeth and braced himself alongside Gaston. He was unprepared when the steerage loosened suddenly.

A grinding of chains and a rending of wood deep in the ship's belly rumbled from below. The lever in Ashton's hands swung free, knocking him off his feet. Scrambling up, he recaptured the lever; it felt curiously slack in his grasp.

"*Cassé*," Gaston shouted above the storm. "The rudder is broken. We are at the mercy of the waves now." The Frenchman crossed himself and glanced fearfully to the west. Nothing was visible through the heavy squall, yet Ashton was aware of the jagged rocks piercing the shoreline, and the deadly *chevaux de frise* the British had placed in the bay.

Ashton relinquished his hold on the tiller bar. He had never felt more tired, drained, and beaten. Not even the foulest-tempered horse had ever fought him like this.

"Go take some food to your wife," Gaston said. "The galley fires will have been put out, but there is plenty of beer and wine and biscuits."

Ashton patted him on the shoulder and walked toward a ladder. When he reached the hatch, the wind rose to a deafening howl. He glanced back, horrified to see that the mainmast was cracking. The huge beam gave way like a tall pine beneath a wood butcher's axe and crashed to the deck, bringing the mizzenmast with it.

Gaston's body lay crushed under the toppled mast. Bellowing for assistance, Ashton dragged the limp, bloody form free. A young and terrified crewman joined him.

"*En bas*," the man cried, gesturing, and they shared the burden of Gaston's body.

Ashton caught at the rail with one hand and placed the other around Gaston. The *Languedoc* rolled and the port side sank down into a huge swell, inundating the three men. The wave was so deep and so slow to retreat that Ashton thought they would all drown. His tired, raw hand clung to the rail.

At last the column of water rolled away. Ashton's lungs nearly exploded as he gulped for air. The young crewman was gone.

Cursing, Ashton carried his burden alone, battening hatches behind him. Men clustered around Gaston, some weeping openly for their loss. Ashton went to find his wife.

Bethany sat on the bunk in the dim cabin, clutching at the sides to keep from being tossed to the planks. She stared at Ashton, and he realized what a spectacle he must appear. Soaked by rain and sea, his loose shirt was plastered against his chest and shoulders. Gaston's blood stained his clothing.

Bethany scrambled up, swaying with the motion of the ship, and came toward him. "An accident?" she asked.

"It's not my blood. Gaston, the helmsman. He was crushed when the mast fell."

"You're shivering. Give me that shirt. You'll be warmer without it."

With slow, weary movements he complied and then, needing no more urging than her proffered hand, collapsed onto the bunk and tumbled into exhausted sleep.

The darkness to which Ashton awoke was meaningless. It could still be the middle of the night or well past dawn. Clouds kept the sky perpetually obscured.

The warm presence at his side brought a smile to his lips. Bethany had been so frightened, and he so drained.

In the galley he found a lot of weary French seamen and grim, quiet Americans. "*Salut,*" he said. "Are all voyages this eventful?"

"Ah," replied Rimbaud, a lieutenant, "but you must admit our life does offer a certain *je ne sais quoi.*"

"Not for this landlubber." Ashton took a sip from a mug of stale beer. "I'm a horseman."

"This one," Rimbaud said, addressing his companions, "this American has the strength of five. He proved that yesterday, working the tiller, then bringing our own Gaston to us."

The Frenchmen lifted their cups in a sober salute. Ashton did likewise, then went topside. Through a curtain of gray rain and the occasional flashes of lightning, he could still see the English fleet of Black Dick Howe.

The billowy clouds of fair weather were piled against a sky of sharp azure. At dawn the storm had departed, leaving death and wreckage in its wake.

In the cabin where he had passed a restless night, Ashton felt his leaden heart lift at the sight of his sleeping wife. In slumber her bright beauty was gently muted, though no less striking. He would have liked to stay and kiss her to wakefulness, but he had other pressing tasks.

His first was to convince d'Estaing to put Bethany and the other hostages ashore. But the count refused to spare an ear for him. He had a dismasted ship to be towed back into harbor.

British vessels plagued the French fleet. Working feverishly, the crew managed to put two of the stern guns in working order. They might have started working on the other eighty-eight, but toward evening a new threat appeared.

"The *Renown*," someone shouted from astern. The approaching ship belched iron balls at the *Languedoc*, ripping holes in her broadsides. D'Estaing shouted an order above the cannonade. The proud colors of the *Languedoc* were struck in surrender.

"Not yet," Finley begged the count. "Let us stay and let our sister ships defend us."

"We are nothing but a wreck of splintered timber with no steerage," d'Estaing said. Lieutenant Rimbaud brought forth a sealed coffer of official papers. The Americans looked on in frustration as d'Estaing emptied the contents over the side. "The English will not find our secrets," he said.

Bethany prayed that, in the purple twilight of the peaceful evening, no one had seen what she had observed from the tiny portal in her cabin. By the time she had donned her gown and raked order into her hair with her fingers, she was certain the tender boat bobbing in the dark waters about fifty yards distant had not been remarked upon.

She left the cabin to find Ashton, to ask him to escape with her. Resolute and no longer afraid of the French sailors, she went to the top deck toward the stateroom. Within, she heard voices.

"You must understand my position, General Sullivan," d'Estaing was saying. "My first obligation is to my fleet."

"It would take so little time," replied a gruff voice. "Just give us twenty-four hours—"

"No," d'Estaing said. "Take Newport on your own, if you must."

"With what?" Sullivan bellowed. "The storm wasn't much kinder to us than it was to you. The wind blew down every tent. Our powder got wet. Dozens of men under General Greene and myself drowned, lying under fences, covered with water."

"The British are no better off."

"I say they are, damn your eyes. If you desert me now, I'll be forced to retreat."

A fist crashed down on a table. "*Alors*," d'Estaing barked, "you do not understand. You are a tiny part of our war with England. We are much more concerned with our interests in the West Indies."

"What of the alliance?"

"I must put into Boston for refitting and then go on to the West Indies. Those are my orders."

"Orders be damned!" Ashton cut in. "Newport is ours for the taking if you'd just extend your support another day."

"You Americans are brash. Insubordinate. Leave me now. We sail for Boston at midnight. And as to your request on behalf of the hostages, I must say no. I shall need the Tories for prisoner exchanges. They come to Boston."

Ashton exploded from the stateroom. He stopped short when he saw Bethany.

"I will not go to Boston," she stated. "I'd sooner swim to Aquidneck, and don't think I can't."

"D'Estaing will come around," Ashton said wearily.

"He will not. Ashton, I want to see Henry again. I want to go home." She took his hand and drew him to the rail.

"There's an abandoned tender out there. We could swim for it and be home by sunup."

He shook his head. "Love, I can't leave now. I have to go back in and try to reason with the admiral. Wait for me below."

Ashton watched her march away, her back stiff, her chin held high. Finley passed her and gave a low whistle. "Your wife looks none too pleased with you," he remarked.

"With good reason."

"Don't look so glum," Finley said. "Newport will be ours as soon as we convince d'Estaing to stay and fight. It is the fulfillment of our dream, Ashton!"

"Maybe I'm following the wrong dream, Finley." He watched Bethany disappear belowdecks. "The right dream just walked away from me."

Her eyes fastened on the faint shape of the tender, Bethany stole across the deck and found a rope ladder. She fixed it to a cap and swung it down to the waterline. Twenty-four hours indeed, she thought. She wasn't about to remain on this wreck a moment longer.

She slipped into the chill waters. Her gown immediately dragged at her, so she set her skirt and petticoat adrift. The idea of going ashore in her shift was daunting indeed, but she had learned to cope with all manner of disapproval.

Striking out with sure strokes, she concentrated on the muted sounds of the ocean and her own rhythmic breathing. She tried not to think about the sharks she knew infested these waters. According to sailors' lore, the beasts could strip a body of flesh in a matter of minutes. She forced herself to focus on a feeling of satisfaction. She had gained freedom all on her own.

Just as her strength began to give out, she collided with the sodden wood of the supply boat. Panting and relieved, she heaved herself up and over the side.

And found herself sprawled across two dead bodies.

She recoiled in horror and scrambled off the lifeless forms of a man and woman. Huddling as far from them as possible, she peered through the gloom. Cannonfire or musket shot had shattered the woman's face. The man's chest was a dark, gory hole. And his face . . . was one she recognized.

Bug Willy. He had undoubtedly been smuggling supplies and had brought a female companion along, probably a starving refugee from the wharves. He had probably offered her a pittance to sell her charms to a sailor.

Bethany surprised herself with her presence of mind. The stench and the feel of slack limbs and formless flesh should by rights have brought her to her knees with revulsion, yet her mind worked with clarity. The woman's dress was of cheap stuff, but it would serve Bethany well enough. The fabric tore as she removed it. The hair had a color and texture so like Bethany's own that she shivered.

She choked out a disjointed prayer and heaved the bodies over the side. A piece of the boat's stern came away.

Filled with a sense of urgency, she picked up the oars and began to row.

Finley understood all too well the awe and fear he observed on the faces of the sailors of the *Languedoc*. Ashton Markham was a man not of this earth.

On the deck, beneath the splintered shafts of the masts and amid the tangled coils of useless rigging and shrouds, the men stepped back to give him a wide berth.

He was a fearsome sight—hair wild and plastered to his pale cheeks, eyes alight with a beastlike rage, his entire frame shaking from hours of swimming the bay in a desperate search for his wife.

The search had yielded flotsam from the tender and the gruesome remains of his wife. Finley shuddered. The cover

of night could not disguise the fact that marine scavengers
had mutilated Bethany's body. Only a few strands of dark
blond hair remained to identify her. The hand that had
worn a wedding ring was missing.

When he could not stand his friend's pain any longer,
Finley snatched up a sodden sailcloth bag and emptied its
contents heedlessly on deck.

"No," Ashton whispered in a voice Finley had never
heard before. "Please don't take her from me—"

At a gesture from Finley some of the sailors stepped forward, their faces pale and horrified in the moonlight. They
managed to enshroud the remains in the sailcloth bag.

"Let her go, Ashton," Finley instructed hoarsely. "Let
her go, so she can be at peace." He fastened the bag
securely and, leading Ashton like a child, brought him to
the rail. Placing the bag in his arms, Finley urged his friend
to say farewell.

Ashton clutched the dark, wet bundle to his chest.

"Think of your son, Ashton," Finley whispered. "Henry
will need you now more than ever."

His words seemed to penetrate the chilling mask of
grief. With sudden resolution Ashton slipped the bag into
the bay.

Taking his friend by the shoulders, Finley led him away
from the rail. The older man's heart ached at the sight of
his shattered friend, and he remembered Chapin, the son
he had loved more than his own life, the son he had lost to
the same war that had taken Bethany from Ashton.

*Ah, Abby, thank God you came along to save me from
myself.*

But who would be there for Ashton?

A sailor pushed a flask into Ashton's hand. Ashton
turned away. He heard Finley say something in a pained
voice, but the sound seemed to come from a great distance,
as if the message were shouted from a world Ashton no
longer belonged to. He dropped the flask, certain no mortal

portion could dull his grief. With slow, shaking steps he trod the length of the deck, stopping only when he reached the rail at the bowsprit.

"Bethany." He whispered her name to the night sky and heard the faint sound like another's voice die on the gentle soughing of the wind.

Dissatisfied at his attempt to send her name to the heavens, he muttered a curse. Slowly, as if awakening from a nightmare, he raised a trembling finger to his face, feeling his own tears for the first time in his memory.

Bethany had urged him to cry, years ago when he had lost his father. You've made me weep now, love, he told her silently. You've made me weep now.

He spoke the name of his beloved again, this time with a scream that poured from his throat like an onrushing tide of agony.

24

Bethany sat, aching and dry-mouthed, beneath an overhanging bank on the mainland side of the Sakonnet. A stiff northerly wind and the strong surge of an incoming tide, combined with hours of dogged rowing, had delivered her safely from the bay.

She was proud of herself for escaping a humiliating and unnecessary trip to Boston. But, her fatigue-battered brain reminded her, the cost of freedom was dear. In fleeing the *Languedoc* she had also fled Ashton, doubtless destroying the healing that had taken place between them.

Aquidneck lay at the opposite bank, a mile to the west. Weary to the marrow, hunger pangs gnawing at her belly, she eyed her surroundings. The bank gave way to a thick wood draped in an early morning shroud of fog. She knew Tiverton lay to the north, Little Compton to the south.

Muddying the gaudy cherry lutestring dress she had pilfered from Bug Willy's woman, she gained the top of the bank and paused, gulping the mist-thick air of dawn. Upriver, barely visible through the haze, she saw a flotilla of boats slipping silently across the river from Aquidneck. Unable to tell whether the transports were American or British, she scrambled to the shelter of the woods.

She struck out northward for Tiverton, where Miss Abigail lived now. The state of the town shocked her. Gutted by fire, it was a place of outcasts. Mildewed sailcloth battened across cellar holes provided scant shelter. Charred board shacks and brush lean-tos lined the muddy track.

The townspeople, miserably clothed in homespun rags, scurried northward, women burdened by crying children, old men carrying pitchforks and spades. She spied a number of soldiers, most of the Negroes clad in the buff and blue of the patriots. They were shouting at the townsfolk, urging them to evacuate their shelters.

Clutching the immodest bodice of her red dress, Bethany approached a man beside a blackened cellar hold. "Please," she said softly. "What happened here?"

At first she thought he had not heard her and began to repeat her question; then she realized his body was convulsed by eerie, voiceless laughter. The man raised a face so marred by smallpox that she had to force herself not to wince, reminded of the disease that had killed William.

"You don't know?" the man asked.

She shook her head. "I—I've only just arrived."

"Have you not eyes to see?" he demanded. "War!" The word was a bitter burst of sound. "That's what's happened, missy. If you know what's good for you, take to the woods. The Negro regiment's here to warn us the British and Hessians are coming in from the river."

The King's army and their hired German killers no longer meant sanity and security to Bethany. She plunged after the fleeing townsfolk and did not stop until a sight even more appalling than the devastated village arrested her.

A rag-clad woman, her face twisted with agony, unwashed children clinging to her skirts, stood in a clearing, aiming a rusty flintlock pistol at a horse.

Bethany ran forward and seized the woman's arm. "Would you shoot this poor beast while your children watch?"

The woman wrenched free. "Better I kill the mare than leave her for the Redcoats to take."

"What would an army want with one farmhorse?"

"'Tis all they need to tote one of their big guns. Christ." The woman wiped her eyes. "I don't like doing away with Bridie any more than you do."

"Perhaps you could outrun the soldiers."

"With this brood of mine?" Her eyes flicked back to the river road. "For God's sake, they're the enemy! 'Pon my faith, how can I give them this horse?" Her hands looked small and clumsy wrapped around the pistol. The barrel wavered; then she fitted it against the horse's broad brow.

"Abel," the woman said, "take the little ones into the woods and wait for me." While the children left, her finger, its nail chewed to the quick, tightened on the trigger.

"No!" The cry ripped from Bethany's throat.

"Wait!" A basso bellow mingled with her voice.

It was Justice Richmond, clad in the frock and breeches of the Negro regiment. He and Bethany reached the horse at the same time. "I'll see to the horse, ma'am." He took the bridle. "Take yourself and your children safe away."

The woman closed her eyes briefly, her lips moving. Then she nodded, stuck the pistol in the top of her apron, and surrendered the horse. Justice immediately boosted Bethany up onto the horse and mounted behind her. The mare grunted and shied, then started off at a reluctant trot.

"I am taking you to the Piper farm," Justice said. "It's safer there."

"What are you doing here?" Bethany asked.

"Joined up with Chris Greene's regiment. We're trying to protect General Sullivan's command as he withdraws."

Withdraws. So the Americans could not make a stand, because the French would not stay and back them. Bethany felt no satisfaction at the news.

They emerged from the woods into a clearing planted with tassel-topped corn. In the distance stood outbuildings and a small house. Primroses, with yellow heads closed against the morning damp, grew in clumps in the dooryard.

Justice helped Bethany down. "You take care now, ma'am."

"Won't you stay, Justice?"

He shook his head. "I got fighting to do." He turned the horse and disappeared into the woods.

As she approached the house, Bethany heard a vague rumble, like distant thunder. Dear God, was she hearing cannon fire? Shuddering, she went to the Dutch door, the top half of which was open to the foggy morning air.

She caught a glimpse of a woman sitting at the kitchen table, her face obscured by dark hair tumbling neglectedly down her back; a shapeless sacque dress was draped over a belly big with child. In her hands the woman held an iron instrument. A bullet mold, of all things.

Bethany frowned. Finley's brother was a widower, so who was this stranger? Suddenly self-conscious, she knocked softly on the doorjamb.

The woman turned. Bethany felt her eyes widen in wonderment. "You—"

"Close your mouth, young lady. We are not a flytrap."

Butterflies scattered through the grass-sweet air around Ashton. Leaves, tickled by the summer wind, sang a soft, restless song.

Ashton's eyes were riveted on the scene below the knoll where he and Finley stood. A hundred yards distant, against a brake of verdant woods and misty sky, a battle raged.

"Damn," said Finley, puffing with exertion from their hike inland. "I thought when d'Estaing put us ashore we'd find the Americans victorious."

At first the rebels had approached the British lines with confidence, even cockiness, mocking the enemy's formal fighting style. Then a six-pounder had been pulled in on a field carriage.

All joking had ceased.

Ashton watched the British cannon recoil, spitting iron into the American ranks, raking down lives in the blink of an eye. He glanced away. The man he had been before losing Bethany would have been appalled at the carnage. The man he was now felt a strange, joyless pride in the rebels who stood their ground, refusing to yield even as they faced the deadly cannonade.

His glance caught a movement to the right. "Wonderful," he said dully. "The cavalry has arrived."

The company rode up the knoll in haphazard fashion, some men allowing their horses to stray and graze. One of the men spurred his mount to a gallop, calling Ashton's name.

Beneath an oozing bandage were a pair of familiar hazel eyes. Ashton felt a shock of pain so intense it took his breath away. Bethany's ghost haunted her twin brother's broad grin.

He had no chance to tell Harry about Bethany. "Captain Tarnover was killed by snipers," Harry said, and his second-in-command took to the wood." He drove a fist into the palm of his hand. "Damn. We were going to charge the cannon, but none of us knows a thing about doing it." He rode back to join his company.

The disorganized company looked incapable of treeing a squirrel, much less mounting an assault on a well-guarded gun.

Swearing, Ashton looked back at the battlefield. A new contingent of British appeared at the right flank. The Redcoats were led by an officer on a prancing midnight stallion.

"By God," Ashton whispered. "He's on Corsair." The

horse danced wildly. Tanner sawed on the reins. "You fool," Ashton muttered. "Corsair's not battle-trained."

But the Thoroughbred was trained to obey—by Ashton's own hand.

"Let's go," Finley said wearily. "I don't want to stay and watch this. We'll come back to help the wounded when it's all over. My brother's farm is three miles to the south." He started down the hill, then paused, looking back. "Are you coming, Ashton?"

He shook his head. "I'm staying, Finley. I'm going to lead the charge on the cannon."

Finley spread his hands. "You? Lead a charge? Good God, Ashton, you swore you'd never take up arms against another man."

"That was . . . when I still cared."

"What of your son?"

"He has no need of the person I've become. Harry will raise the boy."

"God, Ashton, you'll be sliced to ribbons." He looked fearfully at the Redcoats, who formed a bristling wall of bayoneted Brown Bess muskets around the cannon. Then his eyes returned to Ashton. "You know that, don't you? You know that, and you're not afraid."

"No," he replied with total honesty. It was easy to be brave when he had nothing left to live for.

"You haven't got a horse," Finley said in disgust.

Ashton's smile was a humorless ghost about his lips. "Oh, I've got a horse." Turning, he placed his fingers to his lips and gave a single high-pitched whistle.

On the battlefield below, Corsair rose, pawing the air with his forelegs, jerking his head back in the sly old trick Ashton had never been able to school out of him.

Tanner lost his grip on the rein and fell to the ground.

Ashton felt a dark surge of victory as Corsair broke free of the battle confusion and thundered up the hill toward his master.

*   *   *

Bethany sat sipping a mug of strong chicory brew, trying not to sway with exhaustion. She could not speak of her ordeal on the *Languedoc*. Her feelings were still too raw. She could not probe the wound of her emotions now.

As she calmly continued molding bullets from melted lead, Abigail spoke of her marriage to Finley, her elation over the babe. Even the constant thunder of distant cannonfire did not seem to disturb her.

Watching the small hands deftly wielding the bullet mold, Bethany realized how much Abigail had changed— from an impoverished gentlewoman to a farmer's wife, an expectant mother.

"I had no idea the Royal Army was in such dire need of bullets," Bethany commented.

Abigail blinked in surprise. "Bethany dear, these are for the Americans." She took up a jackknife and began trimming the sprues off the new bullets.

"But you're a Tory!"

Abigail smiled. "I'm an American. And if you think about it, Bethany, so are you. Perhaps it all began long before our time, in the minds and hearts of the very first people who settled here. This rebellion is not about Englishman against Englishman, but about another breed of men entirely. Men who never thought of themselves as English."

Images crowded into Bethany's mind: Finley, an ordinary printer changing into a fire-breathing patriot; mobs surging through the streets of Newport demanding their rights; Goody Haas spinning flax and weaving linen in her own house rather than shipping it to England; the poor, fleeing woman in the woods who would have killed the family horse before letting the enemy take it.

Her swirling thoughts turned inevitably to Ashton. Ashton, bursting with pride as he held his infant son to hear the reading of the Declaration of Independence. Ashton, riding missions so dangerous even the Committee of Safety had begged him to stop.

Her husband, she realized, was no more an Englishman than a draft horse was bred to run races.

She looked across the table at Abigail. Bullet molding was repetitive and boring, but Abigail seemed not to mind.

"What if the reb—the Americans are defeated?" Bethany asked.

"We won't be." Abigail scraped the sprues back into the melting pan. "If it takes a hundred years, we'll fight that long." A sad smile curved her lips. "I'm not trying to force you to change your mind, Bethany. But look what you've become in the past four years. Is there anything about you that even vaguely resembles an Englishwoman?"

"You sound like Dorian," Bethany said ruefully. "He gets disgusted with me."

"Do you still credit that scoundrel's opinion?" Abigail demanded. "Is it not enough to know he staged the raid on Seastone and tried to have your husband hanged for the deed?"

Bethany fell still. The color dropped from her face. Her stomach turned to a cold fist of dread. "What did you say?"

"Oh, dear God. Harry didn't find you, did he?"

"I haven't seen my brother since Henry's birthday in April."

"He was coming to show you proof that Tanner planned the raid." Quickly Abigail related the information she and Harry had pieced together.

Bethany nearly stopped breathing. Her tears had the sting of Dorian's betrayal, the burn of humiliation that she had allowed herself to be duped by him, and the searing heat of remorse, for she had blamed Ashton for a crime he had not committed.

As Bethany mentally reeled like a ship in a storm, Abigail said, "I also discovered Dorian is no gentleman, but the son of a London tanner. At a young age he joined a traveling carnival. He excelled at horse tricks and caught the notice of an English lord, who bought him his commission."

"Ashton must hate me for not believing him," Bethany said.

"When he doubted you, did you hate him?" Abigail asked.

Bethany shook her head. Loving Ashton had always been as natural and necessary to her as breathing. "I must go to him, but I don't even know where he is," she said in despair. "He might be on the way to Boston for all I know."

"He's not," said an angry male voice, "though I'm beginning to wish he had gone with the French."

"Finley!" Abigail jumped up and hurried to embrace her husband.

He stared at Bethany. "What the hell are you doing here?"

Bethany was confused by his temper and far too weary for explanations. She stood up. "Please. What about Ashton?"

"A fine time to show wifely concern. You should have thought of him when you staged your own death. Did you never consider what that would do to the man?"

"What a bizarre accusation, Finley. I did no such thing."

His shoulders slumped. "Maybe you didn't mean to, but a body—a woman's body—was found. Ashton believes you died."

Bethany's stomach lurched as she recalled Bug Willy's woman. She buried her face in her hands. "Where is Ashton?"

"Grief has turned him into a cold-blooded killer. Or maybe a suicide. I didn't wait around to see which. He plans to lead a charge on the British cannon." Finley rubbed a hand over his weary brow. "He fears nothing, because he thinks he's lost you."

Horrified, she started for the door.

"Bethany, no," Finley said.

Abigail took his hand. "Do you think you can stop her now, my love?"

*   *   *

Seated on Corsair at the head of the small company that had adopted him as its commander, Ashton felt a primal surge of power. He was empty of softer sentiments, as if Bethany's death had drained the humanity from him.

Was it only yesterday that he had held her in his arms, made love to her? He could still taste her on his lips, still smell the scent of her hair.

He hurled away the thoughts and glanced down at the sword sheathed at his side. Would he be able to slice through human flesh with that blade?

He drank deep gulps of the hot summer air. He considered, with odd clarity, the very real possibility that he would be dead in the next few moments. And he didn't care.

His hand was steady as he unsheathed his sword, raised the blade high, and yelled an order.

The bright green leaves of summer and the bloodred heads of poppies made a swirl of color as the horses galloped down the slope. Ashton's heart rose to his throat. His blood pounded with a dark, awful joy.

They thundered past the American ranks and plunged into the British defense. Coming up from the side was a soldier brandishing a bayonet. Ashton's sword whistled as it sliced the air, meeting cloth and flesh and blood. A fierce cry ripped from his throat.

He became aware of the burn of powder and the flashes of gunfire all around him. A musket ball buzzed past his ear like a wasp. The sounds and smells and danger made him feel furiously, achingly alive.

Soldiers cursed as they fled from him. He probably looked as fierce as he felt. A man hating himself, hating life, must be a fearsome sight indeed. Another soldier came on. Ashton swung his sword low. The blow reverberated to his shoulder. The blade dripped crimson. Blood spattered the ground like the poppies of summer.

Around the cannon, Ashton's horsemen cantered to and fro, bellowing, brandishing swords and pistols along with curses. The smell of gunpowder seethed in the area. The rebels closed in, hacking, thrusting, shouting with mindless rage, their purpose so intense that they seemed impervious to attack. A few moments later, a cacophony of whoops rose from their ranks.

"The devils're retreating!" Harry shouted, his jubilant face and bandage burned by powder.

Ashton pulled his horse to a stop and surveyed the trampled field around the big gun. Butterflies hovered over the lifeless body of a fallen Englishman. The pounding in his head subsided. He was stunned by the violence that had possessed him during the charge. While around him the Americans tossed their hats in the air, Ashton felt hollow.

In the past few minutes, he had learned what war could be, what battle could make a man do. He took Corsair off to the side, into a shelter of trees.

He heard the cold, sharp click of a pistol being cocked and looked up to see Dorian Tanner.

Laughter flowed in silky mirthlessness from Dorian's angrily curling lips. "I've waited a long time for this day. Now Bethany will be mine, and I'll have complete control of Seastone. And your son."

Ashton did not have the energy or the inclination to tell Tanner that Bethany was dead. From the corner of his eye, he saw a flash of red. Good God, how many other Redcoats were lurking in the trees?

"The boy will forget you," Tanner promised, "before you're cold in your grave." His finger curled around the trigger.

Ashton felt stonily calm as he gazed at his executioner.

A final sneer slithered over Tanner's lips as he prepared to discharge the pistol.

A blur of red flung itself on Dorian's firing arm. The pistol exploded with a streak of white light and sulphurous yellow smoke.

Ashton instinctively went for Tanner, stunning him with a kick to the temple. Then he grabbed for the other figure.

His big, blunt-fingered hands closed around her small, trembling ones. His unbelieving eyes locked with her tear-wet ones. And then his thankful lips melded with hers in a brief, fierce kiss.

"Bethany. I thought you—"

"I know," she said, weeping. "It was all a terrible mistake." Her palm cupped his cheek. "So many mistakes. Abigail explained it all, about the raid, about Dorian. . . . Can you ever forgive me?"

He hauled her against him and filled his arms with her beloved, trembling warmth. "God. What a question."

"Ashton!" Harry bellowed from the battlefield. "Let's go! We're giving chase!"

"No!" Bethany clutched at Ashton. "Please don't go."

Coldness touched his heart. "Still the Loyalist, pet?"

She looked proud and weary as she faced him. "I'm as American as you are, Ashton."

"Where the devil are you?" Harry's voice called through the smoke. "We're leaving now!"

"Don't go," Bethany said again. "Your skill is with horses. You can help win this war another way." Tears spilled down her face. "We'll train horses for the cavalry at Seastone. If you'll live with me there."

He gathered her against him and rested his chin on her head. "I'll agree on one condition." Pride and adoration filled his chest. "You have to let me spend the rest of my life showing you how much I love you."

She looked up at him. Her eyes danced with a happiness that might have driven the gods mad with envy. "You do love me, don't you, Ashton?"

"Aye, my sweet. You can't know how much."

"But I can. Oh, yes, I can." Their kiss was long and all-enveloping, healing them in a way mere words could not, their souls fused, bonded by love and trust and a sudden unity of purpose they had never known until this moment.

He glanced down at the defeated Redcoat. "Let's leave him to defend his treason on his own." Ashton took Bethany's hand in his and reached for Corsair's reins. "Let's go get our son, love."

Epilogue

Newport, Rhode Island
11 July 1781

On the steps of the schoolhouse Bethany sat with her husband and tilted her gaze to the evening sky. Fireworks burst overhead, saluting the arrival of the Comte de Rochambeau's fleet. The force had come to liberate the war-ravaged city and to drop the final curtain on the war that had dragged on far too long. Distant bells tolled in welcome, and the guns in Newport's earthworks and batteries saluted the French.

Her gaze returned to the garden, wandering contentedly over the slowly opening petals of the pale yellow evening primroses Ashton had planted three summers earlier.

She was reminded of an even more distant time, the summer of 1775 when Roger Markham had died and she had felt the first stirrings of love for the man who had captured her heart, broken it, and healed it again with his love.

"You look far away," Ashton observed, closing his warm hand over hers.

"I was just thinking of how we used to sit together in this very spot."

"Maybe in years to come you'll tell your students about what we've lived through these years, about Miss Abigail, the schoolmistress who was a spy; about your brother's exploits with the cavalry." His eyes darkened with memory. "The hanging of Dorian Tanner for high treason might even appear in history books."

She lifted his hand to her lips. "What about my own husband's heroism? Surely the chroniclers will write of your charge on the British cannon in the Battle of Rhode Island."

"I'd rather we made our own private history right here."

In front of them, Henry played in the grass with his toddling sister, Abby, and the spaniel dog called Liberty. Abigail and Finley, over from Tiverton for the celebration, strolled along the path beneath the lilacs, their daughter Sally swinging between them.

A distant whinny from the stables brought a smile to Bethany's lips. The horses of Seastone, once fabled for their domination on the racing green, now were destined to bear patriots to victory. Her heart rose as a new shower of fireworks colored the sky.

"Like it?" Ashton's deep whisper stirred silky tendrils near her ear.

She shivered deliciously. She would never grow tired of him, his taste and the sound of his voice, the splendor of his touch. "Mmm, yes," she murmured, fitting her hand around the curve of his thigh.

"Lusty wench," he teased. "I was talking about the *feu de joie*."

"Lovely," she said. "A proper fuss for our saviors, but I much prefer the view right here." Her glance moved lovingly over the soft, starlike primroses drenched in dew. As a host of circling moon-colored moths came to sample the fragrance of the flowers, she leaned up in the evening light to kiss her husband.

COMING SOON

Move Heaven and Earth by Christina Dodd

Fleeing the consequences of scandal and tragedy, Sylvan Miles arrived at Clairmont Court to nurse Lord Rand Malkin back to health after his return from battle. As he taunted his beautiful caretaker with stolen kisses, the dashing rogue never expected her love to heal his damaged soul.

From This Day Forward by Deborah Cox

After falling in love with Jason Sinclair through his letters requesting an obedient and demure mail-order bride, Caroline Marshall decided she would make him the perfect wife, despite her strong-willed, independent ways. She met him in the wilds of the Amazon jungle and together they discovered a love more blissful than either ever imagined.

Lady Vengeance by Sarah Eagle

On a mission to find her brother, still missing in action from the War of 1812, Celia Tregaron ventures from Baltimore to London to confront Marcus Knowles, the Earl of Ashmore—the man responsible for sending her brother to war. Matching wits and flaring tempers did nothing to cool the battlefield of desire that smoldered between them.

Fire in the Dark by Susan Macias

As head of her family's ranch, Regan O'Neil had no time to spare for love—until the wickedly handsome gunslinger Jackson Tyler returned home to claim what was his. Although helping Regan meant risking his own heart, Jackson could not deny the passion that was destined to light up the darkest of nights.

Loving Mollie by Jeane Renick

Stranded overnight in an airport, Mollie McDeere is astonished to encounter world-famous musician Gray Walker. More than a gorgeous celebrity, he is the high school sweetheart who abandoned her years ago to pursue his dream. On an adventure that spans Boston, Malibu, and Hawaii, the two search for the love that eluded them so long ago.

Seasons of Love

A collection of heartwarming stories from beloved, bestselling authors. Find love for all seasons in *Winter Moon* from Elaine Barbieri, *Gentle Rain* by Evelyn Rogers, Karen Lockwood's *Summer Storm*, and *Golden Harvest* by Lori Copeland.

Harper Monogram **The Mark of Distinctive Women's Fiction**

GLORY IN THE SPLENDOR OF SUMMER WITH

HarperMonogram's

101 Days of Romance

BUY 3 BOOKS, GET 1 FREE!

Take a book to the beach, relax by the pool, or read in the most quiet and romantic spot in your home. You can live through love all summer long when you redeem this exciting offer from HarperMonogram. Buy any three HarperMonogram romances in June, July, or August, and get a fourth book sent to you for FREE. See next page for the list of top-selling novels and romances by your favorite authors that you can choose from for your premium!

101 DAYS OF ROMANCE
BUY 3 BOOKS, GET 1 FREE!

CHOOSE A FREE BOOK FROM THIS OUTSTANDING
LIST OF AUTHORS AND TITLES:

HARPERMONOGRAM

____LORD OF THE NIGHT Susan Wiggs 0-06-108052-7
____ORCHIDS IN MOONLIGHT Patricia Hagan 0-06-108038-1
____TEARS OF JADE Leigh Riker 0-06-108047-0
____DIAMOND IN THE ROUGH Millie Criswell 0-06-108093-4
____HIGHLAND LOVE SONG Constance O'Banyon 0-06-108121-3
____CHEYENNE AMBER Catherine Anderson 0-06-108061-6
____OUTRAGEOUS Christina Dodd 0-06-108151-5
____THE COURT OF THREE SISTERS Marianne Willman 0-06-108053-5
____DIAMOND Sharon Sala 0-06-108196-5
____MOMENTS Georgia Bockoven 0-06-108164-7

HARPERPAPERBACKS

____THE SECRET SISTERS Ann Maxwell 0-06-104236-6
____EVERYWHERE THAT MARY WENT Lisa Scottoline 0-06-104293-5
____NOTHING PERSONAL Eileen Dreyer 0-06-104275-7
____OTHER LOVERS Erin Pizzey 0-06-109032-8
____MAGIC HOUR Susan Isaacs 0-06-109948-1
____A WOMAN BETRAYED Barbara Delinsky 0-06-104034-7
____OUTER BANKS Anne Rivers Siddons 0-06-109973-2
____KEEPER OF THE LIGHT Diane Chamberlain 0-06-109040-9
____ALMONDS AND RAISINS Maisie Mosco 0-06-100142-2
____HERE I STAY Barbara Michaels 0-06-100726-9

To receive your free book, simply send in this coupon **and** your store receipt with the purchase prices circled. You may take part in this exclusive offer as many times as you wish, but all qualifying purchases must be made by September 4, 1995, and all requests must be postmarked by October 4, 1995. Please allow 6-8 weeks for delivery.

MAIL TO: HarperPaperbacks, Dept. FC-101
              10 East 53rd Street, New York, N.Y. 10022-5299

Name_____

Address_____

City_____State_____Zip_____

Offer is subject to availability. HarperPaperbacks may make substitutions for requested titles.
                                                                    H09511